PRAISE FOR *COMBAT MONSTERS*

"A beautifully wide-ranging look into a world of glorious monsters ... A brilliant approach to the subject matter, filled with compelling, well-crafted stories."

—SEANAN MCGUIRE,
New York Times bestselling author of
the October Daye series

"*Combat Monsters* is a challenging and rewarding read. War is always terrible, but the added dimension of supernatural creatures gives these stories a whole different slant on 'what if.'"

—CHARLAINE HARRIS,
New York Times bestselling author of
the Southern Vampire Mysteries

"Herz makes good on the fascinating premise of his latest anthology, bringing together twenty high-octane stories that add terrifying monsters to the battlefields of World War II ... Fans of alternate history and military horror will want to check this out."

—*PUBLISHERS WEEKLY*

COMBAT MONSTERS

ANTHOLOGIES BY HENRY HERZ

Beyond the Pale
Coming of Age
The Hitherto Secret Experiments of Marie Curie
The Festival of Lights
Wink
Red Stars and Shattered Shields
Combat Monsters

COMBAT MONSTERS

UNTOLD TALES OF WORLD WAR II

EDITED BY HENRY HERZ

BLACK STONE PUBLISHING

Published in 2025 by Blackstone Publishing
Cover design by Bookfly Design
Book design and chapter illustrations by Candice Edwards

Any historical figures and events referenced in this book are depicted in a fictitious manner. All other characters and events are products of the author's imagination, and any similarity to real persons, living or dead, is coincidental.

Printed in the United States of America

First edition: 2025
ISBN 979-8-8747-4843-2
Fiction / Anthologies (multiple authors)

Version 1

Blackstone Publishing
31 Mistletoe Rd.
Ashland, OR 97520

www.BlackstonePublishing.com

To the brave men and women who risked or lost their lives defending democracy and freedom. May we all strive to be worthy of your sacrifices.

CONTENTS

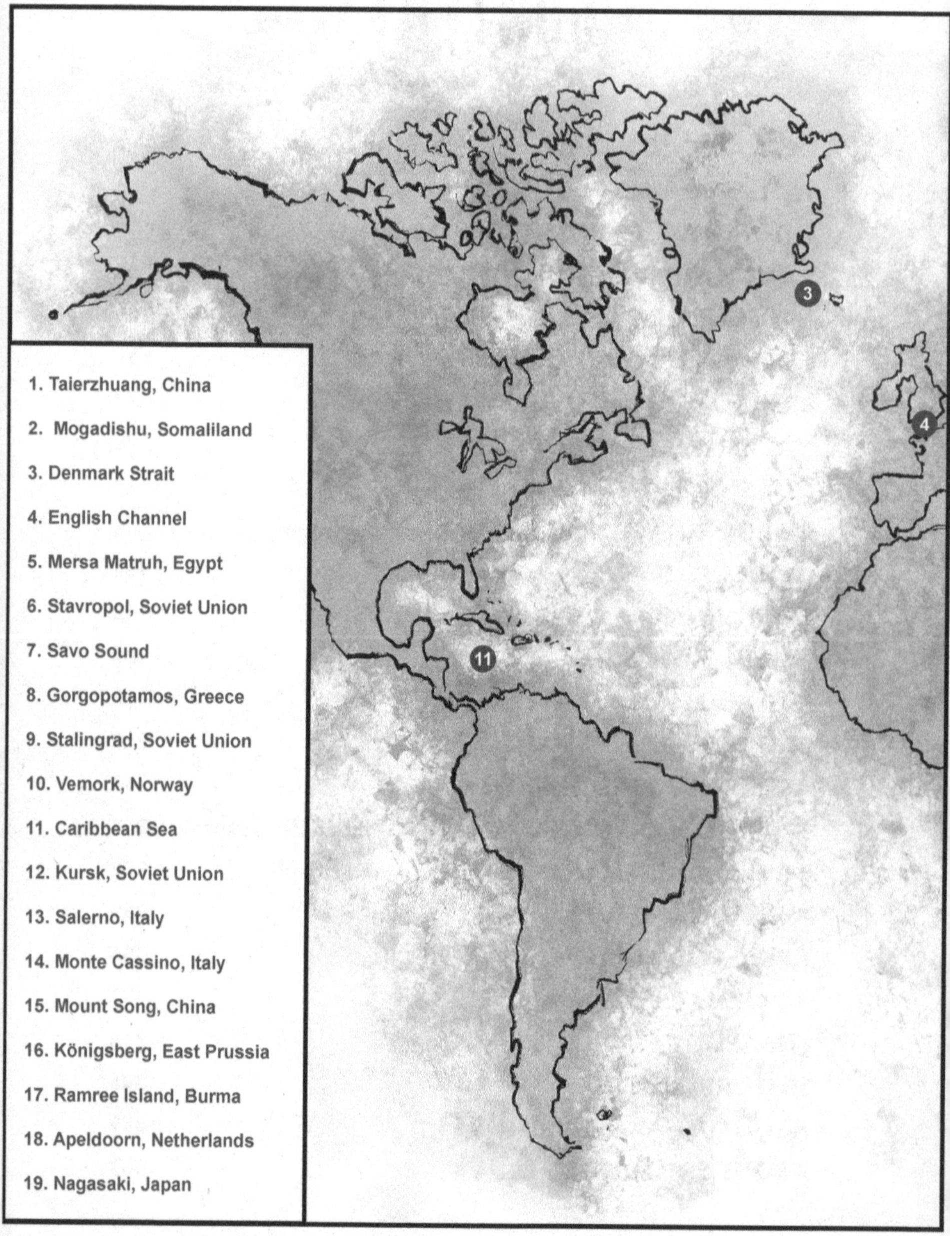
1. Taierzhuang, China
2. Mogadishu, Somaliland
3. Denmark Strait
4. English Channel
5. Mersa Matruh, Egypt
6. Stavropol, Soviet Union
7. Savo Sound
8. Gorgopotamos, Greece
9. Stalingrad, Soviet Union
10. Vemork, Norway
11. Caribbean Sea
12. Kursk, Soviet Union
13. Salerno, Italy
14. Monte Cassino, Italy
15. Mount Song, China
16. Königsberg, East Prussia
17. Ramree Island, Burma
18. Apeldoorn, Netherlands
19. Nagasaki, Japan

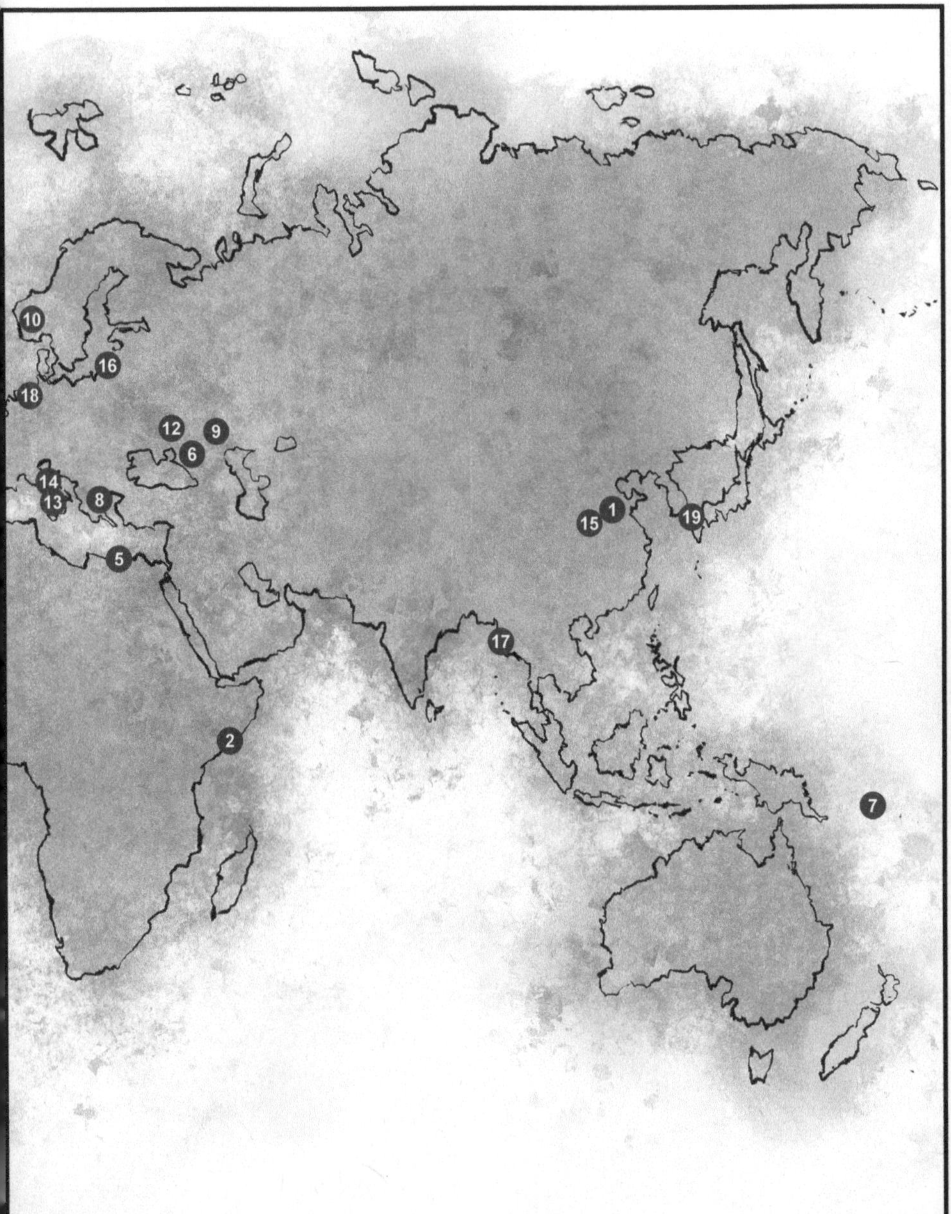
10
16
18
12
9
6
14
13
8
5
2
1
15
19
17
7

INTRODUCTION

JOSHUA PALMATIER

War.

It's only three letters, but it's an ugly word. It conjures up images of death, of brutality, of the human spirit pushed beyond its boundaries. It evokes feelings of trauma, of pain, of anguish so deeply felt it scars the soul. When I say the word, I can taste acrid gunpowder in my mouth, burning my tongue. I breathe in choking black smoke, feel its tendrils seeping into my lungs, destroying as it goes. I hear screams—bellows from those dredging up courage from their bones to do what must be done, howls from those who have been wounded, shrieks from those whose minds have been broken. I smell fear; I smell blood; I smell suffering. All the senses are engaged with immediate and horrific details.

And yet war can also be a forge. The intensity of emotions on the battlefield can mold and harden and temper. Bonds can be formed—of friendship, of comradeship—deeper and stronger than at any other time or any other place. A soul that is lost can find sudden purpose. A sinner without hope can find redemption. An unbeliever cast down into despair can find faith. War can be transformative. It is a cauldron of change, both physically and mentally, individually and sometimes globally.

It's because of this that war provides fertile ground for the imagination. Battlefields are hellscapes, no matter whether you're on the ground in the trenches, within the metal walls of a tank, or winging through the skies above in a bomber. And hellscapes have a tendency to warp reality. Time behaves differently. Perspectives twist. Distance and shape, light and shadow—all of it transforms into something unstable and untenable.

It takes no effort to realize why war—in any shape or form—is a hotbed of inspiration for speculative fiction writers. The displacement from reality experienced by those thrust into conflict—whether they be soldiers or civilians—lends itself to the mysterious, to the fantastic, and to the horrific, of course. Stress opens the mind, allowing in what almost everyone would discount as out of hand in other situations. The unbelievable becomes seen, becomes tangible, becomes *real*.

It can also become an escape.

Most famously, scholars believe J. R. R. Tolkien's writing in Middle-earth was influenced by his experiences in World War I; he reluctantly admitted to certain connections eventually. Scholars also suggested that *The Lord of the Rings* was an allegory for World War II, which Tolkien denied. If nothing else, it isn't hard to believe that Tolkien may have created Middle-earth in an attempt to make sense of the realities of the Great War that he experienced, to give the atrocities a different perspective. What better way to deal with the trauma of battle than to flee, at least mentally, to a different world? To give the honor, the valor, the sacrifice its own otherworldly sheen?

In this anthology, twenty authors explore the unreality that is war, specifically focusing on World War II, with settings from across the globe. You, dear reader, will experience the biting temperatures of winter on enemy soil, awaiting an attack on a power plant via hellhound. Or perhaps you'd rather traipse the sands of the North African desert with a mythical serpent on the loose? Maybe you'd rather slog through a knee-deep swamp on a South Pacific island with something that is definitely *not* a crocodile trailing behind you. Experience a Japanese attack on a Chinese village where the civilians are aided by a qilin; attempt to take out a strategic bridge in Greece when the enemy has its own troll; or search for U-boats in the waters off Cuba with the help of vicious mermaids. In these pages, you will visit the waters off Guadalcanal, the bombed-out villages of Italy, the front lines of Germany's invasion of the Soviet Union, and the frigid seas surrounding England. You will encounter monsters of every kind, from vampires to werewolves, sea serpents and krakens, witches, and even ordinary humans—sometimes the worst monster of them all. You might even discover the *real* reason we used Fat Man on Nagasaki. Sometimes these monsters are fighting for the Axis; sometimes the Allies. Often, they aren't fighting for either side; they are simply enraged at our invasion of their space. In every case, though, they help turn the tide and decide the outcome of the battle.

War. It distorts our sense of reality, defies our expectations, exposes us to the harshness and bitterness of the world. Will you have the stamina and the fortitude to survive?

Prepare to have your mind blown.

WOLF REMAINS

JANE YOLEN

They found the wolf,
dressed in a Gestapo jacket,
carefully buried near the remains
of the Warsaw Ghetto.
It was hard to know
if he had been an officer
or an escapee.
Perhaps he had been a werewolf
who ran with the partisans
and buried in his slaughter's clothes.
The jacket was two sizes too big,
and he carried a knife, not a Luger.
A miracle, some said;
a bad joke, claimed others.
But I know for a fact
that a female wolf
had been chased from the site
after two days of howling his death.

THE NIGHT THE MOON BURNED

MARY FAN

CHINESE COUNTRYSIDE, JANUARY 1938

Years later, Weiyang would come to think of the Chinese countryside where he had been born as timeless, with its open skies and hardy plants—emerald in the summer and silver in winter. But in January 1938, only the present mattered. Because if he lost focus in the moment, he might miss a stray voice, brief movement, or crunching footstep that could indicate the presence of Japanese invaders coming to raid his village.

Ignoring the bitter cold, Weiyang wandered past now-barren fields. Being a lookout had been a lot easier the past summer, before the winter had taken away most cover. If he was lucky, any Japanese soldiers or scouts who spotted him would see only a skinny farm boy, too harmless to pay attention to. If he wasn't, well, being small for thirteen wouldn't save him. Children far younger than him had been slaughtered for less.

Shimmering clouds rippled above, and the afternoon sun ducked between them, sometimes shining bright, sometimes veiling itself. A haze seemed to hang over Weiyang, though it wasn't exactly fog—more like distant smoke drifting in. He wondered if it was possible for it to have floated all the way from the fallen cities of Shanghai and Nanjing.

A flash of light caught his eye. He froze. The flash—again. Maybe sunlight glinting off a weapon . . .

A faraway voice rumbled through the air, as soft as distant thunder during a gathering storm. Weiyang couldn't make out the words, yet the sounds were so foreign; they must have been spoken in Japanese. And if he stood there a moment longer, whoever they belonged to might come into view. He'd see for certain if it was the enemy . . . and they'd have a chance to shoot him before he could warn anyone of their approach.

He took off running.

As he sprinted toward the village, anger flooded his veins. The Japanese had raided the village twice before—last time, they took an entire year's worth of grain. There was hardly anything left to steal. Already the people were on the brink of starvation. How would they survive if the enemy took what little remained?

At least last time the lookout that day had managed to warn everyone in time so they could all escape or hide before the invaders arrived, and the Japanese had been content to take their spoils and leave without searching for anyone. The first time they'd come, taking the village by surprise, many had been injured, and some had died—including Weiyang's father.

Weiyang was certain he'd reach home with enough time for everyone to hide or escape again. But what if the Japanese, unsatisfied with how little there was to take, wouldn't simply leave this time? What if they thought the village was hiding more food somewhere and started hunting people down, or burning everything so there'd be nothing to return to?

He started shouting the moment the low rooftops came into view. "The enemy is coming! The enemy is coming!"

People stopped what they were doing and vanished from

sight, ducking into the buildings or racing away. In the summer, they might have sought cover in the tall fields, but in the dead of winter, there was no place to hide but inside.

Weiyang continued shouting until he reached his family's residence in the middle of the village. His mother, aunt, and siblings—an older sister and a younger brother—were already inside. All five of them ducked into a tiny room at the back and barricaded the door with the old furniture kept inside. He wished they could have vanished between the cracks in the floor or somehow transformed into motes of dust to avoid being found. When the Japanese came, this room wouldn't hide them for long, yet they had nowhere else that could conceal them.

Hearts pounding, breaths short, they waited. No one dared speak a word. Weiyang listened for any sign of movement, wishing he had a way to see what was going on outside.

Moments trickled by like a light rain collecting in a ditch, pooling slowly but eventually becoming undeniably deep.

Finally, Weiyang couldn't stand it any longer. "I'm going to see what's going on."

"Weiyang!" Ma gave him a stern look.

"We can't hide in here forever."

Ma started to argue again, then pursed her lips and nodded.

Clutching a knife—meant for cutting vegetables, not fighting—Weiyang opened the door slowly and slipped out.

Voices drifted in from the street.

"Do you see anything?"

"There's no sign of anyone."

"The enemy is never this quiet."

By the time Weiyang crept outside, half a dozen others were already there, looking tense yet bemused.

An older man spotted him and pointed. "You! You're the one who called the warning. What exactly did you see?"

Weiyang furrowed his brow. "I saw the light glinting off their weapons and heard—"

"But did you *see* the enemy?"

"No."

The man made a derisive noise. "Everyone, come out of hiding! There is no raid. The boy was mistaken."

Weiyang scowled. "I was not! I—"

"Then where are they?" The man barked out a harsh laugh. "Must have been some animal that scared you."

Weiyang wanted to protest further but had nothing to say. Hours must have passed, and the expected raid never took place.

Ma emerged from the house with a weary look on her face. "Don't worry, Weiyang. People are annoyed right now, but I'm sure they'd rather hide for no reason than be caught by surprise."

"I'm sure they were out there," Weiyang muttered.

Ma put a hand on his shoulder. "I don't blame you for being anxious, though I'm glad you were wrong. We don't have enough to eat as it is."

Xiaoyi, Ma's younger sister, approached. "That's why we should accept our uncle's invitation to join his family in Taierzhuang. At least we won't starve there."

Ma nodded with a sigh. "I think you're right."

Weiyang pinched his lips. Ma and Xiaoyi had discussed moving several times since Ba had died, with each conversation inching closer and closer to the inevitable. Now, it seemed, their minds were made up.

As the two women began discussing the practicalities of relocating south to Taierzhuang—an ancient walled village by the Grand Canal linking the Yellow River and Yangtze River—Weiyang found himself wandering back the way he'd come. He was certain the Japanese had been out there—he was *certain*.

Yet everyone was giving him mocking or irritated looks, and even his mother didn't believe him.

Clenching his teeth, he picked up his pace and marched out of the village, past the same barren fields he'd rushed through to give his warning, until he found the spot where he'd stood when he'd glimpsed the flashes and heard the voices. Then he drew a breath and strode in the direction the invaders should have come from, hoping to find some sign they'd been there. Maybe they'd been passing by while heading in another direction, or maybe they were just scouting out the area—whatever the case, he needed some sign to prove he hadn't been imagining things.

The haze seemed thicker than before, possibly because the sun was beginning to set. At first he thought the dark gray splotches scattered across the ground had to be shadows. But as he drew closer, he realized they were ashes, mingled with blackened and shapeless chunks of what looked like metal.

Frowning, Weiyang leaned down and touched them. There was no mistaking the dry texture or the burnt smell. *What could have brought charred, melted metal all the way out here?*

A movement caught his eye, and he looked up with a start. A hazy figure loomed in the distance. Gasping, he jumped to his feet.

Though the figure was only vaguely visible, he recognized it at once. A fierce head like that of a dragon, with a single antler protruding from its forehead. Long whiskers curving toward a powerful, tigerlike body standing on four hoofed feet. Pointed ears rising above a heavy mane, and a long tail ending in a thick tuft. Even from a distance, it looked large—larger than a horse, for sure. It appeared gray in the haze, yet Weiyang knew it had to boast many colors in the light. And it was the most beautiful thing he'd ever beheld.

A qilin—an ancient and revered creature. Known for its

benevolent nature, yet also for the terrifying power it wielded against those who dared attack that which it protected.

He blinked, stunned. *That's impossible . . . Qilin aren't real, only in stories . . .*

"Let's move!" a faraway man shouted.

The qilin vanished from sight, seeming to dissolve into the haze.

Though the moment had seemed frozen, Weiyang had probably only glimpsed the creature for a second or two. He wondered if he'd imagined it . . . if the others were right after all, and he was starting to see things that didn't exist.

TAIERZHUANG, CHINA, MARCH 1938

Though two months had passed since Weiyang arrived in Taierzhuang, he had yet to become accustomed to the sight of all the soldiers. He never knew whether to feel comfort or dread in their presence—comfort because they were there to fight the enemy, and dread knowing they would have to.

His adult relatives often discussed the state of the war, and from what he'd overheard, the Japanese were aiming to strike the great city of Wuhan. They believed taking down such a prominent target would force China to surrender once and for all. And Taierzhuang stood in the Imperial Japanese Army's way.

Sitting at a desk in the cramped house, Weiyang couldn't bring himself to focus on the lesson book Ma had ordered him to read and instead stared out the window at the uniformed men marching down stone streets.

"Weiyang!" Ma entered, her brow sweaty from housework. "I told you to focus!"

"What's the point?" Weiyang scowled. "It's only a matter

of time before the enemy breaches the village walls and kills us all. I thought we were supposed to be safe here."

"So did I." She sighed. "I didn't realize coming here would take us so close to the fighting. But if we'd stayed back home, we'd have starved by now. The news isn't all bad though. Our soldiers are holding off the enemy. I believe they'll beat them back."

Weiyang clenched his teeth and didn't reply. It didn't seem right to point out that the enemy had, so far, been nearly unstoppable.

Ma drew closer and glanced over his shoulder. Faint greasy marks from where Weiyang had repeatedly drawn his finger across the polished wood smudged the desk.

She furrowed her brow. "What have you done here?"

"Sorry. I'll clean it." Weiyang rubbed his sleeve against the desk.

"It looked like a qilin."

He shrugged. Ever since that evening in January, the image of that hazy creature had remained firmly in his mind, as solid as the stone statues that often depicted it. He hadn't told anyone of what he'd seen though. He still wasn't sure himself whether it had been real or not, and if it wasn't . . . well . . . he had no desire to invite his siblings' mockery. The more he heard about the war—the villages destroyed, the innocent people slaughtered—the more certain he was that he'd imagined the qilin. If such a powerful being were on their side, how could such things happen?

Ma placed a hand on his shoulder. "Have you been listening to the rumors, then?"

"Rumors?"

She nodded. "Our soldiers managed to beat back the enemy at nearby Linyi. Some claim it was because a qilin appeared and unleashed its righteous wrath upon the invaders."

"What?" Was it possible the creature he'd seen was real? "That isn't possible. If a qilin were fighting for us, the enemy would have been destroyed by now."

"A qilin would not fight *for* us but *with* us. Such a great creature would not obey orders from a human—any human. But it would cooperate if it deemed the cause worthy. I believe what they're saying . . . The qilin are protectors, and we're in great need of protection right now. Yet it would be beneath them to fight our battles for us."

Weiyang recalled the ash on the ground where the enemy should have been, and the distant voice that had called right before the qilin had vanished. "So perhaps one chose to assist the army but only acts in important moments. It wouldn't appear on every battlefield but might agree to . . . for instance . . . strike a small unit seeking to pillage an already desperate village."

Ma gave him an odd look. "It's possible—"

A loud explosion outside cut her off—a flash of fire, a cacophony of shattering wood and stone, a veil of black smoke dimming the daylight.

Weiyang jumped up and ran to the window. Screams and cries textured the air and were soon drowned out by an ear-shattering mechanical roar. Above, Japanese planes cut across the sky. And from them, more bombs fell.

Distant between the columns of smoke rising from crumbling buildings, the shouting soldiers, and the fleeing villagers, a large, shadowed figure loomed—one nearly as tall as the burning one-story building it stood beside. Weiyang stared, certain he had to be looking at an illusion yet unable to convince his eyes that they were lying to him. The dragon-like head and tigerlike body . . . the single horn . . . they must have been the silhouette of a broken building. The flames that seemed to glow from it—a fire ignited by the bombs, for sure.

"Weiyang!" Ma pulled him away from the window. "Get to the basement! Now!"

She shoved him toward the door.

Shaken from his reverie, Weiyang sprinted out of the room and into the next. And yet as he passed by another window, he saw it again—the shape that looked so much like a qilin.

He ran out the door and into the street before he was fully aware of what he was doing. He had to see for sure. Maybe the rumors were true. And maybe if the great creature were really fighting with them, the war wouldn't feel so desperate. Maybe it would chase away the low-flying bombers with its flames and—

A great *boom* splintered the air, and a blast of heat knocked him off his feet. He landed with a cry but scrambled to get up. The smoky figure still loomed in the distance yet didn't move.

"I see you!" he cried. "Why are you just standing there?"

The creature turned its head, and though its features remained obscured, there was no mistaking the two gleaming eyes that met his.

Still rushing forward, Weiyang tripped but quickly recovered. "Please, help us!"

The qilin dissolved into the smoke, fading as quickly as a dream.

"Come back!"

He stumbled to a halt, stunned. The qilin couldn't have abandoned them, could it? Had it been called away by one of the many shouting soldiers?

Another explosion sounded nearby. He jumped, suddenly realizing how exposed he was. He ran back toward his uncle's house, but he stopped in shock.

A burnt-out shell stood in its place.

Icy shock gripped his chest. With an agonized scream, he rushed forward, only to be thwarted by the heat of still-burning flames. He tried to peer through them, to see if someone, anyone, might have survived. His mother . . . his family . . . they'd gone into hiding below . . .

A loud *crack* sounded above, and he jumped back in time to avoid flying sparks from a charred beam that fell before him.

All around him, desperate citizens raced to put out the fires or try in vain to rescue those beneath the rubble.

Barely able to see through the blur of tears, Weiyang searched every face, hoping against hope to find his family among them.

Many civilians would flee Taierzhuang that day, but Weiyang was not among them. Lost and overwhelmed, with the streets turned to rubble all around him, he'd sought shelter in an abandoned building, too fearful to flee, even knowing that the next bomb might collapse it on top of him.

Though the roof of the house had been blown off and the walls reduced to jagged blocks, a little pocket of safety remained in a storage space beneath the floor, accessible via a narrow crack between fallen bricks that only a skinny young boy could crawl through.

There he remained, with only overheard chatter to inform him of the world outside, as the Japanese surrounded the entire village and the Chinese soldiers within its walls fought to keep them out. Too frightened to emerge, he wept silent tears for the family whose bodies would never be identified amid the ashes and blood. If only he hadn't run out, seeking a creature that had no use for him. If only he could have been with his family when the house went down . . . and with them still.

He'd join them soon enough, he was sure. Yet he was too scared to face the battle that would send him to them.

And so he cowered for days, subsisting on what little remained in the storeroom, waiting for an end that seemingly would never come.

Where was the great supernatural beast that was meant to be defending China? Why hadn't the qilin used its awe-inspiring powers to chase away the invaders for good?

Or maybe there'd never been a qilin at all, and the rumors were just rumors, spread by fools like himself who longed so much for a miracle they saw hope where there was none. The soot- and sweat-stained soldiers who rushed past certainly never spoke of calling upon a qilin for aid.

The days blended into an unending wash of noise and smoke and gunshots and terror. On what Weiyang would later learn was March 26, the Japanese finally breached the village via the northeastern gate, not far from where he hid.

Listening to the noises of battle outside, he was certain that his time had finally run out. Fear melted into relief as he waited for the inevitable—a shell that would collapse the husk of a building on top of him, an enemy soldier who would find him and kill him with a bullet he never saw coming, a fire set elsewhere that would crawl into his hideaway and swallow him.

Yet it didn't come . . .

Why didn't it come?

As daylight turned to darkness outside the small hole through which he perceived the world, the gunfire died away and the noises of battle quieted.

Weiyang crawled up to the opening and peered out, wondering if the fighting had stopped because there was no one left.

Though it was difficult to make out much amid the chaos that had once been a village, he glimpsed the Chenghuang temple in the distance, incongruently beautiful with its stately columns and eaves that flicked in the corners. Japanese soldiers retreated into its painted walls—perhaps seeking shelter for the night.

A sudden wave of fury consumed Weiyang. That temple was dedicated to the Chenghuangshen, the god of the city walls—the very walls the invaders had destroyed. He'd never paid much mind to the religious talk that Ma and Xiaoyi engaged in, yet the enemy's bold irreverence enraged him in a way he hadn't known possible.

Or perhaps it was himself he was enraged at—the coward who'd spent days hiding in a hole, like a rat, while his countrymen fought for the nation's survival against the seemingly invincible force that had already taken two of China's most magnificent cities. Whose family lay rotting beneath the house that should have protected them, unburied and unavenged. Who listened and watched helplessly as brave Chinese soldiers died just beyond his secret shelter, close enough that he could smell their blood and see the light vanish from their eyes.

No more—it all would end that night. For Weiyang, at least. And he wasn't planning to leave alone. Beneath the waning moon, merely a sliver but with edges as sharp as knives, he would at last take action.

Soon the invaders would be asleep inside the temple they'd desecrated. The Chenghuangshen would rather see it reduced to cinders than provide shelter to the enemy.

When the night had stilled, Weiyang emerged for the first time in days and crawled along the rubble to the nearest fallen soldier. After taking the dead man's rifle, he searched the blood-stiffened uniform's pockets but didn't find anything useful. Staying pressed against the ground to avoid being spotted by any enemy watchmen, he crawled to the next body. There he found what he'd been looking for: matches.

Any sign of fear or weakness had evaporated from his body

the moment he'd seen the Japanese enter the temple; in fact, he could no longer feel his body at all. A strange hum filled his head as he made his way silently toward where the enemy slept.

A guard stood watch near the entrance to the temple, and he clung to the shadows for cover. Though he kept his breaths as silent as possible, even his heartbeat felt too loud. Moments wafted by with the breeze, until finally the guard stepped out of sight.

Weiyang sprinted forward before he had a chance to think about what he was doing. In his mind, he'd already pictured his next actions so many times that he felt as if he'd already performed them: rushing up to the structure, dropping the rifle to have both hands free, lighting the match, and throwing it against the vulnerable wood.

The tiny flame seized a corner but hardly seemed large enough to take down the entire building. He reached for another match but froze at the sound of approaching footsteps.

He whirled in time to see the enemy soldier aiming a gun at him. His own was on the ground—there was no way he'd reach it in time.

So this was how it would end. Already the meager flame was flickering out. It seemed somewhat fitting that Weiyang would die along with it.

Inexplicably, the fire burst into an enormous red-and-yellow column, reaching out with golden tendrils and seizing the enemy soldier before he could fire. The man's clothes burst into flames, and he screamed and flailed, the gun clattering to the ground.

Weiyang jumped back from the searing heat. Yet even as the enemy burned mere feet from him, none of the flames touched him. His eyes widened. Like a drop of wet ink soaked into a piece of paper, the fire had spread from a lone match into a gargantuan, inescapable swath, merciless to the cries of those trapped inside. The flames reached so high they seemed to touch the sky above, and the moon that watched from its celestial perch.

Pounding footsteps shook the ground, and then it appeared—the qilin. Tall and proud, it emerged from the conflagration that had been a temple. In the firelight, its brilliant red, gold, and green hues glowed. Fire ringed its magnificent mane and the tufts of its tail and hoofs. Its lone horn glinted as if covered in stars.

"What are you doing here, boy?"

Weiyang spun at the man's voice. A Chinese soldier—a commander, judging by his uniform—approached with several others trailing him.

He waved at Weiyang. "Get out of here!"

Then his gaze moved to the qilin, who remained before the burning temple, and he nodded.

To Weiyang's shock, the qilin nodded in response. After a blinding flash of light, it vanished from sight.

"The battle waged on for days more." Looking back decades later, Weiyang still couldn't explain how he'd survived it. His memory of that time would come and go as vivid flashes—images devoid of context or story. Though that wasn't an answer that would satisfy the curious expression in his granddaughter's eyes, it was the only one he could give. "I was lucky to make it out. Sometimes I would glimpse the qilin in the smoke or the fog."

His granddaughter gave him a skeptical look, her brows low over her eyes. "I don't understand how the Chinese army could have a qilin fighting with it without there being any records," she said, her Mandarin tinged by her broad American accent. "You're making this up."

Weiyang smiled. "Much happened during the war that wasn't recorded, that no one will remember except those who lived it. I knew the night I saw the qilin that the invaders would be driven out, and the homeland would triumph. It would take years, and there were no easy victories, but no matter how desperate things appeared, I never doubted again, knowing the qilin was out there, battling alongside our soldiers."

KINJE'KITILE AND THE JINTU

EUGEN BACON

SOMALILAND, JUNE 1940

Yours is a ritual older than time. It disrupts endless conversations with souls in your head. Once it's done—the ceremony of appeasing the ancestors—you can start the past over. A clean sense of balance toward the present and the future.

Your preparations begin the night before with a flick of the lion's tail—an old male it was, having abandoned its females, too idle to hunt. You found it rotting at the lip of a borehole. Snipped a clutch of its mane, the whole tail, its claws, and some skin right before the hyenas came. The laughing beasts devoured the corpse whole, gobbled it mane to bone, chortling like fools even as they greedily ate and clashed.

The ancestors bring sanity since the *bazungu*, the white devils, came. They brought along their religion, together with conversion, even of babies. Slapping their fresh-born foreheads with the names of saints sanctified by the Vatican. Instead of Shija, Tatu, Vita, Kwara, or Acha—names that carried the history of a victory, a marriage, or a clan—children skipped to church clutching Bibles and shining in their Sunday best, no longer identifiable with their tongue-mangling names like Bartholomew, Apollonia, Januarius, Bonaventure, or Alphonsus.

You rub your face with a powder made from dried crush of what you took from the lion. You wear it in beads around your waist. Today you have secured the intestines of a black cat and the eyes of a sun lizard. You drink them—*aiaiai! Chuchuchuchu!*—our ancestors. The taste never gets better.

You venerate the ancestors for their blessing. There he is, your lover, the great Omukulu, whose spear you anointed for the 1907 Maji Maji Uprising against the colonial Germans, but the white man's bullets still got him. The year is now 1940. You were young with your gift then, unheeding of the precise instructions of the ancestors, made them angry, and they refused to listen. None of the bullets turned to water, as you promised. The rebellious dear ones who took the fight to the *bazungu* felt firsthand what a firearm can do to a human body.

You appeased the ancestors over and over with the fresh blood of spotless cockerel on their graves and smeared on your face, with the fresh dung of a baby elephant all over your skin, with the umbilical cord of a baby in your headwrap and the ashes of a female agama, the long-tailed lizard with her eyes that saw the dead, crushed into your millet porridge. It took forever until your hair was speckled everywhere with natural ash of the gods.

But even Omukulu was forgiving that the magic you gave him did not defeat enemy bullets. Now he has a message for you. You listen closely—this is important. His words echo over and over, ringing to your core:

I am coming. You are coming. We are coming.

Kokorikooo!

Bazi wakes by the crow of a rooster. Must be a new one; he doesn't remember this crow. He looks at his wife, Wetu, then touches the sleeping triplets—Nili, Pili, and Dili—one by one by their hair. He refused baptism, the new names flint-eyed Father Pius was suggesting for him, his wife, and his daughters. Assisi! Loyola! Basil! Alexandria! Deuteronomy! Names even Father Pius wouldn't touch for himself. The shrewd priest would have much to say about what Bazi must do today.

Wetu stirs. The bubs sleepily take turns on her big breasts. Her dark skin is shiny with sweat—it's another humid night. Bazi could take the steam in the air and wear it like a uniform. But he has another to put on.

"It's early," Wetu says, reaching for him. "Is it—?"

"Not yet," he says. He kisses her brow. "Be back soon."

He goes outside the servant quarters, washes his face, brushes his teeth at a basin, running water from a tap. His men don't have such luxury in their dormitory tents—they wash from pails. Men who trust him like a father, an elder brother, for his rank despite his age. Sometimes he feels like a traitor. Enjoying what little perks the British *mzungu*, Lieutenant Blake, deems fit to hurl at him like a bone to a hungry dog. Bazi takes it, the bone, but it's not he who is hungry. It's the men. It's his wife and children. He is a husband and a father now. Too much responsibility to refuse the dry bone.

He sounds the horn. The one the missus of Lieutenant Blake heartily dislikes.

He assembles the men, inspects their khaki uniforms. Today he is too distracted to scrutinize their beds, whose sheets are not folded back just right. It is not the time for discipline, although they will need it where they're going.

The cook sounds the bugle. The men line up with mess tins

for steaming porridge and a crust of bread. It is nothing compared to what Bazi will eat in the officers' mess: toast, muffins, baked custard, croissants, and fruit washed down with coffee. He saves leftovers—for Wetu and, through her, for the suckling triplets.

He meets Lieutenant Blake at the stairs to his manor. It's a tall, rectangular house with a pitched roof. A house that did not bellow with the pelt of rain like the servants' quarters with its corrugated iron roof.

The heavy door opens. The black wood of Lieutenant Blake's house is sculptured with masks and flying tilapia.

"*Afande*!" says Bazi.

He salutes the officer, who returns the salute.

"*Jambo*," Lieutenant Blake says in greeting, using bad Swahili rather than saying the refined *hujambo*.

"Sir," says Bazi.

He refuses to respond in anything but English to Lieutenant Blake's broken Swahili.

The manor has an attic, a basement, many hallways, and windows everywhere. A silk curtain stirs upstairs. Missus is watching from the second floor. Bazi knows the curtains are silk because Wetu cleans the house and cooks for the *bazungu*. She wraps her triplets around her body, bolstered by her ample breasts and bottom, as she scours floors, wrings bedsheets, stirs stew. The lucky one of the triplets gets her bottom, sits on it as if it were a throne.

The only argument he has with Wetu is when she says the British *bazungu* are better than the German ones. As far as Bazi knows, a *mzungu* is a *mzungu*. Worse when they're many, and they become *bazungu*. Nothing is pure; no one is pure, except a newborn. But even the triplets have mastered the art of conniving and negotiating. One of them will yowl at full lungs—as the other two are fast asleep—refusing to shut up and going all throat, flailing arms and legs, until Wetu capitulates, keeps the peace by giving in to the yowler's demands rather than risk waking the others. It's a dog-eat-dog world, survival for the loudest.

Lieutenant Blake's house has many rooms—each child has their own. The children are only two. There's young master Eric, with the eyes of a cat, and the girl, Sue Ellen, who has yellow hair like the ears of ripe maize. Missus schools them in the sitting room. Bazi can hear them repeat their alphabets and numbers when Lieutenant Blake insists on inviting him for cider on the wooden porch with rocking chairs.

The mess filled with the *bazungu*. Over breakfast, Lieutenant Blake reaches across the deep-tanned afromosia wood and outlines, with a finger, the battle plan he has laid on the table. Bazi is the only Black man who eats in the mess, but that is not what he's thinking. The thing on his mind is that what Lieutenant Blake is sharing on the map isn't quite a battle strategy. It's a travel plan. The simplest one to share with a Black man.

"We'll take a bus from Tabora to Mwanza." Lieutenant Blake points on the map. "From Mwanza, we'll take a ferry on Lake Victoria to Kisumu." Lieutenant Blake points at a new circled dot. "From Kisumu, we'll take the East African rail all the way up to Somalia."

"Somalia is our destination, sir?"

"Yes. Somalia."

Lieutenant Blake looks at Bazi as if he's borderline stupid. The way he talks to him, perhaps he imagines Bazi is a stuffed ostrich in a museum. He leans in close to inspect Bazi, anticipating beady eyes to move. His gesture from a pasty face the color of baby yams represents the *mzungu* of a generation that's no different from the one that came with colonizing sticks—a stick is a stick; it hurts when you beat one with it. His and Bazi's is not a forever kinship. When the *mzungu* is old, he will forget Bazi. Hello, hello? Who are you? Right now, or later, he prefers Bazi in a glass case, stuffed like a bird, poised as if about to peck the brightest berry. Bazi would prefer to peck the eyes.

"Not Abyssinia, like you said before?" Bazi asks to confirm.

Lieutenant Blake shakes his head vigorously.

Bazi is just grateful that the expedience of war has guaranteed the *bazungu* do not propose that his men ride donkeys that flicker gray and white ears, or navigate the humps of camels, burps and farts all the way to Somalia.

"There are already troops deployed to fight the Vichy French in Madagascar," Lieutenant Blake is saying. "Others are in Burma fighting against the Japanese. The King's African Rifles needs to be here." He points at the encircled Somalia on the map. "The Abyssinian campaign needs us to be here." Now, he leans yet closer to Bazi. "I want you to tell me the boys are ready."

"They are men, sir," says Bazi. "All of them have passed their rites of passage from adolescence into manhood."

"These men. They're ready?"

Lieutenant Blake's piercing eyes the color of the sky.

"As ready as anyone can be."

Bazi does his best to keep a straight face. He doesn't say that the men need more than bayonets. It's a dialogue he's tried to bring up many times, but the *bazungu* will not trust the Black men with rifles. What are bayonets in a war that's not hand-to-hand combat?

He and his men are doomed.

Only Kinje'kitile can help.

You eye the tall thin man standing outside your hut, a clutch of three black cockerel squawking murder in his hands. His uniform has a white collar and cuffs. He reminds you of Omukulu in his youthfulness and beauty.

"I was expecting you, Bazi," you say.

If he is startled at any of your words, he doesn't show it. He's a calm and measured one. And that is where the similarity with the great Omukulu ends. Omukulu was an impatient one, too unquestioning of his strength, of his spear, of your potions.

You collect the chickens and tell him, "Come inside."

You spit at the ground he has stepped from to ward off evil spirits.

He takes a three-legged stool, faces you with deep velvet eyes that look steadily at you without terror, unlike others who come seeking love potions, wealth potions, health potions, submissive-wife potions, calm-the-in-law potions, baby-maker potions . . .

"You're a virile one," you say.

Despite himself, you see this. He allows himself to be disarmed and raises his brow.

"Young man," you say. "You have suckling little uns. You're not here to ask me to help you make more babies."

At this, his strong, beautiful face breaks into a smile. "Only if the ancestors wish to gift me more to carry my name."

"Is that why you're here, for a son?"

"Not right now."

"Then what do you seek of the ancestors today?" you ask him.

"That is a good question, and I hope you will have an answer." He contemplates his hands, then meets your gaze. "Help from you, our mother, Kinje'kitile. Tomorrow we go to battle. The *mzungu* is asking for the impossible in battle," he says.

"The impossible, mmmhh?" you say. "Then we shall give him the impossible."

You sacrifice the cockerels, one after another, then mingle their throat blood with snake oil and crushed quills of a porcupine.

"I am a vessel," you chant, banging a charmed gourd on his

head. He does not flinch. You circle him three times this way, three times that way.

"I am a vessel of the ancestors; we will be joined," you chant.

At this, he hesitates.

"Our mother, Kinje'kitile. I am a married man, and I love my wife and our three children. Please bear with me, but I cannot have intercourse with you." He speaks in earnest, dusk eyes apologetic, wringing his hands at the shame of denying you an ancestral wish for bonding.

It brings out your biggest belly laugh and mirthful tears.

"You sound like you have heard something," you finally say.

"I heard—"

"Relax, our son," you tell him. "Our joining that the ancestors seek is of a different kind. Nothing for you to worry about."

You give him instructions, and the feathers of the sacrificed cockerel.

Kokorikooo!

Bazi wakes by the rooster's crow. Wetu stirs beside him. The bubs sleepily take turns on her big breasts. He loathes to distract them from her. But he must. He puts his finger into each tiny mouth in turn, feels them suckle, suckle, then replaces his finger with their own digits, and gently pushes each tot away from him and Wetu on the big mattress.

"It's early," Wetu says, reaching for him. "Is it—?"

"Yes," he says. He kisses her brow. "But first there's something we must do."

He pulls out now-dried feathers.

"My love, will you trust our ancestors and lay on these?" he begs.

She shifts, complies without a word.

He draws the calabash with the potion made of throat blood, snake oil, and crushed porcupine quills. He scoops some with his fingers, rubs it on his penis, until he's hard. Wetu is curious, parts her kitenge, the wrap, before he even asks. He rubs the potion inside her, then mounts. It lasts seconds, and first there is a terrible pain, as if a bread knife is shaving him skin by skin. Then the pleasure of his explosion takes him by surprise. Sweetness climbs from his toes to his crown, all the way to his groin, at the same time that Wetu's euphoric cry tells him all he needs to know. They cling to each other.

The babies are unruffled and fast asleep, sucking a thumb, a forefinger, an index finger, respectively.

He feels . . .

More.

He feels . . .

Many.

You feel . . .

More.

You feel . . .

Many.

The day is hot and wet as they march to the bus. Lieutenant Blake is shiny in a military coat full of buttons. Bazi is shiny in his khaki uniform with a white collar and cuffs. His men are shiny in their khaki shorts and safari boots. Bazi is the quartermaster and can be lavish with his men's uniforms, without dragging Lieutenant Blake into it. Because the officer would rather deal with him as if he were an unstriped army private, not the three-striped quartermaster he is.

The *bazungu* have a peculiar habit of naming vessels.

On a green and yellow bus named *Mercy* that sighs on a bumpy road and dirt trails, Bazi avoids conversation, like Kinje'kitile said. They stop for a herd of great big elephants with tree legs and a lot of ears. He spots kudus and sees if he can distinguish the uniqueness of curve patterns in their horns. He and Lieutenant Blake use a special toilet pail, self-cleaning with the reek of chemicals. But his men must stand against a tree or crouch in scrub alongside a narrow road. Bazi thinks of olden stories of the man-eating lions of Tsavo, and he imagines the approach of a rank smell before he sees a strong-legged beast the color of gold, its teeth like knives, claws for killing. It's not sniffing the air and pulling back its lips but rather pounding toward him, seven feet long, seven hundred pounds heavy, the yellowest eyes seeing only him. How does it feel, he wonders, to be in the jaws of a creature with a fecund odor worse than that of a deceased cow rotted for days in the heat and humidity of a tropical climate, and to know it will eat you alive because it's too ravenous to crush your throat with a single bite? They say lions like to eat stomachs first. He thinks of Lieutenant Colonel Patterson, who shot those man-eaters after they had terrorized 150 workers on the East African railway and then sold their maned bodies to a museum for the cost of a castle. He wrote a book.

On a ferry called *Savior* on Lake Victoria, a blue-black giant, slow moving with age, he stands near the bow, uninclined to take the tiny seats for officers on the rest area deck or in the air-conditioned cabin, knowing that his men are stewing somewhere lower in the boat's belly. The ferry is a simple one, not a warship. He tries but fails to find sleep in the first-class cabin with its single berth. He's grateful it's not a dhow like the ones made of wood planks and hanging coconut-leaf sails, masts of Indian teak. The dhows that Arabs used along the Indian Ocean to transport slaves, disposable cargo tossed out to sea if the ocean was too turbulent. He flushes the cabin toilet with guilt, wonders what facilities are available to his men who trust him so.

Still on the ferry, he thinks back to Missus, on the mansion's second floor, gazing at him with the eyes of a cheetah as he waited for Lieutenant Blake to emerge through the heavy black door with its masks and leaping tilapia. He sees her in his mind, billowy cotton gown over a petticoat, white linen apron. Sternly directing Wetu to cook this or that, this way or that, ignorant that the missionaries had already imposed upon his wife a home economics course that covered food science, sewing, health, wellness, and how to raise an obedient child. Wetu knows how to casserole antelope; bake duck pies (moist inside, layered golden crust outside); and garnish twice-cooked goat. But Missus prefers overfried tilapia (to kill the bilharzia) and sugar-boiled maize lavish with butter and cream cheese—terrible milk that's too sour; it's bad enough that, already, it's hardened for chewing rather than drinking. Sometimes the surface of the cheese is foul-blue or moss-green and has invisible animals running along it. The canned variety in the officers' mess is more palatable, with its taste of raw nuts, charcoal, and unripened mango all at once.

He remembers his inner rage the day Wetu was nearly in tears when she put coconut milk in Eric and Sue Ellen's rice pudding, and Missus made a wholesome racket. Bazi raged inside but still smiled at Lieutenant Blake, accepted an ice-cold cider, the calming liquid's mist reaching the outside of the glass, as they sat on the porch with rocking chairs. He smiled, but he wanted to strangle the white man with his bare hands.

The *bazungu* complain that it is humid, but they dress their children in woolen jackets with collars and cuffs. Sometimes Bazi watches Eric, a lonesome child, kick about a rubber ball and knows he will never play with Bazi's daughters once they learn to dribble and pass coconuts around to each other with their feet. His girls will never know to prefer soda or lemonade instead of a fresh squirt of goat milk. He and Wetu will teach them to snack on steamed groundnuts, not imported biscuits and embellished cakes. They'll grow up to cook and eat chicken without throwing away the heads, feet, and gizzards, like Missus directs Wetu.

In Kisumu, they board a train called *Grace*. His men are in a carriage with benches three-people tight. Bazi insists on sitting with them rather than in the "quiet" carriage (for reading or ignoring people), a luxury reserved for officers. Bazi is not an officer with his three stripes, but he holds the highest rank of an African soldier, and it warrants a special allowance. It's the third day of travel, and white or Black, they're beginning to smell like the wet hide on the buttocks of a man-eating lion. More soldiers join them from Kenya, Uganda, and Nyasaland. Not long now before they're in Somalia. He is grateful they're not traveling all the way to Burma. He does not regret sitting with his men.

SOMALILAND, JUNE 1940

You wait. You wait.

You felt the joining that resurrected your lover, the great Omukulu, into your bed chamber. *Aiaiai! Chuchuchuchu!* Our ancestors. The clawing pain, then a pleasure that coursed through your buttocks and soared you in a chime of ululations. Now you wait; you wait with rolling eyes, seeing what the young man Bazi sees, being what he is, on a bus, on a ferry, on a train.

You are . . .
More.
You are . . .
Many.

They hit the ground running in Mogadishu. Thousands of soldiers from the British colonies, a mixed battalion of whites and Blacks surging with rifles and bayonets. It's hot like an oven, and their boots are impediments. The sound of machine-gun fire belches toward him. Bazi sees an explosion of red, a face torn from a soldier's head. Another head topples over. Arms and legs disconnected from bodies everywhere. He sees the white-eyed fear in his men, who still trust him and will do so to their deaths. In between strides, he touches his groin and chants over and over the words Kinje'kitile taught him to say.

"I am a vessel. I am a vessel of the ancestors."

You're running alongside a stampede of soldiers surging with their sharp bayonets. It's a desert; your boots are burning bricks. You rip at them; now you're running barefoot. *Ratatatata*—machine-gun fire shouting at you. Blood, bones, skin on your face. It's blood and bones and skin that births you, births them, births us. You are a vessel; we are a vessel. We feel the great rock python and the porcupine inside us growing with shadow and speed, and we're Omukulu and we're Jintu—a devouring beast.

Bazi is more famished than he's ever felt, and there's food scattering everywhere, humans screaming as he screams—as he laughs—as he tears them with bare hands. Devours them hair to bone.

Their bullets do not touch him.

You rush your ravening jaws toward the enemy, and darkness engulfs them. They're screaming. You're laughing. We're screaming.

Ratatatata, staggered now. The guns' coughing and chocking mingled with a symphony of

high-pitched
laughing and screaming
silence that
falls.

Silence.

Silence.
Silence.

And so it was. The King's African Rifles and the rest of the soldiers in the British-led force of colonial units that joined the Ethiopian guerrillas later spoke, baffled, of what happened on the battlefield in Somalia. How they saw a mighty haze that first shrieked like a dying cockerel, stank like a porcupine, but slithered and writhed like a gigantic rock python as it gulped everyone but them. How the haze of the monstrous snake dissipated, but a god-awful smell stayed wrapped around each man for days. How the Italian troops simply vanished.

Lieutenant Blake took a chartered flight back to Tabora. Bazi accompanied *all* his men (no casualties of war) on a train, a ferry, and a bus all the way back home. Back to the servants' quarters, where his wife, Wetu, and the triplets—Nili, Pili, and Dili—waited. He received a medal called the African Star—also awarded, due to his unshakable doggedness, to his men. His wife, Wetu, clipped her hair, left it au naturel. Never touched the *bazungu*'s fake hair, curly kits, or relaxers—whatever the fashion trending. She still cooked and cleaned for Missus in the tall, rectangular manor with its pitched roof and black wood door sculptured with masks and flying tilapia.

Lieutenant Blake's spawn Sue Ellen married a steel tycoon in London. Eric threw himself off a sturdy rope, but—mollycoddled from infancy—he wasn't skilled enough with a noose to kill himself.

When Lieutenant Blake visited his daughter in Great Britain, he saw the taxidermy mounts of the man-eating lions of Tsavo, a duo preserved to date in a museum, alongside a stuffed ostrich. He pondered for a moment if perhaps it were better had they also made a manikin of Lieutenant Colonel John Henry Patterson.

He leaned close to peer at the bird, and a beady eye moved.

Yours is a ritual older than time. It disrupts endless conversations with the ancestral souls of your lover, the great Omukulu and his demon spirit, Jintu, in your head. You flick the ancient lion's tail.

Now you wait.
To jump-start
the past
over.

AUTHOR'S NOTE

The made-up Jintu monster is derived from African mythical creatures comprising multiplicities. For example, Rompo has "the head of a rabbit, arms like a badger, legs like a bear, a skeletal middle, and human ears." Popobawa is a shape-shifting one-eyed bat creature with a god-awful smell. In Swahili, *mtu* means "person." A "monstrous person" is *jitu*. When I was a little girl, my mother would get me to gobble dinner by threatening that Bichwa will come get me. *Kichwa* means "head." *Bichwa* is a "monstrous head." I borrowed this nightmare of my childhood, the three-headed monster in a billowy shadow, to craft a beast derived from a threesome: the throat blood of a cockerel mingled with snake oil and crushed quills of a porcupine.

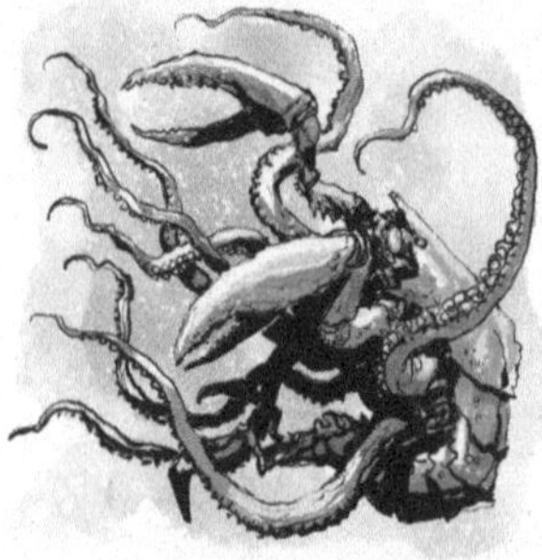

THE FOURTH MAN

JEFF EDWARDS

NORFOLK, ENGLAND, PRESENT DAY

The penitent was late.

Amid the quiet gloom of Saint Mary's, Father Kemble waited in the confessional—steeped in the odors of mahogany, wood polish, and a lingering trace of pipe smoke from an earlier parishioner.

Try as he might, the priest couldn't avoid connecting the aroma of tobacco to its owner. He knew which member of his congregation smoked Briarwood Reserve. And he remembered what sins the man had revealed in this very confessional.

The priest was disappointed by his failure to isolate sin from sinner.

He wished the privacy screen could provide true anonymity, as some of his flock clearly desired. It's a difficult thing to lay bare one's moral failings. How eminently understandable that some people wanted to avoid recognition when divulging whatever transgressions they were most ashamed of.

But Father Kemble had eyes, ears, a nose, and an inquisitive nature.

He couldn't keep his mind from assembling clues. Inevitably, despite his intentions, he would puzzle out the identity of whomever knelt on the other side of the screen.

Tonight the priest's curiosity was more stirred up than usual.

Bishop Exley had asked him to stay late, to hear the confession of someone the bishop had not named. The request had been parsimonious with details.

Possibly it was a celebrity. Someone who needed more than ordinary discretion.

Father Kemble wondered if it might be one of the lesser royals. Officially, the House of Windsor was Anglican, but there had long been rumors of a few Catholics around the fringes of the royal family.

His speculations were interrupted by the sound of an opening door.

The penitent had arrived.

Father Kemble heard footsteps crossing the narthex. Entering the nave. Slow. One heel dragging a bit. Accompanied by an irregular tapping of wood against flagstones.

Unbidden, the priest's mind recognized the sounds and conjured up an image of the approaching parishioner. Not a celebrity. It was the man Father Kemble had privately dubbed Mr. Two-Canes.

An elderly gentleman who wore old-fashioned houndstooth tweed and hobbled along on a pair of matched walking canes.

Father Kemble had seen the old gent often—at the back of the congregation—coming and going in his slow painful way. Never interacting with the people around him.

A man who isolated himself. Who listened to the Word of God but refrained from Communion. Who never spoke to his priest, or to anyone, as far as Father Kemble could tell.

No one even seemed to know the fellow's name.

But here the old gentleman was, shuffling into the

confessional. Pulling the door shut to join the priest in shadowed solitude. Lowering his arthritic body to kneel on the padded step.

When he spoke, the man's voice had the rasp of a rusty hinge. As if he'd gone so long without talking that he'd almost lost the knack. "The bishop . . . tells me you have an open mind."

Father Kemble said, "I try to keep my preconceptions in check."

"I suppose that'll do," said Mr. Two-Canes.

There were several seconds of labored breathing before the penitent spoke again.

"Can you give absolution if you don't believe the sin was real?"

"I'm not sure I understand."

"If I confess to a sin and you think I'm mistaken, or that I imagined it, will you grant forgiveness?"

Father Kemble thought before answering. "A penitent who confesses to a priest is confessing to the Savior. It is Christ—through the priest—who absolves."

"So, you won't withhold absolution if you don't believe my confession?"

"Our Lord doesn't forgive imaginary sins."

"The sin was real," said the old man. "But I doubt you'll believe that."

"It might be better," said the priest, "if you say what you came here to say."

"I was the fourth man," muttered Mr. Two-Canes.

"I'm sorry? The fourth . . . *what*?"

But the penitent responded with the opening words of the Sacrament of Penance and Reconciliation. "Bless me, Father, for I have sinned. It's been more than eighty years since my last confession."

DENMARK STRAIT, MAY 24, 1941

Oliver James Lightoller was a fool on a fool's errand.

No.

An idiot who'd muddled his way into a meat grinder.

He crouched behind a gunwale on the signal bridge of the battle cruiser HMS *Hood* as another German shell came screaming in. Whether it was an eight-inch round from the heavy cruiser *Prinz Eugen* or one of the big fifteen-inchers from the battleship *Bismarck*, Oliver had no way of knowing.

His expertise was in things other than naval warfare, and he was too cold for this nonsense.

The incoming round fell short by thirty or so yards, hitting the water in a huge geyser of spray. Maybe the shell detonated. Maybe not. Whatever sound the projectile made was lost in the thunder of the *Hood*'s forward batteries. Enormous fifteen-inch guns belching fire and steel in a deafening cacophony.

Breath coming out as steam, Oliver chanted quietly, "Hail Mary, full of grace. Hail Mary, full of grace."

Despite his greatcoat and thick woolen trousers, he was chilled to the bone.

His mission—if it could be dignified with such a word—was as absurd as the bundle of mythology books in the rucksack on his back. As ridiculous as the letter of credence buttoned into his breast pocket.

He'd been given strict orders to carry the books and the letter on his person at all times.

The letter could be shown when needed, but the SOE had classified the books as "Most Secret." Oliver was not to reveal their titles or contents—except in the last extremis of necessity.

The next Nazi shell hit the mark, exploding somewhere aft, maybe on the boat decks. Shrapnel and shock waves cutting through topside sailors like a scythe through wheat.

Half deafened as he was, Oliver could make out shouted orders and the cries of wounded men in the respites between incoming and outgoing salvos.

Something crashed into his gunwale with the force of a sledgehammer. The steel plating buckled but didn't give way.

Oliver went arse over biscuits, tumbling across the deck.

He came up, partially dazed. Aching in a dozen places, bleeding from abrasions to his face and hands. A rip in one trouser leg, where some flying fragment had torn wool without hitting flesh. A lovely aperture through which the frosty air could get at him more easily.

Scrambling back into the shelter of the gunwale, he cursed himself for letting them talk him into this madness.

Hail Mary, full of grace. Hail Mary, full of grace.

They'd pulled him out of RAF training just after he'd completed his first solo. He'd made a respectable two-point landing—taxiing the de Havilland trainer plane off the runway—already picturing himself in the cockpit of a Spitfire or a Hurricane.

The SOE men had been waiting in the revetment. His boots had barely touched tarmac before he was bundled into a government car by the gruff agents.

A frustrating ride to Central London, the agents ignoring questions, never uttering a word after they had him in the vehicle.

On arrival, they'd hustled him through the sandbagged entrance of Sixty-Four Baker Street, into the heart of the Special Operations Executive. (Variously nicknamed as the Baker Street Irregulars, Churchill's Secret Army, and—Oliver's favorite—the Ministry of Ungentlemanly Warfare.)

Oliver had been ushered into the office of Sir Frank Nelson himself. There, the trainee pilot had been given a strange invitation.

Sir Frank had spun him a tale about the Nazi high command's obsession with the occult. Spirits. Demons. Magical artifacts.

According to trusted sources, Hitler and his cronies believed that supernatural forces could make the Wehrmacht invincible in battle.

A bunch of horsefeathers, Sir Frank had said. But senior members of the Third Reich believed in such mystical hugger-mugger. *That* was the important part.

With a spot of preparation, it might be possible to exploit Nazi superstitions. Nudge Jerry into some ill-conceived action upon which His Majesty's forces could capitalize.

That's where Oliver came in.

His academic specialty at King's College London, and later at Cambridge, had been Teutonic nautical mythology. He'd made himself into something of an authority on pre-Christian Germanic gods, monsters, and denizens of the seas.

At this moment in history, Britain needed an expert in Nordic sea myths more than it needed another Spitfire pilot. Or so Sir Frank had claimed.

Who was Oliver to argue with the knighted genius behind British special intelligence?

But—genius or not—the head of the SOE had dispatched Oliver on an errand as deadly as it was silly.

Here Oliver was, freezing his buttons off, ducking barrages of German naval artillery. Raising his head occasionally to peek at . . .

What?

Precisely what was he expecting to see?

Nixies manifesting as curvaceous mermaids? The Viking sea spirit, Fossegrim, lounging half naked in the wave tops?

Nothing.

That's what Oliver expected to see.

Nothing.

Because there was nothing related to his academic field here. Nothing he could hope to accomplish, except—if the battle went on much longer—possibly wetting his knickers.

If they'd allowed him to finish RAF training, he might have done something useful. Perhaps he'd have shot down a few Messerschmitts. Or one of the Heinkel bombers that were pounding London.

If Oliver died in the cockpit of a Spitfire, his death might serve a purpose.

But dying at sea with a satchel of books on his back would do nothing for his country. Nothing for anyone.

He risked another glance over the gunwale.

A haze of smoke. Showers of seawater from impacts, large and small. Morning clouds the color of iron. Huge waves, black as a tomb.

The German shells mostly seemed to be falling short. But he saw nothing of use to an intelligence operative, or a scholar, or whatever Oliver was supposed to be.

Hail Mary, full of grace.

The first sign, when it came, was a smell—pungent enough to overpower the odors of scorched steel and cordite.

A miasma of watery putrescence. Like the iodine stench of spoiled fish or the rotting seaweed reek of dock pilings on the Thames at low tide.

Long and pallid, a shape slammed wetly onto the deck near Oliver's makeshift shelter. It was a sinuous rope of living tissue. Snakelike muscles under a sheath of pale blubber.

Twisting. Squirming. Probing with a tactile intelligence that was disturbing.

As he watched, the tentacle—for that's what it was—gripped a stanchion. The sickly white thing coiled itself around the pole like a bullwhip, dripping slime and seawater.

The distal surface of this appendage was lined with rows of suckers, like the tentacles of cephalopods. Near its tip, the quivery mass was the breadth of Oliver's calf. But the size tapered to much greater diameters away from the apex. Closer to the creature's body, the cross section rivaled a redwood tree.

Between one breath and the next, more tentacles rose from the water to join the first. Fumbling for purchase on HMS *Hood*'s armor plating.

The stench was stronger now. A fetor of decayed marine life. Effluvium of some ancient leviathan, risen from endless depths.

This was insane! Things like this could not happen.

Creatures of myth were not real!

But he was looking at one.

Other people saw the thing too. Topside sailors pointed. Shouted.

And suddenly, Oliver understood. *This* was what he'd been sent to find. This legendary monster dragged into reality from forgotten lore.

Because he had an inkling of what the creature must be. If his suspicions were correct, it was a monster long known to Viking seamen. One that crushed the hulls of ships like eggshells.

He understood why God had inspired Sir Frank to send a researcher of obscure legends on this unlikely mission. And why the much-feared *Bismarck* could not be defeated in battle.

The academic in Oliver wanted to dig into the rucksack, retrieve his books, and verify his growing sense of certainty. But German shells were still incoming, and there was a supernatural monstrosity trying to wreak its will on the ship. Not ideal conditions for a bit of research.

In any event, there was no time. Before he could do or say a thing, the unholy behemoth delivered its coup de grâce.

With a shriek of rending steel, an enormous bladelike form

rammed upward through the deck forward of the mainmast. Punching through crossmembers, bulkheads, and armor like a spike through tinfoil.

Oliver caught an eyeblink glimpse of the shape. A monstrous claw, as if from a crustacean of gargantuan scale. Pale as the tentacles of the great beast. Its chitinous surface encrusted with barnacles, coral, and the accretions of centuries.

A fraction of a second later, this vision was torn away as munitions belowdecks erupted into a colossal explosion. Claw, tentacles, and warship all disappeared into a shroud of fire and smoke.

Oliver was blown off his feet. Catapulted into the air.

Insensible, his body pinwheeled through space until the sea rushed up to engulf him.

His wits were slow in returning. As he became conscious of his surroundings, he found himself drifting atop the charred remains of a kapok life raft.

He had no memory of finding the raft. Or of dragging himself out of the water. If someone had assisted him, they were not around to accept his gratitude.

Soaked to the skin, he was even colder than he'd been aboard the *Hood*. But he was out of the water. Prolonged time in that icy brine would have ended him.

Between bouts of uncontrollable shaking, he formulated a plan. If his books and the letter remained legible after their saltwater baptism, he knew what he needed to do.

When the crew of the Royal Navy destroyer HMS *Electra* took him aboard some unknown time later, he was close to hypothermia but utterly resolute of purpose.

He'd been the fourth man rescued from the sinking of the *Hood*. The other three—Signalman Ted Briggs, Seaman Robert Tilburn, and Midshipman William Dundas—would be recorded by history as the only crewmen to escape the destruction of the British flagship.

Shivering in the midships passageway of the destroyer, swaddled in blankets, and drinking hot coffee from an enameled mug, Oliver knew he would not be remembered as a survivor of the lost battle cruiser.

Officially, he'd never set foot aboard HMS *Hood*. Officially, he was not aboard HMS *Electra* now.

Per the records of the Royal Navy, there was no such person as Oliver James Lightoller. His existence was acknowledged by only those few people who knew about his mission.

He gulped down the last of the coffee, nearly scalding his throat in the process. Handing the mug to a sailor, Oliver motioned toward a junior officer. "Ensign! I need to see your commanding officer."

The ensign looked around. "What was that?"

"Take me to your CO," said Oliver.

This brought a frown from the ensign, who was not accustomed to taking orders from bedraggled civilians.

Fumbling under blankets and greatcoat, Oliver pulled forth the sodden letter. He didn't attempt to unfold the wet paper. "Your captain needs to see this *immediately*."

Five minutes later, Lieutenant Commander Stuart Austen Buss—called "captain" by naval tradition, despite his actual rank—read the water-soaked document.

Oliver stood in the man's tiny stateroom, dripping on the

polished deck, trying to appear infinitely more confident than he felt.

Captain Buss glanced up. "What am I supposed to make of this?"

Not a brazen person by temperament, Oliver had spent his time on the raft thinking about this moment. Preparing to abandon his placid nature.

Any signs of timidity would set the tone for every interaction with the man who now regarded him with a skeptical eye.

Oliver had to come across as someone entitled to the extraordinary privileges he was about to demand.

He nodded toward the soggy paper. "Is something unclear?"

The captain's eyes returned to the document. "What exactly is meant by 'cooperation without hesitation or limit'?"

Oliver tried to inject steel into his voice. "If I tell you to ram your ship into an iceberg, you ask which one, and how fast."

"I'll need confirmation from my superiors."

"You've got it in your hands," Oliver said. "That letter is signed by the First Sea Lord, and the director of the Special Operations Executive. The seal and signature at the bottom belong to His Majesty the King."

"I've never heard of anything like this," said Captain Buss. "It's irregular. *Highly* irregular."

Oliver nodded. "I don't imagine the King lends his authority to ordinary matters."

The captain tapped the second paragraph of the letter. "What about *this* part? Surely you don't expect to control what goes into my ship's logs?"

"The Royal Navy expects exactly that," said Oliver. "So does British Intelligence and the Crown. No one is to record my presence aboard your ship. No logs. No reports."

Captain Buss raised an eyebrow. "If I refuse to go along?"

Oddly, Oliver's conversation with Vice Admiral Holland aboard the *Hood* had been far less contentious. The admiral had read the letter twice, asked a handful of insightful questions, then granted Oliver the run of the flagship.

Now, with an officer of much lower rank aboard a ship a fraction as powerful, Oliver was meeting resistance.

He was tempted to back down. Hope that Captain Buss would provide assistance when asked.

But the thing that had wrecked HMS *Hood* was still out there. No one had a prayer of defeating *Bismarck* until that beast was laid to rights.

"You should probably shoot me," said Oliver. "Toss my body overboard. Because if word gets back to Baker Street that you ignored these orders, I suspect you'll be tried for treason."

"Is that supposed to frighten me?"

"It will if you're smart enough to wear that uniform."

The captain read the letter a second time. He reached the end and started again at the top. Examining every word. Every comma.

Finally, he handed the waterlogged paper to Oliver. "What are your orders?"

"I need somewhere private to look over my documents," said Oliver. "A desk or table to lay things out."

Captain Buss stood up and cleared his own papers off a small desktop. "Will this do?"

"Your stateroom?"

"Evidently, what's mine is yours."

"This will be fine."

"Shall I have someone bring you tea?"

It was likely meant as sarcasm, but Oliver treated the offer as genuine. "I'd rather have dry trousers."

The captain saw himself out, leaving Oliver to dig the books out of his bag. Seawater trickled from the old volumes onto the captain's desk. Under other circumstances, Oliver would have been mortified by the mess, but he had no time for fastidiousness.

He started with Günther Brecht's *Mythos und Schatten*. The thin pages felt as delicate as wet cobwebs.

After Brecht, he moved on to Viktor Rydberg's *Undersökningar I Germanisk Mythologi*. By the time he got to Jacob Grimm's *Deutsche Mythologie*, Oliver had confirmed the identity of the monster to his satisfaction.

Norse seamen had called it the *hafgufa*. Christian Franz Paullini had named it the *monstrous marinum*. Francesco Negri's term had been *sciu-crak*, which had likely inspired the common name . . .

Kraken.

Details of the monster's appearance varied from one tale to another, but most descriptions were of a mountain-sized sea crab or lobster, with arms like a gigantic octopus. Precisely what Oliver had seen.

He now had an idea of what he was up against but no clue of how to fight the thing.

For that, he turned to Georg von Holst's *Arkane Riten geheimer Bestien*, a guide to rituals for summoning and banishing entities from Teutonic myth.

Like the other volumes in his pack, Oliver had always regarded this book as an academic reference. A glimpse into the superstitions of a prescientific culture.

That was before he'd seen the kraken.

Discovering the monster had been a challenge to his academic beliefs. Recognizing that Norse legends might be true was a blow to his spiritual faith.

Then again . . . the God of Abraham hadn't claimed to be

the *only* god. Merely the *greatest* of gods. More powerful than Ba'al. Capable of rendering judgment on the gods of Egypt. To be exalted above all others.

Oliver had always interpreted scriptures about other gods as denouncements of false religions. But what if other gods existed?

Improbable as it seemed, Oliver had survived an encounter with an alleged creation of Njörd, the Viking god of wind and wave. If the kraken was *real*, how many other fantastical things in these books were *also* real?

He opened von Holst's book.

Forty minutes later, he went in search of Captain Buss.

Some of the components for the ritual were easily come by.

The *Electra*'s gunnery officer kept a horsehair brush in his shaving kit. First problem sorted.

Captain Buss volunteered the sword. His Royal Navy dress saber had an ornamental blade that would struggle to cut butter. No Viking raider would have considered it a battle-ready weapon, but it *was* a sword. Second problem sorted.

Sadly, Oliver knew exactly where to find the blood of a virgin. Third problem sorted.

Arranging the fire wasn't difficult. A small one would do. A puzzled sailor had supplied a good-sized cook pot containing wooden pieces from an ammunition crate. The fragments were splintered and should catch easily when Oliver applied a match. Fourth problem sorted.

The tricky bit turned out to be the animal heart.

Captain Buss asked his confused crew to search storerooms, lockers, and personal effects for a tin of lamb heart, beef heart, or anything similar.

When that failed, the captain sent flashing light signals to the destroyers HMS *Icarus* and HMS *Anthony*, who had joined *Electra* in searching for survivors of the *Hood*.

"In need of animal heart. Type of animal not important. Tinned meat will suffice. Cannot explain further, but requirement is urgent."

Both ships returned negative replies. No animal hearts aboard *Anthony* or *Icarus*.

Captain Buss—not happy to find himself in such a position—ordered his navigator to plot a course to intercept the cruiser HMS *Norfolk* so he could repeat the odd request. Apart from not wanting to abandon the hunt for survivors, Buss was not looking forward to explaining his urgent need for a cut of meat.

Forbidden by the letter from revealing the source of this weird requirement, he'd have to dream up an excuse to make the request seem reasonable.

His teeth were clenched as he grumbled to himself, "Which iceberg? And how fast?"

Oliver suppressed a smile.

But the captain was spared by a signal from *Icarus*. A lieutenant aboard the destroyer had found a tin of beef heart at the bottom of a seabag. He'd surrender it now, in exchange for a steak dinner from Captain Buss when *Electra* and *Icarus* returned to port.

Buss grudgingly accepted.

When all was in readiness, the *Icarus* maneuvered across HMS *Electra*'s bow. Not a close pass but near enough that a bundle thrown over the fantail of *Icarus* could be recovered by sailors with boat hooks aboard *Electra*.

The bundle consisted of two life vests lashed to an oilskin bag containing the tinned beef heart.

Fifth problem sorted.

The sixth problem had Oliver worried. He wasn't sure he could do what was required. But he couldn't even attempt it until sundown, so he concentrated on preparing the fantail.

The enclosure on the fantail consisted of canvas tarps stretched from stanchions to deck pad eyes. It formed a lidless three-sided box between the aftermost gun and the stern, with the open end facing aft.

The sides were not high, but they were tall enough for Oliver's purposes. He'd be sitting for the ritual. His actions would be hidden from the topside lookouts.

When he'd described this setup to Captain Buss, Oliver had used the fire to justify his need for an enclosure. The canvas would shield his small flame from the winds and conceal whatever light escaped the cook pot.

The true purpose was to hide the ritual from observers. According to von Holst, the rite must not be witnessed by nonbelievers.

Oliver wondered what the crew made of his presence aboard their ship and his bizarre activities. This stranger—dragged from the sea—who made outlandish requests that the captain inexplicably granted.

By now Captain Buss would have concluded that Oliver was a lunatic. None of Oliver's demands could make the slightest sense to the pragmatic navy man. But Buss was a loyal officer. He followed orders, even when he didn't understand them.

Oliver waited in the enclosure until the last sunlight was gone from the sky and the stars glittered between gathering storm clouds.

It was time.

Even with the canvas sides as windbreaks, starting the fire took some doing. He struck nine matches before he got a splinter of wood in the pot to catch. He nurtured the flames until he had a solid little blaze going.

Sitting cross-legged on a navy blanket, he could feel the cold of the deck seeping through the folded layers of wool.

He began the chant, so low that the repetitious phrases were nearly inaudible in the wind.

His pronunciation was not good. He'd spent years learning to read and write Old Norse but little time speaking the language, so he was certainly bungling the articulation.

It would probably suffice. According to lore, Asgrim the Oath-Keeper had performed the ritual after losing half his tongue and most of his teeth. If the gods could understand *that*, they could forgive Oliver's poor elocution.

The words were almost hypnotic in their repetition. "Lord of the waves, hear my call. Lord of the winds, hear my call. Lord of the waves, hear my call . . ."

Continuing the incantation, he opened the tin of beef heart. The wet-copper odor of raw organ meat gave his stomach a twinge.

On the deck next to the open tin, he laid the horsehair shaving brush.

He'd spent twenty minutes with a file, bringing the tip of the captain's sword to the sharpest point the ornamental blade could support.

Before him lay four of the necessary components: Flame. Sword. Hair. Heart.

Pulling back his left sleeve, he raked the tip of the sword down his left forearm, breaking the skin just enough to bring a thin line of blood.

The final component. Blood of a virgin.

He passed the blade through the fire, speaking in Old Norse. "Flame of the faithful. Sword of the valiant."

In his ears rose a thrumming buzz, like a hive of angry bees.

The horsehair brush went into the fire. Bristles curling in the heat. Catching flame. "Hair of the swift."

Something was happening.

Holding his bare forearm above the pot, he allowed a few drops of his blood to fall sizzling into the flames. "Blood of the untouched."

The deck vibrated beneath him. The waters around the fantail roiled and foamed.

He felt a rush of panic. Should he stop this? If he put out the fire and dumped the cook pot overboard, would everything go back to normal?

When he saw tentacles rising from the waves, he knew it was too late. His call had been answered.

The tentacles emerged from the sea like quivering columns of aquatic flesh. Pointing toward the sky.

Rising to the port side of the ship. To starboard. Aft. Surrounding the fantail of the destroyer like a forest of beslimed albino tree trunks.

Oliver paused, unwilling to complete the ritual.

Above him, the tentacles began to writhe. Tips curling downward. Bending inward toward the ship. The clenching fingers of a titanic fist.

Even if the deadly claw did not appear, HMS *Electra* would soon be crushed by the constricting tentacles. Her officers and sailors killed.

And the kraken would continue ripping British warships apart. Littering the seafloor with corpses and broken ships.

Oliver crossed himself and spoke below a whisper. "Forgive me, Lord."

He drew the beef heart from its tin—the heavy wad of meat squelching with unpleasant juices. The heart seemed to grow hot. To pulse in his hand. Like a thing alive. Infused with dark power.

Raising his voice, Oliver chanted in the archaic Nordic tongue. "I bring the flame, and the sword, and the hair, and the blood."

He hesitated. Revolted, not by the physical act that must come next but by the oath he was about to swear.

The kraken's tentacles drew inward, their tips crossing in the air above the ship. Becoming the arches of an unhallowed cathedral.

Contracting. Squeezing inward. Downward. Droplets of seawater and slime falling onto the deck. An unclean baptism that deposited sins rather than washing them away.

Oliver bit into the animal heart. Tore at it with his teeth until a chunk of raw flesh filled his mouth.

Gorge rising, he forced himself to swallow this loathsome mouthful.

With the animal's blood wet upon his face, Oliver spoke the words he had been dreading.

"Master of wind and waves, I have made the sacrifice you demand. I renounce all gods but Njörd. I swear upon my life to hold you above all other gods."

Something like a convulsion passed through Oliver's body. Because he *meant* the words as he said them. He was forsaking the God of Abraham.

The ritual could only be performed by one with no intent to deceive. Oliver was pledging himself to this pagan deity.

The tentacles were a tunnel now. Blotting out stars and storm clouds.

"In exchange for my fealty," intoned Oliver, "send this spawn of the depths to slumber for seven lives of men."

He spat into the fire and hurled the animal heart through the narrowing space between two tentacles.

As the gory object disappeared into the sea, a spasm shot through the arms of the monster.

They twitched.

Uncurled.

Retreated limply, to vanish beneath the waves.

The kraken would sleep for seven lifetimes of man. This, Oliver knew. Because, like the unconscious Goliath now sinking toward the seafloor, Oliver was the servant of an unholy god.

He slumped onto the deck, awash with seawater and fluids more vile. And he cried the tears of a man who has no right to ask forgiveness.

SAINT MARY'S CHURCH, PRESENT DAY

"I broke faith with my God," whispered Oliver Lightoller through the privacy screen. "I raised another god in his place. Violated the commandment that comes before all others."

Father Kemble sat in silence, trying to figure out if any part of this story could be true.

The elderly penitent made a sound that might have been a cough. "You don't believe a word . . ."

"It doesn't seem very *likely*," admitted Father Kemble.

"So, we're back to where we started," said the old man. "Can you offer absolution if you don't believe the sin occurred?"

"This all happened in 1941," said the priest. "Eighty years without attending confession. Why is it important to you *now*?"

The old man sighed. "You won't believe this either."

"Maybe I will . . ."

"I realize now that God—the *Christian* God—won't let me die with this on my soul."

"Like the wandering Jew of biblical legend?" asked the priest. "Condemned to live until the end of the world because he taunted Christ on his way to crucifixion?"

"Perhaps," said the old man.

"You believe the Almighty has cursed you?"

"I did the thing he forbids above all."

"My heart wants to believe you," said Father Kemble, " but my brain tells me such things are not possible."

"When your soul disagrees with your intellect, which voice does God want you to heed?"

The priest said a silent prayer for guidance.

His prayers often went unanswered, or the responses came in some form that needed time to understand. But every now and again he felt the answer in his bones. Plainly, as if the Lord was speaking directly to him.

This was one of those rare occasions.

"I won't assign penance," said Father Kemble. "You've suffered a lifetime of atonement."

The old man's voice broke. "Then you'll . . . *you'll* . . ."

The priest responded by commencing the liturgy of absolution. "Give thanks to the Lord, for he is good."

Beginning to weep, Oliver Lightoller made the customary response. "His mercy endures forever."

"Your sins are forgiven," said Father Kemble. "Go in peace."

"Thanks be to God," whispered the old gentleman. A ragged exhalation came from his side of the screen. The sound of a weary soul releasing eight decades of despair.

Father Kemble waited for the forgiven man to exit the confessional. To hobble with his twin canes into a life no longer crushed beneath an unbearable burden.

But the door didn't open.

The priest gave the old fellow a few minutes to collect himself.

Still no movement.

Father Kemble opened his own door and emerged from the confessional. He tapped on the door to the penitent's compartment.

No answer.

When he opened the penitent's door, he knew what he'd find.

The soul of Oliver Lightoller, Mr. Two-Canes, had flown this earthly realm, leaving only the empty vessel of his mortal remains.

Father Kemble crossed himself, said a prayer for the departed, and went to the phone to call 999.

How much of the extraordinary story was true? Were there *really* other gods out there?

The priest decided that it didn't matter. One God was all he needed. All *anyone* needed.

He lifted the receiver and began to dial.

THE NIGHT CREW

PETER CLINES

ENGLISH CHANNEL, FEBRUARY 1942

Doctor Ken Kraft, professor of history and folklore, temporarily seconded to the US Department of the Navy, tugged his ratty cap a little lower and turned up the collar of his coat against the cold. He leaned against the stack of crates, trying to look more like the other dockworkers scattered around the Dieppe pier, and risked another glance out at the foggy English Channel. Just a glance. He'd been warned looking anxious would draw attention.

He'd also been warned not to stare at the squad of German troopers farther down the dock, but that was even harder. Five armed Nazis, right over there. Smoking. Talking. Looking bored. But if they had any idea what he was doing here . . .

Someone punched him in the arm and waved at the crates behind him. "You're staring again."

"I have to look at something."

Dar Carter slumped against the crates next to him and made a show of yawning, unbothered by the cold, the soldiers, or the lack of ship. "Then look at anything that isn't them or the ocean."

Lean and muscular, with a week of stubble across his square jaw and a long scar that ran down his left cheek, Carter easily passed as a dockworker or crew boss in his own borrowed clothes. Kraft's academic peers and contemporaries often referred to Carter as an overly active historian. In less polite circles, they dismissed him as a mercenary treasure hunter. Either way, he knew the location of every historical site in Europe and Africa, including dozens people had thought lost for centuries. And a few most assumed were just the stuff of myth and legend.

Which was, of course, how they'd both ended up working for the navy.

Carter flipped a length of discarded rope back and forth between his fingers, tying assorted knots, untying them, and then twisting the rope around again. Kraft watched for a few moments, then found his own piece of rope. It gave him something to focus his mind on that wasn't the German soldiers. Or the cold.

Another half hour passed before the muffled clang of a bell worked its way out of the fog. All eyes on the dock turned to the sea. Carter gave him a nudge. "Don't get too excited, but I think our ride home has arrived."

The ship was a shadow, then a dark outline, and eventually it pushed out of the fog and collected details around itself. Kraft saw two short masts and a heavy wooden railing. Heard the chug of a small engine. A handful of figures moved on the deck, tossing orders and confirmations back and forth in at least three languages. Kraft guessed the *Sea Ghost* was all of a hundred feet from bow to stern, going off the men and the assorted crates lashed down on the deck.

"It looks . . . old," he said.

"Did you think they'd send a battleship to collect us?"

"No, but perhaps something made in this century."

Lines were flung off and tied off, anchors dropped, and a heavy boarding ramp run up to the deck. A barrel-chested man in a black peacoat strode down onto the dock. He rearranged the sheaf of papers in his hand as the harbormaster approached. The soldiers moved closer as well.

A tall, lanky man in a dirty sweater carried a smaller crate under one arm. He got halfway down the ramp and shouted back up to the deck. Men came down in pairs, lugging larger crates between them. Most of the dockhands backed away.

"What do we do?" whispered Kraft. "Do we go on board, or—"

"We wait," Carter told him. "They know what they're doing."

Kraft fumbled with more knots as the cargo was unloaded. The barrel-chested captain shared a few semifriendly laughs with the harbormaster and the soldiers. Handed his paperwork and an envelope to the harbormaster. Got the paperwork back. Talked some more as he opened the smaller wooden box that the lanky mate brought him. Handed out bottles to the soldiers. Gave an extra one to the sergeant.

It took them almost half an hour to finish the whole ritual. By the time he walked back to the ramp, most of the ship's deck had been cleared of cargo. Thirty more minutes and another six crates had been hauled up out of the hold. The lanky mate in the dirty sweater put his fingers to his lips and whistled. The dock crew perked up, and he shouted a few commands in French. He pointed at a stack of crates on the dock, then up at the ship's deck. Three of the dockhands joined the crew, carrying the boxes up the ramp.

The mate walked over, pointing at the crates behind Kraft and Carter and calling out in French, "You two. What are you waiting for?" He got closer. Switched to English. "Picking up a schoolteacher and a man with a scar, delivering them across the Channel. Guessing you're them?"

Carter nodded.

"Good. Get these crates on board. Those first three go on the deck."

Kraft glanced back at the crates. "What?"

"Men going on board empty-handed look suspicious," said the mate.

"But dockhands lugging crates look normal. Of course."

"You must be the teacher."

Carter barked out a laugh.

"I'm Paul. Skipper will talk with you after we get underway. Now get moving," the mate added, switching back to French and raising his voice a bit.

They carried three crates onto the *Sea Ghost*, working around the other dockhands. Then helped with one that took a man on each corner. Then some smaller ones all went to the hold. Another large one for the deck. The work helped Kraft to warm up.

Paul stopped him on the dock. Pointed out one last crate. "Take it to the hold. Stay on the ship."

Kraft nodded his understanding and hefted the crate. Walked it up the ramp and down into the *Sea Ghost*'s dim hold. He set it down, turned, and ran into another crew member.

They stared at each other for a moment. Then Kraft automatically stuck out his hand. "Kraft."

The other man, pale in the dim light, looked at the hand. Studied it sleepily. "Abramoff," he said with a thick accent. "New?"

Kraft's mind spun, unsure how to reply. "Earning my passage."

Abramoff smirked. Wrapped his fingers around Kraft's hand. The man's grip had the chill of the winter sea in it. "Welcome, lubber."

Kraft headed back up on deck. Found Carter tying down some crates. The crew moved around them as the *Sea Ghost* cast off. Anchors cranked up. Lines coiled. The deck shuddered as the engine thumped and pushed the ship back into motion. Kraft faked a yawn and a stretch, used it to look back at the docks. The soldiers toasted each other with cups. The dockhands hauled away the cargo that had been unloaded. No one seemed to have noticed him and Carter staying on board.

Then the shoreline faded into the fog, and they were on the Channel.

Carter ambled over to stand near him. "Feeling better?"

"Better to be heading home. Less good that we're doing it by sea."

"What you need is a drink. For that matter, so do I."

"It can't be more than ten in the morning."

"Are you saying you don't want one?"

Images from the past weeks flashed through Kraft's mind. "Do you still have your flask?"

"No, so hopefully our captain will be in a gracious mood when we talk to him."

They watched the sea for a while, and Kraft felt some of the tension slip away from his body. One of the deckhands walked by. Checked the knots they'd tied. "Good work," he said. "You serve on a ship before?"

Kraft shook his head.

"Not for a long time," said Carter.

The hand nodded again. Frowned up at the cloudy sky. Barely enough sunlight made it through for Kraft to tell where the fog ended and the gray clouds began. "Never good when it stays dark," said the hand. "God willing, it breaks before the night crew wakes up."

"Shove off, Castro," said Paul. He'd come up along the ship's port side. "You've got work that needs doing, and none of you should be talking to these two anyway."

Castro glanced up at the sky again, traded looks with the mate, and went to check the next set of crates lashed to the deck.

"Skipper'll see you boys now," said Paul. "Follow me."

He led Kraft and Carter back to the cockpit, a cabin of wood and glass built around the ship's wheel. A set of double doors made up most of the rear wall. A simple cross hung above the ship's wheel, and electric lights had been mounted in the corners. A compass. A modern clock. A two-way radio.

The captain stood with one hand resting on the wheel. A pair of wire spectacles balanced on the tip of his nose, and he studied a leather logbook through them. He'd hung his peacoat on a hook, but somehow his barrel chest looked even wider and heavier without it. He gave them a glance, read a little more, and the book slapped shut in his hands. He dropped it on a wooden counter and swept the spectacles from his face. "This them?"

"Aye, Skipper."

The captain dismissed the mate with a nod, and Paul vanished back out to the deck.

Kraft stepped forward. Held out his hand. "Doctor Ken Kra—"

"No," said the captain. "No names. Best for all of us if me and my crew don't know anything about you."

Kraft let his hand drop.

"It's his first time," said Carter.

The captain barked out a laugh and set both hands on the ship's wheel. "I'm Gordon. I'll get you home. That's all that matters." He pointed at the bridge's window. "Fifteen knots should get us to Folkestone in five hours. Call it six with the fog, but if we're lucky, it'll lift soon. Best if you stay out of sight and out of the way. There's cold sausage and cheese down in the icebox if you're hungry. Cook's not with us on this run."

"I don't suppose you've got anything strong to drink?" asked Carter. "My companion and I have had a . . . well, you wouldn't believe us if we told you."

"I don't want you to tell me. And the *Sea Ghost* is a dry ship. Can't risk a sloppy crew these days."

Carter sighed. "Fair enough."

Kraft cleared his throat. "If I may, Captain Gordon—"

"You may not. My business is discretion. We've already talked as much as I usually do with passengers."

Carter glanced at Kraft. Smiled. "Your business of smuggling people and goods across the Channel."

"Someone has to do it," said Gordon. "And our Allied friends look the other way as long as we pick up the occasional extra cargo or passenger for them. In your case, they even paid a little extra."

Kraft cleared his throat. "Is this why you have such a . . . classic ship?"

"She's solid as stone. Barely sixty, and more than half of that in dry dock up near Scarborough. We rechristened her and put her back to sea for Dunkirk."

"I thought it was considered bad luck to rename a ship."

"Worse luck to leave her with a name she didn't deserve anymore. The *Sea Ghost* made three trips in four days. Rescued almost four hundred men. That sound like bad luck to you?"

Carter nodded approvingly. "Sounds like a ship with some life left in her."

"Damn right she is. Her engine's not much, but she can get us close to twenty knots on a calm sea. The masts are strong if we want to go quiet. These days, lots of companies are calling up older freighters from their fleet to cut potential losses, so we don't attract much attention."

Kraft looked around at all the wood. "Aren't you worried some Nazi captain might get bored and take a shot at you for fun?"

"No. Too many of them are clients. Plus, she's about the same length and beam as a German E-boat, so with sails furled we can usually slip by in fog like this." He gestured at the gray skies outside the cockpit. "Besides, torpedoes cost money. They're filthy Kraut savages, but nobody wants to explain to their superiors that they wasted a perfectly good torpedo just to sink some old junker."

"Sounds a bit like you're daring them to call your bluff."

Carter slapped him on the back. "You've described almost a third of all military strategy, Kraft. Good job."

"Skipper?" Paul was back at the hatch, his brow furrowed. "We've got a ship coming up on our starboard."

"Patrol boat?"

Paul shook his head. "Bigger."

"Another freighter?"

"No, Skipper."

Gordon scowled, gestured for Paul to take the wheel, and grabbed his coat before heading out the door. Kraft and Carter followed. They moved down past another deckhand and paused at the rail. Kraft squinted into the light rain. The distant shadow reminded him of the *Sea Ghost* before it had slid out of the fog back at Dieppe. But even to his untrained eye, he could see the shape in the mist was much larger.

"Christ on a crutch," muttered Gordon.

"That's a battleship," Carter said.

"Can't be."

Kraft tried to estimate the shape's speed and course. "Maybe here to escort us home?"

Carter shook his head. "I don't think it's one of ours."

"Nonsense," said Gordon. "The Krauts wouldn't send a warship into the Channel. It'd be suicide."

Kraft stretched out an arm and pointed out a shape off to the left, past the looming silhouette. "Is that . . . another one?"

Carter and Gordon turned. Stared at the faint shape. "It's not possible." Gordon glared at Carter, then Kraft. "What did you two do back in Europe?"

"Nothing that'd warrant two battleships," Carter assured him.

"Well . . ." Kraft began.

"Are they moving to cut us off?"

"Can't tell," said Gordon. "We won't be past them in time. Best bet is to change course, try to stay ahead of them." He headed back to the cockpit.

"Are we fast enough to do that?" asked Kraft.

Carter studied the distant shadows, growing larger in the fog. "I sincerely doubt it."

"Do you think they've spotted us?"

"Maybe. We spotted them. Let's hope Gordon's right, and they think we're an E-boat."

A low buzz grew in the air. Both men looked up at the gray clouds as the engines grew louder. Kraft thought he caught a glimpse of planes but couldn't be sure with the rain hitting his eyes. "Are you certain they're not after us?" he asked after a minute.

"If anyone even knows about us, at best they think we're two American spies. We wouldn't be worth sending two battleships into the English Channel."

"Three." Kraft pointed. "That's another one, yes?"

"I think that one's a destroyer. Smaller. Probably an escort ship. Probably not the only one."

"They must be trying for the North Sea."

"Looks like. Don't know if they're bold as all hell or plain stupid."

The *Sea Ghost* leaned to the side, forcing water out of its way as it turned. Kraft took a few steps toward the stern as his view of the battleships swung away. "What will they do if they identify us?"

"No idea. Maybe Gordon's right, and no one will bother wasting a cannon shell on us. Or maybe they'll think we could give their position away, and they'll blow us out of the water."

"Pleasant."

More engines buzzed in the clouds above them, followed by the rattle of distant gunfire. Carter walked along the rail, heading toward the stern, trying to keep the distant ships in sight as the *Sea Ghost* came about and picked up speed.

Kraft went the other way, toward the front of the ship. Sea spray and rain pushed against him, and he knew his clothes would be soaked through soon enough. He tried to picture a map of England in his head as he moved across the water-slicked main deck, wondering if—

A scream rang out over the chug of the engine and the rush of the sea. Kraft moved forward and tried to see through the rain. Had someone been injured or fallen overboard or—

Three things hit him at once, jumbling his mind and paralyzing his feet.

Paul, the mate, half ran, half slid across the deck toward him. "Back," he yelled. "They're awake. Get inside."

Two ships, each as big as the *Sea Ghost,* headed toward them. Maybe half a mile away and closing fast.

Beyond Paul, maybe twenty feet away, two crewmen crouched near the front mast, half hidden by cargo. One had fallen, and the other, a man in a tattered coat, bent over him, trying to get him back to his feet. A sheet of rain crashed down on the deck, and when it cleared, Kraft saw the tattered man was kissing the other's throat.

Centuries of folklore and legends and half-believed stories rose up in Kraft's mind.

"Move!" shouted Paul, giving him a shove. His heels slipped on the deck. The mate grabbed his arm and dragged him back toward the stern.

Kraft saw the tattered man tear at the other's throat. Saw the blood. He focused on following Paul, and his other sleeve snagged on something.

The something yanked him back.

He turned and saw Abramoff, the pale man from the hold. Recognition blossomed in Abramoff's eyes as well. Then someone slipped past Kraft and slammed two quick punches into the pale man's face.

Carter.

Abramoff had time to grin before Carter cracked him alongside the head with the piece of wood in his other hand. The pale man roared and leaped back.

"Go, Kraft!"

He turned and didn't see Paul anywhere. Ran as fast as he could along the railing. A wave sloshed across the deck, and his mind lit up.

Carter slammed into him, knocking them both down. Carter rolled to his feet, dragging Kraft up after him. "They're vampires."

"One of them ripped a man's throat open."

"They got the mate as well. Paul. One of them dragged him over a stack of crates just as I found you."

Kraft pointed at the water sloshing back and forth across the deck. "Running water. Might slow them down."

"Smart man. We should get to the captain."

"Agreed."

Carter led the way along the wooden railing. "How are there vampires on a ship?"

Kraft turned his head and realized just how many crosses were in the cockpit. Some scratched into the walls. Others had been hung but blended in with the wood. Small ones on the doorframe. Dozens of them circled the floor of the cockpit, stretching out to the walls. Several looked new, but his historical training told him some of them had been there for years.

"So we'll be safe until the Nazis blow us out of the water," said Carter.

The captain shook his head and pointed out the window. "We're already in range of their guns, and they haven't shelled us yet. This soup's thick enough—with the sails down, I think *they* think we're one of their escorts."

"That won't last forever. Someone's going to notice we're not an E-boat."

"Maybe. But they're focused on speed right now. If we play this right, I can keep us on the south edge of their group and break off before we reach the strait."

"Assuming the vampires don't kill everyone before then."

"The clouds'll lift soon enough."

"And then the Germans will see who we are, and they'll kill everyone."

"We can do this. I can push her up into the red; we'll do twenty, maybe twenty-two, knots. She's done it before. We'll be another shape in the fog."

Kraft crouched and ran his fingers over a cross gouged into the deck by the door. His almost-numb fingers could still feel the decades of wear that had smoothed the shape's rough edges. "Captain, you said the vampires were part of the original crew."

He nodded, and more than a little guilt clouded his face. "I believe so, yes. They were asleep inside the bulkheads and parts of the hull for all the years she was in dry dock."

Kraft nodded. Looked at Carter.

"I'd guess they're the night crew we heard mentioned earlier."

Carter glanced back. "No, I mean, how are they on a ship? I thought vampires hated water. Needed to sleep in the soil of their homeland, all that."

"I have no idea."

"You're supposed to be the brains of this operation, Kraft."

They followed the light shining out of the cockpit windows. Saw Gordon inside. "Perhaps they have soil somewhere on the ship," said Kraft. "Hidden in a crate or somewhere in the hold."

They burst into the cockpit and pulled the doors shut behind them. Gordon looked over his shoulder at them. "Two E-boats just passed us. I think with the fog they—"

"We have other problems," said Carter.

Gordon turned. Saw their faces. Realized they were alone. "The night crew?"

Kraft nodded.

"You knew there were vampires on your ship?" growled Carter.

"I knew there were . . . other crew members. The original crew, I think."

"The original crew?"

Gordon shook his head. "They don't come out often. A few hours after we're underway, and only if it's night. They act a little tired or drunk, but they work. And they're gone belowdecks as soon as the sun's out."

"Well, they're not tired anymore," said Carter.

"They killed Paul and at least one other man," said Kraft.

Gordon muttered something under his breath. "The rest of the crew will be in the galley. They know the drill if the night crew wakes up. It's protected." He waved a hand at the walls around them.

"Vampire sailors. Their 'native land' is the sea. They were helpless in dry dock, started regaining their strength once they put her back in the water." A cold breeze raced through the cockpit. "And they're here."

Abramoff stood outside the cockpit by the now-open doors. Another pale man with a beard stood by him, staring eagerly at Kraft. A third man with thick stubble and a heavy cap moved by the rear cargo. The man in the ragged coat, his chin wet with blood, looked in through a side window. Through the front window, another figure stood atop a low stack of crates between the masts.

Carter moved, placed himself between Kraft and the door. "Stay back."

Abramoff reached his hand through the cross-covered doorway. His fingers twitched like a hundred ants were biting at them. The hand withdrew. "Can't stay in there forever."

"I'm sure we can last until the sun comes out," Carter said with a confident smirk. "Fog's probably going to burn off anytime now."

A grin stretched across Abramoff's face as well, showing off long teeth. "Petrofsky. Up top. Thicken the soup."

The vampire with the cap grunted and leaped up. Kraft heard his boots hit the wooden roof of the cockpit, caught a glimpse of him scurrying up the mast. A few moments later, a heavier layer of fog rolled down out of the sky. The sea vanished in the mist, and the front end of the *Sea Ghost* grew hazy.

Gordon muttered something and checked the compass.

Abramoff looked up at the charcoal sky. "Sun won't be coming out quite yet, it seems."

"We're all going to die," said Kraft.

"Aye. You are."

"No." Kraft swung a hand through the air. "*All* of us are going to die. Us and you. Humans and vampires."

Abramoff's grin faded, and his brow furrowed.

Kraft pointed past the vampires, toward the stern. "The vessels closing on us? They're our enemy. A ruthless enemy. And if they detect us here, if they see through your fog, they'll destroy this ship."

The vampires looked at each other.

Carter stepped back and gave Kraft a small nod of approval.

"Then we should kill you and flee with the ship," said Abramoff. "She's ours anyway."

"It's my ship," growled Gordon. "I'm the captain."

"We don't have long before the Germans reach us," said Kraft. "You can't get in here to kill us, and you don't have the time to try to figure out how you could. What matters right now is we share a common goal. Survival."

The bearded vampire leaned forward, muttered something to Abramoff in . . . Russian? Abramoff answered in the same language, then focused his attention on Kraft again. "What are you suggesting?"

Kraft took a breath. Collected his thoughts. "You are bound to the ship, yes? Because the sea is your homeland."

"Correct," said Abramoff. As he spoke, the vampire with the bloody chin licked his lips.

"So stay in your homeland on a different vessel," said Kraft. "Take a new ship for yourselves and leave this one for us."

Abramoff raised a bushy eyebrow. "What are you . . ."

Then he turned to look over his shoulder at the approaching fleet.

"Your . . . your man above keeps the fog heavy," continued Kraft. "We come alongside one of their ships so you can board them. We sail away. You have a new ship."

"One loaded with a large crew that isn't prepared to defend itself from you," added Carter, pointing at the circle of crosses carved into the deck. "A crew that hates Russians."

More muttering from the vampires out on the deck.

Abramoff studied their faces. "What's to stop us taking one of those ships and turning its guns on you?"

"I'd hope common courtesy," said Kraft, "but I assume you'll need time to take control of the ship. We should be long on our way by then. We survive. You survive."

Abramoff looked back at the approaching battleship. "Six of us can't man a ship that size."

"You could," said Carter. "Convert some of the crew to your cause, or however you like to call it. And you'll have your own battleship. Captain."

"They're almost on us," said the blood-chinned vampire, a bit of unease in his voice.

Kraft put his hands behind his back. "What will it be?"

Abramoff took a half step back from the cabin entrance. Turned his head to the bearded vampire, even as he kept his eyes on Kraft.

Kraft heard a few quiet snatches of Russian. He wished he'd practiced the language more.

The vampires moved forward. "Agreed. Get us to one of the large ships, and we'll leave you."

"Then clear out," barked Gordon. "Let me see."

Abramoff stepped away from the doors and shouted a Russian command.

Kraft glanced back. The vampires had all stepped away, and he could see the German ships looming behind them, barely hidden by the fog now. A quarter mile, if even that. A deep rumble grew beneath the gray sounds of waves and rain. Big engines getting closer. They were already as loud as the *Sea Ghost*'s chugging motor.

Gordon checked the compass. The clock. His map. "This is going to be tight. We're almost at the Strait of Dover."

"Narrowest part of the Channel," Carter said, seeing Kraft's bafflement. "And the heaviest armed. If the Allies have any idea what's going on, there's going to be a lot of guns firing at this fleet."

"So they'll be firing at us."

"You catch on quick, Kraft. I like that about you."

As he spoke, he reached out, took hold of Kraft's collar, and gave him a little tug back. He'd been leaning forward to look at the approaching ships. He'd almost stretched his head out the cockpit doors, past the ring of crosses.

"Do you think we can't trust them?"

"I think they're vampires, and they're hungry. It's not so much a trust issue as common sense."

"Coming up on our port side," shouted the blood-chinned vampire. "A hundred yards and closing!"

Gordon leaned on the wheel, and the *Sea Ghost* responded as the German warship caught up to them.

The steel prow stood almost three times the height of the *Sea Ghost*'s deck, and it made a wake that rocked their smaller ship. Kraft saw a porthole go by. And another. What would happen if a German sailor chose this moment to look outside? How quick could the battleship's crew react?

The *Sea Ghost* altered course again, turned into the heavy wake, and slid closer to the German battleship. Maybe twenty feet separated them now. Almost two hundred feet of rain-soaked steel hull had gone by them, enough that the ship's bow had almost vanished back into the mist, even though there was no sign of the stern yet.

Carter swore in a language Kraft didn't recognize. "It's the *Scharnhorst*," he said. "Beast of a ship."

"Closer," growled Abramoff, back at the doorway.

"I can't get us closer," Gordon shouted over his shoulder.

"We can't jump. We can't cross the water."

"If we hit their hull, they'll know we're here," said Carter.

Gordon shook his head. "We hit the hull and catch on a seam, she'll rip us apart. She's ten times our size."

"You need to be close enough to touch it?" Kraft asked the vampire.

"Aye."

"Are you strong enough to cushion against the impact? All of you together?"

Abramoff looked at him. Gave a sharp nod.

"Then do it. We'll get you close enough."

Abramoff barked out another Russian command, and the vampires leaped to the railing. One dropped down from the mast, trailing fog behind him, and landed on the deck like a man jumping off a high step. They spread out near the middle of the *Sea Ghost*.

"As close as you can," Kraft said to Gordon. "Don't worry about hitting them."

The captain scowled. Looked at the wall of steel sliding past them through the water. Gave the wheel a quarter turn. The *Sea Ghost* moved closer. Fifteen feet. Ten. Kraft could see weld lines. Rivets on portholes.

Abramoff straddled the railing, leaned in, and slapped his hands against the steel hull. Then the bearded vampire followed suit. Then Petrofsky. They heaved and shoved at the wall of metal, the railing squealed, and the *Sea Ghost* leaned hard, the masts tilting away from the larger ship. Kraft slipped, fell toward the wall, and Carter grabbed his arm. Water sloshed up over the deck, and the groan of straining planks rivaled the low thrum of *Scharnhorst*'s huge engines.

Kraft went to step forward, and Carter pulled him back again. "Not until they're on the other ship."

The *Sea Ghost* bounced in the battleship's wake, and water crashed down on the deck again. The vampires worked their way toward the stern even as the big ship moved past them. Petrofsky swung his legs, placing both feet against the steel hull. He hung there for a moment, then crawled a few feet up the side of the *Scharnhorst* like a spider on a window.

The blood-chinned vampire was next. Then the bearded man. One by one, the vampires let the German battleship carry them away, dangling from the side of its hull. Last was Abramoff. He glanced at Kraft, gave a grin and a sharp salute to Gordon, and then he was on the *Scharnhorst*, climbing across the hull, closer to his crew. One of the vampires tore a porthole free from the ship, dropping it into the sea, and they all began to pull at the metal hull.

"Go!" yelled Carter.

Gordon spun the wheel, and the *Sea Ghost* leaned hard to the side as she moved out of the battleship's wake. This time, Kraft and Carter both hit the wall, and one of the crosses fell between them. Gordon spun the wheel again, the ship leveled off, and he slammed the throttle down. The ship lurched in the water.

The battleship, now over sixty feet away, seemed to pick up speed as the *Sea Ghost* slowed and stopped. Kraft caught a last glimpse of the vampires through the haze. They'd twisted the metal of the hull away, making a hole big enough to walk through. Another three hundred feet of hull plowed past them, churning up the water, and then it was gone in the fog.

A fog, Kraft noticed, the thickest of which seemed to be moving along with the *Scharnhorst*.

"We'll let them pass us," said Gordon. "They'll draw fire from Dover, and then we can double back."

Another looming shadow, a second battleship, came out of

the light gray fog, but the *Sea Ghost* was a good hundred feet away from it. The sounds of engines echoed across the water, and the rough chop slapped against the wooden hull. It took a minute for the big ship to pass them, and then a third battleship appeared and headed up the Channel.

Carter stepped over the line of crosses and out of the cockpit. Kraft followed. Carter stuck his hands in the pockets of his jacket as the third battleship faded into the fog. A sound of distant explosions echoed back at them. "Sounds like a lot of big guns," he said.

"Will they stop them?"

Carter shrugged. "The German fleet's shrouded in the vampire's fog now. Decent chance they'll make it to the North Sea."

Kraft shifted his feet on the deck. "Dear God. We've set a vampire battleship loose on the Atlantic."

"Doubt it. They'll probably convert a few dozen of the crew, butcher the rest, and then the Germans will sink their renegade ship and come up with some 'rational' story to explain losing the *Scharnhorst*." He gestured after the ship. "You saw that hole they tore in the hull. Two bits say the Nazis claim it was hit by a torpedo or wandered into a minefield."

"Hey!" shouted Gordon. "Get the crew out of the galley. Tell 'em the night crew's gone, and they need to get back to work!"

Carter laughed and headed for the ladder that led below deck.

Kraft stepped back to the shelter of the cockpit, one last question gnawing at his academic mind. "Captain Gordon?"

"You'll get to Folkestone before sunset," he said. "Don't you worry."

"It's not . . . I was curious. You said you thought the night crew was part of the *Sea Ghost*'s original complement?"

Gordon shot a glance at him. "I did."

"Why? What happened?"

"Dark things. Before she was dry-docked, the crew vanished, and she ran aground. The captain was found right here." He tapped his foot on the deck. "Dead at the wheel. Tied himself to it to stay upright."

The image sparked a half memory in Kraft's mind. "What was her name before? The name the night crew knew?"

"Back then, they called her the *Demeter*."

BREAKOUT

LEE MURRAY

MINQAR QAIM, EGYPT, JUNE 1942

Looking up from the small black box in his hands, Lance Corporal Ernst Hoffman of General Field Marshal Erwin Rommel's German Afrika Korps tugged at the collar of his olive infantry tunic, desperate for the tiniest flow of cool air, but the action provided little relief from the stinking heat of the North African desert. Ernst tucked the device in his jacket pocket, took off his soft hat, pulled a scrap of fabric from his trousers, and wiped the sweat from his temple, his movements as unhurried as he could make them so as not to alarm his companions. Because it wasn't only the broiling conditions that were making him perspire. Their charge had escaped, and under Ernst's watch. If their captive couldn't be found quickly, it would spell the end of Ernst's military career. Worse: he could face the firing squad, and his comrades with him.

The Desert Fox might be fair, but he was not always forgiving.

When he'd replaced both the hat and the fabric, Ernst squinted against the glare, scanning the scrappy terrain for their quarry. "See anything?" he called to Private Otto Schmitt, who at twenty-two was the same age as Ernst.

Schmitt lifted an identical electrical device, then shook his head. "Nothing yet."

"Meier?"

Private Walther Meier turned his attention from his own device. "The signal's still there and strong enough. We should be seeing something."

Schmitt swore under his breath. Ernst didn't blame him. Every moment they were out here away from their unit increased the risk. It didn't do to linger. There were just the three of them.

"He's hiding," suggested Meier.

Schmitt spat a gob of phlegm on the sandy ground. "Or lying in wait somewhere, preparing to ambush us."

Despite the heat that rippled about them, Ernst stifled a shiver. Yes, they were close, and any number of Allied soldiers were likely to be close too. They needed to finish this.

"Go left, then, Meier. And you, Schmitt, go right." He pointed to a rocky outcropping a hundred meters away. "We'll shepherd our quarry toward that cliff."

Schmitt grumbled something under his breath, but he moved off anyway. He knew the stakes as well as Ernst did.

Meier gave Ernst a startled look, pursed his lips, then set out to the left.

Ernst took a deep breath and trudged forward, Meier and Schmitt growing distant as they flanked him. In his pocket, the signal got louder, relentless bleeps that stabbed at his brain even as the sun hammered through the fabric of his field cap.

Come on . . .

He glanced across at Meier. At only seventeen, the stocky soldier had intuition enough to unsling the long metal prod from his back and hold it out before him.

Good call. It wouldn't do to be caught flat-footed. Ernst swung a metal prod from his own back. He didn't switch it on. Not yet. Couldn't risk draining the battery. Not wanting to call out and alert their quarry, Ernst had to trust that Schmitt would glance across and follow their lead.

Brandishing the prod, Ernst kept on, keeping time with the blips from the black box.

Forty meters.

Thirty.

Twenty.

Soon the three of them were in spitting distance of the cliff and of one another. They should have seen something by now. Ernst's knees trembled and his pulse thrummed in his temples. Where was he? Holed up somewhere?

Meier shouted.

What? Ernst swung about.

Meier ran forward.

Ernst ran too, although he dreaded every lumbering step on the uneven sand. Sweat stung his eyes. By now, the beeping had become a continuous whine.

Meier pulled up. Ernst stopped just seconds later, his lungs heaving.

The collar! *Oh Jesus. The collar.*

Schmitt arrived, his K98k rifle held before him.

Ernst frowned at the rifle. Rommel's pet was not to be harmed.

"Fuck," Schmitt said.

Ernst turned off the detector. Meier and Schmitt did the same.

They stared at the evidence. A scaled snakeskin, rough and reeking of musk, stretched thirty meters across the sand.

In all their time as its guards, Ernst and his comrades had

never seen the creature shed its skin. Perhaps even the Führer's scientists did not know this.

Schmitt prodded at the casing with his boot, just below the useless collar, and turned over the horned head.

Ernst almost jumped; it was as if the serpent's empty eye sockets were laughing at him. Just a beast, yet it had bettered Ernst. Evaded them, right under their noses. How would they find the monster now? And if they did, without the collar, they only had the electric prods to control it, since Rommel did not want his pet injured. Already, the beast had killed the enemy in the hundreds. Maybe even in the thousands. Whispers had it that the British might have won their Operation Crusader had Rommel not had the serpent in his arsenal. And now it was loose . . .

Ernst swallowed the vomit that threatened to choke him. The monster had been right here. Where they were standing now.

"Must have passed right beneath us," Meier said, reading Ernst's mind.

"We would have heard it," Schmitt replied.

"No," Ernst said, unclasping the collar and buckling it around his waist. "The new skin would still be soft and flexible—not horny and dried out like this one. It would be quieter." It occurred to Ernst that the creature would also be bigger. Grown fat on prisoners of war. Why else would it need to shed its skin?

"Maybe it'll come back of its own accord," Meier said.

Schmitt rolled his eyes.

"Well, it's possible," Meier insisted. "Back home, my dog used to sit by his bowl every night at suppertime, regular as clockwork."

Suddenly, the soft rumble of an engine sounded behind them.

Allied vehicle? Ernst dropped to his belly on the sand. "Down!" he hissed. But it wasn't the British. Ernst almost wished it were.

Instead, the general field marshal's pet serpent exploded from the sand. It loomed like a glistening tower above them, rasping its new scales.

Still standing, Schmitt fired his K98k wildly. The serpent merely swayed, Schmitt's shots going wide. The monster struck, fast for a creature of its size, its fangs sinking deep into Schmitt's torso. The jaws clamped down, crushing him. Impaled on those deadly blades, with the creature's venom coursing through him, Schmitt was helpless. A rag doll. His eyes bulged in terror. Tears of blood leaked from under his lids.

Meier was up and already running across the sand when it turned its attention to Ernst.

Their battered, machine gun–armed Chevrolet thirty-cwt. patrol truck hidden in the dunes, Artie Potaka lay huddled under the shade of his greatcoat, baking in the Egyptian sand alongside their NCO, Toa Jenkins, a B Company penny diver from Rotorua, and Aperahama Thomas of Southland's Ngāi Tahu tribe. Formerly farmers and a mechanic, now members of the British army's Long Range Desert Group, they were watching the road.

The Axis was on the move. That much was clear. Panzer tanks, half-tracks, sidecar motorcycles, and trucks—some towing 88mm flak guns, and others transporting infantry—thundered by them, kicking up a cloud of sand. Perhaps fifteen minutes passed. The vehicles kept coming. Tanks and more tanks. Crawling across the land like giant insects.

"Fuck. That's not good," Toa whispered eventually. "Our

boys are out there." He meant the Second New Zealand Expeditionary Forces. With the Germans making a push toward Cairo and the canal zone, their Kiwi compatriots had been called back from Syria to join the British Eighth Army. Part of the Fourth New Zealand Infantry Brigade, the Eighteenth, Nineteenth, and Twentieth Kiwi Battalions were holed up on a rock called Minqar Qaim, with instructions to delay Jerry as long as possible.

"What if Jerry pulls that coil tight around our unit? It'll prevent our boys from joining the rest of the Eighth," Toa went on.

Coil. Artie felt a surge of understanding. *There.* This explained the dreams that had been haunting him for months. Nightmares of a giant taniwha-serpent-monster that coiled and slithered in the darkness. It hadn't made sense to him at all, because taniwha lurk in seas and waterways, not in the sand. Struggling with insomnia, Artie had shared his concerns with soft-spoken Aperahama, who'd claimed it was shock and grief that brought on the monsters. All those boys from home gunned down in battle, their wairua-spirits left to roam this wasteland. Some said as many as a thousand had perished in the bloodbath of Operation Crusader. Aperahama's theory was a good one, but this made more sense. Not an echo of the past, Artie's dream-taniwha was surely a harbinger of what was to come: a warning.

"We need to go," Toa said. "We need to get word to Major General Tiny Freyberg."

"We're supposed to watch this road," Aperahama replied. "Give an account of the ordnance."

Toa snorted. "It's bloody *heaps*, bro. Enough to pummel our boys to dust. There's your account. We gotta go."

Artie nodded. You didn't have to be a matakite-seer to work out that Rommel's boys had the upper hand here. Their Kiwi brothers were in deep shit. Already it might be too late.

Toa gestured to the rear, and the three of them scuttled backward on their bellies like beetles, then turned and scrambled over the bank. Ran for the truck. Artie pulled off the camouflage netting, uncovering the vehicle, with its little kiwi hand-painted on the side, as Toa hoisted the antenna. While Artie bundled up the netting, Toa bashed out a message, then hauled the antenna in again. Meanwhile, Aperahama had clambered onto the flatbed behind the Lewis gun. Then Toa was cranking up the engine. Artie barely had time to stuff the netting under his seat next to his flat patu-club, jump in, and grasp the casing of the Browning MK II machine gun, before they were jolting and careening up and down the dunes, keeping ahead, and out of sight, of that deadly enemy train.

They were almost there, could see the Minqar Qaim escarpment rising before them on the horizon, when Aperahama gasped. "Over there," he called.

Toa pulled the Chevrolet into a shallow valley, where a German soldier crawled on his hands and knees in the burning sand. His tunic open, he was young, just a boy. Younger than Artie anyway. His lips were chapped white, and he'd lost his cap a while ago, because the top of his head was pink and blistered. He was delirious, gibbering away to himself.

"Careful." Toa brought the truck to a stop, the engine still turning. "Could be a trap."

It didn't feel like a trap. No sign of a weapon. Nor any comrades.

Artie got out. Behind him, over the soldier's babble, metal graunched. Aperahama swung the Lewis gun around to the side, giving him cover.

The German soldier also noted the movement because he clutched his hands together, clearly begging for mercy.

Artie handed him his canteen.

The babbling stopped as the soldier gulped at the warm liquid, spilling droplets on his tunic. Artie snatched it back. "Hey, hold up." They didn't have water to waste. The land here was harsh and just as keen to kill them as Rommel. "What do we do with him?" he called over his shoulder to Toa.

"Leave him. You saw the panzers. The Germans are on their way."

Artie shook his head. There was no mana in leaving an enemy to die like this. It was beneath them. "Jerry might not find him," Artie replied. "Poor bugger will die."

"And if they do, he'll tell his mates that he saw us," Aperahama said quietly.

"Yeah. They'll know they've lost the surprise," Toa agreed. "Right now they reckon they have us, so they can take their time."

Wild-eyed, the German scrabbled forward. He grabbed at Artie's pant leg and gestured for the truck. "*Schlange, eine Schlange*!" he burbled.

The hair prickled on Artie's neck. He twisted his body, shaking the soldier off. "What does that mean, you reckon?"

Aperahama shrugged.

"*Bitte nimm mich mit. Bitte . . .*" the soldier pleaded, his eyes flickering across the dunes.

"Let's take him with us, then. Hand him off at Minqar Qaim," Toa said.

Artie nodded. "Come on, then," he said to the German. "Looks like you're coming with us."

"He got a name?" Aperahama asked.

Artie didn't bother to look—just gave the soldier's dog tags a tug. "The usual," he replied. "Blood type A."

Toa grinned. "Such a popular name."

"Meier," the soldier said, catching on. "*Mein Name ist Walther Meier.*"

"Right then, Meier," Artie said, giving the man his hand and hauling him to his feet. "You're a guest of the Libyan Desert Taxi Service. Don't be giving us any trouble now."

The monster lifted her horned head, watching as the vehicle rumbled over the dunes, taking her prey with it. She'd been enjoying the chase too, and the creature was almost spent. She rattled her scales in annoyance. Still, it was no matter. The trail of fear was palpable. She had only to follow it. She lowered her head and unfurled her coils, sidewinding across the sand, low and invisible in pursuit of that delectable scent. *Wait.* She slowed, flicking her crimson tongue. Another scent hung in the air, thicker and cloying with rot and despair. *Interesting.* She considered the vehicle bouncing across the plain, then sidled away to explore the new odor.

By the time Artie and the boys reached Minqar Qaim, word had already got out that the enemy was near. Seemed earlier in the day, seeing the tiny dots of the enemy column far off in the distance, a couple of sections had ventured out under the lead of Second Lieutenant McLean, taking with them a bunch of 7-pounders to give Jerry a blasting. Only having been thoroughly outgunned, they'd come scurrying back, with the Hun, in hot pursuit, stopping infuriatingly out of range of the Allied artillery. The enemy's long-range shelling had continued most of the morning, focused mainly on the tanks, while the poor infantrymen hunkered in their sangar firing posts and trenches, roasting like pigs in a hāngī.

Artie, Toa, Aperahama, and their prisoner made it in during a short lull in the shelling around midday. Immediately, Toa went off to find HQ to confirm their report and to find out where to surrender Meier. Artie and Aperahama kept their heads down under a rain of shells while they waited for him to return. The hours stretched on. Artie wondered if Toa had copped one. It was close to midnight when he got back, and by then the shelling had quietened, the enemy settling in for the night.

"Well, what did Tiny say?" Artie demanded.

"Nothing. It's Brigadier Inglis in charge now. Freyberg took some shrapnel to the neck earlier. Still breathing, but he won't be shouting orders for a while."

Aperahama shook his head and crossed himself.

"But it's like we thought," Toa went on. "This rock is surrounded by bloody Germans. Our boys are giving it back to them, but at this rate, the ammunition won't last much more than half a day."

"Yeah, we heard," Artie said. The blokes hunkering around them had said as much.

"Lieutenant Colonel Gray says we're to break out—to head for El Alamein right now, under cover of darkness. Colonel Love is moving the Māori battalion up as we speak. Orders are to leave our bedrolls behind, take any transport possible, and move out, quiet as quiet." He lowered his voice. "And take no new prisoners."

"Ah, heck," Artie said.

They all looked at Meier. Hunched tight against a rock, the German was muttering under his breath. Anyone could see the poor bloke was half mad with terror. There was a chance the boy had deserted. If that were the case, his fate was grim.

Toa puffed his cheeks. "Could be dangerous to leave an enemy at our back though," he said slowly.

Artie rubbed at the bristles on his chin. "No time to stow him with the other POWs either."

"Yeah, I don't reckon he'll take much room," said Aperahama.

Artie smiled. They were LRDG A Squadron, T1 patrol. They didn't answer to Gray.

So they tied a gag around Meier's mouth, tightened the rope around his hands, and put him back in the Chevrolet. By the time the rest of the Māori boys had rolled in an hour later, they'd gained another four passengers: three Kiwis—Dunny, Weepu, and Creighton—and a Brit.

"Let's get out of here," Toa said softly.

"Lead on, Macduff," said the Brit.

With the Chevrolet's lights off, Toa drove them out into the darkness.

Artie had no idea how many trucks were in the convoy. Maybe a thousand. It was hard to tell in the dark. With Gray and their Eighteenth Battalion in the lead, the Fourth Brigade moved in an eerie column—trucks, Bren carriers, even ambulances—nine abreast across the plain, like warriors in a haka war dance. They made for the German line, with men clinging to every available vehicle. Those without wheels ran alongside in groups of three. Each man as silent as he could be. The air hummed with tension. Artie winced at every stray clang, gear change, and inadvertent yelp. The Grant tanks were the worst, and one of them was only running on one cylinder. What an infernal racket. How could Jerry not know they were coming? Surely, they were running to the slaughter.

Dangerous thinking. Artie must have conjured their enemy

into wakefulness, because moments later, tracers whistled overhead, too high to find them yet. Jerry was stirring though. Perhaps he'd caught a whiff of petrol in his nostrils.

The shells started in earnest then. Haphazard. Wild. Ducking, Artie gripped the side of the truck and pushed down the surge of fear. Even a stray bullet could be deadly.

Still, the Fourth Brigade kept on. Heading east. Hoping to sneak through the German lines.

An explosion blasted to their right. A nearby truck had taken a hit. Spewing flames, the truck slowed to a stop. Screams echoed across the plain.

"Get us out of here, man," the Brit hissed, but Toa was already swerving, driving the Chevrolet out of the burning light and off to the right. Artie looked back as a survivor leaped from the smoking chassis. Then the soldier was gone, lost to the shadows. Only the flames still roared, orange sparks swirling and snaking into the inky blackness.

"Lucky break," said Dunny. "They're firing at shadows."

"Not so lucky for the dead," Aperahama answered.

"Shhh," Toa whispered. "I reckon we're close to the line."

More shells struck the earth around them. Light flashed, briefly exposing the plain. They were alone. Where was the rest of the convoy? Either they had strayed too far or the rest of the convoy had turned off somewhere. With shells exploding all around them, there was no time to look. They would have to regroup later.

Assuming they survived.

Toa drove like a madman. Artie and the others were flung every which way. They nearly lost the Brit when they hit a rock and were shunted sideways, but Dunny reached out and grabbed him by the tunic, and between them, Artie and Dunny, they hauled the man to safety.

It was like something out of a moving picture.

Their relief was short-lived. Another shell hit the ground right in front of them. Shrapnel zinged. The trusty truck took the brunt of it, but a stray hunk of metal hit poor Creighton full in the chest. Blood glutted from the wound. He slumped into Toa. Artie pulled the body off, but the damage had been done. For an instant, Toa lost control. The vehicle hurtled full speed into the darkness, striking the corner of a canvas tent, Artie only realizing what it was when the coarse fabric whipped past his cheek.

They'd found the enemy line.

Toa stamped on the brake and wrangled the steering wheel. The truck thundered on, pulling out stakes and dragging the tent a distance with them. They crashed into a parked motorcycle. Then another tent. A medic tent! Artie glimpsed the red cross as they tore through a gap in the canvas, the motorcycle still tangled in the grill. The Chevrolet jolted to a stop inside the medic tent, the bike jammed in the undercarriage.

Artie was thrown out. Winded, he lay on the ground beside the truck and Creighton's twisted body, his Enfield rifle digging into his back and a strange unease washing over him. It was too quiet. Where were the shouts of alarm? Where was the enemy?

Artie struggled to his feet. Then Toa was beside Artie, grasping his upper arm. *What?* Artie swung about. The medical tent was dim, lit only by a couple of lamps, but the reason for Artie's dreams, and that uncanny quiet, was clear.

"Taniwha," Toa whispered.

"Jesus," the Brit choked.

Startled, the serpent-monster rose on its coils, the horned head grazing the canvas apex of the tent. Artie would have stumbled if Toa hadn't been holding him. Dunny scrambled for cover, ducking behind a wooden crate.

The thing was huge. A creature of legend. It swayed, its white belly glistening in the lamplight, and a stale stench wafted over Artie. *Oh, hell.* Bodies lay scattered before the giant serpent—sick and wounded German soldiers and a couple of medical staff, dead or paralyzed, their torsos riddled with paired stab wounds. Given the monster's barbed smile, Artie doubted Allied bayonets were the cause.

They had interrupted the monster's meal.

Artie's own stomach twisted, and his heart pounded hard. They needed to get out. *Get out, get out, get out!* Only the truck was covered in ropes and canvas, and the motorbike was tangled under the wheels. They were going to have to clear the debris if they hoped to drive out of here.

"Aperahama," Toa said.

Aperahama was already moving; he grabbed a surgical knife from a nearby tray and sliced at Meier's bonds, then gestured frantically to the German to help him clear the mangled bike out from under the truck.

Which left Artie and the others—Toa, Weepu, Dunny, and the Brit—to hold off the beast. And they needed to be quiet about it, or it wouldn't just be a monster they were facing: They'd bring the whole panzer division down on them.

Meier pulled down his gag and shrieked, "*Die Schlange*!"

Damn it!

Aperahama slapped a hand over the boy's mouth. Thankfully, there was no answering shout. The boy spoke German. Any living Germans nearby must have discounted his yells as the ravings of a fevered mind. But the monster had heard him, because it turned its ugly head, fixing him with slitted yellow eyes, and the boy went quiet.

Time stilled for a breath, the way a kāhu-hawk stops its wings to glide on the wind.

The creature lunged.

Aperahama shoved Meier bodily, and the pair tumbled to

the dirt. Fangs the size of fenceposts slammed into the truck's bonnet, denting it and splashing milky liquid over the metal.

No time to fret about the noise, Artie dove forward, past Aperahama, who was dragging Meier under the chassis. Snatching his patu-club from under the seat, Artie leaped onto the bonnet. He raised the greenstone weapon and hacked at the monster's head. The blade of the club struck one of the spiky horns, digging deep, almost severing it. The blade stuck. Artie was forced to let it go or risk being pulled off the truck.

Now he was face-to-face with the monster.

Artie fumbled to unleash his Lee Enfield. *No shooting. Bayonet. Hurry!* The serpent undulated, drawing back, about to strike again. Artie's fingers were thick. Slow . . .

Dashing in, Toa slashed at its coils with his bayonet.

Artie shivered, his panic rising.

Toa's steel blade had merely slid across the armored scales. But he'd gained the monster's attention. It swung to face him. Toa backed away.

Then Weepu leaped in to take up the attack, the up-and-under thrust of his bayonet tearing off a scale.

Artie didn't wait around; he jumped off the truck.

Aperahama and Meier were on their feet too, rushing to clear the pranged motorbike. Where was the Brit? Had he run?

The serpent shifted its coils, its head hovering in place. It narrowed its yellow eyes.

Artie spied the Brit facedown in the dirt. He must have been bowled over, crushed under the coils when the creature lunged. Unconscious or dead?

Weepu edged closer, felt for his pulse. Dead, then.

Toa was rummaging around in the surgical equipment. What could he do with a scalpel that couldn't be achieved with a bayonet? For the monster, the hacked horn and lost scale were like losing a nail. Still, they didn't need to kill it—just hold it off for a while.

The snake hesitated as if it couldn't decide which of them to strike first.

The net!

Artie dove again for the truck, grasping for the camouflage net.

Toa had seized a bottle of clear liquid. *Alcohol.* He clambered on the crate, unstoppered the bottle, and tossed the liquid at the serpent, hitting it in one eye. Blinded, the serpent thrashed its coils at the crate, toppling it. Toa jumped away, but Dunny was left exposed.

The serpent attacked. Artie had never seen anything move so fast, the acceleration causing his patu and the horn to be cleaved off in the strike. Then those fangs were plunging deep into Dunny, who didn't even have time to cry out. His legs fluttered weakly. His eyes closed.

Sweet Jesus!

Toa was back at that surgical tray.

The snake drew its fangs out of Dunny, who flopped to the ground.

"Weepu!" Artie called softly. He hoped the soldier would understand. Dragging one end of the net, Artie ran right under the monster's belly, turned swiftly, and ran up onto the shifting coils behind the monster's head. The serpent gnashed at the net.

Then Weepu was there, net in hand, running up the other side. They stood on the monster's back and hung on with all their might, hauling the net into the monster's maw like a bit in a horse's mouth, entangling the fangs. Artie's hands burned. His arms ached. The monster thrashed and bucked. The ride was bumpier than the Chevrolet. How long could they hang on?

Dragging the motorbike carcass clear, Aperahama signaled frantically to Meier to start up the truck.

Meier leaped into the driver's seat. Turned the ignition. *Nothing.*

Artie clung on to the net. Prayed for a miracle as the monster turned in on itself, looking to throw him off, its coils shifting in a wave under Artie's feet.

Toa lifted something from the tray: morphine syrettes.

Aperahama flung open the dented bonnet. He scanned the engine and pulled out a twisted piece of metal. "Meier," he whispered.

This time, the engine thrummed to life.

Thank the gods.

Aperahama rushed to slash an opening in the canvas. Meanwhile, Toa ducked and darted, searching for that bare patch left by the missing scale. He jammed a bunch of syrettes into the exposed flesh.

The snake twisted again, the horned head on the move, looking for Toa now.

No! Artie pulled back on the net with everything he had to keep those fangs away from Toa. But if they were going to get on the truck, eventually Artie and Weepu had to let go of the net. Would the morphine be enough to slow the snake? The medicine was meant for men.

Aperahama was already there, about to swing up behind the Lewis gun, but Meier stamped on the pedal. The Chevrolet plunged into the night.

Curse the man.

Artie wanted to cry. It was over then. They were dead. Maybe Weepu and Artie could hold on long enough for Aperahama and Toa to escape. But Aperahama and Toa took up their warrior stance and brandished their bayonets. They weren't going anywhere.

The snake was still thrashing. Was it tiring a little?

Weepu whimpered beside him. They were exhausted. It would not be long now. Perhaps there was something else Artie could do. Matakite had been known to speak to taniwha. What did they have to lose?

Drawing in a breath, Artie sent the snake a silent inoi-plea: *Tēnā, ka tohu koe ki a mātou, ko tā mātou hiahia, ka wehe noa. Please. Spare us. We wish only to leave.*

The monster turned its good eye on Artie. Something flickered in those yellow depths. Had it understood? Artie wondered if it wanted to be here even less than he did. Suddenly, the snake tossed its coils, throwing them off like a cow flicks off flies.

Artie scrambled in the sand, his hand closing on his patu. *Get up or die.* Dizzy, he staggered to his feet. Turned. Took his place beside the others.

The serpent spat out the pesky net. Rattled in annoyance. It loomed above them, its single horn scraping the roof of the tent and considered them for an instant; then it ducked its head and wound slowly through the slash in the canvas.

Artie couldn't believe it. He lowered his patu in relief. Beside him, Toa's ragged breathing joined his own.

All at once battle chants of "*ka mate, ka mate*" pierced the still of the encampment. Their Māori brothers had reached them.

Artie looked at Toa, Weepu, and Aperahama, an unspoken agreement passing between them. They readied their bayonets to join the Kiwis as they broke through. Alamein could wait until tomorrow. They would crawl there if they had to.

Parting the canvas, they ran into the night.

A hand-painted kiwi on its side, the damaged truck flew across the plain. At the wheel, his foot flat to the accelerator, Meier giggled with relief. He was alive! And free. Who could have imagined he would escape Rommel's monster a second time? He tried not to think of the men he'd left behind. Men who'd saved his life more than once. They'd likely be dead now. Still, war was war, wasn't it? It was a prisoner's duty to escape. To create chaos. Well, he'd certainly done that. Meier chortled. History was told by survivors, at least that's what his grandfather always said.

The truck shuddered, a strange clunking emanating from somewhere deep in the engine. Meier ignored it. But the clunk quickly became a piercing whine, the noise penetrating his bones and setting his nerves on edge. Soon the truck rumbled to a stop in the dunes.

"Fuck."

It wasn't the gas. Meier had seen his captors fill the truck from a tank before they'd left Minqar Qaim. Something must be stuck in the works. He got out and lifted the bent-up bonnet. Looked at the engine. That Māori engineer would know what to do.

A quiet scrape sounded behind him. Pebbles shifting somewhere.

Meier whirled. Peered into the gloom. With its broken horn, the dark silhouette was unmistakable.

The monster sidewinded toward him, its musk filling his nostrils.

Meier's heart sank into his boots.

NACHTHEXEN

BISHOP O'CONNELL

VORONEZH OBLAST, SOVIET UNION, OCTOBER 1942

Vera Belik, navigator and newly graduated from the Engels School of Aviation, rode in silence down the rough road in the old supply truck. The only words the driver, Comrade Sergeant Morozov, had spoken had been to introduce himself and tell her to get in the truck loaded with supplies for the 588th Night Bomber Regiment.

That was two hours ago.

She'd grown used to being ignored. It was preferable to the harassment and mockery that she'd received since volunteering, not all of which came just because she was a woman. Like many Ukrainians, all she'd known about the Nazis was Communist propaganda when they'd been allies. As such, many had hoped the Nazi invasion would lead to independence. There was little love for Russia and the Communists after the *Holodomor*, the Great Famine.

It hadn't taken long to see the Nazis were somehow even more evil. The things she'd seen before fleeing her home left her feeling foolish for ever having such a hope. As such, she'd signed up for a chance to kill Nazis, not out of loyalty to Moscow. But as far as the commissars were concerned, she was a dedicated and loyal Communist.

The distant sounds of war, amplified by the silence in the truck, left her mind free to run. The only thing she'd been told about the 588th that she believed true was that every role was done by women. Not just pilots and navigators but also ground and support crews. That singular fact was what she clung to in hopes of finding some sort of camaraderie.

They arrived at the airfield—the loosest possible definition of the word—after another hour of silence. Vera managed to keep from smiling when she saw a group of women in their late teens or early twenties, of an age with her, approach the truck.

"Stay in the truck, Comrade," a dark-haired woman said to the driver. "We'll unload the supplies."

Comrade Sergeant Morozov smirked and lit a cigarette.

"You're our new navigator?" the woman asked Vera.

"Yes," Vera said, getting out of the truck. She went to attention and gave a salute. "Lieutenant Vera Lukianovna Belik, flight navigator."

The other women gave a nod and set to unloading the truck quickly and efficiently.

"Welcome to Digora, Comrade Lieutenant," the woman said, returning the salute. "I am Sergeant Svetlana Sychyova Yegorovna. I'm in charge of ground crews. Comrade Colonel Bershanskaya will be in her command tent." She pointed to a collection of canvas tents, one slightly larger and less threadbare than the others.

Vera saluted again. "Thank you, Comrade Sergeant." She grabbed her rucksack and hurried to meet her new commander, her pilot, and hopefully, soon begin bombing Nazis.

Snow crunched under her oversized boots, which, like her

uniform, were cut for a man. At least the fabric stuffed inside the heavy footwear kept her feet warm. It wasn't terribly cold yet, but she knew it would be soon enough. When she reached the tent, she took a moment to look at the line of Polikarpov Po-2s. The cloth and wood biplanes were all battered—and far from the best Russia had to offer—but to Vera Lukianovna, they were beautiful.

As she turned away, something about the planes caught her attention. All of them had been painted with various kinds of flowers, but several sported large sunflowers on the fuselage. The small spark of hope hidden in her heart swelled at seeing the symbol of Ukraine openly displayed.

After a moment, she drew in a breath, stood up straight, and knocked on a tent post.

"Enter," came a voice from inside.

Vera stepped inside to find the famous regiment commander, Lieutenant Colonel Yevdokia Davidovna Bershanskaya, a woman in her late twenties with short brown hair and keen eyes. She was speaking to a younger woman with short blond hair, and a woman pushing forty with short dark hair. They shared a laugh and turned to Vera.

"Lieutenant Vera Lukianovna Belik, flight navigator," she said, saluting. "Reporting, Comrade Colonel."

"At ease, Comrade Lieutenant," the commander said. "You have excellent timing." She motioned to the older woman. "This is Deputy Commander Yevdokiya Yakovlevna Rachkevich, our commissar, and this"—she nodded at the blonde woman—"is Comrade Major Natalya Fyodorovna Meklin, your pilot."

"Welcome to the 588th, Comrade Lieutenant," Yevdokiya Yakovlevna said.

"The Night Witches," Natalya Fyodorovna said and offered her hand. "Comrade."

Vera recognized the Ukrainian accent but kept from smiling. She shook the offered hand. "Night Witches?" she asked tentatively.

"A moniker from the fascists," said Yevdokiya Yakovlevna. "They believe our silent and precise night raids can only be attributed to magic."

With practiced ease, Vera kept her face neutral.

"Accepting such a foolish assumption and ridiculous title serves to further crush their morale," Yevdokiya Yakovlevna said.

Vera nodded. "I understand, Comrade Commissar. Very wise."

"I don't know what they're teaching at Engels these days," Colonel Bershanskaya said, "and I don't care. We're unlike any other regiment in the Red Army. We do things differently. Our first rule is be proud you're a woman."

Both Yevdokiya Yakovlevna and Natalya Fyodorovna stood a little taller and nodded.

"Yes, Comrade Colonel," Vera said.

"Our mission is simple," Bershanskaya said. "We're tasked with harassing the Nazis all night long, depriving them of sleep, and destroying all the material we can."

"And we are very good at our job," Natalya Fyodorovna said, chuckling.

"So good, even Comrade Stalin himself has taken notice," added Yevdokiya Yakovlevna.

"I won't let you down, comrades," Vera said.

"I know you won't," Colonel Bershanskaya said and turned to Natalya Fyodorovna. "Comrade Major, show Comrade Vera Lukianovna to her bunk and introduce her to the rest of your flight." She turned back to Vera. "She will also brief you on the specifics of our current mission. Get rest, if you can. Our nights are long here."

"But not as long as they are for the fascists," Yevdokiya Yakovlevna said and chuckled.

"Dismissed," Colonel Bershanskaya said.

Natalya Fyodorovna saluted. "Yes, Comrade Colonel." She turned to Vera and gestured to the tent door. "After you, Comrade."

"Comrade Colonel, Comrade Commissar," Vera said, saluted one last time, and then turned on her heel and exited the tent.

Natalya Fyodorovna followed and then led the way down the row of tents. "Ukrainian, yes?" she asked when they were away from the tent.

"Okhrimivka," Vera said. "You are from the North, I think."

"Lubny," Natalya Fyodorovna said. "All the women of our three-aircraft flight are Ukrainian, by suggestion of the comrade commissar."

"I see," Vera said.

Natalya Fyodorovna stopped. "I'm not suggesting you can speak freely around her, but as far as political officers go, Yevdokiya Yakovlevna is perhaps the most understanding and least dictatorial I've ever met. I've seen her just happen to be looking the other way during transgressions others would've reported."

"She is still Russian, though, yes?"

Natalya Fyodorovna nodded. "She is, as is our commander." She lowered her voice. "They are as decent as any Russian can probably be, but never forget they are Russian first."

"You needn't worry about that," Vera said.

Natalya Fyodorovna resumed walking and came to a stop at the second to last tent. "This is home until we get sent somewhere else," she said and opened the flap.

Vera stepped inside to find six cots, four of them occupied by women Vera's age—two blondes, two brunettes, all of them smoking. One looked up from reviewing a map; another discreetly moved the paper she'd been writing on out of Vera's line of sight.

"Sisters," Natalya Fyodorovna said. "This is Vera Lukianovna, my new navigator. She's from Okhrimivka."

Some of the tension in the tent eased a little.

Natalya Fyodorovna gestured at the two blondes. "Lyudmyla Semenivna and her navigator, Maryna Ruslanivna. They're city girls, from Kyiv."

"Yes," Maryna Ruslanivna said through a grin. "Because of the Nazis, we have to slum with uncultured swine like you, Natalya Fyodorovna."

Everyone laughed.

"Nadiya Antonivna, navigator," the brunette with the map said and nodded to the woman who'd tucked away her paper. "Oleksandra Yuriyivna there is my pilot. Best in the regiment."

"This is true," Oleksandra Yuriyivna said, "by far."

"We've discussed your slanderous lies before," said Lyudmyla Semenivna. "You are perhaps third best, second if Natalya Fyodorovna hasn't had her tea."

There was another round of laughter and some playful exchanges, but Vera didn't catch it all.

Natalya Fyodorovna motioned to an empty cot at the far end of the tent. "That is yours; mine is the one next to it."

"Thank you," Vera said. She went to it, sat down, and began going through her meager possessions. A loud "mewrawr" sounded from Natalya Fyodorovna's cot, and Vera turned to see a small ball of black fluff staring at her with bright green eyes.

"That is Nastya," Natalya Fyodorovna said, picking up the kitten and petting it. "She is my copilot and bodyguard."

The other women laughed as though there was a deeper joke Vera wasn't privy to.

"She's very sweet, but I didn't know we could have pets," Vera said. "May I touch her?"

"You should ask her," Natalya Fyodorovna said and looked down at Nastya. "What do you think, my love? Would you permit Vera Lukianovna to pet you?"

The other women leaned forward as if very interested in what was transpiring. Vera wondered if perhaps she was about to experience some hazing ritual but decided if she was, best to get it over with.

The kitten, for her part, eyed Vera for a long moment with far more intelligence than Vera had ever seen in an animal.

"*Mawr*," Nastya finally said and began to purr.

"That means you have been given permission," Natalya Fyodorovna said and smiled.

"Thank you, Nastya," Vera said and pretended not to notice the exchange of looks between the others. She reached over and scratched behind the kitten's ears.

After a moment, Nastya reached out for Vera.

Natalya Fyodorovna's eyebrows rose. "She wants you to hold her. Very impressive. She's usually quite selective."

"I'm honored," Vera said and took the small cat, cradling it. As Nastya purred, Vera ran her fingers through the cat's soft fur.

The other women gave Oleksandra Yuriyivna a look and chuckled.

"Nastya won't let Oleksandra Yuriyivna hold her," Natalya Fyodorovna said in a faux whisper.

Oleksandra Yuriyivna narrowed her eyes and waved a hand. "Bah, she probably smells of sausages."

More laughter.

Vera handed Nastya back and settled in, while Natalya Fyodorovna explained their mission and how things worked. Currently, they were protecting the city of Vladikavkaz from advancing Nazi forces. They flew at least ten sorties a night, though on a good night they could do as many as sixteen. Their three planes would fly together. While two distracted the searchlights and ground fire, the third crew would idle their engine, glide in silently, and drop their bombs. Then they would accelerate and get clear before doing it twice more until all had dropped their ordinance. Mission complete, they would return to base, refuel, rearm, and do it again.

Vera knew from her training that their Po-2s would have no radios, guns, or parachutes. The official explanation was weight restrictions, but most agreed such equipment was reserved for the men. Vera's training was to navigate using a flashlight, a compass, a map, and a stopwatch. Any communication between the planes was via signals with the flashlight.

"Thankfully," Natalya Fyodorovna said, "the Luftwaffe have been focused more on the larger bombers and fighters to the west, but there's no telling how long that may last."

Everyone knew the Po-2's top speed, ninety knots, was slower than the stall speed of every Nazi fighter. That, combined with superior maneuverability, did much to level the playing field. Vera suspected pilot skill played no small role as well, but the men would laugh when such was mentioned.

"Which is why I carry this," Lyudmyla Semenivna said and held up a Nagant revolver. "Any Nazi pig who gets close to me finds out how good of a shot I am."

Natalya Fyodorovna rolled her eyes and looked at Vera. "You focus on getting us to our targets; Nastya and I will worry about the fascists."

Vera nodded and didn't mention she was less afraid of being shot than the plane catching fire from tracers. The fabric skin of the Po-2 was flammable, hence the nickname, "flying matchstick." She could deal with being shot, but burning alive was a fear born from generations of women in her family burned for being *vid'ma*. Of course, most had indeed been witches, but they'd never committed the dark acts they were accused of.

She touched her chest where, under several layers of clothing, hung the amulet her mother had passed on to keep her safe.

"We have a couple of hours before preflight checks," Natalya Fyodorovna said. "Try and get some sleep."

Vera settled into her cot and closed her eyes. Years of hardship had taught her to sleep anywhere and anytime she could. A quietly whispered spell helped. In moments, she slipped into a deep sleep.

She woke to find Natalya Fyodorovna gently shaking her.

Vera blinked, wiped at her eyes, and sat up. She could just make out the fading daylight outside. "It's time?"

"Yes," Natalya Fyodorovna said. "Ready to kill some Nazis?"

"Always," Vera said through a vulpine smile. She stood, stretched, and did a double take at her bunkmates. "Are you wearing makeup?"

"Eyeliner of a sort," Maryna Ruslanivna said and held up a pencil. "We burn the tip and use the graphite and ash."

Vera looked at the pencil and then at the dark lines drawn around the eyes of each woman. Something about them sent shivering tingles through her body, much as she felt whenever her mother or grandmother wove one of their more subtle magics.

But it couldn't be, could it?

"Always be proud you're a woman," Nadiya Antonivna said. "Would you like me to do your eyes?"

"Next time," Natalya Fyodorovna said. "We have to get to our mission briefing." She turned to Vera. "Get your gear."

As the tent did little to block the cold, and a need to scramble to the aircraft could happen without warning, Vera—like everyone else—slept with her clothes and boots on. She grabbed her helmet, goggles, gloves, and the satchel holding her navigating gear. The maps would be provided prior to each mission, for security reasons.

Vera turned to her pilot and nodded. "Ready—"

Nastya poked her head out of Natalya Fyodorovna's coat and meowed softly.

"She's eager to get in the air," said Natalya Fyodorovna.

"Is it safe for her?" Vera asked, genuinely concerned.

Everyone laughed and exchanged knowing looks.

"Yes," Natalya Fyodorovna said. "It is safe, but we both appreciate your concern. Now, come."

"Yes, Comrade Major," Vera said and saluted.

Another round of shared glances, and Vera knew she'd made a mistake.

"You are new," Natalya Fyodorovna said, not unkindly. "You are also Ukrainian, as are we, so we understand the need to play along. Around the others, we are all loyal party members, proudly fighting for Mother Russia." She gestured around her at the tent. "But this place is for us, and we do not wear masks here."

"Unless, of course, you truly are a loyal Communist," Lyudmyla Semenivna said, hand resting on the revolver holstered on her hip.

Vera spat on the ground. "I despise the pigs who starved our people while never missing a meal themselves. I'm here because the Communists let me fly and give me bombs to drop."

A round of nods was exchanged, and Natalya Fyodorovna patted her shoulder. "Then you are welcome. Now we must go, or we'll be late."

The six of them—seven, if you counted Nastya—made their way to the command tent. Maps were handed out, and they were briefed with the other pilots on their targets for the night. Vera made notes on the map of confirmed, and suspected, antiaircraft batteries and landmarks to watch for. As the pilots were briefed on possible Luftwaffe threats, Vera and the other navigators did their calculations and coordinated the bombing runs.

They also made note of the best places to put down, if need be.

Again, Vera touched the amulet under her layers of clothing.

When the briefing ended, there was the usual propaganda from the commissar. Everyone, as loyal Communists, nodded and cheered. Thankfully, it ended quickly, and the crews left for their respective planes. It was still an hour before it would be dark enough to set out, but it was impossible to inspect an aircraft in the dark. The ground crews would, of course, see to the plane and its operational status, but no pilot worth the name would fly in something she hadn't inspected herself.

Excitement and anxiety roiled Vera's stomach, and she took a deep breath. The cold air was heavy with the smell of fuel, grease, and burning wood.

She calmed a little and reminded herself of the spells she had prepared that would, hopefully, ensure that she and her pilot would survive, even if their plane was hit.

The tricky part would be getting the *vid'ma* marks onto the plane without anyone noticing. If anyone did, she would say that she was checking for tears and imperfections that might impact their airspeed and thus require adjustments to her calculations.

It wasn't a surprise to learn the three planes that bore the most sunflowers belonged to her bunkmates. As they approached, the ground crew finished securing the two bombs under the wings.

When Natalya Fyodorovna set to checking the plane over, Vera set her satchel in her seat, palmed a charcoal pencil, and casually positioned herself on the opposite side of the plane from her pilot. The best place to put the marks would be near the flowers; she could do them small enough that they'd look like an embellishment to anyone not looking too closely.

Vera began whispering the incantation and then froze in shock and astonishment.

There were already *vid'ma* marks on the plane.

A lot of them.

All were carefully hidden in the flowers, and Vera could just sense an active charm that would cause most to ignore the symbols, even if looking for them. She only recognized maybe half of the marks, but the ones she did were potent and would've taken most of an hour to cast properly.

And from the look of them, they had been.

She took a step back, her mind reeling. That's when she saw the bombs also had *vid'ma* marks. Again, she didn't know all of them, but they seemed to be related to increasing the power of the bombs and making them more accurate.

It took Vera a moment to realize she was just standing there, gawking like a fool. She composed herself, turned, and came face-to-face with her pilot and Nastya, both of whom were eyeing her.

"Is something wrong, Navigator?" Natalya Fyodorovna asked.

"Merawr," Nastya said, her eyes narrowed.

Fear and panic seized Vera's heart. She opened her mouth, but it took a second or two for words to tumble out. "I was, um, checking integrity of, um—damage to the skin could, um . . ."

Natalya Fyodorovna arched an eyebrow, clearly unbelieving.

Vera swallowed, stood up straight, and waited for what would come next.

Natalya Fyodorovna might be a fellow Ukrainian, but many of the women in Vera's family had met their end at Ukrainian hands. Vera decided she would go along peacefully, at first, but she would not go quietly to her own execution. She didn't know a lot of spells, but she had a few that would make sure that she wouldn't die alone.

That's when the realization came, and Vera's mouth fell open.

"I hadn't dared hoped that my new navigator would also be a *vid'ma*," Natalya Fyodorovna said, a fierce, proud smile on her face. She embraced Vera and kissed each cheek. "Welcome, my sister."

Vera was dumbstruck. "I, uh, you're also—?"

Natalya Fyodorovna nodded. "I am. As are the others in our flight, half a dozen ground crew, three other pilots, and one other navigator." She touched the black lining around her eyes. "What you missed out on gives us perfect night vision, which combined with our enchanted bombs ensure we send the Nazis running with fear at the sound of our brooms."

"So many?" Vera asked, then looked around and leaned in closer. "But how have the others never seen or deduced—?"

"They see only what they want to see," Natalya Fyodorovna said. "Our commander, even the commissar, suspect." She shrugged. "They probably know at this point, but they say nothing. We bomb with accuracy and wreak much havoc."

"I don't believe it."

"Meow," Nastya said and began to purr.

Natalya Fyodorovna smiled and scratched the kitten's ears. "Nastya is happy that you are one of us. But is it so hard to believe? We are women fighting in a man's war, in a man's army, in a man's world. I don't fully trust the commissar, the commander, or many of our Russian comrades, but there are members of my own family I don't fully trust. With our help, these flying matchsticks catch fire far less than they should. This means the pilots and navigators return to bomb more targets." She put her hand on Vera's shoulder. "I'm not so naive to believe when the war ends, if we see the end, that they won't turn on us. But for now they need us, and they know it. So long as we don't make it too obvious, they will continue not to see that which they don't wish to see."

Vera nodded. It made sense, and though on guard, she felt safer and a bit freer than she had in a long time. She lifted her chin and donned a fierce grin. "Then let us go and show the Nazis why they are afraid of the dark."

Nastya let out of a low meowing growl, and they climbed into their Po-2. The engine started up, and Vera smiled. Soon it came time for Vera's flight to depart. The engine throttled up, and they bounced down the rough, makeshift airstrip. Thankfully, the Po-2 didn't require much runway to get into the air. It felt like little more than a dozen feet before they lifted from the ground and headed for their target at treetop level.

The mild cold was biting at full speed in the open cockpit, but Vera still smiled like a fool. There was nothing that compared to flying, and knowing those with her were also *vid'ma* made it all the more exhilarating. Modern witches on modern brooms to rain hell down on their enemies.

The engine and wind noise meant Vera needed to shout at Natalya Fyodorovna, but they also used shoulder taps to note when it was time to make course changes.

When they neared their target, Vera tapped Natalya Fyodorovna's shoulder, and they began to climb, the other two planes following suit. When they reached the desired altitude, Natalya Fyodorovna idled the engine. Silently, they banked and glided toward their target.

At the same time, Lyudmyla Semenivna and Oleksandra Yuriyivna broke off and swooped down. Almost immediately, antiaircraft fire erupted, and tracer bullets streaked by. The two pilots rolled and banked, deftly avoiding the incoming fire. It looked a bit like a dance, and Vera started to sing "*Rozpryahayte, khloptsi, koni*"—"Unhitch the Horses, Boys."

Natalya Fyodorovna joined in at the chorus. When they released the bombs, Natalya Fyodorovna shouted, "*Slava Ukraini*!" ("Glory to Ukraine!") throttled the engine up, and banked hard to the right.

Vera turned in her seat and watched, smiling as Nazis ran or were thrown by the blasts. She smiled more when the secondary and tertiary explosions went off.

All three planes regrouped, next letting Lyudmyla Semenivna and then Oleksandra Yuriyivna drop their bombs. Then, as quickly as it had begun, all three turned and sped back to base.

They landed and taxied to their waiting ground crews. Natalya Fyodorovna killed the engine, and the four women around the plane set to work. In minutes, the aircraft were rearmed and refueled. The next target wasn't far from the first. As before, through singing and shouting, they dropped their bombs, flummoxed the antiaircraft guns, and returned to base, before doing it again and again.

On their fifth run, an Fw 190, the most fearsome German fighter, buzzed them in route, but they all evaded its fire as it raced by.

On the third pass, it got too close.

There was a flash from Lyudmyla Semenivna's plane, and a streak of orange hit the Nazi plane, punching through the wing and fuselage. It sped off, trailing black smoke, and Vera could just make out Lyudmyla Semenivna shaking her revolver and shouting something.

"You didn't think that was an ordinary pistol, did you?" Natalya Fyodorovna shouted back to Vera.

By the twelfth run, Vera was worn out. Based on the hour and the sky, this was likely to be the last run of the night. Everything went as before, singing and shouting included, but when Oleksandra Yuriyivna made her run, a gun emplacement opened fire, one that had been silent.

The singing stopped as Natalya Fyodorovna desperately twisted and turned the plane one way, then the other, trying to evade the trail of bullets. Vera watched streaking tracer fire tear through the wing and even the fuselage. More than once she heard a bullet whiz by her ear and thought she could feel the heat of the tracer round.

As soon as Oleksandra Yuriyivna had dropped her bombs, she and Lyudmyla Semenivna tried to draw some of the fire away.

The Nazis manning the gun wouldn't be deterred. They'd clearly been waiting until they knew there would be no more bombs to drop.

More gunfire erupted from new spots, blocking their return path.

Despite the twisting and turning, Vera plotted a new course and shouted it to Natalya Fyodorovna.

"That is away from the base!" she shouted back. "And deeper into enemy territory!"

"I don't see another option!" Vera shouted back.

"Damn it!" Natalya Fyodorovna shouted.

They turned, the other two planes following suit, and made a run for it. Vera knew their fuel didn't allow for much leeway, but they only needed a couple of miles.

Just as she was directing Natalya Fyodorovna on the next turn, more gunfire erupted from behind them, shredding their wings. Seconds later, two Fw 190s raced by, banked, and turned to come back around.

"We're not going to make it back to base in the plane," Natalya Fyodorovna said. "Make sure your harness is tight."

Vera did so and reached into her jacket to grip the talisman.

Using wing movements, Natalya Fyodorovna signaled the others to break off and return to base. After a moment of hesitation, they did so. To cover their escape, Natalya Fyodorovna turned her plane and put it between her sisters and the Fw 190s.

Despite everything, Vera felt relief when she saw the other two planes vanish into the darkness. Fear that she was going to die nibbled at her guts, but her thoughts fixed on Nastya. She whispered a quiet prayer that the kitten would be okay.

To focus her mind, Vera began calculating the best route to get back to base on foot. She'd barely finished when the Fw 190s opened fire again.

Natalya Fyodorovna did her best to evade, but the plane had lost maneuverability from the damage, and too much strain might have pulled the thing apart.

Bullets riddled the limping biplane as the fighters sped by again. This time, the Po-2's engine spat black smoke, sputtered, and died.

"Hang on," Natalya Fyodorovna shouted. "I'm going to put us down in that clearing."

Vera turned one way and then the other, but she couldn't see a clearing. Instead of panicking, she closed her eyes, gripped the safety straps, and trusted in her pilot.

Tree branches snapped and cracked against the landing gear, sounding like thunder. Then the fabric skin of the plane tore apart.

The battered Po-2 shook and jerked, but Vera kept her eyes closed.

The wooden frame of the plane groaned and flexed before breaking.

They dropped, and her stomach leaped into her throat.

Luckily, they were close to the ground, slamming down hard only a moment later. The plane slid and bounced along the hard, frozen ground before coming to rest.

Vera opened her eyes and took a quick mental inventory of her body. Her shoulders hurt, but she could move. Likely she'd pulled some muscles and would have bruises from the safety straps, but otherwise she was okay. That's when she realized her boots were touching the ground.

The bottom half of the plane had been entirely ripped away.

She freed herself, shoved her map and compass into a pocket, clambered from the wreckage, and went to check on Natalya Fyodorovna.

Her pilot was conscious but dazed. It looked as though she'd smacked her head against something. Vera patted down Natalya Fyodorovna's jacket and found a rattled but uninjured Nastya.

"Can you move?" Vera asked.

"I think so," Natalya Fyodorovna said.

"Then come—we need to get away from the plane before the fighters come back."

Natalya Fyodorovna unfastened her harness, wincing as she did, but said nothing.

Vera helped her out of the plane, and the two of them hurried to the cover of trees. They'd only just caught their breath when the chattering of machine-gun fire sounded from above, and a barrage of bullets tore through the remains of their Po-2.

Neither of them moved for several minutes.

The silence of the night remained unbroken by the sound of engines.

"I think they're gone," Vera said.

"We need to get back to base," Natalya Fyodorovna said. "Do you know how far and which direction?"

Vera checked the map and then the compass. "A little over thirty kilometers that way," she said, pointing to the southwest.

Natalya Fyodorovna had pulled Nastya from her coat and looked her over. "Are you okay, little sister?"

Nastya meowed fiercely.

"Thirty kilometers," Natalya Fyodorovna said. "Five hours." She checked her watch. "The sun will be up in just over two. Until then, I will guide you. Give me the compass."

Vera handed it over and put her hand on Natalya Fyodorovna's shoulder.

Natalya Fyodorovna drew her revolver. "Keep quiet unless it's absolutely necessary," she said and led the way through the trees.

After sunrise, they took a short break, and Vera checked the map to get her bearings. It was harder at ground level, but the mountains helped orient her. Natalya Fyodorovna had kept them on track, and it looked as though they were about two hours from base and half an hour from the front lines.

She told Natalya Fyodorovna as much, and they were about to resume their trek when the sounds of snapping branches and men talking came from ahead of them.

They both crouched, getting as low as they could.

Vera's heart pounded so hard she was sure it could be heard all the way back at base.

It wasn't long before she could make out German, and though she didn't speak much, she recognized the word *Nachthexen*—Night Witches.

The Nazis headed right for them.

Natalya Fyodorovna swore silently, leaned in close, and whispered, "Stay down and stay quiet."

Vera nodded.

Natalya Fyodorovna drew back the hammer on her revolver,

though Vera knew it—and its paltry seven bullets—wouldn't do much good against Nazis with submachine guns.

Vera swallowed and tried to slow her rapid breathing.

Natalya Fyodorovna was a beacon of calm, and it spread to Vera, lending her, what seemed at the moment, unjustified confidence. The stone-faced pilot opened her coat, drew out Nastya, and lifted the kitten to her lips.

Vera presumed Natalya Fyodorovna was making her goodbyes before sending the kitten to fend for herself in the woods.

"We need your help, little sister," Natalya Fyodorovna whispered. "I wouldn't ask if we had another option."

Nastya licked Natalya Fyodorovna's nose and let out a low growl, much deeper than a kitten had any right to make.

Natalya Fyodorovna set Nastya down, and the cat sped off silently.

Vera gave Natalya Fyodorovna a questioning look.

The pilot just motioned for her to wait.

The Nazis drew so close that Vera could smell their foul body odor.

A blood-curdling roar sounded from behind them, followed by shouts of surprise; rapid gunfire, and then screams like Vera had never heard.

She shrank herself as small as she could as the terrible sounds of shrieking men, chattering gunfire, and bellowing roars filled the air.

Just as abruptly as it started, it ended.

The sudden silence was like a physical blow.

Vera opened her eyes, unsure when she'd closed them, and took a breath she didn't know she was holding. The air was thick with the smell of gunpowder and blood.

Natalya Fyodorovna stood over Vera, hand out. "It's over. We need to get out of here before more Nazis come," she said.

Vera accepted the offered hand and was pulled to her feet. She froze in disbelief.

Not even ten meters away were the torn, bloody remains of Nazi soldiers. Vera didn't know how many, because they'd literally been torn to shreds. In the middle of it all sat Nastya, licking a paw clean.

Natalya Fyodorovna picked up the kitten and tucked her back into her coat. "We are *vid'ma*. We have many friends, and not all are of this world."

Vera smiled and scratched Nastya behind her ears. "Thank you, little sister."

Nastya purred and rubbed her face against Vera's hand.

"Let's get back to base, yes?" Natalya Fyodorovna asked.

"Yes."

As they hurried along, Vera felt pity for the Nazis, but only a little. It was, after all, as her mother had said: "When you put evil out into the world, it always comes back home."

GODS OF THE SEA

TORI ELDRIDGE

SOLOMON SEA, PACIFIC OCEAN, NOVEMBER 1942

"No change. No change. Rapid fire," Nalu Kali'i shouted, doubtful that the gunner's mate or any of his fellow seaman could hear him above the salvos of outgoing American gunfire and the explosions of incoming Japanese shells.

The US task force, led by Admiral Callaghan, had only made visual contact with the enemy ten minutes ago. They had steamed for an hour through heavy squalls into the Savo Sound, north of Guadalcanal. Confusing reports and visual impairment from the rain and the inky-black night had led to dramatic changes in orders and direction. By the time the Japanese bombardment fleet and America's counterforce had visually confirmed the other's presence, both had lost their formations and intermingled dangerously close. Sailors on both sides were pent up and ready to explode. So when searchlights from two Japanese battle cruisers lit up the light cruiser USS *Atlanta*, both sides immediately opened fired.

Nalu lowered his binoculars as tracers, star shells, and muzzle flashes obliterated his night vision. Although only a seaman apprentice, he had been assigned lookout battle station for the antiaircraft gunners. With a Japanese destroyer passing alongside, he directed fire at the smaller guns on the enemy's deck.

Destroyers and cruisers changed directions to avoid collisions with enemy warships and friendlies. Some torpedoes struck before their warheads could activate, while those fired at greater distances blasted through hull armor and caused engine rooms and magazines to explode. A battle that should have been fought at a distance devolved instead into the naval equivalent of a barroom brawl.

The deck tipped starboard as the destroyer USS *Barton* executed an abrupt high-speed turn to port.

Nalu crashed into the curved metal gun shield.

A Japanese destroyer exploded.

The *Atlanta* took heavy fire and burst into flames.

Frigid seawater splashed onto the deck, but Nalu's face beneath his MK II talker helmet was already wet from rain and combat-tension sweat.

Never in six months of combat duty had Nalu gone on a mission to stop an attacking Japanese force, and certainly never in a chaotic melee of warships changing direction and passing each other at twenty to thirty knots. If not for his keen eyesight and hearing, Nalu might have been stationed out of the elements. But although the 5-inch, .38-caliber guns were loaded from inside their turrets, the 1.1-inch and the 20mm antiaircraft guns were loaded and fired topside. Someone had to keep their eyes on the enemy and their ears on the communications channel. Tonight one of those someones was him.

"Action starboard. Rapid fire!" he shouted into the microphone as the *Barton* turned toward a new target.

Another enemy destroyer passed so closely that Nalu could see a Japanese sailor staring back at him through binoculars, before the muzzle flashes and smoke from the *Barton*'s 5-inch guns hid him from view. The repetitive pounding and thunderous booms throbbed inside Nalu's skull despite the headset protecting his ears. He ducked behind the gun shield as bullets hit steel above his head. The seconds seemed to last forever as the two destroyers passed. Then the *Barton* dug in for a hard starboard turn.

Nalu scanned the momentary darkness before new explosions of light erupted and whipped through the sky. With enemy ships and his own destroyer in frenetic motion, it was hard to predict where the next target would be.

A massive Japanese battle cruiser lay dead ahead. Its searchlights had drawn heavy American fire, like Japan's other Kongō-class beast. The *Hiei* and *Kirishima* had escorted the aircraft carriers that bombarded Pearl Harbor. Nalu bet these ships were them. With 14-inch main guns and displacing 27,000 tons, the Imperial Japanese Navy battle cruisers dwarfed the 1,620-ton *Barton* and the 6,720-ton *Atlanta*.

Nalu shouted for his 1.1-inch gun crew to standby as *Barton*'s 5-inch guns blasted from the fantail. The centerline quintuple torpedo tube mounts finished their rotation and fired the first fish off the port side. The deck vibrated from the launch and rattled with more force as three additional fish shot out of their tubes.

Nalu spotted something he couldn't understand.

A massive iridescent form darted and splashed between the ships.

Only sections of the scaly creature could be seen as they rolled above the surface and reflected the light. Then it dove, whipping a great tail in the air, reappearing behind itself as if making a giant loop. A fearsome head burst out of the water, jaws open, tendrils trailing from its face like a beard. Glacial-blue eyes flashed in hatred. It dove beneath the *Barton* and smashed its powerful tail against the hull.

The impact of the hit knocked Nalu and the rest of the gun crew off their feet. Before he could process the impossibility of what he had seen, salvos of gunfire peppered the ship. The noise was deafening, even to Nalu's protected ears.

The *Barton*'s engines cut abruptly.

A US light cruiser swerved across their bow.

Nalu grabbed hold of the gun shield and heaved with relief. A broadside collision could have fatally damaged them both. As the cruiser steamed away, the *Barton* came to full stop. It was dead in the water until the engineering crew could bring it back to life.

As Nalu raised his binoculars to search for the next threat, a powerful force slammed into the destroyer's side. A torpedo explosion hurled Nalu over the gun mount and onto the upper deck, where secondary explosion shock waves from below punched the metal platform into his back. Most of his gun crew lay broken and lifeless. The aft funnel screeched above him as it split. A sheet of metal hurtled downward and sliced through a gunner's mate's chest.

Nalu choked on his cries as he scrambled away, head turned, struggling to breath. His body shook as violently as the ship.

He crawled to the railing in time to see the massive serpent circle for another charge. Before it could attack, a second torpedo shook the destroyer like a quake. The engine room exploded and broke the destroyer's spine. A moment later, the midsection of the ship buckled upward, struck by a ferocious power from below, and catapulted Nalu off the deck.

He tumbled through the night, disoriented by the strobing lights and menaced by flying scraps from his shattered destroyer. With the barest sense of up and down, he tried to correct himself as if diving off a cliff, but he slammed into the water. As his life vest buoyed him to the surface, he shielded his head from falling debris.

Years of big-wave surfing back home had strengthened Nalu's lungs and taught him to remain calm when knocked from his board and buried beneath the waves' weight. It had also taught him to expect additional hazards as he rose. So instead of floundering at the surface, he wiped the oil and water from his eyes as he gulped in the air. The two halves of the *Barton* sank into the turbulent waters.

He kicked his powerful legs to boost himself higher in the water for a better view, spotting other survivors bobbing amid the wreckage. Dozens of bodies. Some of them struggled. Others did not. Many were scrambling toward the buoyant remnants of Carley floats or balsa-wood life rafts. If the survivors could band together, they might draw enough attention to be rescued before they all drowned.

A concussive blast knocked back his head and spiked shards of pain through his eyes and his ears. Smoke stung his sinuses as he struggled to breathe. He fought back the darkness creeping into his brain and forced himself to swim. He had just grabbed the life-vest collar of an injured sailor when a nearby US destroyer made a violent turn. Steaming too fast for a rescue, it headed in their direction at a murderous speed.

"Hey!" Nalu yelled, waving an arm at the towering bow as if he could ward off the ship.

The injured man screamed.

The destroyer continued its turn and shoved them both with its wake. Then it plowed straight through the remaining survivors.

Nalu cried out in horror. Hadn't the destroyer's lookouts seen the *Barton* sink? Hadn't they seen the survivors waving and screaming in the oily wreckage? What had caused the destroyer to mow down its own? As star shells, tracers, and searchlights streamed through the sky, and muzzle flashes and torpedo explosions lit up warships all around, Nalu wondered which of these threats had forced the destroyer to turn.

The injured sailor slapped the water with his hands, crying and shouting obscenities into the night.

Nalu remained silent and watched the movement of the tides. He had surfed the winter waves at Pipeline, Waimea, and Sunset Beach, and he recognized the feel of the water when a new ride approached. He had also survived enough shark encounters to remain vigilant for predator attacks. The undulating motion of the water as the flaming oil and debris rose and fell was more terrifying than any back-crushing wave or man-eating shark.

"Quiet," Nalu said, grabbing the sailor's hands before they could slap the water again. "Something's coming. We need to be still."

The massive creature he had spotted from the deck cut through the water, causing pulsating wakes and mountainous flashes of iridescent scales. When the sea dragon's head breached the surface with its jaws open wide, Nalu clapped his hands over the sailor's mouth to stifle his scream. He swallowed his own cry as the serpent devoured all the bodies in its path, both living and dead. When it circled for more food, its wake shoved Nalu and the sailor farther away. It vanished.

"What the hell was that?" the sailor asked, wiggling free of Nalu's firm grip.

"I don't know, bruh. But I saw it from da deck before da second torpedo hit. I think it struck us from below and broke da ship in two." Although boot camp had eradicated Nalu's pidgin English, fear and disorientation from the explosions had brought the Islander twang back into his speech.

"Not possible," the sailor said.

"Oh yeah? Tell it to da serpent that just ate thirty of our guys."

The thunder of naval guns punctuated his shout as, all

around them, warships exchanged fire. Some were miles in the distance, others a few thousand feet away. The bursts of violent engagement brightened their surroundings, then plunged them into darkness like a slow, erratic strobe. During a brief illumination, Nalu saw blood dripping from the man's head.

"We need to get out of da water before you and da rest of those bleeding bodies attract hungry *manō* to us."

"Hungry what?"

"Sharks, bruh. We gotta move."

Twenty yards away, a Carley float burst through the water like a breaching whale. Since the sailor couldn't kick, Nalu pulled him against his chest and swam backward through the debris until they bumped into the raft. The netting inside was torn, and the plank bottom was gone. Only the buoyant oval ring, with its cork insulation around an air-filled copper tube, and the netting that encircled the outermost canvas remained.

Nalu hauled the sailor onto the float and noticed a gash in the man's thigh. "You okay?"

"Yeah, buddy. Thanks. I thought I was a goner for sure."

"Your leg looks pretty bad."

He coughed out a laugh. "It feels a fuck of a lot worse."

"I hear you, bruh. I'm Nalu."

"Sam."

"Okay, Sam. Pull your legs out of da water and rest them on top. Put pressure on da wound. I'm gonna swim ovah to those bodies. See if anyone is alive."

"What about the sharks?"

A tremor of fear rose up Nalu's spine. He scanned the expanse of darkness, steeled himself for the task, and shrugged. "I still gotta check."

He swam with swift, clean strokes to minimize the disturbance and tried not to think about predators below. The dim battle glow made that hard. Bodies floated like a banquet for sea life. Every wave cap looked like a fin. It was only a matter of time before *manō* came to feast.

As he approached the first cluster of gray kapok life jackets, he whispered a prayer. "*Aloha ahiahi, manō.* It's me, He'enalu Keli'i from Hawai'i. Our family *'aumākua* is one of you. Please accept my respect and allow me to pass."

Would sharks in these waters care about his guardian ancestor back home? Surely not, but it made Nalu feel better to show them respect.

He swam through the spreading debris, but every sailor he reached was dead. If there were survivors, the destroyer's wake had pushed them out of sight.

"Hello? Anyone there?"

Nothing answered except distant gunfire and explosions. Nalu might have chanced a shark attack to keep searching, but he couldn't leave an injured sailor behind.

"Nalu!" Sam yelled.

"Yeah. I'm coming back."

"Any survivors?"

Nalu didn't answer. It felt disrespectful to shout the sad news.

When he reached the gray float, he climbed onto the opposite side from Sam. The fact that he was alone answered Sam's question. Safe for the moment, they watched the battle in silence as warships they couldn't identify fired, exploded, or sank. Would another ship, friendly or enemy, swerve out of the melee and plow into them?

As the battle continued, the warships spread farther apart, leaving Nalu and Sam alone with the dead. He rubbed his throbbing temples and winced. In addition to a probable concussion, the explosion had burned his face and the sleeve and skin of one arm. Although nothing felt broken, the shock waves of the blast and impact of the water had battered his muscles into tenderized meat. He worried about brain damage as his vision blurred and cleared.

On the other side of the floating ring, Sam moaned.

Alone, with no options or help, Nalu puzzled through the mystery of what he had seen.

"I know what it was," he said. "Da creature we saw."

Tracers brightened the sky as Sam shook his head. "You didn't see a creature. Neither did I."

"Yeah, we did. I heard stories about it growing up in Hawai'i. My best friend was half Japanese. His uncle took us camping and scared us with ayakashi tales."

Sam's sudden movement rocked the Carley float. "Are you Japanese too?" The darkness couldn't hide the fear and suspicion in his voice.

"I'm Hawaiian and a quarter Chinese, but after Pearl Harbor, da haole on O'ahu sneered at me all da same. But tell me, bruh, what difference would it make if my ancestors or me had immigrated from Japan? I still hauled your ass out of da ocean. The Japanese living in Hawai'i or on da mainland didn't bomb those ships in Pearl Harbor."

They sat in silence.

After a while, Sam spoke again. "What did you call those tales?"

"Ayakashi. It's what da Japanese call supernatural phenomenon near da surface of da sea. They can appear as demons, spirits, or—"

"Sea monsters?" The sailor sounded skeptical but afraid.

"I know it sounds nuts, bruh. But my friend's uncle described serpents like that. I'm pretty sure what we saw was Ryūjin."

"What's a Ryūjin?"

"Not a what, bruh. Who. Ryūjin is Japan's dragon god of da sea."

The float bucked. Sam muttered and cursed. "Dragon god? Are you kidding me? We don't have time for this shit."

Nalu steadied their raft. "Seems to me like we got all da time in da world."

"Oh yeah? Well, it seems to *me* that the explosions might have messed up your brain. Do you even know who you are?"

"Of course I do. Seaman Apprentice He'enalu Keli'i. I came aboard the *Barton* last month. I was standing lookout for da gunners when—"

"Cool down, okay?" Sam peered at him as a salvo of distant gunfire lit up the night. "SA Kelly. Yeah, I seen you around."

Sam had pronounced *Keli'i* the American way, omitting the glottal stop between the *i*'s. Normally, He'enalu would let it go. But if this was the last time anyone spoke his name, he wanted to hear it correctly or not at all. "Call me Nalu."

"Okay," Sam said as the darkness returned. "Sam Forester, radioman third class."

"Radioman, huh? Get to hear all da chatter? Guess you know more than me."

Sam scoffed. "Not about sea serpents."

Star shells illuminated the sky, revealing trails of toilet paper and other mundane items bobbing amid the oil-slicked debris.

Both sides ceased fire, and darkness swallowed the sound and the light. An eerie calm focused Nalu's thoughts as he breathed in the stench of oil, chemicals, and steel mingled with the tang of seawater and blood. Although he couldn't see it, the horror remained. So did the truth of what he had seen.

"It might not have been Ryūjin himself," he said. "But if da sea dragon god sent monsters to help Japan, it will take more than torpedoes and guns for our side to survive."

"You mean win, right? Stop the Japanese bombardment? Keep them away from Guadalcanal?"

If the Allies lost this battle, the Imperial Japanese Navy would dominate the sea with their aircraft carriers and take back the much-valued Henderson Field. The lives, planes, and ships the Allied forces had lost during Operation Watchtower would be for nothing, as would the hardships suffered by the US Marines on Guadalcanal.

"No, bruh. I meant what I said. If da Japanese get one sea god fighting for them, we need a sea god fighting for us."

"And do you happen to have the phone number of a friendly sea god handy?"

"Don't make jokes. Not about this. Not when a giant serpent rammed our ship and ate our guys. We live in a magical world. My people respect this. So do the Japanese."

Nalu blocked out Sam's questions and racked his memory for the *oli*, *mele*, and *moʻolelo* about Kanaloa that his parents had chanted, sang, and told. The Hawaiian god of the sea and long-distance voyages was the second most powerful of Hawaiʻi's pantheon of gods. Kanaloa and the ocean were one and the same. From him, the sea creatures and characteristics of the ocean emerged. He could manifest in many *kino lau* forms like whales, dolphins, or heʻe, the elusive squid the ancient Hawaiians believed could make sickness flee. The word *heʻe* also meant to slide or—as in Heʻenalu's name—to surf on the waves. If any supernatural being could face down the Japanese sea dragon god, it would be Hawaiʻi's benevolent god of the sea.

If I speak from da heart with aloha and respect, will you travel all da way to Guadalcanal for me?

He opened his arms to the darkness and chanted for the god to stand upright on the solid floor where the squid lies flat.

"e Kanaloa i ke kū,
Kūlia ke papa,
Kūlia i ka papa he'e!"

He alternated between English and 'ōlelo Hawai'i as his language skills allowed. He praised Kanaloa and identified himself with the full Hawaiian names of every ancestor from both sides of his family as far back as he could trace. He explained why he—a *kanaka maoli* of a foreign sovereign nation, annexed by America, and striving for statehood—had joined the US Navy to fight against the enemy who had attacked Kanaloa's home. He described their mission and the dire state of affairs, and how the Japanese sea dragon god had joined the battle to help the enemy win. As the golden glow of dawn spread across the sky, Nalu rasped his final plea.

"*E 'olu'olu e Kanaloa*, I beg you to come."

All around him floated the detritus of war that had not sunk into Kanaloa's domain. Would Hawai'i's sea god rise from the ocean bed where the squid lay flat? Would he race all the way to the Solomon Islands to help one of his own?

Nalu dropped his arms and wept.

Sam pointed to the receding ships in the east. "They're leaving us."

A burst of gunfire thundered to the west, where several US warships still engaged the enemy between and beyond Savo Island and the northwest tip of Guadalcanal. Nalu squinted into the sunlight. Even with his keen eyesight, he couldn't tell their side from his. What he could see, all too clearly, were the sharks circling his raft.

"Get your legs out of da water!" he yelled. Nalu clung to the waterproof canvas as Sam rocked his side of the buoyant oval ring.

While salvos of gunfire continued to the northwest, the circling sharks took turns ramming their float. Sam's legs slipped off the edge.

Nalu beat the water on his side to attract the sharks to him. The commotion acted like a feeding bell, calling more and more predators toward himself until a shiver of three dozen sharks circled. Soon one of them would come in for a bite.

Nalu grabbed hold of the net and jumped into a squat. Although Sam yelled at him to get down, Nalu had better balance and control if he stayed on his feet. But as the largest shark charged, a disturbance agitated the water, scattered the shiver, and raised Nalu and the float high on a wave. Below them, the sea dragon undulated. The creature was so enormous and close that all Nalu could see were its spines and scales, sparkling like billions of faceted aquamarines.

After what seemed like forever, the shimmering body slimmed into a powerfully propulsive tail. It took all Nalu's strength and skill to balance the float through the turbulent chop while his injured raftmate struggled to hang on. When the raft settled, Nalu let go of the net and rose to his full height for a better view as Ryūjin charged toward the warships exchanging fire to the northwest.

A new disturbance on the horizon drew Nalu's eyes. He had seen mass splashing like this many times before, but it had never covered so vast a space. He dropped back to his knees and cheered as a mega pod of dolphins and pilot whales descended from the north and curved west to intercept Ryūjin.

"What's happening?" Sam yelled.

Nalu looked at him and grinned. "Kanaloa sent his emissaries to fight Ryūjin."

Ryūjin must have heard the vibrations in the water, because he turned and attacked. The nimble dragon sliced into the enormous pod, thrashing and whipping the animals into the air. Dolphins and pilot whales dropped like hail. Waves formed. Geysers shot to the sky. Ryūjin churned the water into a whirlpool as he spun.

Nalu wrapped his arms and legs around the buoyant tube as his side of the oval ring rode fifteen feet up a wave. Directly below him, Sam dragged in the water, his arms caught in the net. They locked eyes in that moment of inertia when the raft could tip either way. Then a new surge pushed behind the wave and flipped Nalu's side over the top. He let go of the tube, snagged a handful of netting, and plunged feet first into the trough. If he hadn't flexed his arm, his shoulder would have dislocated when the float yanked him back up.

Nalu sucked a quick breath before choppy waves hit his life raft and flipped it again. Rather than smack on the water repeatedly, he let go. He would have swum beneath the turbulence as he did through big waves, but his life vest kept him on top. Yards away, Sam smacked against the water like a rag doll in an irritable child's hand.

"Sam, let go!"

A force hit Nalu from behind. A second impact snagged his life vest and dragged him underwater at great speed. He caught a flash of aquamarine scales before the stinging flush of ocean water caused him to squint.

The undulating serpent spiraled and bucked.

Nalu lost all sense of direction as he tumbled with the beast. Despair roiled in his heart. Ryūjin wanted him. Kanaloa did not.

Determined pilot whales rammed into the serpent and freed Nalu from his entanglement in its spines. The shredded life vest had lost some buoyancy, drawing him more slowly toward the surface than before. But Nalu didn't have the energy to kick. After a lifetime of surfing, the ocean was finally calling him home—until a gentle mouth closed on his torso, and Kanaloa sped him toward air.

Nalu woke to the thunder of machine guns in the sky, explosions on the sea, and his arms stretched over a curved plank of wood. The sun hung low. Ryūjin and the pod of rescuers were gone. So were the oil-slicked remnants of the *Barton* and any sign of the Carley float or Sam. His back, no longer protected by his life vest or shirt, baked in the heat. If not for his already deep tan and Polynesian blood, he would have suffered a terrible burn.

Although his salt-caked skin stung, he crawled onto a fragment of the balsa-wood boat as F4F Wildcats and Japanese Zero fighters maneuvered like hummingbirds overhead. The aerial combat centered around bombing or protecting Japan's dying battle cruiser, which, after suffering extensive damage during the previous night's battle, had lingered for a last-ditch bombardment on Henderson Field, or perhaps it simply could not escape. Regardless of the reason, the protective escort of destroyers still presented a threat.

Nalu sucked in the smoky air and managed a raspy shout at the rescue boats far to the east. His parched throat made him cough. A futile effort. Even at full voice, they wouldn't have heard.

How could he warn them about Ryūjin? How could he let them know Kanaloa had fought on their behalf? He wasn't the only one in trouble. If the Japanese regained Henderson Field, the Allied forces would lose a base vital to the war effort. Tears rolled down his face as the USS *Bobolink*—a minesweeper turned tugboat—towed damaged warships to safety, and boxy Higgins boats rescued survivors luckier than him.

Hope vanished with the sun. He had done all that he could. But it wasn't enough.

Fourteen-inch salvos fired from the battle cruiser shook its damaged hull, while clouds of smoke marked the hits at Henderson Field. Buzzing aircraft approached. Ryūjin leaped from the water and snapped at a low-flying plane. The dragon's teeth grazed a wing and sent the Wildcat cartwheeling along the surface. When the nose dug into the water, it flipped onto its back and disintegrated. As Ryūjin lunged at another Wildcat, a smaller pod of pilot whales rushed in to attack. Smaller sea serpents and giant barracuda came to Ryūjin's aid. Without their previous numbers, the whales were soon overwhelmed. The sea dragon god killed dozens in a swirling attack.

Suddenly, the waters buckled upward, and a giant tentacle smashed the battle cruiser's burning deck. The heavy strike broke the ship's spine. Grasping tentacle hooks and suckers did the rest. The ocean's surface glowed as the flaming wreckage sank, illuminating Kanaloa's fearsome new form. Larger than any giant squid, the Hawaiian sea god had transformed himself into a fantastical creature thrice the size of Ryūjin.

In the gleam of twilight, the sea dragon and his serpents dodged through the tentacles to ram and tear at the triangular-shaped head. Kanaloa spun like a propeller and cut through his foes. Blood, gore, and water shot into the air.

Body parts fell around Nalu like bloody rain. Choppy tides swept him off his plank and pummeled him from all sides. As he struggled to stay afloat, Ryūjin leaped out of the waves. A gash had opened its right side from the front to hind leg. The sea dragon god screeched in fury—or anguish? It dove into the water and bolted away.

Nalu would have cheered if he hadn't been struggling to remain afloat. He had never been caught in rough seas like this before, not even on the sailing voyage to Moloka'i in an outrigger canoe. But as an enormous wave was about to crash on his head, something wrapped around his legs and yanked him below. Nalu pinched his nose against the rushing water as he was dragged at high speed. When finally released at the surface, Nalu breathed in the fresh, salty air below stars twinkling in the dusk.

He floated in silence, one tiny, exhausted person in an unfathomable sea.

Had Kanaloa fought on his behalf but abandoned him to die?

Why hadn't the god left him with his fellow sailors and warships at the bottom of Savo Sound? At least then he wouldn't have died alone.

As stars grew brighter in the darkening sky, Nalu imagined himself on a surfboard in Waimea Bay on a gentle summer night. He could hear the laughter of his family and friends as they played music and sang on the beach. The scent of grilled fish floated on the breeze. Nalu had lived a good life. He needed to open his heart and make peace.

With no voice or strength left to chant, Nalu closed his eyes and prayed. He thanked Kanaloa for answering his call and fighting with the Allied forces against Japan. He thanked the god of the sea and long-distance voyages for protecting him over the years. With gratitude in his heart, He'enalu Keli'i from O'ahu asked for one final boon.

"*E 'olu'olu e Kanaloa*. Please, take me home."

With Hawai'i firmly in his mind, the ocean wrapped him in a comforting embrace.

GORGOPOTAMOS BRIDGE

HARRY TURTLEDOVE

GORGOPOTAMOS, GREECE, NOVEMBER 1942

I had a syrinx—panpipes, if you like. One of Zervas's andartes guerrillas sprawling around the fire with me had a bouzouki—a lute, if you must. Another had a fiddle. When I raised the panpipes to my mouth, the fiddler asked, "What'll it be, Konstantin?"

"You know 'Christos Milionis'?" I blew the first few notes to give him the tune in case he didn't.

But he nodded and played along with me. So did the andartes with the bouzouki, though he said, "You like the old ones, don't you?"

"They're real. They're true." I played a little more, then lowered the pipes and started to sing: "Three little birds are perched on the ridge by the klephts' stronghold. One looks at Armyro, the other on to Valto. The third, the fairest, sings a dirge and says . . ."

A lot of klephtic brigand songs start with the three little birds. They're an easy way to let people know what's coming—and to let the lazy fellow putting the song together do it without thinking very much. Always watch out for the third bird. He's the one with the bad news.

We went through it. A Turk was hunting Milionis. They knew each other. They drank together. Then the Turk told him the sultan and his agha generals wanted him. Milionis answered, "While life is in Christos, to Turks he does not do homage." They charged each other, fired at each other, and both fell dead.

I know. Hell of a cheerful song.

No Greeks doing homage to Turks these days. But the Italians, the Bulgarians, and the Germans all had their feet on Hellas's neck. Taking orders from Italians was embarrassing. Humiliating. They didn't beat us in 1940 or 1941 either. The Bulgarians were just vultures, pecking at what somebody else killed. The Germans . . .

The Germans, the Nazis, they frightened me, and I've seen a thing or three in my days. You know how cancer can turn a big, strong man into a pain-wracked skeleton before it finally kills him? The Nazis were a cancer to humankind. They made the Turks seem like gentlemen by comparison. When a Greek says that—well, it explains why I was where I was.

Napoleon Zervas stood up and ambled over to me. On the way, he tossed aside a rib of mutton he'd been gnawing on. He was past fifty and could have dropped some weight. His big, bushy beard made him look like a klephtic captain anyway. He wore a Greek army tunic with bandoliers crisscrossed on his chest, Italian trousers, and German marching boots. His men's eyes followed him when he moved. They were *his* men, the way a long-ago kapetan's men followed him.

He set a hand on my shoulder. "You know all the old songs, Karaghiosis. You sing them well too."

"Thanks. For somebody who can't sing, I'm not too bad."

Zervas chuckled. A wolf would have chuckled the same way. "You sing them like you lived them."

"They all happened a long time ago. The *Tourkokratia*'s a hundred years gone, a hundred years and then some."

"I know." Zervas studied me. His eyes were like a wolf's too—yellow-brown and very intent. "May I ask you a question?"

"Kapetan, you just did," I observed.

That tickled him. He chuckled again, less carnivorously.

I set the pipes on my leg and spread my hands, inviting him to go on.

"Why do you call yourself Karaghiosis, after a silly shadow puppet? Most andartes give themselves fierce handles. Keravnos there—" He looked toward the fiddler.

I nodded. His nickname meant *Thunderbolt*.

Napoleon Zervas—with a name like that, he needed nothing fancier—went on, "Even the Communist kapetan, he goes by Aris, for the god of war."

He sounded disgusted. He also sounded nervous. Aris Velouchiotis, who sat by some other fire in the field, had almost twice as many men from his ELAS resistance group here as Zervas and his EDES did. The commanders didn't trust each other. Neither did their fighters. EDES was Zervas's personal band. ELAS was something else, something closer to a real army, and Velouchiotis an officer in it.

Getting them to work together at all had taken the English a bit of doing, or more than a bit. But I didn't have to deal with that, not from the question he'd asked. "Why? Because somebody told me *Karaghiosis* means 'dark eye' in Turkish."

I looked up at him. The fire was failing, but it gave enough light to show him my right eye was blue, my left brown.

He grunted. "All right. Fair enough. One of the emperors—Anastasios the First—had eyes of two different colors."

I remembered Anastasios. Zervas knowing about him surprised me. He'd climbed through the ranks; he hadn't gone to any fancy military college. And my answer satisfied him, which was what I mostly wanted. I yawned. "By your leave, I'm going to roll myself in my blanket."

"Yes. Go ahead. I'll do that too. More marching tomorrow." Zervas didn't fancy marching. As I mentioned, he wasn't a skinny man. But then those wolf eyes caught the embers' glow and lit up. "And tomorrow, night fighting."

We were about fifteen kilometers from where we needed to be by nightfall. We mooched along by squad and section, never too many of us at once. I limped along—my left leg is longer than my right. A cobbler had made me a built-up boot like Spud Odell's, but it helped only so much. Still, I kept up.

By then, a year and a half after the Nazis had overrun Greece, people were used to seeing andartes on the road. Chances were they wouldn't report us to the Italians in the village or to the Germans helping them guard the bridge over the river with the same name, Gorgopotamos. If they did, they'd regret it as long as they lived. That wouldn't be long either—one more reason (aside from despising Italians and hating Germans, I mean) they'd keep quiet. Yes, fear is a weapon.

The bunch I was with would've given any nice, orderly Wehrmacht officer a stroke. No two of us wore the same clothes. We had German rifles, English rifles, Italian rifles, Greek rifles, shotguns from farms, whatever we could get our hands on. Most of us were at least as shaggy as Zervas. But we were there. That counted more than all the rest put together.

Another dirt track straggled out of some gaunt trees and joined our slightly wider one. Along it came some of Aris Velouchiotis's ELAS men. They were as motley as our gang; only three or four of them wore the same kind of brimless beret. Those Mavroskoufides Black Caps were Aris's tough boys.

They looked at us the way you'd look at half a worm in your apple. Zervas's fighters eyed them the same way. Greeks don't get along with other Greeks any better than they get along with foreigners.

I coughed a couple of times. I was with the EDES men, but not exactly part of them. I wasn't exactly part of ELAS either. But I was well above six feet tall, hobbled, and had mismatched eyes. I stood out, in other words. At the moment, I was giving them the blue eye, the cold one.

Wanting to forestall infighting, I said, "We're all going the same way now. Everything else will keep till later."

"And who are you to tell us that?" one of the Black Caps asked. He had a machine pistol, a Sten gun—a mess of trouble in not much space.

I took off my own cap and scratched my head. Communist or not, the Black Cap crossed himself when I did. No one ever accused me of being handsome. For one thing, my hairline comes down to within a finger's width of my shaggy eyebrows. For another . . . never mind. I'm not handsome, that's all.

"They call me Karaghiosis these days," I said, as mildly as I could. "Who're you?"

He didn't answer me, or not exactly. Instead, he muttered, "They ought to call you Kallikantzaros, because you look like a goblin."

"It's November," I said. "Till Christmas, I'm supposed to be sawing the trunk of the world tree, not blowing up a bridge. We're all in this together, or else we're not. Are we? Feathers or lead?"

"We are." He kept quiet about the rest, which was smart. However you answer *feathers or lead*, you're wrong if a kallikantzaros wants you to be. He generally does too. And then you regret it.

But one of the fellows in the ELAS group asked, "'Feathers or lead?' What manner of question is that?" He spoke the kind of Greek that hasn't been heard in Hellas since before Great Pan died, if he did die. I can talk that way too, but I don't. People nowadays have trouble understanding when you do.

I don't know why I didn't spot him right away. He was almost as tall as I am, and his beard wasn't black or grizzled. It was the color of fire. I must've been slow that morning. I should have noticed him sooner, but I didn't. Sue me.

"Major Woodhouse, it's short for 'Which is heavier: A pound of feathers or a pound of lead?'" I said, in standard spoken Dimotiki. That Woodhouse spoke Greek at all felt like a miracle; none of the other British special forces with us did.

"Is it not so that they should be of equal weight?" Not only did he speak something more like Classical Attic than even modern Katharevousa Greek but he thought like an engineer. Well, he was an artilleryman, so it came naturally to him.

I let it go. If I am a kallikantzaros, I'm a softie. "Never mind," I told him. "Your friend followed me well enough." I looked at his friend with the cold blue eye again. "Didn't you?"

"We *are* all in this together," he said, speaking very quickly indeed. Fear *is* a weapon. A kallikantzaros is unlikely to put the fear of God in a man, but another kind of fear will serve.

And so we all ambled past the village. Major Woodhouse, I saw, wore a full British uniform. That worried me less than his ginger whiskers. These days, folks used whatever clothes they could find or steal. A red beard? Maybe people who saw him from a distance thought he had Franks in the woodpile. Or maybe they just minded their own business. Keeping your head down and your mouth shut is one way to get through an occupation.

The bridge lay a couple of kilometers past the village. Gorgopotamos means "rushing river," and it had carved out quite a canyon over the centuries. The bridge carried the one and only railway line between German-held Thessaloniki and German-held Athens. Taking it out would hurt the Nazis—oh, less than it would have before Rommel started falling back in North Africa, but even so.

We were in Italian-run land. Greeks hated and scorned Mussolini's heroes at the same time. Some of the eighty or so men guarding the bridge wore coal-scuttle helmets and Wehrmacht uniform field gray, but most of them were Italian conscripts who didn't want to be there. We'd brought twice as many, near enough.

When night came, we'd see what the guards had in them. Till then, we ducked behind shrubs and tall grass that screened us from the bridge and from the road. We waited for the sun to set.

Zervas and Aris both came by to check on their groups. They were smart commanders: They took nothing for granted. Somebody told me they were distant cousins, though they hadn't met each other before this operation. I'm not sure that's true, or that they knew about it if it was.

Daylight guttered out. "We are to move at the fifth hour of the night," Major Woodhouse declared.

Two men said the same thing at the same time: "What's he talking about?"

"He means eleven o'clock," I explained.

"Why doesn't he say so, then?" one of them asked. If Woodhouse heard that, he didn't follow it, which was bound to be just as well.

Some of the andartes moved out before eleven o'clock—the fighters who were going to cut the telephone and telegraph lines. If the bridge garrison started screaming for help, we'd have more trouble than we wanted.

Then the men who were left split into three units. One headed straight for the northern garrison. The other crossed the river at a ford upstream from the bridge and made for the other detachment of Italians and Germans. That left the English demolition party—and me.

I'd wondered whether Zervas or Velouchiotis would want me somewhere else. I aimed to get huffy if they did. Something told me this might not go as smoothly as the leaders—and the Englishmen—expected. I listened to that little voice. It wasn't always right, but when it was . . .

We slid and scrambled down the steep sides of the canyon to the riverbank. I learned some English bad language I hadn't heard before. The way Woodhouse cursed in his old, old Greek would have made Aristophanes blush. Or more likely, it wouldn't. Aristophanes wasn't much to look at—horse-faced and sobersided, you'd guess. Then he'd open his mouth. He talked just the way he wrote: filthy and funny, all stirred together with a big spoon. I liked him. He thought I was almost as ugly as Socrates, or maybe the other way around. After all this time, who remembers for sure?

Right on schedule, the fireworks at both ends of the bridge started. One of the English officers said something in his own language. Woodhouse translated for me: "Once the vile, cistern-arsed Italians and their German friends are beaten, we go forward to do that which is necessary."

I nodded; I'd gotten the gist of it myself.

Only the vile, cistern-arsed Italians and their German friends weren't to be beaten so easily. They fought back as hard as they could. And each garrison turned out to have a machine gun or two, so they fought back pretty hard. Machine guns are the concentrated essence of infantry. You can't charge them across bare ground, not unless you want your womenfolk wearing black for the next year.

But in the dark, you can sneak up on them. A couple of grenades went off by the north end of the bridge, and the machine gun there stopped chattering. After that, I heard screams. And I heard soldiers trying to surrender. From the shrieks that followed, they didn't have much luck.

The garrison on the south side of the bridge would have heard those shrieks too. Nothing makes you not want to give up like knowing what will happen if you do. So they kept fighting for all they were worth. They even turned their Breda around a couple of times and sprayed bursts along the bridge to make the andartes think twice about rushing along it to take them from behind.

Woodhouse's superior—the senior Englishman—was a lieutenant colonel named Myers. The longer the fighting went on, the more he fumed. He wanted to get on with the important part of the business: dropping the bridge. He fidgeted. He fumed. Finally, he muttered, "Ah, to hell with it."

Woodhouse helpfully translated for me: "*Eis korakas.*"

Nobody would've said that for centuries, but never mind.

"I speak English," I said, also helpfully. I'd learned a long time ago, from other Englishmen who fought to help make Greece free. Woodhouse didn't have Lord Byron's Scots burr. I still miss Byron across more than a century. I have too many centuries these days, and too many people I miss. Byron was handsomer than I am—well, most people are—but, like me, mad, bad, and dangerous to know, as a lady friend of his famously said.

Moonlight—Selene was a couple of days past full—showed his eyes widen. "Why didn't you say so sooner, damn it?"

"I didn't need to. And besides"—I wanted to kiss him on the forehead to show him what a good boy he was; only something told me he wouldn't understand—"I love to hear you speak Greek."

He spluttered, even though it was true. Myers, meanwhile,

waved toward the bridge. "We haven't got time to waste," he said. "We'll blow it now, even if the guards aren't finished yet. With any luck at all, they'll be too occupied with our friends to pay attention to what we're up to."

With any luck at all . . . I'd heard that mournful phrase too often. Hell's bells, I'd said it too often myself.

But Myers gave the orders because the British had the demolition expertise. We scurried forward. Everything at the north end of the bridge stayed as quiet as the tomb. The English sappers got to work placing their charges at the base of the first support column, which rose from the riverbank.

They worked with unhurried haste, like men who knew what they were doing and had done it more times than they could count. Then they hustled back, trailing a wire behind them. Woodhouse hooked up the detonator, handing it to me. "Care to do the honors? It's your country, after all."

It was only a bridge. I couldn't blow up all the occupiers in my country all at once, the way I wanted to. I'd had that it's-not-enough feeling before, when the Turks were making Greece do what they wanted, not what it wanted. We took a devil of a long time to get rid of them. With any luck at all—you see? I even said it myself—the Italians and Germans would leave faster. Blowing the bridge would help.

I pushed down the plunger.

There was a sharp, short *boom*, bigger than a grenade going off, but not a lot bigger. The sappers knew their business—they used just enough, not too much. Suddenly, the support didn't. Down it came, and the bridge sagged like an old man with too much ouzo in him.

I didn't think the blast made the garrison at the south end notice us. But when they turned their machine gun around again, they sure did notice the bridge had gone off-kilter. They didn't need to be geniuses to work out how that happened. When they weren't too busy doing other things, like trying to stay alive, they started shooting at where they thought we were. We did our best not to be there. I've been shot before. I don't recommend it.

Then Lieutenant Colonel Myers said the words I didn't want to hear: "This isn't good enough, boys. The way it is, even the bloody Italians could fix it lickety-split. We've got to take out the next column too."

Major Woodhouse sighed. "No rest for the wicked."

"That's 'weary,'" Myers snapped.

"You say it your way; I'll say it mine," Woodhouse answered. "Sir."

The next column rose from the river. The moonlight illuminated foam swirling around its base—the Gorgopotamos does live up to its name. After the sappers got done grousing, they readied fresh charges and splashed into the water to set them.

Which turned out to be more complicated than we'd looked for, and not just because the garrison kept shooting at us when they found the chance. Giving the Italians some backbone turned out not to be the only reason the Germans were playing Horatius here.

Something reared up out of the Gorgopotamos as soon as the first Englishman got his boots wet. Apparently, the Germans had brought a river troll from the north to help them hold the bridge. It was taller than a man and wider than a man, with shaggy hair on the outside and muscles underneath. The moon showed me what I would have guessed anyway: It was uglier than anything that had never been accused of being a kallikantzaros. It roared like—like what? Like a furious troll, that's what. And it charged.

I gave Major Woodhouse credit. He had reflexes a viper would have been proud of. The troll couldn't have taken more than a stride or two before he put most of a magazine from his machine pistol into it.

Other Englishmen shot at the troll, too, with rifles or pistols.

It didn't care for that, not even a little bit. It roared again, louder than the first time, and staggered as if Woodhouse had kicked it in the belly. You shoot an ordinary human being twenty or thirty times, what have you got? Chopped meat, that's what. The troll was not an ordinary human being. Well, I already knew as much. If Woodhouse didn't, he figured it out in a hurry, because the troll straightened up and kept on coming.

"I say!" he said. Some of what followed was in English, some in ancient Greek. I learned some more from the former and goggled at the latter. Socrates would have admired it, and he was not a man who admired much. I also goggled at how fast Major Woodhouse could slap in a fresh magazine. Swearing a blue streak didn't slow him down a bit. Then he squeezed the trigger. The range was shorter now. I think every round hit home.

The bullets hurt the troll. It staggered again and roared some more. It didn't fall over though. It was supposed to. Or I thought so anyway. Somehow nobody'd given the troll the news.

Which meant whatever sense smells trouble for me had known all along what it was smelling. If the bridge was going to get properly wrecked, I needed to be here to help the ordinary human beings. The Englishmen were all yelling and shouting. I gave a yell myself: "Hey, stupid!"

The troll didn't pay any attention to the excited sappers. Me, it noticed. When it did, I wondered if I wanted it to. There was always the chance I'd get wrecked instead of the bridge. I should have worried about that before I opened my big mouth, which wasn't nearly so big, nor so toothy, as the troll's.

You always think of these things too late.

No help for it, not anymore. Wondering just what kind of fool I was making of myself, I ran toward the brute, not away from it. It swung a haymaker at me, like the boxer Max Schmeling. Even thinking about a damned German was plenty to angry me up.

The troll missed. I stepped closer and gave it a good one to the side of the head. I may have broken a knuckle; it had the thickest skull I'd ever punched. It didn't like getting smacked at all—even less than it liked getting shot. Don't ask me why. Because I packed a hell of a punch (which I do)? Because I wasn't exactly an ordinary human being myself? Never mind. *Why* didn't matter. *What* did.

A different kind of noise came from the troll. Distress? Surprise? I didn't know for sure; I wasn't taking notes. I didn't have time. But different. I hit it again—this time in the belly, thinking that would be softer than its head. And it was, but not enough to keep my fist from hurting when I punched it.

I drew back my hand in a hurry; I didn't want the creature grabbing me. A funny thing . . . it had taken most of two magazines from Woodhouse's Sten, plus odd bullets from several other sappers. It should have been bloody all over. It should have been, but it wasn't. My fist was clean in the moonlight.

Did the bullets ricochet? Did they just fall down? They couldn't all have missed. The troll wouldn't have roared when the Englishman fired at it if they had. I had questions, no answers.

Even thinking about them didn't pay. While I wasted split seconds doing it, the troll swung at me again. And it connected. I don't know if it broke ribs; bruise them enough and you'll feel as bad as if they're broken, even if not for so long. I said several unkind things, all of them on the exhale. I didn't have Major Woodhouse's splendid vocabulary, but I was very sincere.

And now I was very angry. I had this big Germanic thing in

front of me, and I could hit it. I smacked it in the face with my left hand, the one I hadn't hurt yet, and something crunched and crumpled under my fist. I wasn't imagining that—the troll wailed, if a *sub-sub-bass* noise counts for a wail.

I hit it again and again and again. It hit me a couple of times too, but I hardly noticed. I seemed to get stronger every time I struck it, the way Antaeus did when he wrestled while touching the ground. Well, river mud anyway. I was touching *my* ground, *Greek* ground. I belonged there. The troll didn't. And we both understood that.

I heaved the troll up over my head.

Behind me, Major Woodhouse and a couple of other sappers gasped. That wasn't the kind of thing an ordinary human being was likely to be able to do.

I slammed the troll down into the river as hard as I could. And I waited, ready to fight some more if it came up again.

But it didn't.

Woodhouse's eyes were as big as gumdrops. "In sweet Jesus's name, how did you do that?"

"I've got no idea," I said, which was true enough. I didn't much want to talk at all, if you care to know something else that was true. I felt weak and sick, the way anybody's liable to after the fighting's over.

A bullet cracked past a meter or two above my head, which reminded me the fighting wasn't over here yet. I pointed toward the second support column with my chin. "Blow that damned thing, will you, so we can run away?"

"Right," Woodhouse said tightly and sketched a salute, as if I were his superior. He looked surprised at himself even as his right hand dropped to his side.

I was more than surprised; I was bloody gobsmacked, to borrow his phrase. British soldiers didn't go around casually saluting andartes. I knew that only too well, and so, plainly, did Woodhouse. To Englishmen, Greeks counted for wogs: useful and handy tools for the Defense Ministry, but not worth respect.

Of course, Woodhouse understood how things worked. But just for a moment, he'd forgotten, and his right hand lost its cunning and betrayed him into treating me more like a man than a wog. He did what any officer would: He tried to pretend it never happened. Turning to his men, he bawled orders.

They splashed through the shallow water and started to set their charges. Then they discovered they had another problem: The base of that column wasn't shaped the same as the first one had been. They had to mess about with their explosives before they got them the way they wanted. Meanwhile, of course, the Italians and Germans at the far end of the bridge kept firing at us when the andartes weren't keeping them too busy.

After what seemed a very long time and was probably five or ten real minutes, Woodhouse held out the detonator to me again. "One more time?"

"You've got the *gamemeno* thing. You do it," I said.

So he did. One more *boom* among so many, and down came the Gorgopotamos bridge, cradle and all. "That's more like it!" Lieutenant Colonel Myers exclaimed. In a way, I agreed with him. Mussolini's military engineers, or maybe Hitler's, would be a long time restoring the bridge. In another way—

A stone kicked up by a falling span had missed my head by much less than that bullet I mentioned a moment ago. Some ways to go seem stupider than others. That one stood pretty high on the list.

Major Woodhouse caught my eye. A grin flickered across his face. "Daddle," he offered.

I grinned too. Yes, he knew his Aristophanes, even the bits that weren't filthy. "Let's ske," I replied.

"Daddle," he said again.

"Together!" I urged, and we both said them that way: "Let's skedaddle!"

Skedaddle we did, all of us. The andartes were already making tracks. When we caught up with some of them, we found out they'd taken only four wounded, none hurt badly. Quite a few carried rifles or machine pistols better than the ones they'd used before.

We hadn't gone more than a kilometer—a kilometer and a half at most—when a fresh racket of gunfire came from the railway line behind us.

"What the devil?" I said.

"Somebody from the village came out and told us he'd heard a trainload of Italian soldiers was on the way to the bridge," one of the andartes said. "Aris sent out an ambush party to slow the bastards down. I guess they're doing it." The way he spoke of Velouchiotis told me he was an ELAS man.

By the time the sun came up, we'd got back to the hills. We were all proud of what we'd done—the Englishmen, Zervas's fighters, and Aris's too. It wouldn't win the war, but it gave the occupiers a good kick where a kick would hurt the most. It would bring more men to the andartes. No one step does everything you want. But you have to take each and every one, or you lose. Not even I knew what would go into the next one.

I expected I'd find out.

AUTHOR'S NOTE

Use of the cranky, charismatic kallikantzaros Konstantin Karaghiosis (Conrad), from *This Immortal*, was with permission of the estate of Roger Zelazny.

GRIGORIY'S ARMY

CATHERINE STINE

STALINGRAD OBLAST, SOVIET UNION

"You come in here often but have never told me your name," remarked the ruddy-cheeked waitress as she served Grigoriy his vodka and minced-fish patty with boiled potato in the crowded canteen. "I'm Oksana. Who are you?"

"*Gri-gor-iy,*" he said haltingly, averting his eyes from her gaze. She shone so brightly with her piercing blue eyes and red hair like maple leaves in fall that it stunned him. Her curvy body—barely contained by her faded, flowered apron—made him shake. Her sturdy arms, which hauled firewood and heavy trays brimming with meats, goulash, and bowls of hot borscht, made him worshipful. Women lived in a higher realm—one he had not yet found the courage to explore, though he was twenty-nine.

When he stole a glance at her, his neck heated up. She was taking in not only his face but the expanse from his broad shoulders to his trunk-like legs in their muddy work boots. "You're the owner of that forest that old Eduard tried to farm. Bless his soul. I heard he passed a few years ago." She waited for Grigoriy to say something, but he only gave a faint nod. "I've heard someone cleared out many kilometers of brush. That it's now full of sugar beets and winter wheat. Did you clear it by yourself?"

Grigoriy gave a slightly firmer nod.

"Cat got your tongue?" she asked with a raspy chuckle and gave his hand a tap.

"I have no cat to feed or take my tongue," he replied with a poker face.

To which the woman broke out in guffaws. "A strange bird, aren't you?" Others within earshot laughed as well—three men in overalls to one side eating goulash and a toothless old woman with a white-bearded man slurping borscht at the other neighboring table.

"I am strange, but not a bird," Grigoriy mumbled, knowing that couldn't be what she meant. *Could it?* Ever since the accident more than eighteen years ago, his brain was broken. Well, not broken as much as divided, like opposite riverbanks on the Volga. He knew things that no one else did when it came to cells, to blood, to tiny things swimming and squirming under microscopes, to how gradually and methodically he created beasts with genetic enhancements.

Yet Grigoriy failed to grasp the simplest of things. Things that other people knew even in childhood. Words strung together fast, human connections, affiliations, how to start conversations, and how to explain more complicated aspects of life than which items he needed from the communal stores. When people talked over each other in a debate, he only heard noise, like steam shrilling from a factory smokestack. He could tell by people's wide eyes, followed by their surprised laughter, that he was a misfit.

Grigoriy stumbled to his feet, his meal barely touched. He lumbered out of the canteen and felt eyes on his back, including Oksana's keen stare that burned like fire.

As he hastened down the dirt road lined with pine, larch,

and maples, his face cooled, his heart slowed. He thought he was more like the creatures he was building than a bird. All he wanted was to get back to his beasts—part bear, part human—enhanced by his own DNA.

Before Grigoriy's accident, when he was a boy of ten, his father, a biologist for the Russian Empire and the Soviet state that followed, took him to the lab as often as he could. Grigoriy was fascinated by the petri dishes; the slime molds; the chromosomes that divided and multiplied, that formed patterns of infinite beauty. His father relayed numbers and equations and formulas. Back then, Grigoriy had a supple brain for these things. Sucking information in and running it through his mind like a gigantic calculator.

When his father took seriously ill in 1923, he told little Grigoriy about his frustrated dreams. He admitted that he'd experimented with how to enhance humans for longer lives, for greater muscle strength. He'd made progress, but there was no time left. That since Grigoriy's mother had passed at his birth, Grigoriy would have to go to his uncle Eduard's southeast of Stalingrad when he died. Grigoriy had wept in the backyard with tall apple trees. Gazing up at a particular fruit, the sun's rays forming a golden crown over it, Grigoriy had a desperate, dreamlike hope. He hauled over a ladder leaning against the house. Climbing up, he reached way too far for that golden apple, whose mineral juices might magically save his father from the grave.

Instead, Grigoriy's feet slid off the rung, and he smacked down to his own near-death. Blood poured from his head, under his shirt, and blackness closed in.

When they wheeled him from neurosurgery and tucked him under crisp sheets with a tangle of wires and blinking machines on all sides, a pale doctor told him softly that his father had died. Grigoriy wept bitterly. His head throbbed. He had not saved his father. For weeks after, Grigoriy's tearful lids swelled until his eyes were mere slits. And his brain was quite broken.

"You are lucky to be alive," Eduard said, when he fetched the parentless boy and ferried him to his forest cabin outside Stalingrad.

For many months, Grigoriy was paralyzed by grief and mired in confusion. The grief lifted after a year, but his brain . . . well, it *changed*.

Grigoriy now *knew* things but couldn't begin to use his words or written math equations to explain them. Not even to his old uncle Eduard, the man growing ever feebler with a wasting disease. They would sit by the fire, Eduard covered by a thick Soviet blanket, Grigoriy drinking milk fresh from his uncle's cow.

"Your numbers," Eduard would start. "What is five multiplied by twenty?"

Grigoriy knew but could most easily show it by raising his hands ten times with all ten fingers outstretched.

"How will you help clear the forest to farm if we can't discuss it?" Eduard lamented.

"I . . . *can* . . . talk," Grigoriy insisted slowly. But he worried. For if he was too clumsy to stand on a ladder without falling, he doubted he could fell even one tree.

Then, at nineteen, Grigoriy was finally over his grief enough to pore through the boxes of his father's research he'd taken years ago. Grigoriy sipped vodka by the fire and marveled at the reams, while old Eduard rasped on the couch.

In images like sped-up film reels, Grigoriy saw how he could move well beyond this data. Create super-engineered beasts that ripped trees from their roots, smashed them on boulders into usable sections with their brute strength, and hauled them to the sides of the new fields. "I see it!" exclaimed Grigoriy as Eduard breathed his last.

Grigoriy buried his uncle on the land and carved his name in a rock.

He began to collect jars and bowls for petri dishes. Eduard had hoarded many metal and glass oddments in his cabinets—tubes, valves, and hollow rods. In dazzling visual flashes, Grigoriy saw how to craft them into laboratory tools. He boiled and wrapped them in sterilized towels. When he went to the doctor in town to get an infected molar pulled, Grigoriy pocketed hypodermic needles, sedatives, and antibiotics when the dentist was called into another room.

Neighbors would ask nosy questions. "When did Eduard pass? Is this your land now? What is your assigned kolkhoz plan? Has the collective discussed it with you?" Or less nosy questions, like, "Can I trade you two goats for a cow? Some kale seeds?"

Remembering how a colleague of his father's got imprisoned for activities forbidden by the state, Grigoriy toiled for months to dig a secret cellar lab. Once completed, he moved down equipment and strung up lights. He covered its entry with a square of flat pine planks and threw a rug over it.

At night, in his cavern, he sat as stunning, instructive images filled his head. He suddenly understood a multitude of things he was sure hadn't yet been discovered. How DNA spiraled in a helix twist, how its codes were heritable. How one could snip the twisted chain and deliver a new section into the body like an arrow to a bull's-eye target. Then have this new section magically connect the two cut pieces. Designing new creatures from the old.

He began to extract his own DNA, his chromosomes, the best of what made him human. He sedated bears that shambled close to feast on berries and nuts. While they slept, he injected engineered

DNA that migrated into their helix chains. He bred bears in large cages, sparing them no luxury—Eduard's thick blankets, the best greens, fish from the fertile stream, more nuts and berries, this time with pots of honey bought with money saved from his father.

The first time he led an engineered bear from its cage and into the field, his heart felt as if it were beating out of his chest. What if the beast lunged at him? What if the commands he had drilled into the bear-workers didn't stick? Nothing held it here. It could easily run. Or maul him.

"My good bear." Grigoriy craned his neck up to see the gigantic thing, standing on its hind legs. He was so close he could've touched its thick fur. One swipe of its saber claws and Grigoriy would be slashed into raw strips. It stared down at him with eerie, glowing eyes. Grigoriy tapped at the bark of a pine tree. "Rip this tree out and carry it over there," he said in a tremulous voice, pointing to the field's edge.

The gigantic brown bear hesitated. It stared down at Grigoriy, snuffling. It studied the tree. Grigoriy held his breath as the bear lumbered over to the old pine and wrapped its monstrous forearms around the trunk. It only took three yanks for the tree to be ripped from the ground, its wide root mound shedding dirt and pebbles.

Grigoriy gasped as the bear rambled over to exactly where Grigoriy had pointed and dropped the tree with a huge thud.

Rushes of shock and excitement shuddered through Grigoriy.

The bear stood uncertainly, wagging from side to side. Finally, Grigoriy remembered to give the next command. "Good work, bear! Go back to your cage den. You get a treat!"

The bear ran back on all fours, its maw slavering. It hopped into its pen.

"Good work, bear!" Grigoriy wept with pure joy as he tossed it a generous portion of dried pike. Now the other bears were howling for treats. "You are all my good bears!" he exclaimed, so ecstatic that every bear got a hunk of dried pike that morning.

Over successive breeding, he crafted the bears for more perfect field work. They became more compliant. They understood more commands: fetch, gather, plow, sleep. He also learned how to speak to them silently—after all, their minds had parts of his in them.

Now a crew of thirty, they cleared fields and carried gargantuan trees like tent poles in their mammoth arms. Their standing height stretched to the second floor of his barn. Their skulls were as big as an elephant's. Their stamina in snow and rocky terrain was like an alpha corsac fox gliding over the steppes.

The fields cleared, Grigoriy and his beast-bears planted and harvested bounteous crops of beets, winter wheat, barley, and kale.

More people at the collective asked questions. "I saw gigantic bears in your field. One looked to be carrying a tree. Did my eyes deceive me? Have they attacked you?"

Grigoriy would simply nod like the simpleton they assumed he was. He was not stupid. Far from it. But he was slow to speak, to react, also rendering him unfit for service in the Red Army. Grigoriy hated the idea of war. He rarely read the papers, though he knew enough that they were conscripting soldiers to fight the Nazi invaders.

STALINGRAD OBLAST, SOVIET UNION, SEPTEMBER 1942

Then, one day, when Grigoriy shopped for boots at the collective store, a husky NKVD captain with coal-black hair and heavy brows cornered him. He demanded they go outside behind a dense hedge.

Grigoriy saw the pistol in the man's holster, and his stomach dropped. He sensed the axis of his world tilt.

"We know what you've been doing, Comrade." The man studied Grigoriy with glinting black eyes. "The *Stavka* has a proposition." Of course, a proposition from the *high command of the Soviet Armed Forces* was in reality an order.

Grigoriy's throat tightened. "What is that?"

The man held out a photo of a soldier wearing an angular eagle and forked-cross insignia. "Do you recognize the uniform?"

"Huh!" blurted Grigoriy. *The strange insignia.* Two Wehrmacht soldiers in the same tall boots and odd, curved helmets had trespassed onto his fields last month.

They had cursed in German, "*Was zur Hölle*?" and "*Lass mich los*!" ("What the hell?" and "Get your hands off!"), as his beasts scooped them up.

With uncanny speed, the beasts pinned them to the ground, their rifles tumbling aside. The beasts delivered the kicking soldiers to Grigoriy's door in their gigantic woolly arms. Denuded of weaponry, and taken with no warning, the soldiers' evident terror and hunger exceeded their outrage. "*Geben Sie uns etwas zu essen*," ("Give us food,") one had begged. He'd given them food and told them to leave, but not before taking their weapons, ammo belts, and field jackets.

"Yes, I have seen Nazi soldiers," he admitted. "No one should raid another's land. But I am no soldier."

The captain raised his pistol and pressed the barrel to Grigoriy's forehead. "You may not be a soldier, but if you do not help the Red Army liberate Stalingrad, you will be executed, Comrade."

"What m-must . . . I do?" Grigoriy stuttered.

"Change your worker bears into lethal warriors to decimate the enemy."

"But how?" Grigoriy continued to play dumb.

"We are not blind. We know who your father was. We know what bioengineered creatures you've developed in your cellar. We are sure your strange talents can greatly help the war effort. I will accompany you back to your farm and monitor your progress. The *Stavka* is watching. You have three months."

STALINGRAD OBLAST, SOVIET UNION, JANUARY 1943

Snow gusts and bone-breaking cold blew in, piercing through thick, padded military gear. Just before they left, the NKVD captain and two additional comrades had explained to Grigoriy that the Soviets had surrounded the German Sixth Army at Stalingrad.

"It is time for you to prove your worth," said the captain to Grigoriy. "You must order your monster bear troops to punch through the German line inside our comrades' encirclement."

"Yes, I see," Grigoriy said uncertainly.

The captain frowned, his black brows curved over piercing eyes. "With a break in the enemy line, our brave infantry will not only destroy the Nazis but hopefully prompt the surrender of the trapped and starving German, Romanian, Italian, and Croatian troops. Do you understand?"

Grigoriy nodded, straining to take in the complexity of the battle plan. "Where will I be during the battle?"

"You will be there. Our NKVD men will protect you."

Grigoriy was struck with terror, though he didn't dare show it. He couldn't quite fathom how he would be close enough to his bears to shout orders. He had trained his bears to recognize the distinct shape of Wehrmacht helmets and the spread-winged eagle symbol on the right breast of their uniforms. Still, he did have the unspoken connection. He could speak silently to them. They read each other's emotions, thoughts.

Grigoriy led his now forty-strong warrior-beasts, further enhanced with steel-tipped claws and steel armor. Three NKVD escorts, there both to protect Grigoriy and ensure he followed the battle plan, trudged with them through the moonless, snowy night toward the city outskirts.

A couple of dazed Soviet wanderers, whose homes had been reduced to rubble, stared wide-eyed at them from afar and then ran for cover.

The ruined buildings and abandoned vehicles they trudged past looked absolutely haunted. Grigoriy imagined them as mausoleums full of tortured snow ghosts.

His handlers and the assault battalion of genetically engineered woolly warriors forged on. They slipped past forewarned Soviet checkpoints. It helped that the bears' body armor was painted white to match the Soviets' winter gear—clever chameleon invisibility in this frigid landscape.

In the inky darkness shot through with snow, the NKVD captain told Grigoriy to order individual scout bears to neutralize German lookouts. Grigoriy gave the silent order. He added, "Seek out the helmets in dirt trenches!" At once, a posse of ten raced out, each finding its hidden victim. With savage slashes of steel-tipped claws, they tore apart the German lookouts, more concerned with not freezing to death in their foxholes without a fire than keeping watch.

Behind the line of Grigoriy's bruin assault battalion crept 120 grim and battle-hardened men of the Fifth Guards Rifle Regiment, thick white jackets protecting them from the minus-thirty-degree cold. In their gloved hands, they carried submachine guns. All were under strict orders not to fire until the engineered monster bears began their attack. The captain had explained to Grigoriy that the elite Ninth and Thirteenth Guards Rifle Regiments would trail the Fifth. And that behind those units waited entire infantry and artillery divisions. That the latter would remain silent until the assault began. The element of surprise was paramount. So the battalion clambered slowly and quietly through Stalingrad's rubble, around shattered vehicles, and over body parts of soldiers, frozen in the drifts.

To prevent the bears from individually attacking, rather than in a coordinated effort, Grigoriy gave them a whispered but stern order: "Only attack on my command."

He conveyed other silent words of encouragement. *Good bears, my bears. Your loyalty and patience will be rewarded.* He sensed the bears' coiled tension, their eyes, enhanced with mined owl DNA, glowed against the cold blackness. With infrared night vision, they were capable of seeing Nazi helmets from hundreds of feet away.

Grigoriy felt the beasts' low-frequency growls in his chest the moment their eyes locked onto the German defensive line. Even through the dense snowfall, the dark of night, and smoke from a smoldering building, the beasts found their prey.

"Attack," Grigoriy whispered to his bears. He and his NKVD minders were crouched behind a burned-out truck. *Go! Charge!* He added silently, directly to make sure this essential command was obeyed.

His beasts galloped with preternatural speed, almost *flying* toward their prey. Their nine-hundred-kilogram weight—a literal ton—irrelevant. He'd enhanced them with hawk and fox DNA, injecting it over and over. Still, he was astounded at their speed, for there had been precious little time to train and equip them. *Attack! Go!* Grigoriy urged, his heart racing, his nerves jangled.

Like avenging angels, the bear-beasts charged the German

positions. Oddly nimble, they zigzagged in their approach, hurdling over crushed vehicles, bent fences, and half-toppled walls, even smashing right through them. The Nazi forces gaped in momentary shock at the huge, armored monsters and their thunderous, feral roars.

The stunned Germans began to open fire. Grigoriy heard the rifle *plinks* from soldiers behind barricades or within abandoned buildings, the menacing growl of heavy machine guns spewing ten rounds per second from sandbag nests. It seemed to Grigoriy that much of their firepower missed its mark. No doubt their quivering horror of his bear-warriors badly impaired their aim. And even when the monstrous wave of bears grew so close it was impossible to miss, their thick steel armor deflected most of the Germans' bullets.

The beasts grabbed Nazi soldiers, tearing their bodies in two as one would twist the top off a jar. They threw the severed heads and shoulders in one direction, the lower bodies and legs in another, spraying blood everywhere. With extraordinary strength, they grabbed machine guns and small-caliber artillery barrels, bending them savagely and rendering them useless. They scooped up Nazi soldiers, squeezing them in gargantuan forearms until they became bloody pulp. Other unlucky soldiers were slashed to pieces, the beasts' already-powerful claws redesigned to be as lethal as butcher knives and almost as long as a man's forearm when extended.

The Germans cowered and tripped over themselves to get away from the roaring, steel-clad monsters. In their panic, some fled into the leveled weapons of the nearby Red Army soldiers, another sure death. Other Nazis kept firing from the few positions not yet destroyed. The bear-beasts dodged as nimbly as Bolshoi dancers yet charged into ruined buildings like crazed bulls, their armor protecting them from all but larger-caliber headshots or strikes to their rear feet. Their power and speed made them a bestial tornado. They raced around walls, tore up half-destroyed stairways, and leaped ferociously on their victims before the enemy had a chance to reload.

Even in the midst of frenzied battle, the warrior-beasts sensed the Nazi soldiers' exhaustion, their hunger, their desperate pain. Their violent shivers from prolonged exposure to the frigid minus-thirty-eight-Celsius temperature and their swollen, blackened feet inside their ruined boots. For creatures knew more than humans assumed. They understood nature versus the blight of civilization in a way that required no intellectual thought. So much of nature communicated via a realm inaccessible to humanity. Like the trees that communicated through roots and fungal systems, or the birds that knew to fly south in formation when winter approached. It was clear that the Nazis were mostly blind and frozen in this dark, mixed with teeming snowfall. But the beasts' redesign drove them to kill even those near death—these spectacular killing machines.

In a bloodstained snowy dawn, the urban battlefield was eerily silent, brimming with broken bodies in rigor mortis, and only two bear-warriors dead—one blown apart by fire from an anti-tank cannon, the other from a barrage of machine-gun bullets.

Grigoriy gave the order to the rest of his woolly troop. "Stop! Return to camp."

The bear-warriors ignored him. They kept obsessively sniffing through the human debris field, searching for breathing soldiers with the eagle and barbed-cross insignia.

Suddenly scared, Grigoriy gave a silent, fierce command this time. *I said stop. Stop now! Bad bears! Stop or no food.* The beasts pawed at the rubble for another twenty minutes. They had gotten a taste for blood, which their genetic reprogramming was amplifying in some unnerving way. Grigoriy had a sinking, dreadful surety that if anything happened to him, the warrior monsters would not stop killing. Like a greyhound trained for the race that often kept running when let free.

Word came soon after this that Field Marshal Paulus had signaled the surrender of the German Sixth Army.

The *Stavka* thanked Grigoriy for his help. They even gave him a medal. Yet they insisted on keeping the warrior-bears despite Grigoriy's stark warning that these beasts would likely kill Red Army soldiers, civilians, women, children, anyone they could grab.

"Killing machines will never stop killing," he stressed. "Their instincts to kill have unnaturally amplified—some snag in my gene editing. They aren't like tanks that you can turn off."

The NKVD men were not convinced. Until one day, as they were leaving Stalingrad and trooping southeast, one of the beasts viciously attacked a homeless Soviet wanderer and then turned on an NKVD soldier, biting his head clear off. The rest of the bear-monsters snarled and roared until Grigoriy shouted desperately, "Stop! Stop! Stop now!" By some miracle, this time it worked. But Grigoriy could not allow another breach. There had been enough gruesome killing for a lifetime.

The battalion waited in a wooded encampment until after midnight. The surviving NKVD captain made a stunning, rare admission. "Comrade Grigoriy, we have concluded that these monsters you created are truly uncontrollable. We will inject the sleeping beasts with a powerful sedative." The captain studied Grigoriy. "But *you* . . . you must once again prove worthy." He said nothing more, but Grigoriy knew what he meant when the captain handed him a submachine gun. He gave a faint nod and took the gun.

Grigoriy gazed sadly down at the row of sleeping giants. He remembered the joy of designing them, of them successfully completing their first farming tasks, even of their incredible skill on the battlefield. His gut roiled, and he wept inconsolably as he aimed and fired at their brains, all down the row. *Pop! Pop! Pop!* Their engineered blood spilled over the snowy forest floor. Yet he was also strangely relieved. The NKVD commander told him the next morning before they parted ways that they might need his service again. He nodded, seething inside.

Grigoriy returned to his farm. He plowed and planted the fields himself—ten times the work than with the help of enhanced worker bears, but deeply satisfying. His rug remained on the trapdoor leading to his cellar lab. Instead of experimenting down there with more chromosomes and mined animal DNA, he sat by the fire with a gimpy hound that had hobbled in and stayed. He named him Eduard the Second.

The first time Grigoriy ventured to the canteen, he was utterly startled when the crowd of diners broke into thunderous cheers. "*Grigoriy, spasibo, nash geroy! Thank you, hero!*"

"Me?" he muttered.

The rosy server, Oksana, hurried over and hugged him. "Our war hero! You saved us! We heard about your bear-monsters defeating the Nazi invaders." The room erupted in a longer, louder round of jubilant cheers.

Grigoriy, who had always pined for acceptance, found himself deeply embarrassed, his face flaming hot.

"Cat got your tongue?" Oksana asked playfully and gave him a tighter hug. She stood on tiptoes and kissed him on his hot cheek. "It doesn't matter that you are strange; you are our hero and a good, good man."

He was sure war was evil. But this war had saved the people, the land. He wasn't sure he was good, but Oksana's embrace was warm and a blessing. He let himself stop worrying, relaxed in her welcoming arms, and hugged her back.

SVART HUND

SCOTT SIGLER

RJUKAN, NORWAY, FEBRUARY 1943

Einar Skinnarland knew that some words had many meanings.

For instance, the word *swallow*.

Swallow: A bird with two tail points, fast and agile enough to snatch insects from the sky.

Swallow: The name of his unit, five men who had endured in the winter forest and risked all to stop the Nazis.

Swallow: To use the muscles of the throat to move something into the stomach.

The last definition was the one now on his mind. It was what he would have to do with the whitish pill in his hand.

"If your capture is imminent, place the L-pill in your mouth and bite down." The setting sun filtering through the trees lit the vapor of Lieutenant Joachim Rønneberg's breath. He shivered despite his snowsuit. "You *must* bite to break it. Otherwise, the rubber coating will allow it to pass through your body. You will still be alive when it comes out later, when the Nazis are torturing and questioning you. Understand?"

The five men of Swallow gave a soft, unified *Ja, Løytnant.*

They'd heard these instructions before, from their own team leader, Jens-Anton Poulson. The men of Swallow had known the consequences of capture for many months, even when they'd first dropped into Hardangervidda for their initial mission—Operation Freshman—five months earlier.

Swallow had been known as *Grouse* then. The team's job had been to direct a pair of gliders to land on a frozen lake. The gliders contained commandos meant to assault the Vemork hydroelectric plant outside Rjukan. Why Vemork was the objective, Einar and the men of Grouse-Swallow did not know.

Both gliders crashed. The commandos inside either died on impact, from their L-pills, or were captured by the Nazis. Einar and his team had been ordered to remain in place, hopefully for another attempt on Vemork. For *four months*, the men of Swallow had hidden, had endured Hardangervidda's bitter, life-taking cold.

Their rations lasted one month. After that, Swallow found a way to survive. And now they sat in a circle, eating rations given to them by the Gunnerside team, listening to Rønneberg describe their likely deaths.

Rønneberg and his six men—five Norwegians and, oddly, one old Englishman—had parachuted in under the shroud of darkness, then spent five days hiking and skiing through the forest. They wore the same gear as Swallow: white snowsuits, white boots, white gloves. In this cold, to be without a snowsuit was to freeze to death. The two units were combining to execute Operation Gunnerside. Rønneberg had collected Swallow's L-pills and issued new ones, just to be sure they operated correctly.

Death by cyanide was supposedly painless. Death by Nazi torture was not.

"We go in tonight," Rønneberg said. "Cover squad is

Poulsson, Haugland, Kjelstrup, and Helberg of Swallow, along with my men Størhaug and Haukelid. Haugland is your radio operator. Poulsson will command."

The named men of Swallow looked at their counterparts, exchanged nods. They were all members of Kompani Linge, Norwegians trained by Britain's SOE—the Special Operations Executive. Most of them had trained together in Scotland, where Kompani Linge practiced mountain climbing in the dead of the night, forded frigid rivers, and survived off the land for weeks at a time.

Poulsson, Haugland, Kjelstrup, and Helberg had lost weight. Thick snowsuits and gloves hid their emaciated bodies, but gaunt faces and sunken eyes showed the price they'd paid to stay here and wait for the next mission. Einar knew he looked much the same.

"I will lead the explosives squad," Rønneberg said. "My men Kayser, Idland, and Stømsheim will accompany me." He gestured at the Englishman. "Mr. Aumont and radioman Skinnarland will stay close behind my squad."

Mister. No rank. If Aumont had rank, he'd have to be a general, because only generals served into their fifties and sixties.

Aumont's eyes were colder than the biting frost. The bit of forehead showing under his parka hood revealed his baldness. How the chubby old Englishman had survived the night drop into the mountains—and the grueling hiking and skiing that followed—Einar had no idea.

There was something off about Aumont. Something . . . frightening.

Jens-Anton sat up straighter, anger on his sallow face.

"The Nazis have two hundred men guarding Vemork," he said. "Even with our knowledge of their patterns and their defensive positions, the chances of getting in, blowing up the target, and getting out alive are slim. Before I risk my men, I want to know the objective. *Why* are we going in?"

A question one was not supposed to ask. But spending four months isolated from the world, skirting on the edge of starvation, and cheating death every day had a way of changing one's perspective. Einar wanted to know too. Everyone in Swallow did.

"All I can tell you is this mission is of the utmost importance," Rønneberg said. "If we succeed, you will be heroes. You will change the course of the war."

He smiled then, a commander's smile meant to placate his troops, to reassure them that he and the chain of command knew best.

"That's not enough," Jens-Anton said. "Not anymore. We didn't survive out here this long to throw our lives away without knowing why."

The commander's smile vanished, its falsity fading to reveal the expression of a man who did not tolerate insubordination.

"Second Lieutenant Poulsson," Rønneberg said, ice in his voice, "you will—"

"Just tell them."

All heads turned to the old Englishman.

"We don't have time to waste," Aumont said. "We are asking these men to accept great risk. Tell them."

Rønneberg's jaw muscles twitched. "They do not need to know."

His words carried no mettle, because Rønneberg feared Aumont. Einar could see that. Everyone could see that.

Who was this old man playing soldier? How could he be dangerous enough that even the legendary Joachim Rønneberg feared him?

"They need to know the stakes," Aumont said softly, calmly. "They need to understand the importance of this mission."

He reached into his backpack and drew from it a yellowed ivory box the length and width of his forearm. Trimmed in brass, dinged and lined with deeps scratches, the box looked ancient. Silver crosses decorated the sides and the lid, which had no hinges. What a strange thing to bring on a commando mission.

Aumont set the box on his lap. "Inside this box is a weapon code-named *Svart Hund*."

Svart Hund—Norwegian for *black dog*.

"If I am forced to unleash it, what these men see could make them run, make them panic," Aumont said. "They need knowledge to stay on course, no matter how terrifying things may become."

Einar bristled, as did the other members of Swallow.

"You think us cowards?" Jens-Anton spat into the snow. "We have endured cold so deep we thought we would die. We have evaded hundreds of men who hunt us every single day. Our rations ran out long ago. We have survived in these woods by eating the flesh of reindeer we killed with spears, because we can't risk the noise of shooting a weapon. We ate their flesh raw, like animals, because we can't risk a fire. We are hardened by war, sir. The men of Swallow have accepted that we will likely die here. What weapon could you produce that could make us run?"

Aumont stared at Jens-Anton, not with anger, not with disrespect, but rather with patience, with measurement.

"I can't tell you what the *Svart Hund is*," the old man said. "Knowing of its existence carries a heavy price. If all goes well, we will not need to use it at all. Knowing *why* it might be used, however, does not. Lieutenant Rønneberg, the men have asked why we are attacking a heavily fortified position. Shall you tell them, or shall I?"

Rønneberg looked away, gazed into the darkness of the surrounding woods.

"You do it," he said.

Aumont's hands moved slowly across the ivory box as he spoke, almost as if he were petting it.

"You men know the Germans are working on a weapon at Vemork," he said. "You have not been told specifically what *kind* of weapon. They are producing heavy water—deuterium oxide, a chemical critical to building an atomic bomb."

Einar hissed in a breath. Could it be true? Before he'd been trapped here in this frozen hell, he'd read about the concept of these nightmarish, possibly world-ending devices in the books of Olaf Stapledon and H. G. Wells.

"Atomic bombs are science fiction," Einar said. "No one knows how to make one."

Aumont turned his gaze on Einar, and Einar felt the same fear he'd seen on Rønneberg. Aumont's eyes were soulless and dark, a pair of portholes into something best not seen.

"The Germans have the knowledge," Aumont said. "They are not alone. Others are working on them too." He looked at the men of Swallow and Gunnerside as he spoke. "These bombs are so powerful just *one* of them can destroy an entire city. If the Germans succeed, we believe they will use their first one on English soil, likely on Birmingham. The city will be knocked flat in an instant. Estimates are that twenty-five to fifty thousand will die immediately, some in heat so intense they will disintegrate in a cloud of ash. A hundred thousand more will die in the days afterward, cooking alive from radiation absorbed in the detonation. The city will be an uninhabitable wasteland for a century. Perhaps more."

The men of Swallow traded disbelieving glances. So, too, did the men of Gunnerside—they had not been told the true nature of this mission. Until this moment, it seemed only Rønneberg and Aumont had known.

A *single bomb* could kill 150,000 people? An abomination. It would not only change the balance of power; it would *end* any semblance of that balance. End it forever.

"After, Hitler will demand England's surrender," Aumont said. "If he does not get it, he will use the next bomb on London. One way or the other, England *will* concede, of that you can be sure. Hitler will then demand the same of the Soviets. If they do not comply, he will use a bomb first on Leningrad, then, if need be, on Moscow."

Einar saw, or thought he saw, the lid of the box open slightly, but Aumont pressed down hard, the briefest twitch of his hand, and the line vanished.

"When the Soviets bend the knee, the war in Europe will be over," Aumont said. "Hitler will turn his attention to the United States. Norway will have no allies left. Your country—and the entire world—will be ruled by Germany. Perhaps forever."

The Nazi occupation of Einar's nation might never end. Could Hitler's Third Reich last the promised thousand years? Who could say. But without opposition, Norway would be subjugated for decades, if not centuries.

Einar's squad mates looked ashen. Perhaps from the potential consequences of this weapon, perhaps from a true understanding of the importance of their coming actions, of the responsibility they had for . . . well, for saving the world.

"*Løytnant* Rønneberg," Jens-Anton said, "is Aumont telling the truth?"

There was a hint of hope in Jens-Anton's voice, hope that the lieutenant would dismiss Aumont's claims as exaggeration, as hyperbole.

"He is," Rønneberg said. "It's true. All of it. The outcome of the war rests on our shoulders."

Jens-Anton pointed at the box. "Our shoulders, and what's

in there? This is madness." He stared into nothingness for a moment. "But if the stakes are truly that high, then I will go." He looked to the men he'd commanded for months, the men he'd led through the brutal winter, through isolation, through starvation. "Who will go with me?"

A question that did not matter, as Rønneberg was ordering them to go, yet every man—Einar included—raised a gloved hand.

The men of Swallow had waited long enough. The time had come to strike.

In the light of a half-moon screened by sparse clouds, Vemork looked like a dark fortress from some ancient fable. The mountain sloped up sharply from behind the massive concrete structure that straddled a man-made offshoot of the Måna River, the coursing water of which drove the facility's turbines.

Only a few lights illuminated small areas of the sprawling building, each bulb topped by a wide circle of metal to hide its glow from above. The Luftwaffe owned the skies here, yet the Germans feared Allied bombers all the same.

The moon's meager glow was a stroke of luck—just enough of it to avoid the pitch-black that could lead to stepping on branches beneath the snow or into a hole that could break an ankle, but not enough for the men of Gunnerside to be seen from a distance by the guards behind the fence, huddling against the cold, or by the snipers on the facility's high points, fighting off sleep and boredom.

Einar and Aumont crouched behind a fallen tree. Rønneberg, Stømsheim, Kayser, and Idland were moving toward the fence.

The relentless chill stung Einar's face. He was exhausted, the endurance left in his emaciated body already taxed, already drained. There were only three ways to reach the facility: come down the mountainside, upon which the Nazis had placed thousands of land mines now covered by snow; a suicidal run across a heavily guarded, single-lane suspension bridge; or descend to the bottom of a gorge, cross the half-frozen river there, and then scale a five-hundred-foot-high cliff. The last was the only real option, an option the men of Company Linge had trained for.

Aumont seemed fine, as if he hadn't climbed at all. Granted, he had not been burdened with a twenty-kilo radio pack, as Einar had, but the man was in his sixties—how had he easily managed an ascent that drained a highly trained soldier a third his age?

Einar leaned closer to the Englishman.

"Your climbing skills are exceptional. Did you train with the SOE?"

Aumont stared into the woods, his eyes barely above the fallen log.

"I did not," he said. "For someone who tried their hand at K2 and Kanchenjunga, the cliff we ascended offers little challenge."

Einar had never heard of Kanchenjunga, but *K2*? The Kashmir peak was mountaineering's ultimate challenge.

Einar's eyes twitched to Aumont's pack. He'd said the ivory box inside it held a weapon, but that box was small, barely big enough to hold a narrow pistol. Explosives of some kind perhaps?

Aumont had shared the secret of Nazi atomic bombs—maybe he would share this secret as well.

"*Svart Hund*," Einar said. "What is it?"

Aumont finally looked at Einar, and Einar wished he'd kept his mouth shut. The old man frightened him more than a bullet.

"A bit of ancient England," Aumont said. "All I will tell you is this—the lesser evil can be seen in comparison with the greater evil as a good. And there is no greater evil than Hitler, my boy."

"Aristotle," Einar said.

The Englishman smiled. "You're a well-read lad."

Einar knew his radio would go unused until well after the attack. *If* Operation Gunnerside succeeded, and *if* they got clear of Vemork and its hordes of Nazis, and *if* they could escape back down the cliff and get clear, then and only then would Einar use it as part of an effort to travel some 320 kilometers to reach Sweden.

Three hundred and twenty kilometers, *on skis*. Escaping after the mission might prove deadlier than the mission itself.

Einar watched Rønneberg's team cut through the fence. Aumont and Einar were ordered to stay where they were and provide support, if needed. What kind of support, Einar didn't know—support with whatever was inside Aumont's ancient box. The cover team was close by, already hidden among the snow-covered trees and rocks.

Rønneberg's quartet had planned to use a side door to gain access. Einar watched them, saw that they found the door locked. The men were not so easily deterred though—they continued on, silent shadows searching for a way in. They found it in a hatch to an access tunnel.

"Here," Aumont said, handing Einar a Bakelite tin. "Spread the contents in a circle wide enough for everyone to stand inside of. Leave a gap that men can walk through. *Make sure* your line is solid, my boy, but also thin enough that you have enough remaining in the tin to complete the circle if and when I tell you."

Einar lifted the lid. In the moon's dim light, he saw a dark, granular material inside.

"Is this gunpowder?"

"Black salt," Aumont said. "Clear the snow away first. Do it quickly, son. Quickly."

Black salt?

Aumont pulled the ivory box from his pack and set it atop the snow.

It struck Einar that, despite being deep in Nazi-controlled territory and carrying an L-pill in his pocket, the thing that scared him most was something he'd not yet seen.

What is inside that box?

In the silence of the night, Einar visually measured the area needed to contain all the men. He walked in a circle, kicking away snow as he did to reveal the frozen ground beneath. When he came around the second time, he started his salt circle.

Aumont quietly muttered something . . . not English, not Norwegian . . . not any language Einar had ever heard. The old man pressed both hands against the box's lid, which vibrated spasmodically, as if something *inside* was trying to force its way out.

"My Lord Jesus," Einar whispered. "What evil is this?"

Aumont laughed, a quiet thing, almost a wheeze.

"One would go mad if one took the Bible seriously," he said. "But to take it seriously, one must already be mad. What I will bring forth, if need be, is older than your Jesus. *Far* older."

The box lid rattled harder. Aumont leaned his weight on it, his locked arms pressing down.

Einar heard something inside, faint, oh so faint. A tiny, thin growl, full of malevolence and hatred.

And then another noise—distant, deep, a *whump* like a giant coughing into his hands. The explosives team had found their mark.

"The telltale sound of success," Aumont said. "Lieutenant Rønneberg has destroyed the heavy water production cells."

Einar looked to the access tunnel just as Rønneberg and Kayser silently slid out of it. Einar took a moment to wonder if Idland and Birger had been killed or caught, then saw them running from another direction—the team had split apart. All four men sprinted for the inner fence.

A gunshot rang out.

From somewhere in the concrete darkness, a man shouted: "*Kommandos! Achtung, wir werden angegriffen!*"

At the facility's high points, two spotlights flared to life, their steadily intensifying beams sweeping across the fence line.

"Ah, a shame." Aumont's arms trembled—he was having trouble keeping the lid closed. "I'd hoped they might slip away unseen. Signal the cover squad, my boy. Bring them here, and if you value their souls, be quick about it."

If you value their souls?

Aumont again muttered in that incomprehensible language—that *inhuman* language.

Einar mimicked the call of the snowy owl. He could do a half dozen calls of birds common to the Hardangervidda. Variations on each call communicated critical information. The snowy owl's call was perhaps the most intense, for it meant: *Urgent! Come to me now!*

An alarm sounded in the facility, one that bounced off hard walls and echoed off the mountainside. The shouts of men joined it. The spotlights swept across the fence—a beam caught Strømsheim just as he slipped through.

That spotlight remained fixed on the spot.

Gunshots. Shouts.

Jens-Anton rushed toward Einar, the others of cover squad spread out behind him, silent predators slipping through the trees. Einar stepped to the gap in the salt circle and waved the men toward him. He yelled to be heard over the klaxon's blare.

"*Right here*," he said. "*Do not* step on the circle! This way!"

He didn't know what Aumont was going to do, but he knew it was something horrible, something *evil.*

Aumont's mumbles grew louder, darker, more sinister in their maddening incoherence.

The lid rattled so hard the old man's locked arms shook, the box's clatter growing in volume and intensity.

The cover squad rushed into the salt circle.

Flashlight beams pierced the woods. Dozens of them. The Germans were coming.

Rønneberg and Kayser reached the circle, with Idland and Birger close behind. Rønneberg didn't need to be told what to do—he saw the circle, and with wide eyes and a heaving chest, he directed the others through the gap to stand with Jens-Anton.

Einar's shaking hands poured salt even before Rønneberg was through the gap.

The circle closed.

The klaxon blared.

Spotlights probed the trees. A beam locked onto the men packed within the circle. They knelt low, as did Einar, and raised their gloved hands to block out the blinding radiance.

Rifles rang out—a bullet struck nearby, missing everyone. The high-point snipers would undoubtedly soon find their mark.

Einar saw a dozen Germans rushing through the woods toward them.

Dozens more would follow.

There was no chance of escape.

Einar pulled off a glove and reached into his snowsuit pocket. His frigid fingers found the L-pill. So light. It felt like nothing. How could something so small be his end?

He raised the pill to his lips.

A hand locked hard on his wrist—Rønneberg, snot frozen to his nose, his eyes wide with terror.

"Not yet," he said.

Aumont shouted words Einar did not understand, words that sounded blasphemous, ancient, and *wrong*. The old man stood and slowly, carefully stepped into the circle, taking his time to make sure he didn't disturb the black salt. Once inside, he extended his arms and held the ivory box beyond the circle's perimeter.

Something flew out of the box as if thrown by an angry man, something long and white that tumbled as it sailed through the air.

A bone . . . a femur.

As it traveled, Einar saw it *grow*. Other bones sprouted from it. Fibula and tibia, then the small bones of an animal's foot. Hip bones, from which expanded a second femur, then a spine. As shoulder bones and a skull grew into place, the first leg blossomed red muscle. In the time it took the femur to arc through the air, spreading flesh turned black—the ebony nothingness of a sealed dungeon, the light-gobbling void of an eclipse's umbra.

The thing landed on all fours just as the darkness rushed up the shoulders, then over the ears and the long maw, and down the forelegs.

A dog.

A dog the size of two men.

A dog made of unholy shadow.

A *black* dog—*Svart Hund.*

It turned toward Einar. A single fist-sized red eye stared out like a hot ember bobbing on a rippling river of ink. The mouth opened, revealing finger-long fangs of onyx.

The dog rushed at Aumont, huge paws eating up the short distance. It leaped, jaws wide, shadow tongue twitching.

As casually as one might pick up cards from the table and see their hand, Aumont pulled the box back to his chest.

The phantom dog slammed into something, as if an invisible wall rose straight up from the black salt circle. *Svart Hund* tumbled away and rolled across the ground before coming to a stop.

Sounds rushed back to Einar's ears, sounds that had been there all along, but they'd passed him by as he stared at an unimaginable demon brought to life in an instant: gunshots, machine-gun fire, the klaxon . . .

. . . and the shouts of the Nazis.

Svart Hund heard those too.

The shadow monster turned and rushed toward the leading German, a sergeant. Einar saw the confused look on his face as *Svart Hund* attacked. Mystical teeth slammed down on mortal flesh and bone. The shadow-beast violently shook its head—the sergeant's left arm tore free and spun away, trailing blood. His left leg ripped loose, bouncing hard against the chest of another soldier.

Svart Hund tossed the sergeant's ravaged, broken body aside. With a growl of the damned, it tore into the Germans.

The crack of a sniper rifle—Kayser cried out, clutching at his shoulder.

"The lights." Aumont was on one knee, his voice weak and hoarse. "Lieutenant . . . the lights . . ."

Rønneberg aimed his rifle toward Vemork's high points. "Take out the lights!" He fired, the others doing the same as fast as they could.

But not Einar. He moved to Aumont, knelt next to the old man.

"The box," Aumont said. "Hold it. Quickly."

Einar glanced at Aumont's hands, saw his gloves were torn, *burned* in some places. Blood leaked from the tears and spread across the off-white leather, dripping down to the boot-trodden snow just shy of the salt circle.

Even as he reached for the box, Einar heard the screams of the Germans and the gurgling, deep-bass roar of the creature. He heard the snapping of bones and the tearing of cloth.

His hands closed on the box just as the spotlights blinked out.

The guns of his comrades fell silent, but not the guns of

the Germans. They fired in mad, panicked bursts. Those bursts quickly ceased, as did the screams and sobbing prayers answered only with rumbling growls before a brutal, ragged end.

Einar held the box in both hands. Inside, a single bone—another femur the same size as the one Aumont had thrown—dirty and dry with age, etched with runes inked in fading black.

Aumont pointed to the ivory lid, which had fallen free.

"Break the circle," he said, his words breathy, struggling. "When you do, take the bone out, turn it the other way, put it back in, and . . . and be ready to close the lid."

Einar's ears placed a distant shriek from where one of the now-dark spotlights rested, where the sniper had been.

A scream from the second high spot: the last sniper.

No more gunfire. No more screams. No more blubbering prayers. Only the sound of the klaxon remained.

"Now, my boy," Aumont said. "Do it now."

Many years later, Einar would allow himself to think of this day once again, allow the memories he forced away to come trickling back. He would wonder at his own bravery. Or perhaps at his own stupidity to follow the instructions of a man who'd called forth a demon.

Einar kicked the toe of his boot through the salt, breaking the circle, sending tiny crystals flying into the night air.

Einar heard the beast's fast steps coming closer, heard its building growl.

He heard the terrified shouts of his comrades.

In that moment, Einar Skinnarland discovered a pure calmness, a silent serenity where his world narrowed to the box, the bone, and his own fingers.

Quickly, smoothly, he removed the rune-covered bone, turned it, and placed it back inside.

For an instant, he felt the hot breath of an animal, smelled the iron tang of blood, and he knew that he'd been a split second from suffering the same fate as the German sergeant; then he felt a weight in the box, so heavy it lurched toward the ground, almost tore free of his hands.

When the box thudded down, Einar slammed the lid closed.

The men of Operation Gunnerside faced no further opposition. In silence, they quickly moved to the cliff and descended. Einar had put the box back in Aumont's pack. Instead of the old expert climber helping Einar, Einar helped Aumont. Aumont's hands were riddled with lacerations, some to the bone. The men had bandaged his wounds.

When they were two kilometers away from Vemork's outer fence, the explosives team—Einar and Aumont included—would embark on the long trip to Sweden. They would keep to the woods and the wilds, avoiding all towns and all people. The cover team would immediately disburse and take individual paths out of Norway, hiding when necessary, always moving toward Sweden.

Everyone had survived. Keyser's wound wasn't bad; he could move on his own.

Rønneberg congratulated the men on altering the course of the war, but his words rang hollow. They'd all seen a thing they'd never thought possible, something that was—in some ways, if not *all* ways—even worse than a bomb that could wipe out a city and kill hundreds of thousands.

They'd seen *Svart Hund*.

Before Rønneberg sent everyone on their way, he let the old Englishman have the final words of Operation Gunnerside.

"I give you a gift," Aumont said to them. "The gift of your

lives. Should you ever mention this incident to anyone—ever—the occupant of the box will know. It will come for you. There is no safe place, in this world or the next. You have seen its hunger, its appetite for souls. It will swallow yours, just as it did those of the Germans who died this night."

Later, Einar would recall little of the grueling trek to Sweden. He would recall little because he observed little. During the entire trip, he ate when he was hungry, he slept when he was tired, but he paid no attention to the countryside.

He had eyes only for Aumont.

For Aumont's pack.

And the impossible thing that lurked inside it.

He had eyes only for *Svart Hund.*

CS-13

GABY TRIANA

FLORIDA STRAITS, MAY 1943

Ensign Mario Ramírez Delgado stood at the bow of his ship, scanning for ghosts. He'd volunteered for the Cuban navy four days after Pearl Harbor, the day his country declared war on Germany, but today—May 15, 1943—reality was starting to sink in.

Though *los Estados Unidos* had supplied Cuba with a small fleet of submarine chasers a few months ago to reinforce defenses against U-boats in the Florida Straits and Caribbean, Delgado was on high alert. Only two days ago, the Germans had obliterated both the American tanker *Nickeliner* and the Cuban tanker *Mambí*. Only eleven survivors. Twenty-three innocent men, now dead.

Seventy-nine, if one counted the merchant ship attacks from last year.

Now his eighty-three-foot *CS-13* was one of three ordered to escort two more merchant ships sailing from Isabela de Sagua to Havana, keeping an eye out for German ghosts. In the wake of the deadly onslaught, Ensign Delgado did his best to keep his crew calm, but he knew something lurked out there. It was bad enough that terror was on everybody's minds. Oil, fuel, and blood still stained the surface of the straits, but now crewmen were claiming to see corpses in the water. Some had spotted flailing arms and legs, survivors calling for help—some bobbing bodies belonging to women.

But that wasn't possible, Delgado thought. When they'd scoured the area—nothing. With six U-boats rumored to still haunt the waterways, he couldn't help but wonder if they were losing their minds or if these visions of phantom limbs and screams were a result of trauma. Some even claimed to see larger mysterious shapes just under the surface. And while Delgado passed them off as shadows created by US Kingfisher floatplanes operating out of Cuba, he knew better.

Under his service white shirt, he clutched the outline of the medallion pressing against his bare skin. Not of *Jesucristo* or *la Virgen María* like the other crewmen—charms of love and luck from their *novias* and wives—but the one from his *abuela*, given to him on his graduation day from the Naval Academy, days before she passed. For protection, she'd said, then asked him to keep it hidden away, like any good Catholic with a dark side would do.

Delgado's eyes narrowed, searching for signs in the water he dared not vocalize, memories from bedtime stories many moons ago. Crowns of pearls, fish tails, bronze skin, tridents . . . vengeance, if you weren't careful. *No,* he thought. *Qué ridículo. Abuela*'s tales were fiction, legends of an imaginative *campesina*. As much as he'd loved her, she'd been a simple woman. The educated knew no creatures swam the seas other than the ones science had proven.

It was 17:15 when a Kingfisher sailed across the bright blue sky, snapping Delgado's attention upward. The Vought OS2U seaplane, about a mile and a half from the starboard stern, dropped a smoke float, flew in circles, and repeatedly cut its engine before starting again. The code was clear—enemy presence.

Not a moment later, the radio crackled with the voice of *CS-11*'s commander. "Enemy sighted!" he shouted. The squadron leader ordered Delgado to head to the smoke bomb site to investigate, as they were the closest.

The convoy of merchant ships turned forty-five degrees port, as Delgado ordered his crew straight to the Kingfisher's smoke float, hiking their easy speed from eight to fifteen knots. Had the American plane really spotted a U-boat, or was this a false alarm? If they'd indeed found a German sub, would he be able to take out such a formidable enemy?

Delgado steeled himself and looked around at his crew, who depended on him. No matter what, he had to keep *una impresión fuerte*, a stony face of resolve and courage. At about nine hundred yards from the target, he stalked into the bridge and ordered his sonar operator, Norberto Abreu, to search for the enemy sub. As he stood by watching the screen, they both caught the small blip at the same time, its sound as crystal clear as the turquoise waters, marked with Doppler effect and whirring of propeller.

"*Submarino enemigo*," Abreu confirmed.

Delgado pinched at the protection charm under his shirt. *Dios mío.* He could not let these men die today, not on his watch. "Prepare the depth charges," he said without hesitation, stepping halfway out of the room to peer ahead through his binoculars. The small crew aboard the eighty-three-foot submarine chaser scuttled into action.

They would use a pattern of three. If oil did not come sputtering to the surface, he would change course and order another round of attacks, but first things first. At the doorway between his deck and the bridge, Delgado felt it—a surge underneath the ship.

"*¿Qué fue eso?*" a crewman asked.

"I don't know," Delgado replied. The claims of shadows, ghostly corpses, and more came barreling into his mind again. Maybe his crew wasn't delirious or haunted by odd visions after all.

"*Alférez*," Abreu said, pressing the headphones to one ear. "Something else. School of fish, possibly dolphins. Whales?" He pointed to small formations on the screen. Delgado knew of dolphins being harmed by sonar. The pulses would become so loud that they'd strand themselves on the beaches to die, but these creatures seemed to be heading toward the target, surrounding the enemy submarine.

"What do you hear?" Delgado demanded.

The sonar operator winced, shook his head, and held up the headphones for Delgado. "A screech? Or . . . screaming? I'm sorry, sir. I'm unfamiliar."

Delgado pressed his ear to the headphones. He could barely make out an elongated, high-pitched noise, like a cross between a dolphin and a malfunctioning, magnified speaker emitting feedback. Of course, that didn't make sense. No submarine made a noise like that. He hated the thought of harming sea creatures, regardless of their species, but his men's lives were at stake.

"Prepare to fire depth charge. Detonation depth one hundred feet," he ordered. "Fire!"

"Firing depth charge, aye, sir."

His crew released the first depth charge as Delgado and Abreu listened. The screeching grew louder, angrier. Delgado dropped the headphones he and Abreu shared, the shriek in his ears so intense that he fell against the metal bulkhead, hitting the back of his head. Immediately, tunnels of darkness closed in around his line of sight. The shouts of his crewman seemed to fade away as watery sounds lulled him.

"Sir!" Abreu's face appeared before his, one arm gripping him by the collar, the other on the headphones. "You all right?"

"Fine, fine." Whatever momentary concussion he'd had, it had passed.

"I'm getting no sounds of sub breakup on sonar."

Delgado rubbed the back of his head. "Prepare to fire depth charge. Detonation depth one fifty," he said, regaining consciousness. Only this time, whenever he blinked, flashes of other movement slid into his vision, not of his crewmen. He remembered long ago, as a child playing on *la finca*, the farm, when he'd hit his head, the same phenomenon had happened. The concussion had caused hallucinations. This was certainly not the time. He shook them off. "Fire!"

"Firing depth charge, aye, sir."

Now, in one layer of vision, he saw the bridge, its controls, the sonar, and Abreu seated at it, wide-eyed and listening for his life. On another layer—over or under the other, he wasn't sure—he saw them . . . several dozen ghosts. Not German, but phantoms of the undersea, swimming about with glinting green scales and black skin with purplish iridescence, slicing through the water, some holding golden staffs.

Golden staffs?

The duality confused him. His grandmother's old stories resurfaced. Frantically, Delgado brushed at his face.

"*¿Estás bien, Alférez?*" Abreu asked.

"I'm fine. Do you still have contact?" Delgado worked to stay focused, but the shapes kept flitting in his periphery. *Women. No—fish. Tridents?* He wanted nothing more than to dissolve the hallucinations at this most critical moment.

"Still hear propellers, sir," Abreu reported. "And that infernal screaming."

On the screen, the blips came and went so quickly that it was hard to tell what was there or if the sonar was malfunctioning, but Delgado could see the blips in his altered vision as fully formed manifestations. And if he closed his eyes, they were clearly there—creatures, lots of them, swimming erratically, without pattern and flustered, like sharks in a feeding frenzy. Just beyond, he could see the enemy looming in the depths as well. The creatures swarmed the submarine, slender feminine arms with human hands, elongated webbed fingers carrying ropes of seaweed and kelp. The sonar blips aligned with his vision, swimming in a circular pattern.

He stiffened. *My God, they're real.*

Thank heavens they were going after the U-boat and not them.

Delgado brushed at his eyes and ears like a beekeeper under attack, only the swarm were these vicious women-fish. Hallucinations or not, mermaids or dolphins, *CS-13* needed to destroy that U-boat.

"Prepare to fire a third depth charge. Detonation depth two hundred fifty feet," he ordered.

In his second sight, Delgado saw the mermaids' faces—piercing gold eyes like citrines shining out of dark faces, coils of long black hair swirling around slick, female bodies glistening like eels. Beautiful and devastatingly horrific, with teeth like vampire fish, fangs erupting from lower jaws. The squadron of *sirenas* nudged the submarine off course, damaging its rudders with their fins. The seaweed and kelp they'd carried were now tangled in struggling propellers.

The mermaids swam away from the U-boat as if working in tandem with Delgado's thoughts.

"Fire!"

"Firing depth charge, aye, sir."

A furious sound echoed through the headphones, and Abreu pulled them off his head. A column of white, foamy water shot up from the surface. At its peak, Delgado saw them—the fish, the creatures with glistening green-purple skin—screeching so loudly they could be heard without sonar. Every last crewman covered his ears. Some mermaids dove back into the water, shot like torpedoes into the depths, and disappeared. Others resurfaced to help the injured ones.

All went quiet. Delgado fought to catch his breath, unsure if the third depth charge had hit or not. "Lookouts, check for surface debris or oil. Sonar, report," he ordered.

"No breaking-up sounds, sir, but there are strange bubbling noises. Listen," Abreu said.

The ensign pressed his ear to a headphone and closed his eyes. Delgado could see them congregating again—the fish-women. *Yemayá's children*, he remembered *Abuela* calling them. They weren't gone. They were there, wrestling in the depths, muscular ebony-violet arms wrapped around two masses, seven meters long, metallic, tube-shaped, with man-made features, so opposite of the organic beings guiding them, deflecting . . .

Torpedoes. Anticipating further depth charge attacks, the U-boat had fired.

Are the mermaids deflecting the torpedoes away . . . or toward us? Delgado wondered.

"Incoming torpedoes."

"Sir?" replied Abreu. "Lookouts haven't reported any torpedoes."

Delgado ignored the sonarman. He knew what he'd seen. "Engine room, flank speed!"

"Flank speed, aye, sir."

"Helm, hard to port!" he ordered and yanked his medallion out, clutching it tightly. "Torpedoes incoming." He didn't know how he saw this, only that he did. The vision was back, pushing at the edges of his view. For reasons he couldn't quite explain, he felt aided, protected, like these creatures were on his side.

"Hard to port, aye, sir."

Delgado held the railing and crouched, covering his head, seeing what the crewmen couldn't—two torpedoes charging through the water at them.

The torpedoes approached the ship's stern, three or four fish-women wrapped around each. Using their tails and tridents, they struggled to redirect them. The torpedoes passed just astern of the *CS-13*. The mermaids released their hold and disappeared into the depths.

Delgado closed his eyes to better see his dual vision, accepting it now for what it was. In the fathoms, he saw many of the mermaids sinking, their tridents descending through the depths, as others collected the injured in their arms. Farther down, something was rising—a massive shadow emerging from the darkness.

"Breaking-up noises, sir," reported Abreu. "We got her!"

As Delgado pried his eyes open to scan the sea's surface, a large pool of oil appeared, spread widely, bringing with it arms, legs, and torsos of men, bloodied green-purple tails, severed fins, and debris. Delgado shut his eyes against the carnage and swallowed. Once again, the sea swelled, the ship pitched, and water washed onto the stern.

His second sight revealed more—below them, a storm brewed. Whorls and bubbles spun through the water. Knots formed in the pit of his stomach as he watched it churn. Delgado saw her clear as the straits, larger than all her children put together, the size of several blue whales, end to end. Raven-haired mermaids gathered around her as a protective army. The skin of her upper body was dark, like carved ebony, eyes glowing yellow with rage, lower half of her body blue and turquoise and covered in scales. Around her neck was a lace shawl of seaweed, around her head a crown of pearls embedded in her hair. She broke the surface with such force the ship nearly capsized.

Raging with ire, the goddess Yemayá, the very one on Delgado's medallion, shouted, a hollow sound echoing across the sea. In her massive arms, she held a broken, battered Spanish galleon of long ago, dripping gold, jewels, paintings, hull fragments of more modern warships . . . a veritable tangled mass of battle junk, broken human skeletons, and a large section of what Delgado could only assume was the destroyed enemy U-boat. The sea goddess's powerful tail wavered back and forth to propel her body out of water, causing high waves that shuddered *CS-13* like a bathtub toy. Delgado grasped for his medallion, but the chain holding his protection charm had snapped. The bauble was gone.

"Yemayá . . ." he uttered in awe. She had come. His grandmother had consecrated her, fused her to his protective charm, and so she'd come. But she was not happy with him. Deep in his chest, Delgado felt a fissure spread, like his heart splitting open. He suppressed the urge to cry, to beg for forgiveness for not quite believing in her for so long. For causing her to anger.

Around him, the crew panicked, some cowering in fear on the decks, others whimpering or crowding into the cabin together in vain. Abreu slid to the floor, his mouth agape with awe.

Behind the orisha mother of the sea, giver of life, patron of women, spirit of *Abuela*'s hidden religion, the late-afternoon sun's rays filtered through the clouds like a crown behind her head. The colossal goddess turned her golden eyes brimming with hurt toward Delgado like she knew him. And in her gaze, yes, he recognized the familiar. From days gone by. From his days on *la finca*. When she spoke, watery foam splashed and gurgled out of her mouth like nonsense to the shivering crew trembling in her shadow. But to Delgado, it was an old lullaby he'd heard as a child on his grandmother's farm.

Turning toward the ship, Yemayá angrily dumped the wreckage and carnage of sea battles into the water near the ship's bow, missing its deck by a few feet. Gusts from the falling debris blew back the deck crewmen's hair and hats. One discarded husk of a rusted old torpedo landed on the deck with a clank, denting the wood before rolling away, splashing back into the ocean. The message was clear: Keep your *trastos inútiles* out of my sea. And with a heave to the side, the goddess dove back into the straits, sending waves in all directions, dousing the *CS-13* in a deluge of salt water.

When the ship righted itself, not a word was spoken. The *CS-13* bobbed for what felt like hours in silence as the crewman sat alone, praying on their rosaries, Jesucristos, and Vírgen Marías. Abreu sat at his station, unmoving. Delgado, with no trinket of his own to pray on, ordered the crew to turn toward shore and catch up with the rest of the convoy. Though the battle had ended, something deep inside him was lost forever.

President Batista was hesitant to officially announce the sinking of *U-176* to world news sources, and Delgado, still rattled, preferred it that way. In fact, the president specifically asked him not to speak of the matter for some time. It made sense—the crew was never able to accurately elucidate what happened on May 15, 1943, and versions of the story kept changing, depending on who told it. As Delgado understood, no country in the Allied forces believed that his small subchaser could have defeated such a formidable opponent anyway, so it was just as well.

A year later, Alférez Mario Ramírez Delgado was promoted to lieutenant. By the end of the *Segunda Guerra Mundial*, Batista had awarded him with the Orden del Mérito Naval Medal of Honor, which flummoxed him. He couldn't, for the sake of him, shake from his mind the visions of the mermaid army surrounding the U-boat, diverting their attention, redirecting torpedoes aimed for him . . . for them. They were alive because of them. Because of her. And this medal, this trinket on his lapel, represented everything that Yemayá never wanted.

On a Saturday in May, Delgado took seven gardenias, a clutch of pearls, seven white roses, seven shells, and some twine, and together tied it all into a wreath with blue and white ribbon. He sailed his fishing boat off the shore of Isabela de Sagua into the straits and stopped at exactly 17:15.

Alone, he scanned the horizon. To show gratitude in person was all he could ever do. When she didn't appear, he said, "Forgive me, *diosa*. I was only trying to protect my home, same as you." He would never forget the injured mermaids or the look of hurt in his goddess's eyes upon showing him the cost of war from the bottom of her ocean. Kissing the wreath, he dropped the offering over the edge of the boat. When again she didn't appear, he reached into his bag, hesitantly pulled out his Medal of Honor, stared at it, then dropped that as well.

The medal spiraled downward.

On his way home under a full moon, a soft wave pushed him along. It swelled to a peak, washed over the bow of his boat, and retreated. There on the deck, glinting under the moonlight, was his *abuela*'s lost chain and medallion.

DAS *MAMMUT*

HENRY HERZ

GREMUCHII, SOVIET UNION, JULY 3, 1943

Two hundred ninety-one soldiers of a Soviet tank battalion, a mix of battle-hardened veterans and raw recruits barely old enough to shave, sat on rows of crude wooden benches in their brigade assembly area. Overhead, a capacious, weather-beaten tent shaded them from the blistering midday sun. Every breath reminded Andrei that no one had showered for at least a week. The olive-drab tent flaps hung limp in the still air like corpses dangling from ropes. A makeshift wooden board stood before them, a map of the Kursk region tacked to it.

Andrei Petrov, a gangly, blond twenty-four-year-old drafted in 1941, was now a T-34 tanker. Through a combination of bravery, skill, and sheer good fortune, he'd survived enough encounters with German armor to be promoted to kapitán and placed in command of the Thirty-First Tank Company. The wartime Red Army offered only two career paths: promotion or violent death. Andrei half listened to the men nearby exchanging theories as to the briefing's purpose. But he knew.

"Attention!" someone shouted from the rear of the tent.

Soldiers scrambled to their feet, the space falling silent as a mausoleum.

The tall, brown-haired battalion commander, Majór Makarov, strode toward the map. Dark burn scars on the left side of his face offered silent testimony to his battle experience. He turned. "At ease, comrades." With everyone seated, he pointed at the map, the battlefront marked with red pencil strokes. "As you can see, our sector bulges westward between Orel in the north and Belgorod in the south."

Uncharacteristically candid for a Soviet officer, he got right to the point. "I have good news and bad news. First, the bad news. We in the First Tank Army have the honor of facing the three deadliest divisions in the German army: the SS panzer divisions *Leibstandarte*, *Das Reich*, and *Totenkopf*." Makarov scowled. "They've recently received the new PzKw V Panther and PzKw VI Tiger tanks. Their frontal armor is too thick for our T-34 guns to pierce." He paced. "Worse, the Panther's 75mm and the Tiger's 88mm cannons outrange ours and will penetrate our tanks' armor. So, it's a knife fight. We must use our greater speed to get close to the Nazi panzers and shoot them in their thinner side or rear armor."

Andrei's shoulders tightened.

Makarov scanned the resolute faces of his men. "Now, the good news. First, you're all brave patriots of the Motherland. You defeated the Nazis at Stalingrad, and you'll do so again. Second, our factory workers have supplied us with far more tanks, artillery, and aircraft than the enemy. Third, thanks to superb intel, we've known about their plans for some time. The Nazis will soon launch a major offensive. Their Ninth Army will strike southward from Orel toward Kursk, while their Fourth Panzer Army and Army Detachment Kempf will drive northward from Belgorod."

The major smirked. "But we're ready for them. Since April, three hundred thousand civilians helped construct three defensive belts at both shoulders of the Kursk bulge, preparing forty-kilometer-deep defense zones. All told, we've dug sixty-eight hundred kilometers of trench and laid over half a million antitank mines. Fortifying each belt are barbed-wire fences, antitank ditches and obstacles, dug-in antitank guns and armored vehicles, and machine-gun bunkers." He slammed a fist into an open hand. "Let them come. Kursk will be their graveyard."

Andrei and the others grunted their agreement.

GREMUCHII, SOVIET UNION, JULY 5, 1943

The morning sun warmed Andrei's face, reminding him of more peaceful times working as a zookeeper in Voronezh and walking hand in hand with his gray-eyed girlfriend, Sofia.

He shook hands with Kapitán Denis Varkov, the stocky, affable commander of the Thirty-Second Tank Company stationed westward of Andrei's Thirty-First. "Lovely morning, eh, Denis?"

Denis nodded, taking a deep breath of fresh air, rich with petrichor from the night's rain. "Indeed, though I fear the quiet won't last."

Together the pair plodded through mud that sucked at their boots. They inspected their companies, reminding the crews to remain alert. Parked turret-down facing south, just behind an east–west ridgeline, their nineteen T-34 tanks stood at thirty-meter intervals just out of sight from the reverse slope—the direction from which the Germans would advance.

A narrow north–south dirt road signified the western edge of the Thirty-Second. Beyond it, a half dozen ZiS-2 57mm antitank guns in bunkers alternated with DShK 12.7mm machine guns in sandbag nests along the ridge for five hundred meters. Two rifle companies rested in covered slit trenches fifty meters behind the tanks. Three hundred meters farther back, six crews readied their BM-37 82mm mortars. Extensive camouflage masked the Soviets, rendering them nearly impossible to see from a distance.

Someday I'll return home to my family and Sofia.

Andrei turned his head at the cawing of passing crows. He gestured with his thumb at the crest. "Denis, shall we check the front again?" The pair clambered upslope until they could scan with their binoculars the terrain beyond the ridge.

A kilometer down the gentle slope grew a tall stand of kalyna bushes near the eastern edge of the road. A half kilometer beyond that stood a seventy-meter-wide grove of spruce trees. During last night's briefing, Majór Makarov indicated Soviet TM-38 antitank mines riddled the road and grassy field to the west of the trees.

At the high-pitched whine of German howitzer rounds passing far overhead, Andrei's pulse raced. He and Denis rushed to their T-34s, scrambling through turret hatches, bidding the fresh air a hasty farewell.

A squadron of German Ju 87 *Stuka* dive bombers screamed overhead but did not attack.

Our camouflage is working.

Andrei glanced at a crinkled black-and-white photo of Sofia taped to the bulkhead. He sighed, fastening the chinstrap of his brown leather helmet. *Forget dreams of the war's end for now. Just get through the next battle. Time to move the unit into firing positions.*

"Driver, start engine," Andrei barked. The 500 hp V12 diesel engine rumbled to life, gray smoke spewing from the two downward-angled exhaust pipes on the rear hull.

Since only Soviet company commanders had radios in their tanks, he raised a signal flag from his hatch, ordering his nine other T-34s to advance the few meters into hull-down position, where their guns could fire from an earth-shielded position at targets on the other side of the ridge.

Radio in one hand, binoculars in the other, Andrei eased his head out of the cramped turret.

Here they come.

"Battalion, this is Thirty-One. Over."

"Go ahead, Thirty-One. Over."

"Enemy armor at one and a half kilometers. Five Tigers west of the road. To the east of the trees, I see five PzKw IV tanks and four StuG III assault guns, both in wedge formation. They've all got long 75s. Behind them are eight half-tracks. Over."

"Understood, Thirty-One. Weapons free. Over."

"Acknowledged. Over and out." Andrei raised the signal flag to open fire. Recognizing his tank could do little to a Tiger's frontal armor, he targeted a PzKw IV, slewing the turret and elevating the gun barrel. "Load AP."

The loader crewman shoved an armor-piercing round into the cannon's breach. "Up."

Andrei braced himself for the cannon's recoil. "On the way." He fired. *Whoomp!* The round missed high. *Shit.* "Reengaging."

The Soviet tanks, antitank guns, and mortars blasted away, creating a bone-rattling cacophony.

A symphony of death.

When an antitank mine shattered the left tread of the lead Tiger, the other Tigers halted. All five returned fire with high-explosive rounds against the camouflaged Soviet antitank positions, now made visible by their own muzzle blasts.

The Soviet tanks and guns focused their fire on the tanks to the east of the woods. Soon a PzKw IV and an StuG were struck. The former exploded, blowing the turret off the tank. A mortar shot struck the stationary Tiger, blasting through the thin roof armor and killing the crew.

"One Thirty-One, this is Battalion. Over."

"Go ahead, Battalion. Over."

"The Germans are marching their howitzer fire southward toward your positions. Assault the enemy's eastern flank immediately. Thirty-Two will be right behind you after they load infantry. Over."

"Acknowledged. Over and out."

Into the lion's mouth. Again. Andrei's heart thumped.

He raised the signal flag for his company to charge. "Driver, move out at full speed toward the panzers' eastern flank." With a roar of its engine, their tank lurched forward, its treads spewing clods of rich earth.

Andrei grabbed handholds as the tank jostled its crowded crew. *At least our T-34's wider tracks make us more agile over muddy ground than panzers.*

Indirect fire from Soviet mortars targeted the remaining Tigers. The German tanks backed out of the minefield and maneuvered to prevent the mortars from bracketing them. The Tigers faced no corresponding difficulty targeting the stationary Soviet antitank and machine guns, eventually destroying them.

East of the woods, the German infantry dismounted from their half-tracks and dispersed. They advanced in practiced choreography to support their tanks east of the road.

Andrei's company raced forward, taking fire while shooting on the move.

Wham! A near miss. Bits of debris plinked harmlessly on the T-34's side armor.

Whoomp! He destroyed a PzKw IV with a shot to its turret. Andrei smiled grimly. He spared a quick glance backward.

Riflemen clung to Denis's nine tanks as they rumbled toward the stand of kalyna bushes.

Smart. The infantry can dismount in concealment and then

keep the German infantry from attacking our flanks with rocket-propelled grenades.

"Driver, full speed through the gap between the two nearest StuGs!" Andrei's tanks swarmed around the German vehicles like angry bees. The turretless StuG assault guns couldn't traverse quickly enough against close-in, fast-moving opponents. Soon the swirling T-34s set them aflame. The Soviet tanks fired at the surviving PzKw IVs.

A T-34 exploded.

Damn.

Andrei radioed the rifle company commander. "Forty-Two, this is Thirty-One. Over."

"Go ahead, Thirty-One. Over."

"German infantry are firing *Panzerschrecks* from the woods. Neutralize them. Over."

"We're advancing toward them as quickly as we can without machine-gun support, Thirty-One. Machine-gun fire from the German half-tracks is slowing us down."

Another T-34 exploded.

Shit. Andrei scanned ahead. Four Tigers advanced from the left side of the trees.

They must've rounded the forest.

He slewed the T-34 turret. "Load AP."

"Up."

"On the way." Andrei fired. The round bounced off the Tiger's front armor plate. *Damn. Without close infantry support, we can't take out the Tigers.*

"Battalion, this is Thirty-One. The Tigers are advancing. Request mortars drop smoke rounds to cover our withdrawal. Over and out." He raised the retreat flag for his remaining tanks. "Driver, fall back at max speed."

Andrei swiveled the turret rearward, firing the coaxial machine gun to keep the German infantry from advancing. He radioed Denis, who confirmed the other tank company's withdrawal.

PROKHOROVKA, SOVIET UNION, JULY 7, 1943

As ordered by Battalion, the Thirty-First Tank Company parked their tanks at the Fortieth Tank Brigade headquarters, twelve kilometers behind the front lines.

A lieutenant approached. He saluted. "Are you Kapitán Andrei Petrov?"

"Yes, Comrade Leytenant."

"Sir, Majór Makarov wants you to report to him at that farmhouse." He pointed. "I'm to escort your company to the field kitchen."

The offer of warm food received hearty agreement from Andrei's men.

His thoughts drifted homeward.

I hope Mama, Papa, and Sofia are getting enough to eat.

"Thank you, Leytenant." Andrei strode toward the farmhouse.

He found the major in a dining room converted to an office, a bucolic wall painting and homemade knickknacks incongruous with the military maps and gear strewn about the room.

Andrei saluted, stiffening further at the presence of another officer.

A general?

"Generalmajór Belsky," said Makarov, "this is Kapitán Petrov."

"I've heard good things about you, Comrade," said the general, sitting on a hand-carved wooden dining-room chair. "At ease, Kapitán. Majór, clear the building. We need *privacy*." His tone added significance to the word.

This can't be good.

"Brave spies died getting us this intel. You must tell no one." He met Andrei's gaze. "Divulging any of this will result in *severe* punishment. Understood?"

"Yes, sir." Andrei's stomach knotted at the implication.

"We've fought the Germans to a standstill, but that only increases our danger." The general unlocked a briefcase, rifled through a folder, and withdrew three aerial reconnaissance photos. "The Nazis have committed a superweapon to the fight, their only *Mammut* land dreadnought. As we speak, it marches from its assembly point in Kiev. Toward us."

Land dreadnought? Marching?

Andrei's eyes bulged as he reviewed the spy photos. Trucks seemed like insects next to *Mammut.* Its tiered, isosceles triangle shape looked like an elongated half ziggurat. Cannon barrels bristled from five levels, a gargantuan steel hedgehog. Four mechanical legs sprouted from both the vehicle's sides, thick as bridge supports.

The general read from a report. "Intelligence estimates *Mammut* is a hundred meters long, forty meters wide at the base of the triangle, and fifty meters from keel to superstructure, excluding antennas. That dish near the top is a Würzburg radar for guiding antiaircraft guns. The fifty-meter-tall antenna is a Rudolf DMG 3G radio."

He flipped to the next page. "Two diesel-powered Wagner water-tube boilers generate twenty-seven thousand horsepower for each leg. The legs provide ten-meter ground clearance, so it can ignore antitank obstacles. The feet are so thick that antitank mines will have no effect. No bridge could support its vast weight, but it can ford streams and shallow rivers." He paused for effect. "What do you make of the turreted weapons lining the two long sides?"

"Sir, the lowest, outermost tier has ten quad-20mm

Flakvierling cannons that can be used in anti-infantry or anti-aircraft roles. I'm not familiar with the larger weapons near the front on the second and third tiers. The fourth tier has eight 88mm *Flak* 41 cannons that can be used in antitank or anti-aircraft roles."

"Very good, Kapitán. The two round turrets in the second tier each house a pair of 380mm *Raketen-Werfer* rocket-propelled mortars. The four rectangular turrets on the third tier each mount two 380mm SK C/34 naval guns, same as on the battleship *Bismarck*."

Jesus.

"Along the vehicle's rear edge, the fifth tier mounts six pop-up 200cm *Flak* floodlights for nighttime antiaircraft illumination. The superstructure above that houses the command center, surveillance and communications equipment, and ammo magazines." He raised his eyes.

Andrei shuddered.

That metal monstrosity will blast a path to Kursk.

"Can our air force comrades bomb it before it reaches the front line, sir?"

The general shook his head. "Men have died trying. Luftwaffe aircraft maintain an outer perimeter defense. Any of our bombers that make it past the Messerschmitts have to survive *Mammut*'s own air defenses. Even then, the bombs have to hit a moving target. And if a bomb strikes the *Mammut*, it must penetrate either 360mm Krupp cemented armor on the vertical-angled surfaces or 200mm homogeneous steel armor on the decks. It's a walking battleship."

Andrei paled. "How do we stop it, sir?"

"That's where you come in, Comrade Kapitán."

Damn. I'll never see my family again.

The general's dark eyes reminded Andrei of a snake's. "Your

records indicate you have animal-handling experience, and your bravery is unquestioned. We possess a secret weapon too . . . one that requires a crewman."

Crewman?

"Go eat something, grab your belongings, and bid your men farewell. You are reassigned. Majór Makarov will appoint a new company commander. Meet me at the motor pool in one hour. Dismissed."

ENROUTE TO KURSK RESERVOIR, SOVIET UNION, JULY 7, 1943

The setting sun painted the western sky purple. As Belsky's adjutant drove the GAZ-64 four-wheel-drive vehicle northward, the general briefed Andrei. "I know this is unbelievable, Kapitán, but a year ago, the Motherland discovered a dragon in a long-abandoned mine near Kursk Reservoir."

"A dragon? Out of fairy tales?" His eyebrows rose.

This just gets worse and worse.

The general nodded. "Zmei Gorynych, to be exact—Son of the Mountain. He's our only chance to stop *Mammut.*"

The junior officer stared at the general, ignoring jolts from road potholes.

"And, to anticipate your next questions, Gorynych hasn't yet fought for us in any battles, because he was asleep. The *Stavka* couldn't be sure they'd be able to communicate with him, how violently he might react when awoken, or how compliant to their requests he might be."

Four IL-2 *Sturmovik* ground-attack fighters swept southward at low altitude, their growling engines interrupting the briefing.

Andrei realized he was holding his breath. "They've woken him, haven't they, sir?"

"Yes. The German deployment of *Mammut* forced headquarters' hand. Fortunately, the dragon speaks Russian. Like humans, he's motivated by greed and self-preservation. He knows the Germans would steal his hoard if they reach Kursk. Headquarters also promised him a Fabergé egg if he stops *Mammut*."

A platoon of KV-1 heavy tanks rumbled by in the opposite direction.

I wish I were back with my unit fighting against men. "What's my role, sir?"

The general chuckled. "Although Gorynych is ancient, he has the attention span of a teenager. He doesn't understand maps or modern military tactics, and he will need to be directed to *Mammut*. You'll also keep him focused. We don't want him stopping to dine on some shepherd's flock. A hot-air ballooning basket's been strapped just behind Gorynych's middle head."

Andrei's heart nearly pounded out of his chest. "Sir, did you say middle head?"

"Yes. He has three."

Dear God, you want me riding a triple-headed dragon.

"Tomorrow you'll meet Gorynych, review the mission details, and practice operating with him. You'll be issued goggles, cold-weather gear, harness, compass, map, radio, and PAU-2 night-vision device."

Andrei's breathing accelerated.

How high does he fly?

"And a parachute, sir?"

"No. You'll stay with him until the mission's complete."

Son of a bitch.

"But, sir, how will we reach the *Mammut* without getting shot up like our aircraft?"

The general nodded. "You'll attack at night. Given we're tracking *Mammut*'s location in daytime and know its destination and speed, we can calculate its heading and nighttime location. The day after tomorrow, at 0145, six Tupolev TB-3 bombers will approach *Mammut* on a reverse heading at twenty-five hundred meters. That'll keep them out of reach of the 20mm *Flak*, but not the 88s, I'm afraid. While *Mammut* concentrates on the threat to their front, you'll glide in undetected from the rear."

I'm gonna throw up.

"What will Gorynych do once we reach the target, sir?"

"You'll direct his tactics. He's immensely powerful. Strong enough to crush cannon barrels. And then there's his breath."

"His breath?" asked Andrei, forgetting in his shock to append an honorific.

Belsky grinned. "Oh yes. He can breathe fire. Imagine a gigantic flying flamethrower." He rubbed his hands in glee.

KURSK RESERVOIR, SOVIET UNION, JULY 8, 1943

Wearing his flying gear, Andrei arrived at the general's tent at 0700, as ordered.

Belsky checked his watch. "Right on time. Come, Comrade Kapitán. Let's introduce you to Zmei Gorynych."

I hope I don't piss my pants. Then again, if I do, maybe the dragon will refuse to carry me.

Andrei shook his head.

That's a cowardly thought. What would Papa think? You're better than that.

As they left the tent, a private approached, leading a Ukrainian Grey on a rope.

In response to Andrei's double take, Belsky laughed. "It's a snack."

Snack?

Sunlight glinted off a shiny new aircraft hangar.

A hangar without a runway?

"Give the cow's lead to the kapitán." The general slapped Andrei's back. "Time for you to make a new friend. Be polite. Show no fear." Belsky led Andrei toward a hangar side door, the cow following Andrei, encouraged by an occasional tug on the rope.

I'm dumbly following you just like the cow's following me.

Taking a deep breath, Andrei crossed the threshold and pulled up short at both the aroma of brimstone and the dragon's size.

In the center of the hangar, Gorynych lounged like a colossal dark green cat. Enlisted men wielding long-handled brushes administered a thorough scrubbing to dragon flanks covered in shield-shaped scales the size of trash can lids. Other than having three heads, the beast's appearance matched Andrei's expectations of a dragon. Gorynych's winged, lizard-like body stretched forty meters from tail to snout.

The middle head yawned. The dragon stretched, revealing an equally wide wingspan and mouths lined with half-meter-long fangs.

Belsky's whisper snapped Andrei out of his stupor. "Tie the cow to that metal post in the floor, and then I'll introduce you. Only his middle head speaks, so that's whom you address."

This must be a bad dream.

The general strode toward the dragon while Andrei hastened to comply. "Good morning, Your Immensity. I trust you slept well?"

"As well as could be expected outside the comfort of my lair, Viktor." His deep, booming voice echoed throughout the hangar.

Andrei's eyebrows rose at the dragon's informal use of a general's first name.

I guess size does matter.

Belsky pressed on, ignoring the impropriety. "I have someone I'd like you to meet—Kapitán Andrei Petrov. And as you can see, he brought you a snack."

Gorynych nodded. "Ah, how nice." The dragon's left head lunged, crushing the poor cow in his enormous jaws and gulping it down in three bites. Gorynych kept his head close to the floor so his attendants could scrub the bovine blood from his snout.

Andrei shivered, imagining a similar fate for himself.

The center head moved to within a few yards of him, the aroma of brimstone wafting from glistening nostrils.

Andrei froze under the gaze of intense amber eyes the size of dinner plates.

"Thank you. Very tasty. Viktor told me we will be working together."

"Yes, um, Your Immensity."

Do I salute? Bow?

The general handed Andrei a folded piece of paper. "After you two are sufficiently acquainted, we"—he glanced at the dragon—"*request* you conduct the following training exercises. If all proceeds as planned, your mission will start at 0130." He cleared his throat. "Now, please excuse me. I have other pressing matters this morning." Belsky departed.

His shock gradually fading, Andrei engaged in polite conversation as one would with a general, starting with a compliment. "Your scales are most impressive, Your Immensity."

"How kind of you, Andrei. They are also protective. With my permission, Viktor had weapon tests conducted."

"Really? How did you fare?"

The hint of a prideful smile appeared on the dragon's middle face. "I don't notice rifle or machine-gun fire at all—20mm rounds tickled, 45mm antitank fire itched, 76.2mm cannon shots were uncomfortable, and 100mm shells were painful. I halted the testing at that point."

"Very understandable, Your Immensity. Your safety is of the utmost concern. I see they've attached a ballooning basket behind your head. Are the straps comfortable?"

And by that, I mean, will the basket stay attached when we're high in the air?

"They are comfortable. Thank you for your concern." Gorynych shook his middle head violently, sending a scintillating ripple of emerald down his muscular neck. The basket remained in place. He winked. "And as you can see, it is quite secure."

The dragon inquired about Andrei's tank battles. In turn, Andrei learned that Gorynych's combat experience was somewhat dated. He'd last been awake during Catherine the Great's reign.

The general said to show no fear. I hope Gorynych has a sense of humor, or this will be the shortest duty assignment ever.

Andrei pulled a cigarette from a crumpled pack and stuck it between his chapped lips. "Got a light?" he asked, trying not to quake.

Gorynych raised an eyebrow and chuckled, the sound reverberating in Andrei's chest.

By the end of an hour's conversation, he extended Andrei the honor of addressing him by name. At that point, Andrei informed the attendants that they'd begin training.

The enlisted men saluted and hauled open the enormous hangar main doors.

Andrei consulted the written list as they strolled outside.

This is insane.

At his request, Gorynych lowered his middle head. Andrei practiced climbing into the basket and strapping in with carabiners.

Now, how will I explain headings to him? Ah, I know.

Andrei showed Gorynych the orientation of his wristwatch numbers. "Twelve o'clock refers to the direction you're flying, you see? So, three o'clock means turn a quarter circle to the right." The sun warmed his face.

Well, no point in putting it off any longer.

"Shall we try some low-altitude flying?"

"Certainly." Gorynych flapped his enormous wings and leaped into the air.

Andrei's knuckles whitened as he gripped the edge of the basket. *Jesus!*

Gorynych executed the practice turns as directed. Since he was unaccustomed to judging smaller distances, they agreed to use "dragon-lengths" as a way to specify altitude. The dragon proved a quick study.

Once past the shock of the novel experience, Andrei found himself grinning with the exhilaration of flight.

Good thing I'm not scared of heights, not that the general would care.

After a lunch involving meals of considerably different sizes, the pair returned to the skies to practice navigating based on radio communications from the command post, call sign Omega. Last, they practiced silently gliding downward at a steep angle and alighting on the rising slope of a hill.

The summer sun set at 2145. They repeated the navigation exercises in darkness, Andrei relying on his night-vision goggles. At 2230, they landed.

Less than four hours until I ride a dragon into battle. I should get my head checked.

The command post updated Andrei on the last known position of *Mammut*. They reviewed the attack plan again. Afterward, Generalmajór Belsky unnecessarily reminded Andrei of the criticality of the mission. He arranged a late-night steak dinner with fresh vegetables and chocolate cake for dessert.

This reminds me of the last time I took Sofia out for dinner. But this fancy food also feels like a condemned man's last meal. Maybe that's true too.

Andrei retired to his tent to rest, gather himself, and write letters to his parents and Sofia.

"Anyone at home?"

Andrei set down his pencil, grinning at the familiar voice. "Please come in."

Beaming, Majór Makarov entered. "The men of the Thirty-First Tank Company send their best."

Andrei stood and shook his guest's hand. "Thanks. It's great to see a friendly face."

"Even better than my handsome face are these gifts." Makarov hefted a heavy canvas sack. "For good luck."

"How kind." Andrei peered inside. "Rope, a bayonet, a flashlight, and three hand grenades." He raised an eyebrow. "For good luck?"

"Ha. Better to have and not need than to need and not have, eh? I'm sorry I couldn't scrounge a bottle of vodka. For celebrating *after* the mission, of course," he added. "I've no doubt you'll make us all proud."

PROKHOROVKA, SOVIET UNION, JULY 9, 1943

At 0130, Gorynych leaped aloft with Andrei into the moonless sky, ascending quickly to an altitude of fifty dragon-lengths. They hurtled southward for ten minutes, propelled by beats of the dragon's mighty wings. War-ravaged farmland passed swiftly beneath them.

Andrei shivered despite the cold-weather gear.

The radio chattered, "Zmei, this is Omega. You're now south and just east of the target. Make your heading 330 degrees true for a rear intercept. Over."

"Omega, turning to 330 degrees true. Over." Andrei took a breath. "Gorynych, please turn us to five o'clock."

The dragon banked to comply.

"Omega, this is Zmei. Maneuver completed. Over." Suddenly, six floodlight beams blazed upward from a point on the ground two kilometers ahead. *Mammut*! With grinding mechanical steps, the land dreadnought shoved aside mature oak trees like a cow grazing through tall grass.

Its immensity took Andrei's breath away, despite his having seen photos. Tracer fire hurtled skyward. Eight explosions lit the sky at twenty-five hundred meters. "Omega, we have a visual on the target. They're firing their 88s to the north, not at us. Over."

A larger airborne explosion trailed orange flames downward. *Damn, they got one of our bombers.*

Nine groundbursts detonated in front of *Mammut*, hurling dirt skyward. A tenth bomb obliterated a *Flakvierling* turret at the bow, but *Mammut* stomped inexorably forward, crushing a farmhouse under one giant foot.

"Zmei, the bombers have dropped their payloads. Commence your attack. Commence your attack. Acknowledge. Over."

"Omega, commencing attack. Over and out."

"Gorynych, silent dive, please. Land us at those back-edge floodlights."

The dragon folded his wings, stooping like an immense hawk toward the steel behemoth. Cold air buffeted Andrei's face. At an altitude of five dragon-lengths, Gorynych flared his giant wings, rapidly decelerating and rotating his lower body forward. His hind talons slammed into tier five of *Mammut*, smashing two of the floodlights. Momentum rotated his upper body and heads forward. His fore talons grabbed hold of the vehicle's superstructure.

Andrei's restraints tugged violently at his torso, his knees buckling from the jolt.

The thumping of 88s firing skyward continued.

"Gorynych, let's smash the other floodlights. That'll help the surviving bombers escape."

The dragon stomped a floodlight with his right rear foot. Soon all six lights were extinguished.

"Excellent. Now, let's take out its eyes and ears. Destroy the radar dish and radio antennas."

Gorynych scrambled to the starboard side of the superstructure. Extending upward, three sets of powerful jaws made short work of *Mammut*'s sensors and communication gear.

Whomp. Whomp. Whomp. Whomp.

"Ugh!" groaned the dragon. Though gut-wrenching, the impacts failed to pierce his scales.

The four starboard 88mm turrets had rotated to engage the dragon. Fortunately, *Mammut*'s superstructure shielded Gorynych from the portside 88s.

He can survive 88mm hits, but I can't.

"Gorynych, destroy the starboard 88s."

Snarling from the painful strikes, the dragon needed no further encouragement. Nimble as a lizard in a tree, Gorynych reoriented himself downward. His heads lunged, snapping jaws deforming cannon barrels like a child gnawing licorice.

The tart odor of cordite drifted over them. "Well done." Andrei suppressed the urge to pat the dragon. "Their command staff operates from the bridge atop the superstructure. Tear it open." As Gorynych scrambled upward, Andrei glanced over his shoulder.

The four naval gun turrets at the bow are rotating toward us! Dragon armor won't stop those huge rounds.

"Hurry!" His hands trembled.

Gorynych dragged a powerful claw across the superstructure, the deafening fingers-on-chalkboard sound making Andrei wince. The massive talons found no purchase in the tiny visibility slits, nor did they penetrate the thick steel. His long tail whipped in frustration. The dragon tried again.

That's not working.

Andrei cast another glance toward the bow. "Ha. The naval guns are too long for the turrets to slew all the way astern!"

Bullets whizzing upward past his head dispelled Andrei's momentary feeling of relief. Two intrepid German crewmen had opened a hatch below Gorynych's line of sight, shooting their pistols at Andrei.

He ducked. *7.62mm bullets can make me just as dead as a 380mm artillery shell.*

His eyes fell on Makarov's gift. An incongruous smile cracked his face.

You clever bastard.

Andrei withdrew two grenades, pulled the pins, and tossed them down at the Germans.

Blam. Blam.

The pistol fire ceased.

Bam!

Gorynych bellowed in pain, so loud it rattled the basket and stunned Andrei.

He ran his gaze along the length of the dragon. The explosion had shredded the tip of the dragon's tail. It dripped green gore.

Damn. The short-barreled 380mm rocket-propelled mortar turrets can rotate fully astern. We're out of time.

The dragon roared, flailing its wings in agony.

Bam!

The second mortar shot blasted a gaping hole in the leathery membrane of Gorynych's right wing. Tattered skin fluttered like curtains in a breeze.

No!

Bam! The mortar shell missed the writhing dragon, hurtling upward into the distance.

Bam! The fourth shot struck Gorynych in the left shoulder, shattering scales and blasting chunks of flesh into gory hail. He roared like thunder, but his left wing hung limp. In agony, the dragon breathed a gout of fire skyward.

That's it!

"Gorynych, breathe fire into the open hatch that's at your waist level. Then we must flee."

Bam! The round blew off the dragon's left head. It's neck spasmed like a decapitated snake.

Roar! The dragon shivered and gasped. "No, Andrei. It is you who must flee. My time is nearly at an end."

Andrei's throat tightened; his mouth formed a thin line.

There's nothing I can do for you now.

He unhooked his harness from the balloon basket and seized the coiled rope. Tying one end to the basket, he tossed the line over the side.

Will it reach the ground?

Strength fading, the dragon backed down the face of the superstructure until his head drew even with the open hatch.

Gloves protecting his hands from burns, Andrei slid to the end of the rope. His feet dangled in the air. He muttered a quick prayer and let go, falling the last five meters to the soft earth.

Bam! The blast shattered Gorynych's right rear foot. He

roared again—this time tinged with fury. As he slipped downward, he arched his middle neck.

Oh, brave comrade.

Andrei turned and sprinted through tall grass toward a nearby pine forest.

Gorynych belched a torrent of hellfire through the open hatch like an enraged volcano, the burst of flame so intense it melted steel.

Bam!

No!

The dead dragon tumbled off *Mammut*. The impact shook the ground.

Andrei ran until a series of earthshaking explosions knocked him down.

He did it! Gorynych ignited the ammo in Mammut*'s magazine.*

He dove behind a fallen tree trunk as shrapnel fell like rain.

Mammut became a metallic funeral pyre, flickering flames honoring the last dragon's sacrifice.

The grass caught fire. Amid the overwhelming odors of brimstone, cordite, and burning diesel, Andrei fled the burgeoning firestorm.

Tears ran down his cheeks. *Poor Comrade Gorynych. Mountains of flesh and steel have destroyed each other. Mother Russia is saved, though at great cost.*

BEST BEHAVE

ANN DÁVILA CARDINAL

SALERNO, ITALY, SEPTEMBER 1943

In the shadow of the cathedral's damaged colonnade, Jorge pulled his helmet lower on his head and wrapped his arms around his body, trying, and failing, to get warm. But how could he complain about the cold? After they'd secured the city's beachhead a few days earlier, his regiment had followed behind the British troops, moving into the city. For a few hours, it looked like the Germans were going to maintain control with their well-placed machine-gun posts and tanks. But when the paratroopers dropped into the city, and the Allied forces surged behind, instead of a fight, they found hundreds of German soldiers skewered through their bellies. Jorge and his friend Miguel had been posted at the cathedral, and when they did their initial sweep, they found a live German soldier hiding in the bell tower near a dead comrade, his eyes wild, repeating what sounded like "boots man" over and over. They carted him away, and the city had been quiet since.

Yes, Jorge knew he'd gotten off easy; he hadn't even discharged his gun.

He shivered again. It was torturous, however, that he could smell the sea and see mountains in the distance like at home in Puerto Rico, but in Salerno it was so fucking cold. Not to mention that it had been raining for two days straight. "What happened to sunny Italy?" he grumbled, already forgetting his pledge to not complain about the temperature.

"Nah, hombre," a voice said from the shadows. "They actually have seasons here."

Jorge jumped a bit: he thought he was alone in the darkened church courtyard, the sun having only just peaked over the eastern horizon. "Well, this one feels like winter."

"I'm here to relieve you. Go get warm," Miguel said, slapping his friend on the shoulder.

"Thanks, man. You get any sleep last night?"

"Slept like the dead. Especially after downing a half a bottle of limoncello with Williams and his crew."

Just the mention of the man's name made Jorge's skin crawl. "Where the hell did he get that?"

"I don't know. Some old man's wine cellar, I think. All I do know is, my head feels like it's in a vise."

Jorge stood for a bit, kicking his boot at loose stones on the ground. Williams was always showing off some delicacy or treasure that he then tucked away into his locked trunk like a damn pirate. Jorge didn't trust the Texan, especially since he never seemed to answer when asked where he got all the goodies. He worried about his friend spending time with him. He didn't say anything though: Miguel was a grown man, after all. "Well, not much going on here, so it should be quiet for you."

"*Perfecto.* See you at mess tonight?"

Jorge shrugged. "I got no place else to be. See you later, man." He stepped out of the shade of the half roof and was surprised to enter a rare patch of morning sun. Eyes closed, he lifted his face to the light and breathed deep. He could almost imagine he was on his family's land in Toa Baja, the sweet green smell of trees in the rain, the screech of seagulls overhead. A cart tumbled off a curb with a loud clatter, yanking him back to chilly Salerno. He sighed and headed east toward the barracks.

A block from the cathedral, he caught the slight scent of lavender on the morning air, then saw the familiar head of coiffed gray hair, string bags of groceries dangling from arthritic hands. He hustled up next to the woman, slinging the rifle over his back. "Signora Acheros, let me help you."

The old lady started a bit when he appeared at her side, but when she saw Jorge's face, she smiled. "Oh, Jorge. Thank you, young man." She handed over the two bags, and her tiny, hunched body sprang back as if released. "Can you come over for some *caffè*? I baked fresh cornettos this morning." They managed to communicate quite well—she with her Italian, and he with his Caribbean Spanish—and besides, baked goods were a universal language.

"Oh, you sure know the way to this soldier's heart!" He smiled big and followed the old woman to her second-floor apartment on Via Benedetto, a few blocks from the cathedral. He'd met her the first day in town when she appeared at his post in the colonnade. Rosary in hand, she had looked around the half-destroyed church with tears damming her eyelids and her shoulders set, as if preparing to weather a blow. She had reminded him so much of his own *abuela* back home, drawn to the church as if it were a magnet, especially during those dark times for her war-torn city. They'd stood and spoken for an hour that day, mostly about what it had been like for her to stay through the German occupation, and then the retaking of the city just a few weeks before, days she'd spent curled up in her bathtub, shaking with her elderly cat.

He set the bags on her neat-as-a-pin wooden counter, the sweet, yeasty smell of freshly baked bread a balm for his homesick heart. He started to empty the bags and put away the precious staples—flour, sugar, and butter—but she gently slapped his hand away.

"*Sedere, sedere.* Sit there, my son. I'll bring you some *caffè*."

He sat at the small table in the window, the embroidered white tablecloth worn, but perfectly ironed. He didn't think Mrs. Acheros had much, but she took immaculate care of what she did have.

She shuffled over on her orthopedic shoes and set a steaming cup of café con leche in front of him, the creamy, nutty scent reaching for him like a handshake from home. She also brought a small china plate with a horn-shaped pastry and a dollop of electric-green pistachio crema cuddled in the center. She always placed the silverware last, laying it gently on the worn linen napkins. He picked up the delicate spoon and examined it. It looked handmade, the silver lovingly polished, a crescent moon nestled in the bottom of the handle, a bloodred crystal in its center. "I've been meaning to ask you about these. They're really unusual. Are they old?"

She laughed. "Oh yes, dear. Way older than even me! They've been in my family for generations." She busied herself setting up her own plate. "When we heard the Germans were coming, and my neighbors tried to talk me into fleeing, this set was the first thing I would have packed. Well, that and my mother's Bible." She sat down with a small groan and a sigh.

"Why *didn't* you leave?" He hadn't asked her that yet, thought it best to just let her talk given what she'd gone through just a few short weeks before, but it had been gnawing at him.

She took some time to answer, chewing her pastry, thinking. Finally, "Because I've always lived here in this city. My people are buried not two kilometers from here. I would not leave my home just because men in faraway countries feel they have the right to take and bomb wherever and whomever they please."

Jorge wasn't certain if she was referring to the Nazis or the Allied forces or both, since men from both sides had been deciding the fate of the small seaside city, but either way, he understood her frustration. He was from the longest-lasting colony in the history of the world, one that had been invaded during his grandfather's lifetime by the very country for which he was now forced to fight. So he stayed quiet instead, just enjoying her company. Sitting in that kitchen with her, he could almost forget they were in the middle of a war. Until he looked closer and saw the layer of dust that settled each day on the windowsills, microscopic pieces of bombed-out stone, shrapnel, and dead bodies.

"This is delicious, Signora. Thank you."

She waved him away as she took a sip from her own cup. "I am so happy to have the company, Jorge." She looked out the window, her rheumy eyes far away. "These are hard times." Then she looked back at him, and her eyes cleared. Suddenly, they were piercing and dark. "But I've seen so much worse."

The town in which she was born and raised had been overtaken by German soldiers, then half destroyed when the Allied forces retook the strategic city, their generals hungering for the city's rails and port facilities. Access like that can decide the outcome of modern warfare. So he couldn't imagine how the old woman could have lived through anything worse, but he let it be and took another sip of his coffee. He'd learned young that people can surprise you with what they bury in their hearts.

"How are things going? Are you getting along with the other soldiers?"

He couldn't help but grin, it was like when he came home from his first day of school. "Well, with my regiment, yes. The

Sixty-Fifth Infantry is all men from Puerto Rico. And the British and Americans are fine. But there is one guy, Williams . . . well, let's just say I don't trust him. I think he's doing some bad things."

"Ah yes. Evil always sticks its bony fingers into someone, doesn't it? But I trust that those people get what they deserve in this life."

He looked at her then, surprised by her words and the tone of her voice, the dark glint of her eyes returned. She always seemed so gentle and pious—"may the Lord forgive them" kind of thing—so this outburst seemed uncharacteristic, a glimpse of darkness under the talcum-powdered, lace-covered exterior. Then again, his *abuela* was similar. She was very hard to make angry, but all the kids knew, when you did, you best get out of the way. He chuckled again to himself.

"Something amuse you, young man?" she asked with a one-sided smile.

He shook his head. "Nothing. It's just . . . when you were talking about bad people getting what they deserve, you reminded me of my grandmother and something she used to say."

"Oh, she must be so worried about you being in the middle of all this danger."

Jorge swallowed. "She passed, right after I shipped out. I couldn't even go to her funeral." And just like that, the scab was pulled off, and the wound bled again. He didn't want to bleed anymore.

As if she sensed it, the old woman brought the subject back around. "What did she used to say?"

He smiled. "She would shake her finger at us when we were kids and say, 'You best behave, or El Cuco is going to get you.'"

She tilted her silver head. "El Cuco?"

"He's like the boogeyman. When we were up to no-good, we were threatened with his wrath. It used to terrify us."

"Ah! We have the same being here, he's called the Babau. My father would make a knocking sound under the table and tell us he was at the door, coming to get us if we didn't clean up or get to bed."

"Why did adults feel the need to terrify us so?"

"I think in part because parents have much less power than they would like. And to teach us right from wrong, I imagine." She took the last sip of her coffee; both plates now held only crumbs.

They sat in companionable silence for a bit, the sun higher in the sky outside the dusty window. "Well, I better get some sleep before my next watch. Let me help you clean—" Jorge stood and reached for the plates.

The swatting again. "Don't you dare. What else am I going to do with my morning?" She slapped his cheek gently, then grabbed a hunk of flesh and twisted. He wondered if they taught all old ladies in every Latin culture to do that. "You're a good boy, Jorge. Thank you for helping me with my groceries and keeping an old lady company."

He smiled, a part of him melting, just a little, at the thought of making his *abuela* proud. "You're keeping *me* company, Signora. You make me feel more at home. *Grazie.*"

As he walked down the narrow apartment stairs, he rubbed his cheek where the echo of her pinch throbbed, and smiled.

He woke to the sound of laughter. Jorge shook his head to try and clear sleep from his brain. He hated being greeted by the makeshift barrack's smell of sweat, bad breath, and flatulence upon waking each evening.

"What the fuck are these, Williams?"

"I don't know. They're weird as hell, but solid silver."

"You got a whole set?"

"Yeah."

Jorge sat up and held his head in his hands. His mouth was cottony, and his head throbbed like it had its own heart. He looked at the clock on the wall—two hours until his next watch. He peeled off his socks; they seemed to have rotted to his now pale feet after the days and days of guard duty in the rain. He let them sit in the air for a moment, examining them for signs of trench foot.

Kevin, one of Williams's buddies, was waving something at Miguel, making cackling witch sounds. The guy's voice was like a fork stabbing the inside of Jorge's skull. He stood up and stretched his back, then grabbed clean, dry socks.

"Man, get that shit away from me! Jorge, back me up here. This is some voodoo Santeria shit, no?" Miguel called to him from across the room.

"Santa-what?" Kevin laughed.

Jorge finished tying his boots in no particular hurry, then made his way over. "What *mierda* are you guys talking so loudly about when some of us are trying to sleep?"

"This shit Williams got is giving me the creeps. These guys don't believe me, but you'll get it."

The minute Jorge saw the spoon in Kevin's hand, a fire roared to life in his stomach.

It was from Mrs. Acheros's set.

"Where's Williams?" he asked, eyes narrowed, the fire licking his chest now.

"I don't know, man. What's wrong with—"

Jorge lurched over and grabbed Kevin by the front of his uniform shirt, one of the buttons popping off and flying across the room like a period at the end of a sentence. "Where's Williams?" he screamed into the freckled, smug face.

"Jesus, Jorge! He—he's talking to the lieutenant!"

Jorge dropped him and ran out of the building, Miguel calling his name behind. His mind and heart galloped as he ran, his boots hitting the pavement with clean *thunks*. He had to make sure she was okay first; he would deal with Williams soon enough. The building door was open, and he took the stairs two at a time, shoving open the apartment door with his entire body weight.

She was sitting in one of the living room's worn, upholstered chairs, her fingers to her forehead where a bruise was forming. He dropped to his knees next to her. "Signora!" Her eyes seemed distant, like she heard him but couldn't see him there. "Signora, are you all right?"

"Y-yes, I think so." She looked over at him. "Oh! Jorge. I'm so glad it's you."

Taking her soft, papery-skinned hands in his, he smelled her comforting lavender scent, but also the salty tang of fear. "Did he hurt you?"

"No, I'm all right. I just tried to stop him when he took my family's silver, and he shoved me to the floor. I-I must have hit my head." She looked around, as if there would be a mark somewhere.

Jorge's rage fire flared again, into his neck now, licking at the bottom of his throat. He looked around the apartment, saw all the drawers in every room hanging open as if in shock, chairs turned over, juice spilled all over the kitchen's tiled floor.

"It was right after you left. I heard a knock at the door, and I thought it was you—that you'd forgotten something." She looked into Jorge's eyes, and he thought his heart would burst. "But this big man, red hair and angry eyes, he pushed his way in and started pulling apart my whole house." She indicated around the apartment with her bony hands.

Jorge gently pulled them into his again, like small birds he wanted to shield from a predator. "It was Williams, Signora. The guy I told you about. But I will get your silverware back. I swear to you."

Her eyes got big and scared then. "Oh no! Son, you must not do that. Men like him are dangerous. They have no morality or beliefs to guide them. They are capable of anything."

His eyes filled then. She was worried about *him*? She had just gotten robbed by the very men who were supposed to be protecting her, and she's concerned about *his* safety. He spoke through a tightened throat. "Don't worry, Signora. I'll deal with Williams."

The black filled her eyes again. "No, Jorge. Promise me you'll stay out of this. I don't want you to get hurt. Good people are always the ones who get hurt by men like him."

He brought her flower-scented hands to his lips and kissed them gently. "I'm sorry, *Abuela*." He didn't correct the error—in that moment, she was his grandmother. "But I can't promise you that." He stood and left, being sure to lock the apartment door behind him.

He wasn't even aware of the walk back to the mess hall. He began to run as he got closer, heat blaring throughout his body, the flames lighting the back of his eyes. He wanted to kill Williams. To choke him and watch the life slowly seep out of his body, then drop his vile corpse to the floor. But he knew that would break his grandmother's heart. But he would make him pay.

He was breathing heavily when he barreled into the mess hall, hundreds of pairs of eyes looking up upon his dramatic entrance.

"Afraid to miss the shit on a shingle, Guzman?" a private asked.

Jorge saw Williams standing with his tray near a central table and stalked over. When he got to the redheaded Texan, he drew his arm back and punched him full on the jaw, the tray contents tumbling and splashing all over, knocking the big man to the ground.

There was a beat of stunned silence, then the volume in the room rose in a wave, guys whooping and yelling and making bets, entertained for the first time in a week. Jorge ignored them and yanked on Williams's shirt.

"What the fuck is wrong with you, Guzman?" the man asked, wiping his sleeve across his bleeding mouth.

"You're stealing from them! You're stealing from these people we're supposed to protect!"

Williams shook him off, then stumbled to his feet. "You're crazy. I have no idea what you're talking about." He looked around at the other men; the whole hall was listening to this like it was a weekly radio broadcast, and they needed to know what happened next.

"You robbed her! Shoved an old woman to the goddamn floor!"

Williams's eyes lit with understanding, and an evil grin lifted the edges of his mouth. "Ah! You're sweet on the old broad. You doing her, Guzman? Gotta thing for old ladies like your grandma—"

Jorge threw himself on Williams then with a loud growl, both of them falling to the floor. He windmilled his arms, punching anywhere he could, determined to beat the man senseless, but then hands were pulling him up, setting him on his feet again, and he was trying to yank his arms free, trying to hit that red, evil face just one more time. But then the lieutenant appeared and stood between them.

"All right, children, break it up. Would one of you like to tell me just what the hell is going on here?"

Williams glared. "Beats me, sir. Ask Guzman."

Jorge's mind was galloping. What was the right thing to do?

Telling on the fucking guy, probably, but soldiers didn't snitch on each other, ever. He narrowed his eyes and shot fire at the Texan. "Nothing, sir. We just have different opinions about who is going to win the World Series this week."

A grin slowly spread across Williams's face, like some sort of cartoon villain. "Yeah, Lieutenant. Everyone knows the Yankees suck. Everyone but George here."

Jorge let out a slow breath. "Sir, may I be dismissed? I have guard duty starting at 2130."

"Dismissed!"

Jorge lit another cigarette. He wasn't even sure he wanted one, but the whole scene with Williams had left him on edge. He would find a way to get him back, but that night he just needed to get through his watch.

To pass the time, he thought about the night before he shipped out. He and his cousin Victor had gotten all suited up and went to see Rafael Muñoz and his orchestra at the Escambrón Beach Club in San Juan. It cost them a small fortune, but Jorge had spent the entire night dancing with a girl from Guaynabo, a tiny-waisted thing in a green silk dress who he was certain he'd never see again. But that one night had been perfect, like a dream.

A stone suddenly skittered across the courtyard, waking him up from his memory, and he whipped his rifle from back to front.

"Who's there?" His voice sounded loud in the empty colonnade.

Nothing.

Just the distant sound of a truck starting up and the slow music of low tide.

Jorge lowered his gun and leaned back against the column. Then, one by one, figures stepped to the side of the other columns around the square—four, five, seven men. One stepped out in front, and Jorge knew who it was despite the deep midnight shadows. He relaxed, but only a little. At least they weren't Germans, but Jorge figured he was about to get the beating of his life.

"What can I do for you, Williams?" he asked, his voice sounding casual and annoyed, though his guard was more than up.

"You can learn to mind your own damn business, George."

The bastard knew how much he hated when he anglicized his name, but Jorge wouldn't let it distract him. "It's wrong to steal from these people, and you know it."

Williams was closer now, just a step between them. "Do I?" He looked around at his cronies, who were moving in beside him. "Men, do we know it's wrong?"

Disparate mumbling from the others.

"We're supposed to protect these people, not steal from them."

"And why should I protect them?"

"So you admit it? The stealing?" If only he'd said all this in front of their lieutenant, but the guy was too smart for that.

Williams stepped closer, until his face was inches from Jorge's, his breath stinking of cheap whiskey and stale cigarettes. "I didn't sign up to stand around and guard an empty fucking town!" He pointed in some random inland direction, and yelled, "I should be where the fighting is! Up front, killing Krauts, but instead they got me babysitting fucking civilians in this bullshit backwater town!"

"Oh, so you think you're owed something? Is that it?"

"Hell yes, I am! Spoils of war."

"What? Are you kidding me?"

Williams poked his beefy finger into Jorge's chest, hard.

"I'm not gonna take the chance that you'll rat to the lieutenant, so me and the boys are here to shut you up . . . permanently."

Jorge realized he wasn't just in for a beating. Maybe he wouldn't see another day. He knew it was in his best interest to keep his mouth shut, but it was almost as if he couldn't control it any longer. "Go to hell, Williams. I'm not afraid of you," he said in the calmest voice imaginable. In his head, he recited the Our Father in Spanish, over and over, working his *abuela*'s rosary beads in his mind as if he actually held them.

Williams pulled something out of his pocket, touched a button, and a long switchblade snicked out, glistening in the moonlight.

They were too close for him to use his rifle, and he had no time to draw his M1 bayonet from its scabbard hanging at his waist. He managed to get one good whack in at the side of Williams's head with the butt of his rifle, but Williams caught his jaw with an uppercut that made his skull ring, the pain flaring behind his eyes. Jorge wrapped a few fingers around the Texan's knife, and they wrestled for a bit, but slowly he watched his arm twist, the feeling of tendons pulling, then snapping like overstretched rubber bands, shooting flames of pain up his arms and into his chest. He tried to wrestle with one arm, but soon dizziness flooded his brain, and he was overpowered, his back against the column, the marble ridges digging into his back.

Fuck. Was this how he was to die and join his *abuela*? Killed at the hands of this yahoo who was supposed to be fighting on the same side? He had never expected to make it home, but to die this way was insult to fatal injury.

As Williams drew the knife back, a loud knocking sound echoed in the plaza.

All the men looked around, eyes wide. Williams froze, switchblade held up next to Jorge's face. "What the fuck was that?"

His eyes turned back to Jorge, and in that moment, the Texan lurched forward, falling into his opponent. Jorge pushed him off, watching Williams stagger, blood dripping from the side of his mouth. He stared wide-eyed into Williams's rigid face as it rose, the big man's feet leaving the ground, dangling like those of a hanged man. Darkness spread across Williams's belly. The other men slowly backed away, faces distorted with fear and panic.

A high-pitched squealing filled the air, and Williams's eyes were almost all whites, the muscles in his face lax with complete and utter terror. Jorge stepped aside to see what had the Texan, but all he saw was blackness. Not like a shadow: void of anything. Like when his little sister cut out paper dolls, and all that remained were people-shaped empty spaces, beings defined by what surrounded them, not the lack of what was within.

Jorge was rooted in place, sounds of Williams's former accomplices fleeing, their childlike screams trailing behind them. He could only stare, terror freezing through his legs, forbidding their movement.

The blackness shoved harder through Williams's stomach, blood and entrails spilling out onto the stones of the courtyard as wet choking noises gurgled from the man's bleeding mouth. Williams suddenly dropped to the ground, like a bored child's plaything, his disemboweled body now resting in a pool of glistening blood.

Jorge spun around, worried he was next, but there was nothing there, not even a void. He stepped over the now still Williams and looked around the colonnade. Whatever the being had been, it was gone.

He knew then what had killed the Germans, how they had died.

He shook himself as if he could clear the whole scene from

his head; he had to report this ASAP, though what he would say, he didn't know.

As Jorge turned to leave, he stiffened as he caught it, rising through the metallic smell of fresh blood. Just a small whiff on the cooling night air.

The delicate scent of lavender.

A TERRIBLE ASPECT

JONATHAN MABERRY

MONTE CASSINO, ITALY, APRIL 1944

The killer crouched in the darkness of a tree.

Dense purple shadows hid him from the soldiers, but they did not hide the soldiers from him. He was as still and silent as the starlit sky, as cold and patient as the moon. His clothes were black, his face hidden behind a balaclava, his eyes invisible behind the lenses of dark goggles. That he could see with clarity despite those lenses was peculiar to him. Anyone else would be blind.

Crickets pulsed in the darkness, indifferent to the soldiers who patrolled the vineyards and walkways around the monastery. Nightjars called to one another, and swifts danced with bats overhead.

The killer, who was currently going by the code name Deacon, heard the birds and the small night rodents, but his attention was focused on the line of trucks that had come up Route 6 all the way from Rome. They were parked with the precision the Germans loved. Two soldiers stood guard with each, one in front, the other in back, both with rifles slung, the barrels around front but pointed down.

Although the soldiers were well trained, that training was intended to stop partisans or Allied commandos. It was not the kind of training that would stop him.

In the darkness, Deacon smiled.

The soldiers worked well into the night, bringing items out of the monastery in an endless stream of small carts and hand trucks. The sentries watched as these things were checked off inventory sheets and then loaded with haste but with great care into the backs of the trucks. Filling the vehicles one at a time.

Precise.

Always precise.

Deacon appreciated this. Precision was a large part of his life, but he was acutely aware that precision and predictability often went hand in hand. Predictability was a very dangerous trait, and it was a chink in the armor of those whose arrogance is propped up by a belief in their own power.

Such beliefs were being challenged, however. Had *been* challenged. Leningrad and Kursk both spoke truth to that power.

Deacon lowered himself from his perch and landed silently on the soft grass. He carried no long gun, preferring a silenced .22 pistol. Lightweight, quiet, and the rounds were sensible for his line of work. They would pierce a skull but lacked the force to exit, which meant that bullet would bounce around inside and do terrible work. Very little mess and extremely reliable. He had knives in various places, including a Corsican throwing-knife in a rear-collar sheath.

He made his way up the slope toward the monastery at the top of Monte Cassino, picking the most difficult route because it made foot patrols awkward. There were lookout posts tucked into the slopes all around the monastery, but he knew how to avoid them.

The monastery's location was a critical part of the German winter defensive line, blocking any Allied march on Rome. The OSS had gotten word to him that the place was to be heavily bombed on the fifteenth. It was just after midnight, which left him only a few hours to accomplish one or both parts of his mission.

One—what the OSS had assigned him—was to find and kill any senior officers billeted there and to collect proof of death. Picking through rubble after tens of thousands of pounds of bombs were dropped was time-consuming and held little likelihood of success. Deacon personally believed the entire plan of dropping those bombs was absurd. Yes, there were Germans at the monastery, but he did not for a minute believe it was an actual command center of great worth.

So, to Deacon, the bombing was of secondary importance, and its impending reality was wildly inconvenient because it endangered his *actual* mission. One self-assigned and with no information shared with the OSS or any office.

His real goal was to find a certain man, *SS-Oberführer* Conrad Schmidt. Not any ordinary officer, but a key player in a special and very secret division called the Ariosophists. Like the Thule Society, they were dedicated to the search for weapons that did not involve bullets or bombs. Dangerous and ancient weapons that could give the failing Third Reich a new lease on life.

His war was personal and also very important, even if history books would never record it. Some things, he knew, were better left out of the public knowledge, and so he fought his war in shadows, both real and metaphorical.

Deacon climbed to the top of the slope, and there he paused to survey the building. The abbey was ancient, and it felt that way. Built in 529—more than fourteen centuries ago—it held its secrets within thick walls. No building that old was only stone and wood. Life bled into the materials, imbuing it with a kind of life that most can feel but not understand.

He understood. He was old too. Far older than he looked. And time had left its marks on him.

At the sound of boots on gravel, Deacon went totally still, pulling his energy into himself, projecting nothing. It was like being nowhere. With nothing on any level to pull their attention, two soldiers on foot patrol passed within a yard of him.

Deacon lay still until they were gone, and then he was gone—up and over the edge, running low and fast toward the closest wall, fading against it, sticking to the shadows. He found the entrance he wanted at a far corner, a small window set low and hidden by flowers. It took him less than four minutes to quietly pry the nails from the wood and remove the frame. Then he slid inside and pulled the frame back into place.

But as he did so, he paused, then lowered the frame. Something had tickled the very edge of his awareness, and he went very still, slowing his breath and channeling all his consciousness into the senses of sight, hearing, and, to a lesser degree, smell.

What was it? What had moved out there in the night?

He looked across the flat ground. It was bare. Then he shifted and leaned out to see the topmost guard post that had been cut into the very top of the hill.

His breath caught.

There had been two helmeted heads just visible over the edge. Now there were none.

The night sounds had all stopped. Even the crickets and

nightjars. There were still the sounds of men talking and the creak of laden carts, but nature itself held its breath.

Something *was* out there. Whatever it was, nature responded to it differently than it did to him, or to the German soldiers. Few things could do that. Usually, it was either a sudden loud sound—of which there had been none—or the entry into the area of a large predator.

He sniffed the night air, and it brought its olio of odors—the fecundity of animals in mating season, vibrant and rotting vegetation, scat of a dozen kinds.

And . . .

There was another scent, nearly hidden beneath the aromas of plants and flowers and newly dug earth. Rich, vibrant, exuding power. But also unusual for this part of Italy.

Dog, he thought at first, but changed that opinion on a second inhalation. The scent was too intense for a dog.

Wolf . . . ?

There were wolves in the Apennine Mountains. Small and rare, usually of about seventy pounds, with a few males heavier than that. He'd seen them, long before the war. But this . . . did not smell like those.

Or, at least, not true Italian mountain wolves. There was an underlying quality that suggested greater size and greater power. Closer to what he had felt when in the presence of Alaskan gray wolf and the Eurasian wolf. They had a similar presence even when sensed rather than seen.

This scent, he realized, was stronger still.

Deacon stood in the inky darkness of the basement, peering out at ground level, watching the shadows. It took a while, but then he saw a piece of those shadows detach itself and creep from one lightless spot to another.

A wolf for sure.

He felt his blood run cold though.

It was a wolf, without a doubt, so . . . why was it running on two feet?

The wolf moved as quickly as caution allowed.

It was not as massive as Deacon thought at first, and yet the power it exuded was towering. Halfway across the flat clearing between the guard post and the monastery, it suddenly dropped down to all fours, hunkering belly-down on the grass, ears lifted to tufted points, nose twitching as it took in the air. Then it turned its face toward one wall. Toward one ground-level basement window.

Starlight turned its eyes a luminous blue-white, and even from forty feet away, Deacon could feel the impact of that stare. Cold and deep. He knew for certain that it *saw* him.

Part of him wanted to replace the frame and vanish into the interior of the ancient building. Part of him wanted to watch to see what might happen next. There were glistening black stains on the animal's muzzle. Blood, turned black by the pale heavenly light.

It was hunting.

It was killing. And it was not doing it the way wolves typically did. Even a lone wolf made noise—growls and snarls as it attacked. Nor were there any screams.

Deacon found that very interesting.

Without entirely knowing why he did it, he moved closer to the window. Allowing himself to be more clearly seen. Exhaling a deep chestful of air, giving scent to the wind to carry to the beast.

Then he walked backward from the window.

He drew his pistol with his right hand and held it down at his side. He slipped a V-42 stiletto with his left. Then he waited.

Nearly a full minute passed with no movement or sound.

And then, all at once, something came in through the window. It moved with the fluid grace of water spilling over a cliff edge, seeming to flow shapelessly and puddle on the shadowy floor. He could make out no detail at all except a complete awareness that it had entered and was there at the base of the wall. He could feel it watching him, though he could not tell if it saw his weapons and understood its peril.

But then the shape changed, rising up from the stone floor, filling out into definite form. Deacon nearly raised his pistol but did not fire. It took quite a lot of effort to stand still and present at least a facade of calm.

Even standing erect, the figure was in silhouette, nearly invisible against the dark wall. It was not standing on all fours, that much he could tell. Nor was it a very tall shape. Short for a man.

Then Deacon cocked his head to one side as he reconsidered. Short for a man. Tall for a woman.

"Who are you?" he said quietly in Italian. He did not whisper, because the sibilant *S* sounds carried farther than ordinary words spoken softly.

A voice replied after a moment. Deep, but only deep for a woman. It was not a man's voice. There was a rasp to the tone. "Don't you mean *what* am I?"

Her accent was not Roman, but closer to that of extreme northeastern Italy, with a faint veneer of Austrian and Slovakian.

"No," he said. "I think we both know what you are."

"And what is that?"

"Do I need to say the words?"

"If you know them, yes."

"*La donna lupo*," he murmured.

The woman took a small half step forward, and now he could see her eyes. There was no light inside the basement room, and the starlight was only visible through the open window behind her, and yet . . . he could see her eyes. Luminescent. Blue-white and entirely unnatural.

"You are not afraid of me," she said.

"I am, actually," said Deacon.

"Not really."

He smiled. "Not really."

She sniffed the air. "You are not Italian. Nor German either."

"No."

"I cannot easily tell what you are," said the woman. "And that is a rare thing."

"We are each different from the rest." He gestured to the building, as if to indicate both the monks and the occupying Germans.

After a moment, she nodded. "We are different from many."

"We are."

She moved forward another step, and it was immediately clear that she was naked. Her body was strongly made, lean, with broad shoulders and hips, a narrow waist, legs as trim and taut as a dancer's. There were scars on her skin, and Deacon could see the marks of whip and blade, bullet and—he thought—arrows.

The woman watched his eyes and touched one of the deeper, older scars. Then she sniffed the air again. "We both have scars," she said.

"We do."

"And we are both, I think, older than we appear. I certainly am."

"As am I."

Another sniff. "You are far older than you look. You may

even be older than me. You know what I am, but I wonder . . . what *are* you?"

"Does it matter?"

She smiled. Her teeth were white and very sharp. "That will depend on why you're here."

Deacon raised his pistol, glanced at it, and then looked at her as he slid it back into its holster. He sheathed his knife as well. "This is one of those awkward moments," he said. "Neither of us knows which side the other is on."

"I think you can guess who I hunt," she said. There were traces of blood on her lips and chin.

Then something occurred to Deacon. "You are *benandanti*, aren't you?"

Something like a mixture of surprise and amusement spread across her face. She lifted one eyebrow. "And what do you know of the *benandanti*?"

"Rumors," he admitted. "Old stories."

"And *what* stories have you heard?"

He sensed that this was more than a question. He saw lines of tension in the muscles of her thighs, and the nails on each hand seemed oddly long. Longer than they had been a moment ago. He regretted sheathing his knife.

"There are stories of them going back many centuries," he said, subtly shifting his weight to the balls of his feet in case he needed to move very fast. "The 'good walkers.' Old families, some going back to Etruscan times, who claimed to transform into monsters in order to hunt evil creatures."

"Evil against evil?"

"No. Primal forces against evil," Deacon said. "Theriomorphs who take the shape of forest hunters."

"Wolves," she said softly, using one fingernail to scratch a line on the top of a heavy wooden packing crate. A spiral of wood rose up where her nail had passed, and the gouge was very deep.

"Yes," he murmured. "Or something like it. It was no wolf I saw outside."

There were strange lights in the eyes above her broad smile. "So why, then, am I here?"

Before he could answer, a sound—distant, carried by echoes—reached them. It was a cry. Humanlike, but not human. Canine-like, but not a dog or wolf. It was something in between, and it was in terrible pain.

They listened as the scream rose, rose, lingered, and then fell away with the sudden drop of a person so exhausted by pain that even screams of any duration were too difficult to sustain. Deacon saw the flicker of empathetic pain in her eyes.

"That is why you're here," said Deacon. "Have the Nazis taken one of your kind?"

"Not the Nazis," she said, the lines of her face straining. "The Ariosophists."

With the Americans in the war and the Allies in France as well as Italy, the Germans' dreams of conquest were crumbling. The Thule Society was one of the covert groups searching the world for items of supernatural power. Another group, less well known but equally dangerous, were the Ariosophists, esoterics who were less concerned with finding relics and holy objects and more focused on finding living *examples* of the supernatural.

"I am very familiar with them," said Deacon. "I encountered a group in the mountains of Ukraine who were trying to find a true *upyr*. Their hope was to curse or infect—I do not know which word truly applies—a group of SS commandos and use them as a new and unstoppable form of shock troops."

Again, her eyebrow lifted. "I heard that an entire SS *Totenkopf* regiment was slaughtered in that region."

"Not quite a regiment," he corrected.

"That was you?"

Deacon merely shrugged. "I suspect you are here on a similar mission."

"What makes you think so?" she asked.

"That scream sounded human," he said, "but only on the surface. There is a quality in it that is more animal than man."

After a brief pause, she merely said, "Yes."

"Are you here to prevent the SS from doing with your kind what they tried to do with vampires in Ukraine?"

"Oh yes. Believe me—you would not want a pack of SS wolves hunting you."

"The thought is genuinely terrifying," said Deacon. "So, please tell me . . . how does it work? Is it from a bite? Is it a kind of infection?"

She shook her head. "It is a gift. It cannot be taken. We must do something."

A scream, short but heartbreaking, tore through the air.

Deacon held up a hand. "If that man is what I suspect he is, then there is still time, and we need to settle matters between us."

She shifted slightly, glancing past him and then back. A curt nod was her only answer.

"What do the SS want with him?" asked Deacon. "Are they hoping to coerce him into bestowing that gift? Can it be tortured out of someone like you?"

"Yes," she said. And he could hear from the pain in her voice how much that answer cost her. "It has been done before. We stopped it once at a great cost. We must stop it now."

"Then it will be stopped," he assured her.

"Is that why you are here?" she asked, giving him a penetrating look.

"In a way," he said. "I am not hunting for *upyr*, nor *benandanti*."

"What then?"

"I am hunting for a man. A very important man whose death would shorten this war by many months. A high-ranking officer whom the Allies think is merely organizing the defense against an Allied invasion of Rome. But he is far more than that. In reality, he is a devoted member of the Ariosophists and has used this monastery as a training center for teams like the one I encountered in Ukraine."

"Ah," she said. "*Generalfeldmarschal* Albert Kesselring."

"No, actually, Kesselring is the commander here, but the one I'm looking for is named Conrad Schmidt."

"I do not know that name."

"He led the team in Ukraine, but he slipped away while I was . . . busy . . . with his men. I do not know how he managed it, but he is apparently resourceful and very dangerous. The American government sent me here on a different mission, which was convenient in terms of logistics and transportation. But this is why I'm here."

"You are not American, then?"

"As a matter of convenience only."

There was another dreadful scream. This was louder but wetter, throatier.

"My kinsman will not last much longer," she said. Then she gave Deacon an appraising look. "We are both here on important missions, but not the same mission. This Schmidt is yours, if you can find him. But the person you hear is, as you might say, one of mine. I am here for him."

The killer stepped closer to her. "My name is Deacon," he

said, offering his hand. "I will help you if you will help me."

The woman paused for a moment, looking not at the hand but into his eyes. "I ask again: What *are* you?"

"Just a man," he lied.

"Only that?"

"That, and a friend."

She took his hand. Her grip was furnace hot and very strong. "I am Lucia Cacciatrice."

"Cacciatrice? That means 'huntress.' Is it your real name?"

"Is Deacon yours?"

"Fair enough."

They shook. Then he went over and replaced the window frame.

"Let's go hunt," he suggested.

"Let's go play," she replied.

They moved through the darkness of the cellar. There were scores of crates, each stenciled with the division that was to take ownership. Most were marked only with the symbol of a mountain and a small swastika. He trailed his fingers over one of these.

"Most of this is art," he said. "Looted from private collections and museums across the face of Europe. These boxes are marked for Argentina." He touched another stenciled with an eagle. "These will be sent through discreet channels to select persons in America. The Allies will not think to look for them there. It's rather a shame that it will all be lost."

"The Allies may recover it once they take this place," said Cacciatrice.

He hesitated, debating on how much he could trust her. His instincts won out over his natural caution. "In a very few hours, the Allies are going to bomb this place to rubble. There will be little left to find."

Lucia Cacciatrice frowned, glancing around at all the crates. "So much lost."

Then there was one more scream. A series of them, really, interspersed with someone shouting in German.

"The goal is to win the war," he said. "Not all casualties are human."

Cacciatrice nearly laughed at that. "I think we can both agree on that."

They reached a short set of stone stairs and paused, listening through the cracked old door as footsteps moved by with the brisk precision of marching men. A patrol.

The door was unlocked, and Deacon opened it very slowly and quietly. They peered out and saw the retreating backs of four soldiers heading away from them.

Cacciatrice pointed to a set of stairs and then flicked her finger upward. He nodded. They exited the cellar, closing the door behind them, and ran to the stairs. Deacon drew his silenced pistol and turned to say something to the woman, but there was no woman on the stairs. Instead, a wolf with hair as black as Cacciatrice's crouched there, eyes blazing with silver light, teeth bared and sharp as daggers.

Deacon smiled.

The werewolf smiled back.

They moved up the stairs as swift and silent as death.

His name was Giantonio, and he was dying.

He knew it.

The torturers knew it.

It was all going to end soon, and with him in some unmarked grave, where his bones would never be found by anyone who loved him. At least it would probably be here on Monte Cassino, on the sacred ground of a monastery. That was something, a small thing, but he clung to it.

Soon, though, was an awful word. Soon could be minutes or hours, and each second of that time was its own eternity.

He was strapped to a chair that was bolted to the floor. His body was draped with chains. Iron chains, not steel. Iron wrapped in silver wire. Like the iron spikes that pinned his feet to the floor. Like the iron nails that had been hammered through the backs of both wrists, securing his arms to the chair.

Iron.

What they used against witches. What they used to keep vampires pinned to their coffins. Not wood. Never steel. Iron. An old bit of wisdom culled from folklore and based in truth.

Iron with a little silver. The only thing that could keep him from transforming, from becoming who he truly was. The only thing that prevented him from tearing these men to red ruin.

There was aconite too. Wolfsbane, some called it. The poison of those flowers weakened him and yet heightened his awareness. It made the pain worse but did not allow him to die from it. One of nature's many cruelties that the Ariosophists prized.

Giantonio screamed and screamed, but with each injury, each insult to his body, each calculated assault, he knew that death was closer. He wanted to die, and he prayed that God or his angels would release him before his will broke.

And his will was so very fragile now. Tissue thin and torn in places.

Already he had given up names of others like him. That, he knew, would likely send him to hell rather than heaven. The pieces of him that the Nazis had cut away to steal those names lay on a table in a neat, bloody row. There for him to see. To know. To count and weigh against how much of him was left to take.

"Please," he begged. Blood, hot and salty, ran over his lower lip and choked his throat. "Madonna, please . . ."

"This can end so easily," said Conrad Schmidt. He was tall and very thin, with gray eyes and thinning hair combed back to hide its paucity. He wore uniform trousers but was naked to the waist, his lean body glistening with sweat, and his pale skin spattered with drops of blood. He held a pair of tin snips in his left hand, their blades still wet and red. "Give me the gift, and this ends. That's all you need to do. One small thing, and then there will be peace. There will be no more pain."

Giantonio bowed his head, feeling warm drops of blood and hot tears splash onto his bare thighs.

"Please . . . just kill me and be done."

"Oh no, my friend," said Schmidt. "You know the rules. Or shall I explain them again? You still have three toes left. Must I take another of them so that you remember how this works?"

There were six soldiers in the room, and four of them laughed at this. The others were stony-faced and silent. All of them knew what the dying man was and what their officer had in mind, both for the Italian and for them. The two unsmiling men had been with Schmidt for years. They knew much. The ghostly symbol of a pale white face was embroidered on their uniforms, and they were not called *Todeskommando* for nothing.

"I . . . cannot . . ." moaned Giantonio. "Please, you cannot ask me to do this . . ."

"Or," said Schmidt, snapping the shears, "we can discover together how little needs to be left of a man to still call him a man."

None of them saw the door open. No one heard it.

The first they knew that they were not alone was when they

all heard the distinct sound of a pistol hammer being clicked back. They whirled and saw a man—tall, blocky, with short dark hair and the coldest of smiles—standing in the doorway with a pistol held out straight, the barrel pointed at the officer.

In flawless German, the man said, "Call out and die."

"Who are you?" demanded Schmidt.

"Does it matter? Put the tin snips down. The rest of you, turn toward the wall and lace your fingers on top of your heads."

Schmidt shifted to put the tortured Italian between him and the intruder. He produced a small pistol from a pocket, doing so with the speed of a professional. Schmidt pressed the barrel against Giantonio's forehead.

"Enough with the brave theatrics," he said. "I think you will drop your weapon. Even if you shoot me, this place is filled with soldiers."

Deacon shot him in the center of the chest, missing the Italian by less than an inch. The bullet hissed from the gun, making hardly a sound, and it punched into—and through—Conrad Schmidt's heart. The officer coughed, stumbled backward, hit a wall, and slid to the floor.

Which was when all hell broke loose.

The soldiers dove for their rifles, which were hung on a row of pegs. Deacon fired at them, but the closest ones got in the way, taking several shots, while the ones behind reached the weapons. Suddenly, the air was ripped apart by the roar of gunfire.

Deacon dove for the floor, sliding in behind the heavy chair on which Giantonio was chained. His dive was only partly intentional, with an attempted roll spoiled by a heavy impact that sent him sprawling. He rolled onto his side, trying to bring his gun to bear, but did not fire because a gray shape hurtled over him and slammed into the nearest soldier.

The impact was more than mass hitting mass. The wolf's claws extended like those of a great cat, and its mouth opened unnaturally wide. The soldier seemed to fly apart as if he were a loosely stitched-together doll. Blood splashed onto the ceiling and spattered the faces of the other soldiers.

Then the moment of shock passed, and those soldiers dove for their guns.

Deacon spun and fired, catching one between the shoulder blades, but as the man fell, he accidentally shoved the others out of the way of the next bullets. One of the stone-faced guards flung himself at Deacon, a trench knife in his fist. There was no time to evade, and so they collapsed backward to the floor.

As they landed, Deacon rolled, twisting his hips to create torsion. He bucked the soldier off him and then chopped sideways and down, hammering with the butt of his pistol. The angle was bad, and he missed the man's throat, but the blow shattered his jaw, and the soldier rolled away, gagged, snarling, spitting teeth.

And all at once, he underwent a process of change that was as rapid as it was terrifying. His pale skin turned a deathly gray, his eyes dulled to a poisonous green, and strings of bloody drool hung from his lips. He looked dead, even rotting, and yet alive in a wrong and dreadful way.

Deacon scrambled back from him, recognizing what it was he faced. It was a *Nachzehrer.* A kind of ghoulish creature that dwelled in the dark gulf between life and death. Schmidt had been very busy, but Deacon instantly understood why the Ariosophist had been hunting for vampires and werewolves. *Nachzehrer* were dangerous, but they were not cunning and could not regenerate from mortal wounds. They might make terrifying shock troops, but a sophisticated army could stop them. An army of vampires and werewolves would be virtually unstoppable.

In one-to-one combat, though, *Nachzehrer* were more than

a match for any man. The very sight of them was enough to make even a seasoned soldier freeze in fear. But Deacon was no ordinary man.

Deacon kicked away from the floor, back-rolled to a crouch, and fired his pistol at the one spot he knew was immediately fatal to the living dead. The bullet struck the thing even as it leaped, taking him above the right eyebrow. The .22 did its malicious work, and the leap transformed into a boneless fall.

Spinning away from the thing, he saw that Cacciatrice had torn into the other soldiers. They were firing at her, and the bullets slowed her, tearing bloody holes in the wolf's powerful chest and shoulders. Even so, she pressed her attack.

Then a second of the *Nachzehrer* revealed his horrific nature as he wrapped a powerful gray arm around her throat and buried wicked teeth in her neck. Blood exploded upward, and the snarl of the beast turned into a howl of agony. The last two soldiers took that moment to train their guns on her, trying to blow her head off.

Deacon ran, jumped, stepped on the thigh of the tortured man to propel him into the air, twisting, and struck the riflemen with his hip. The impact dove them against the wall, knocking the guns from their hands. He landed awkwardly but recovered fast, his own gun lost. He drew his stiletto and wove a net of silver between himself and the soldiers, and within a moment, the silver turned bright red.

He spun away, not needing to watch them die but aching to help Cacciatrice.

But he had underestimated her. The wolf-woman had twisted in the *Nachzehrer*'s grip, and as Deacon watched, the monster sagged backward, his head connected to his body by the spine column alone. Then the werewolf bit through that, and the ghoul's head rolled away.

Deacon immediately set to work freeing the captive. He

found a pair of bloody pliers, and with no pause or apology, he tore the spikes from wrists and feet. Then he used a mallet from the tray of torture tools to break the locks on the chains.

Giantonio slid from the chair onto the floor, gasping, weeping, bleeding.

Then a gunshot, loud as thunder, rang out.

Deacon whirled to see Cacciatrice stagger away from the ghoul, blood running from her neck. Five feet away stood Conrad Schmidt, a smoking pistol in his hand. His bare skin had changed to gray and his eyes to a toxic green.

He was a *Nachzehrer* too.

"I know what this bitch is," he said, kicking Cacciatrice, who had collapsed into a panting, dying heap. "What, I wonder, are you?"

Deacon smiled. "Do you really want to know?"

Schmidt raised the gun and pointed it at Deacon's face. "Tell me."

"I don't have to."

"Is that supposed to be some kind of vague threat?"

"No," said Deacon. "Merely a distraction."

A shadow fell across Schmidt's face, and he turned to where Giantonio had fallen. The man no longer lay there.

Instead, a thing that was part man and part wolf rose up on hind legs. It was missing some of its claws and its teeth. But not all of them.

There were more than enough for what it wanted to do.

The screams were inhuman, and they lasted a good long time.

Deacon stood in the shadows and watched the two wolves run away down the slope. They moved slowly, with evident pain.

But, he noticed, with each step that pain seemed less and less. And soon they were running with grace and power.

It made him smile.

Above him, in the darkness, he heard the sound of aircraft. Many of them, with heavy engines. Bombers.

The Americans were early. If any of Schmidt's work remained, it would be forever entombed beneath the weight of the massive monastery.

That made him smile too.

GUARDIAN OF THE BURMA ROAD

ANDREA TANG

NEW YORK, UNITED STATES, JULY 1937

The day Susannah Yang's brother left home, allegedly to save the lives of strangers for the greater good of the world, she almost killed him ten steps from their apartment fire escape.

"Nathaniel." His legs were longer than hers, but hers were quicker. Suze scurried after her brother, panting, every other step punctuated by his name. "Nathaniel." She inhaled, exhaled, and told herself, very sternly, not to cry. Bursting into tears would only slow her down. "Nathaniel, wait."

Nathaniel didn't wait. He didn't speed up. He didn't slow down. He kept his stride, seemingly heedless of the distance between them.

Suze gritted her teeth and closed it. "Nathaniel. God damn it, look at me, Nate!"

"Language, Suze," said Nathaniel, glancing over his shoulder.

In three rapid strides, Suze caught up to him and seized a handful of his coat. It was the good one, the expensive material that Mother had paid for that Christmas, before they all started fighting with one another. "You can't really mean to leave," said Suze.

Her brother sighed without turning around but didn't pull

free from her grip. Maybe he just didn't want to spoil the fabric. "Don't make this harder than it already is, Suze."

"Don't do that." She tugged harder on the coat, less because she thought she could actually hold him in place and more because the pettiness of it felt good. "Don't talk like I'm the one who's doing this. I'm not the one who fought with Mother and Father day and night to die for people we don't even know." Suze swallowed hard. "I'm not the one who's walking away."

The material in her grip went slack. Slowly, Nathaniel faced her. "I'm not walking away from you, little sister," he said. "I'm walking toward something that needs me more."

Telltale heat bloomed under Suze's skin, then ice. The familiar signs of her dragon's magic curdling in her veins, hungry for an outlet. She breathed out slowly. She'd never been angrier at her brother in her life, but she didn't want him dead. That was the whole point of this stupid fight they were having.

Suze counted one, two, three, until she had the magic back under control, then said, as evenly as she could, "Nothing needs you more than your own family, Nathaniel. Least of all a country you've never set foot in."

Her brother's gaze listed toward the sky. "Our family won't be safe for long. America isn't some magical impenetrable fortress, much as we like to pretend otherwise. Those Chinese forces won't be able to hold off the Japanese invasion forever, and then what? This war swallows countries whole. Europe's been overrun, and now Asia too. How long before war reaches our shores?"

"So you're diving headfirst into war."

He smiled sidelong at her. She wanted to smack the upward curve of his mouth right off his face. Magic twitched toward her fingers. She let go of her brother's coat so she could close her fists. Slowly and deliberately, she breathed in and out, steady as could be.

"I'm preempting the war," said Nathaniel. "At the end of

the day, it doesn't really matter if we're Chinese, or American, or something else entirely. Our family is blessed with an ability ordinary humans lack. An ability that can limit the blood spilled on the battlefield. Do you truly care where those battlefields are, if human lives can be saved?"

"And what if they're saved at the cost of your own?" Suze's nails dug into her palms. Dragon's magic flared over the crescent-shaped cuts they formed. "How much will any ordinary, anonymous human life mean then?"

Nathaniel's answer came without hesitation, like a knife slicing through his sister's heart. "Everything," he said. "A human life means everything."

He turned away from her. That expensive coat flared once over his shoulders. Then it was empty, simply fabric hanging lifeless in Suze's arms.

In the distance, whipping across the glow of a fat white moon, the serpentine form of a dragon darted through the clouds. The Yang family dragons had never been particularly large, adapting their size with each generation to fit into the tiny confines of modern urban life among humanity. This one grew smaller and smaller still, until Nathaniel, at last, was gone.

As the story went, once upon a time, the Yang family had decided to take a crack at being human. It was all the rage at the time, being human. When you were all-but-immortal dragons, existing just short of godliness got old after a century or two. So they'd taken on feeble, two-legged, two-armed shapes and gotten down to the business of finding out what exactly made mortal life as a glorified monkey so thrilling.

The way Mother told it, their illustrious ancestors figured

out within a couple of generations that mortality wasn't all it was cracked up to be. But by then, they'd settled into their nice little human communities, and walking it all back seemed like more trouble than it was worth.

That was the other problem: When you lived in human form for long enough, you started forgetting how it felt to be a dragon. By the time the twentieth century dawned, the most powerful scions of the Yang family couldn't take on their true form for longer than an hour or two before gassing out on magic. And by then, China—occupied as it was with various would-be invaders and the general unpleasantness of colonialism—was looking less and less friendly to dragons. It was, in truth, less than friendly to humans too.

But dragons, at least—even mortal dragons, who were more or less human 90 percent of the time—had more means than most to leave an unfriendly living situation behind.

So the Yangs had arrived on the shores of New York, settled into a nice high-rise on the Upper West Side, and turned a tidy profit using dragon's magic to enchant easy American money right into the coffers of their various business investments. It was a very pleasant existence, the quietly luxurious life that Suze had been born into in that Upper West Side apartment. A comfortable life. A life that no one in their right mind would have thought of giving up.

And then Suze's big brother had gotten wind of the war arriving in China, and he fucked it all up.

The way Suze saw it, the worst thing about the day Nathaniel left home wasn't that near-violent goodbye ten steps from the fire escape. It was the anger he left behind in his wake.

It had permeated every crevice of the apartment for weeks, the anger, sticky and all-consuming, bristling with spiky-edged hurt from everyone who contributed to its invasion of the Yang family household. After its instigator was gone, the anger remained, quieter than before, but worse for it in some ways. With Nathaniel gone, there was nowhere else for the anger to go, so it clung to the walls like mold, killing the family slowly.

Later, when Suze thought back on those weeks before her brother finally left them all behind, part of her would want to blame their parents for all the anger. She'd remember late nights punctuated by slammed doors and raised voices from both Father and Nathaniel, and early mornings waking to the sound of Mother crying softly in the kitchen. Most of her, though, would want to blame Nathaniel.

After all, Nathaniel was the one who'd wanted to leave in the first place. His reasons didn't matter.

Letters began to arrive from overseas, addressed in Nathaniel's hand, most of them for Suze. They piled up unopened on her bedside table for months, until eventually, they stopped arriving at all. Even Nathaniel took hints sometimes.

After the letters stopped, Suze thought that would be the last of her brother's attempts to change her mind. She'd never hear from him again. Nathaniel had given up on his little sister, at long last.

She couldn't have been more wrong.

NEW YORK, UNITED STATES, MAY 1944

The thump on the fire escape woke Suze with a bone-chilling start.

The thing was, when you were born into a family of dragons,

you grew up with a greater-than-average knowledge of things that went bump in the night. That wasn't always for the best. When Suze was a little girl, she'd assumed the worst with every scratch and murmur that emerged from the darkness beyond her bedroom window. The blessing of dragon's magic didn't make a child invulnerable to a fear of the dark. It just made those fears more specific.

So, when the thump on the fire escape was followed by a low, plaintive snarl, Suze's brain raced through a series of possibilities, each less pleasant than the last. It could have been some eldritch, black-winged shape-shifter out there, or some vengeful sorcerer, or a demon crawling, cackling from the bowels of hell itself.

Suze wasn't a child anymore though. These days, she didn't take eldritch abominations or angry sorcerers or evil demons lying down. Dragon's magic crackled beneath her skin, a glow of comfort, as she crept toward the ornate glass door that led out to the fire escape.

When she cracked the door ajar, another snarl greeted her. She froze. That wasn't anger in the snarl. That was pain.

Pain in a voice she recognized.

She gave her eyes a moment to adjust to the darkness out on the steps. Blinking, she stepped carefully out into the chilly night air. Autumn had arrived early this year. The absence of sunshine this late at night also made the fire escape unseasonably cold.

For another moment, neither she nor the midnight visitor on her fire escape breathed so much as a word, the two of them simply taking in the darkness and cold in stiff-lipped silence.

Her visitor broke first, as she'd intended. "I didn't think you would recognize me."

"I almost didn't, at first." She squinted into the dark. "I'm still not sure I do."

The cumbersome, serpentine shape curled up in the corner

of the fire escape rumbled with what Suze supposed must be laughter. Scales shook free from the form, slowly, then all at once, dissolving as soon as they hit the air. Piece by piece, the dragon melted away to reveal the young human man beneath.

Nathaniel Yang, bloodied but breathing, peered up at his sister with a small, ghastly grin. One of his eyes was swollen shut. "Hello, Suze."

"Don't you 'Hello, Suze' me." Suze strode toward her brother in two quick strides that belied immediate worry. Nathaniel hadn't seemed in such a bad way while in the body of a semi-immortal lizard. Cuts and bruises seemed like little more than cosmetic scratches on the mighty hide of a dragon. Insignificant.

They seemed far less insignificant on a mere human body.

"What the hell happened to you?" asked Suze. Dragon's magic twitched beneath her fingertips as she reached for him.

Her brother rasped a laugh. "What do you think? Turns out our Allied forces aren't the only armies with magic on their side."

Suze's fingers paused. "The Imperial Japanese military," she said slowly. "Don't tell me that they . . . that they're also . . ."

"Employing arcane means to win their war?" It was too dark to make out Nathaniel's facial expression, but Suze knew him well enough to hear the wince coloring his words. "Turns out that Japanese sorcerers shouldn't be taken lightly."

Suze sat on her haunches in front of him without touching him. Instead, she coaxed her magic to the surface—just a sliver of their ancient dragons' power—and wafted it toward her brother. It glittered briefly between them, jade green, before finding a home beneath his skin.

Nathaniel sighed. In the dark, Suze saw the tense outline of his shoulders relax as the healing power of her magic coursed through his body, closing the wounds. She nudged her foot against his, when it was done. "Better?"

"Tremendously." He tilted his head back against the fire escape railing. "Thank you."

Suze didn't tell him he was welcome. "What happened?"

"I was assisting the Chinese and American forces along the Burma Road," said Nathaniel. "I was cocky. I thought that dragon's magic would be more than enough to take back Mount Song. We need that route for supply through China, and I thought I'd be the one to win it back single-handedly. Who needs ordinary human artillery barrages when your magic commands fire and rain alike? What could Japan's poor mortal soldiers do in the face of my power?" Chuckling darkly, Nathaniel shook his head. "Hubris, thy name is Nathaniel Yang. Their command didn't take long to catch on to the fact that I was the Allies' secret weapon. And that's when they deployed their sorcerers. I would have died if I hadn't used my last burst of power to flee."

"So you spent it on a dragon's form, and expedited air travel, so you could haul your pitiful, half-dead carcass on to my fire escape."

"I spent it on coming home," said Nathaniel quietly. "I knew you were angry. But I also knew you wouldn't let me die in vain."

"I wouldn't let you die at all," snapped Suze. She ignored the ice-cold clench of her heart. "Mother and Father haven't forgiven you." *And neither have I.* "But they'll be pleased that you've come to your senses, at least."

An odd silence stretched between brother and sister. Then Nathaniel said, even more quietly, "Suze, I'm not staying."

The icy fingers around Suze's heart squeezed tighter. "Don't be ridiculous."

"I'm grateful for your healing," said Nathaniel. "But I haven't changed my mind about where I'm needed."

"You almost died!"

"It's a war, Suze." Nathaniel's tone was infuriatingly droll. "That tends to happen."

To Suze's shame, hot tears sprang to her eyes. "You used me," she spat. "You came crawling back here because it was convenient. You knew I wouldn't be able to tell you no. You tricked me into thinking that you might actually . . . might actually . . ."

Might stay home. Might let them be a family again. Might suck out all the anger clinging like old rot to the eaves of the apartment and return their lives to what they had once been, before a war being fought a million miles away had torn them all apart.

Nathaniel sucked in a breath, like he'd been hit. "Suze, I'm sorry—"

"You're not," she snapped, heedless of the furious tears trickling unchecked down her cheeks. "Or you'd never have dared show your face to me again after the day you left."

"You could come with me."

It was such an unexpected response to her rage that Suze sat shocked into silence for several seconds. "Don't be an even greater fool than you've already been, Nathaniel."

"You could make a real difference out there, Suze," he barreled on, painful hope seeping into the words. "You have no idea what our family's magic is truly capable of. This whole time we've been spending it on petty luck charms, enchantments to keep ourselves safe and comfortable and wealthy where we're convinced violence and poverty can never touch us. We've only been helping ourselves, when we could be helping so many more people. Don't you want that? Don't you want all this power we've inherited to mean something? To do something important, and real, and good?"

"No!" shouted Suze. "I want my brother alive!"

He fell silent. At first Suze thought he'd clammed up with anger or hurt. It had happened often enough, in the days before he finally left, between shouted arguments in the corridors of the Yang family apartment. Then he said, in a low voice, "Suze, they're here."

"What do you mean they're here? Who are you talking about?"

"Hush," hissed Nathaniel. "The sorcerers who attacked me. They must have traced the trail my power left."

"They can do that?" A new, alien terror seeped into Suze's heart. "Complete an ocean's worth of travel in the same amount of time a dragon can ride the wind across the world?"

"I told you," said Nathaniel. "Ours isn't the only side that wields arcane power. Stay here. I'm going to lead them away from the apartment."

"Have you lost your mind?" Suze's fingers snatched Nathaniel's arm of their own volition. "You've barely healed. If you run, and they give chase, they'll only hurt you again."

Or worse.

"I know." In the dark, she caught the curve of her brother's smile. "But you'll be safe. You, and Mother, and Father. It's the least I can do, at the end of the day."

"Nathaniel, don't do this."

"Entering the war was my choice." Nathaniel stood. "But this isn't. Protecting our family was never a choice at all. Tell Mother and Father I'm sorry. And that I love—"

Something rumbled in the distance, cutting him off. The hairs on the back of Suze's neck stood on end. Suze would have called it thunder, but no thunderstorm she'd ever encountered had been accompanied by the billow of black wings blotting out the sliver of moonlight over their heads.

Nathaniel stood. "They're here. We're out of time, I'm afraid, little sister." His hands found hers one last time. "Burma Road. That's where I'll be. Ask for Mr. Liu. He'll know what to do. Find me at the Burma Road. I'll be returning to the front at Mount Song, if I make it through this."

If? What did he mean, if?

What happened next flew through a blur in Suze's conscious mind. Nathaniel slipped once more from her grasp. The billowing black wings dove toward the fire escape—then changed course abruptly as a pale serpentine streak wove like white flame through the dark. Suze screamed Nathaniel's name—or thought she did. She could hardly hear herself over the rumble of those awful black wings, the things in the dark hunting her brother down, as if he were little more than quarry to be caught for sport.

It all took place over the space of two minutes, maybe three. Moonlight reappeared. And Suze was once again alone in the dark.

HENAN PROVINCE, CHINA, JUNE 1944

Nathaniel's point of contact at the Burma Road looked thoroughly unimpressed with Suze. Mr. Liu was a stocky, no-nonsense military sort, with neatly cropped hair and a neatly trimmed mustache, which sat above a mouth that looked utterly incapable of smiling.

"So you're the sister, huh?" Mr. Liu squinted at Suze, looking her up and down, like he was examining a bargain purchase and reconsidering the deal he'd gotten.

"I'm the sister," confirmed Suze. She swallowed hard. "Please, did Nathaniel ever—"

"Still missing in action," said Mr. Liu. "Sorry for your loss."

"He's not lost yet," said Suze, bristling. "That's why I'm here. I don't care about your war. I just want my brother back."

"Hmph," said Mr. Liu, unmoved. "In that case, you'd best start by picking up where he left off. If you intend to find Nathaniel, your best bet is behind enemy lines. If he's not dead, that's where they'll be holding him, and may the heavens bless that boy's soul." A shudder ran through Mr. Liu, disrupting that otherwise uncanny aura of stoicism. "Imperial Japanese sorcerers tend . . . not to give up their prisoners of war easily. They'll die before they yield what they consider theirs."

"So what do you suggest?"

"Suggest?" Mr. Liu barked a laugh. "I'm not suggesting anything. But you're here now, in the belly of the beast." He eyed her thoughtfully. "From what your brother's told me, you're a bit of a beast yourself. The way I see it, the only way out is by tooth and claw."

Fighting a war on foreign shores wasn't what Suze expected.

She'd grown up with dragon's magic cleaved close beneath her skin, the comfort of her hidden inheritance a balm and a weapon in equal measure. She spoke in the language of charms to soothe ailments, repair household items, enhance the curl of her hair or the shade of her lipstick. Magic to serve mundane purposes had always been her birthright, as close to second nature to her as the breath inside her lungs.

Turning a dragon's power toward warfare was wholly different. Suze had never assumed a dragon's form as easily or as contentedly as Nathaniel had. He'd love to fly, to span miles upon miles of endless sky in the space of seconds. Now, Suze found herself flying high above enemy encampments to summon storm clouds and lightning, to split the ground beneath the boots of enemy soldiers. This was a wholly different sort of dragon's magic—the rage of her ancestry channeled through the rage of the earth itself.

Suze liked it.

That was, perhaps, the most surprising part of the whole affair. There was a vicious, purposeful elegance to the magic she hurled from the skies. Power had always been her birthright.

Now, it had some place to go. Now, it had a reason to take shape beyond the confines of her body.

If she could free up the Burma Road, if she could retake Mount Song, then Nathaniel's work here would be done. If she could accomplish what he hadn't, she'd finally be able to bring her brother home.

She just had to find him first. And to do that, she needed to beat the enemy down until they spat him back out from wherever they were hiding him. If the Imperial Japanese sorcerers would rather die than give Nathaniel back to his sister, then Suze was more than happy to grant their wish.

Her fury—cold, precise, and aggressively goal-oriented—roared to spectacular life on the battlefield. The Japanese forces, even backed by their sorcerers, had begun to wilt beneath the combined aerial assault of Allied airpower and Yang family dragon's magic.

Weeks passed, then months. The dying heat of August began to fade toward inklings of September. Suze and the Allied troops pressed onward. They were winning.

And then, one day, a new letter arrived for Suze, its envelope the same color as the unopened notes from her brother that sat piled up on her bedside table back in New York. This one was not written in Nathaniel's hand. It contained news from Mr. Liu, gathered by Allied intelligence officers. It had not been intended for Suze's eyes. But even Mr. Liu, it seemed, had a heart, at the end of the day.

The letter's contents were layered in the author's sympathies, but there was no mistaking the information they honeyed over: Nathaniel's body had been found and identified.

Suze's brother was dead.

"You're running away," observed Mr. Liu.

Suze dropped the suitcase she was packing and rounded on him. "Say that again," she told him, very quietly. "Say that again, and then explain to your superiors why this encampment was razed to the ground by a dragon's storm in the space of five minutes."

Mr. Liu didn't even flinch. "There's no reason to leave. You started something here, Miss Yang, and now, it seems, you intend to leave your work abandoned to flee back to New York, tail tucked between your legs. Or don't the people in your family finish what they start?"

"Don't you dare talk about my family."

"Miss Yang," said Mr. Liu. He looked, abruptly, deeply tired. "I knew your brother quite well. Not the same way you did. Not the same way that I imagine your parents must have. But I knew the heart of the man who chose to fight a war that he didn't have to. A war that, on the surface, was never his. I asked him, once, why he bothered. Why he cared, when he could have lived in safety and luxury in your glamorous American city apartment, without once seeing the heat of battle. Why mere human lives would matter to the descendant of dragons. And do you know what he told me?"

"Mr. Liu, I really don't—"

"*Human lives mean everything,*" said Mr. Liu. "That's what he told me. That all human life is precious." He met her eyes. "There's a reason your ancestors came down from their immortal pedestals to live among us feeble mortals all those generations ago, Miss Yang. And your brother figured it out. You might consider that, before you pack those bags and cross the ocean again. But hey, what do I know? I'm just a mere human mortal in presence of dragons. The decision on what we mean to you is ultimately yours."

He left Suze alone in the empty room, with her half-packed suitcase and her dead brother's words.

Susannah Yang never returned to New York. Letters were sent home to her parents, written in her hand, explaining that she had decided to travel the world in the aftermath of her brother's death. To see if she could learn to see it in his eyes.

They gave up searching for her after a year passed. Letters continued to arrive faithfully at her parents' address in New York in the years that followed, but the girl herself was never spotted again.

During roughly the same month as the runaway disappearance of Susannah Yang, Mount Song was recaptured. The Japanese sorcerers and soldiers retreated. Burma Road reopened to Chinese supply lines. And the second war to end all wars inched agonizingly closer to its conclusion.

In the months that followed the Battle of Mount Song, rumors emerged in small corners of the arcane world. Some said that a dragon had assisted the Allied forces in their victory. Others insisted that it wasn't one dragon, but two, who had deigned to find their small human cause worthy.

No one knew the truth with any great certainty. What everyone seemed to agree on, though, was the sight that a lucky few could catch on select nights, in the shadow of Mount Song: a pale serpentine streak that could be spotted weaving between moonlit clouds late at night.

No one had ever seen such a thing prior to the battle for the soul of Burma Road, but after the supply routes reopened, they spotted that serpentine shape in the sky at least once a week, a tiny god watching over the passage of the mortals beneath its watch.

BOUND AND CHAINED

KEVIN ANDREW MURPHY

DRESDEN, GERMANY, APRIL 1944

Clothilde von Penzlin loved the library and considered it the most splendid of Dresden's many treasures: the elaborately carved sixteenth-century bookcases with their curious creatures; the stained-glass windows painted with saints; and most of all, the books and their mingled perfume of Russian, English, and Spanish leather. Augustus I—Father Augustus—founded it in 1574, taking the collection from the Annaburg Palace, 1,674 bound volumes, to form the new Saxon State Library.

To be German was to be organized.

A great many volumes had been added since the days of Augustus I, and countless catalogs. Clothilde could list them all. It was a pity they had to dismantle the library in order to save it, but such was war, especially now that it was going badly.

Clothilde affixed a label to the crate, destining it for Wewelsburg Castle, stronghold of the SS, where Heinrich Himmler had restyled everything to be like King Arthur and his knights.

She padlocked the crate, then sealed the key in an envelope, kissing it for good measure. Then she felt embarrassed. Was she a superstitious schoolgirl, or a witch, or worse, the former playing the latter?

But truth was, the war had been going on for five years, and one did what one could to stay sane. The books had been taken away as well, secreted in remote *Schlössern* far from Dresden, with almost the last crate being these, requisitioned by the SS, a collection of rare treatises on alchemy and porcelain by Johann Friedrich Böttger, failed alchemist turned successful porcelain maker to Augustus II.

"Is this the last?" inquired a male voice, mellow, albeit stern. Clothilde turned, seeing a figure framed in the doorway, bracketed by barren shelves. Not particularly imposing, barely above average height, soft oval face framed by scholar's spectacles, but his military uniform identified him as SS of the highest rank.

"Herr Himmler!" Clothilde exclaimed in surprise, instead of the usual *Heil Hitler!*

"Indeed," he agreed, "and you must be the illustrious Fräulein von Penzlin." He appeared disappointed but not surprised to behold an aging spinster over a decade his senior rather than the moderately attractive younger woman she'd been during the last world war. "Penzlin . . ." he mused, "a town once known for its witches?"

"Yes, sir," Clothilde admitted with some reluctance. "But where wasn't?"

Himmler frowned slightly. "Pity you aren't younger . . ." He shrugged. "But I still have need of your knowledge." He stepped forward, adjusting his spectacles as he peered down. "Ah, Wewelsburg . . . did you not read my latest?"

"Sir, the last letter I received was a month ago."

"A mail train was bombed. My letter must have been on it." Himmler looked annoyed. "No matter—these should be bound for Houska Castle."

"Houska?" Clothilde racked her brain. "Isn't that in Bohemia?"

"Yes, but Czechoslovakia's now our protectorate, and Houska has an interesting history."

Bohemia was not Clothilde's specialty—her interest lay in *Märchen und Sagen*, folktales and sagas—but she recalled a legend that declared that Houska was built atop a chasm that led directly to hell. More obscure scholarship pointed to Houska being the castle from one of the fairy tales from the Brothers Grimm—*Rumpelstiltskin*, to be exact, the imp who spun straw into gold. "I've heard tales."

Himmler smiled wider. It was not a nice smile. He took a fountain pen from his pocket and uncapped it, crossing out "WEWELSBURG" and adding "HOUSKA." The pen's cap, rather than a Montblanc's stylized six-pointed snowcap—suspiciously similar to a *Judenstern*—instead sported a sinister white skull: a *Totenkopf*, a death's head. Himmler's handwriting was not nice either, a sloppy schoolboy's scrawl, but Clothilde had learned to recognize the distinctive scribble. "I hope the book I'm looking for is here."

"What book?"

"The Agrippa."

Agrippa was a name well known to Clothilde. Heinrich Cornelius Agrippa von Nettesheim was the famous occultist who, in 1533, authored the *Three Books of Occult Philosophy*, codifying Hermetic magic. Agrippa's *Three Books* also drew on Neoplatonism and the Kabbalah, the second a subject a colleague had told her about, how King Solomon had used his seal ring to bind a demon who he then commanded to build the First Temple in Jerusalem.

Clothilde chose her words carefully. "I sent multiple editions of the *Three Books of Occult Philosophy* to Wewelsburg."

"I mean Agrippa's other book." Himmler pursed his lips, then told her, enunciating precisely, "I am referring to a very particular book of Agrippa's that, after his death, ended up being part of a witch trial in Baden in 1574, then passed into the possession of Augustus I and then this library. But in the reign of Augustus II, it disappeared."

Clothilde paused. She had indeed seen such a notation in the catalog from 1574, but nothing of such an elaborate provenance, merely that there had been a book auctioned off as part of a witch trial. "I'd assumed that manuscript was the *Three Books of Occult Philosophy*. Do you believe it was some rarer book?"

"Quite." Himmler spoke with such precision as to make it clear that he intended this to be a masterpiece of dry Berlin wit. "But it's not the book so much as what it is bound in . . ."

Clothilde considered. It was customary, when bookbinding, to wrap the boards in scraps of other older manuscripts. "What was it?"

Himmler gazed through his spectacles, stroking his chin, then at last pronounced, "That is not your concern. Now give me that envelope, which I assume holds the key to the crate with Böttger's manuscripts."

"Of course, Herr Himmler."

Himmler tore it open and, once he had the key and list, tossed the envelope aside and opened the lock. With annoyed precision, he unpacked the crate, crossing each book off the list with his skull-capped pen as he found it, shoving volume after precious volume into Clothilde's arms until the stack grew too heavy, and she had to set it on a research table.

He paused as he came to a relatively modern Meissen porcelain catalog, which had a cover photograph of the famous figurine of Count Brühl's tailor riding a goat, both wearing pince-nez spectacles. "Ah, the *Bockreiter* . . ." Himmler whispered, slipping into Dutch. Clothilde silently translated: "the buckrider." Buckriders were a Robin Hood–style gang of thieves from Dutch and Belgian folklore who allegedly flew through the air on magic goats they'd obtained from a demon.

Himmler excitedly opened the book, but finding that the contents showed nothing but pictures of expensive porcelain, he shoved it into Clothilde's hands and dug to the bottom of the chest, pushing the packing raffia aside, rapping to check for a false bottom.

There was none, of course. Himmler glared at Clothilde. "The Agrippa's not here, so you'll now show me the library's catalogs."

Auditing the catalogs took hours, but the result was as Himmler had told her: The mysterious Agrippa was listed among the final items of the library's catalog from 1547. It appeared in other catalogs, with nothing significant, simply referring back to the 1547 listing, until a final notation in the catalog of 1707: *Augustus II.*

"It appears as you knew already," Clothilde said as diplomatically as she could. "It was checked out by the elector but not returned."

Heinrich Himmler stamped the floor in fury, like Rumpelstiltskin. "I shall have to check the elector's palace, then. The museums. I'm not sure where else . . ." He glared. "You will stay here. Recheck these catalogs, for the Führer will be most displeased if we cannot find the Agrippa. It is crucial to the war."

To question Himmler was tantamount to questioning the Führer himself, but the question still needed to be asked: "Was not the plan to remove all the books, including catalogs, to a location at less risk of bombing?"

"Perhaps the Agrippa is still here, mislabeled."

"Very good, Herr Himmler. I will do my best to search."

Himmler flashed a toothy grin to match the skull on the cap of the pen in his pocket.

A week passed with nothing more eventful than gathering up stray volumes—which Clothilde addressed to Herr Himmler at Houska Castle, including notations. As for the books, while some were rare, none were particularly occult beyond a nice edition of Goethe's *Faust* and an erotically illustrated copy of Keller's *Mirror, the Kitten*, including a lurid chromolithograph of the old witch transformed into a nubile maiden flying up a chimney like Saint Nicholas in reverse, with the caption, in Keller's inimitable prose: *In the dark night, however, a witch often rode up out of this chimney on her broomstick, young and beautiful and stark naked, just as God made women and the devil likes to see them.*

This found favor with Himmler, or at least he had chosen to change tactics from the whip to the sugar bread—literally—for Clothilde received a small tin of lebkuchen along with a letter filled with encouragement, as well as thanks for Keller's book, which Himmler said had brightened his day, and he hoped this gift might brighten hers in turn. With the lebkuchen and letter was a package wrapped with gold paper stamped *SS*.

Clothilde paused. Christmas had been months ago, and the only thing special about this night was that April 30 was *Walpurgisnacht*, when all the witches supposedly danced around the *Hexentanzplatz* atop the Brocken, like in *Faust*, when Mephistopheles took the old scholar there to obtain a youth potion.

Inside, Clothilde found a gold candle and a rustic porcelain candleholder, Swedish in style, with the cutout of a heart above and a stylized six-pointed snowflake below. A *Julleuchter*, a Yule lantern.

Clothilde savored the lebkuchen. Sugar was in short supply with the war, along with everything, and some children were singing *Deutschland ohne alles* instead of *über alles* before their horrified mothers shut them up. *Ohne Butter, ohne Brot* . . . "without butter, without bread . . ."

As for the *Julleuchter*, it was pretty taken by itself, charming simplicity, glazed brown so it looked like lebkuchen, like a gingerbread *hexenhaus*.

Clothilde took the candle, gold as *Goldlöckchen*'s hair in the fairy tale, but stained red as *Rotkäppchen*'s hood. Clothilde realized she had pricked her finger on one of the Yule lantern's windows. Three drops of blood slid down the candle. Clothilde took a match and lit it anyway.

Clothilde sucked her finger as the candle cast its light about her office. Unlike the main rooms of the library, which were sixteenth century, dating to Augustus I, the offices were rococo, enlarged and refurbished by Augustus II, with gilded neoclassical bas-reliefs. A golden youth playing the lyre, a goat-legged satyr playing the panpipes, and a king who, for inexplicable reasons, had donkey's ears.

Clothilde then realized this was not inexplicable at all. The golden youth with his lyre was no youth but the sun god Apollo, also the god of music. The satyr? Marsyas, who challenged Apollo to a music contest. The donkey-eared king could be none other than Midas, who judged Marsyas the winner and in consequence Apollo cursed with donkey's ears.

Most remembered Midas's later legend, where Dionysus granted Midas the power to turn everything he touched to gold. But if Augustus II had made a secret laboratory for his alchemist,

Böttger, where better to hide it than the office that had once been a royal refuge?

The Yule lantern's candle flickered, shimmering across the gilding, and Clothilde reached out and flicked off the electric light. The design became even clearer, with curls of golden music issuing forth from the panpipes of Marsyas, the traceries forming bars of musical notation with notes picked out in gold.

Clothilde could sight-read music, and the reeds of the satyr's panpipes pointed upward so that they resembled piano keys. Fingering was harder, but standing on a chair and pressing the gilded pipes, she found that they were indeed secret buttons, and she was able to play the tune—a jaunty little drinking song.

The panel with the donkey-eared king popped inward, a secret door. Clothilde got down and took the *Julleuchter* with her, entering the dark cobwebbed room. Then she blinked, dazzled as Aladdin in the Cave of Wonders, for rather than gilded ornaments on the panels and plasterwork, everything here was golden—the chairs, the tables, the many ornaments and treasures. The walls themselves told the more famous tale of King Midas, with him turning roses, apples, and even his unfortunate daughter to gold, but it was hard to tell where the bas-relief panels ended and the furnishing began.

On a shelf near the door, Clothilde spied a golden tailor riding a golden goat, the famous Meissen figurine, but gilded all over rather than just highlighted. She tried to pick it up, then realized it was far heavier than it looked—not gilded porcelain, but solid gold . . .

The common story was that Böttger, when he failed to make gold for Augustus, had made white gold instead—another name for porcelain, so precious was it then—for Augustus II was using all his real gold to buy Chinese porcelain. But here Clothilde had clear evidence that Böttger not only discovered the secret of white gold but the secret of making gold itself. The Agrippa, which Augustus II checked out from the library, contained the secrets of alchemy. Small wonder why Himmler was so close-lipped.

She heard a noise then, clanging and clattering, as if from some infernal machinery. Then the secret door snapped shut behind her. The candle flame fluttered with the air movement, almost guttering out, but flickered back to life. Clothilde held her breath, realizing she was trapped, no handle on the panel behind her.

Chains rattled again, somewhere below the floor. Clothilde tried not to panic. Böttger was an alchemist, and along with the secrets of porcelain and gold, he undoubtedly knew poison. Everything in this chamber could be trapped, and from the clanking chains, some mechanism had been activated, making it only a matter of time before her doom fell.

The chains clanked louder, echoing across the room. Clothilde looked to the other side of the gold table laden with golden treasures. A circular stair led down into darkness. She shielded the candle and walked that way slowly, carefully, descending. Down and down, spiraling widdershins like a witch's dance.

When she reached the bottom landing, the candle flame glittered off glassware everywhere, retorts and alembics, vials and flasks and jars. An alchemist's laboratory, Böttger's secret lair! Suspended in the middle of the chamber, hanging from black iron chains and bound with locks, was a book. The Agrippa.

The chains rattled again, the book swaying and swinging as if struggling to break free. Clothilde realized that the Agrippa was not just a book of alchemy but one of demonology, for as she had read in a collection of folklore treatises, the Scots had a legend of a book of magic with a demon bound into it, wrapped in iron chains in just such a manner, and they called the book the Agrippa.

It seemed that Henry Cornelius Agrippa von Nettesheim, rather than eschewing the secrets of the Kabbalah, had embraced them, for his black book was stamped in gold with a six-pointed star in a circle, emblazoned with holy names in Hebrew—Solomon's Seal. The two triangles that made up the star glowed as faces tried to push through—one appearing as a man, the other as a goat.

Clothilde knew the script from *Faust*, having read the play and seen it on stage and screen. "Appear in a form that is pleasing to me, a tailor riding a goat, for that form suits you best."

Suddenly, instead of a black poodle, or an incensed hippopotamus, or any of the other frightening forms Mephistopheles first took in Goethe's play, the book—a large folio, a foot by a foot and a half—ceased shaking against its chains and turned horizontal, level as a hanging table, Solomon's Seal in the center. Like a materialization in a magic lantern show, what appeared in the magic circle was an eighteenth-century tailor, foppishly dressed in a flowered frock coat, riding a goat, both of them sporting pince-nez spectacles, but all in miniature. The tailor modeled a tricorn hat with a candle burning at each corner. More disturbingly, the tailor had goat eyes, while his goat had human eyes. "Who summons us and what sacrifice do you offer?" the man and the goat bleated as one.

Names were power, so Clothilde didn't mention hers. "I summon you," Clothilde intoned, "and as for my offering, three drops of virgin blood as incense and a fragment of consecrated bread." Clothilde spat out the last crumb of lebkuchen she had stuck in her teeth, tossing it into the circle. Lebkuchen was baked atop the same *Oblaten* wafers used for Communion. That seemed close enough to the holy host that witches profaned in their ceremonies.

The goat knelt and lapped up the sugared crumbs, while the

man sniffed the smoke three times. "Delicious!" they bleated as one, then sighed. "Your sacrifice is acceptable, so you shall have three of your choosing: three bags of gold, three secrets revealed, or three chances to guess my name and command me as your servant." Both goat and man grinned, teeth exchanged like their eyes.

"I have gold upstairs," Clothilde told the demon, "and as for secrets I wish revealed, I've far more than three, so I choose to guess your name."

"Very well," said the demon.

Clothilde drew on all her scholarship. "From the three bags of gold, I surmise you're the wicked spirit once defeated by Saint Nicholas, the spirit known locally as Knecht Ruprecht, but in Austria as Krampus."

"Perhaps," the demon allowed enigmatically, then leered. "But regardless, neither's my true name. You have one guess left."

"Well then," said Clothilde, who felt she had prepared her entire career for this moment, "the only possible name left is . . . *Rumpelstiltskin*."

"A witch told you that!" screamed the demon, exactly as in the fairy tale. "A witch!"

"Two brothers, actually," Clothilde admitted, "but their intelligence may have come roundabout from a witch."

"The bargain is made regardless," spat both goat and man. The shackle holding the chained book to the ceiling suddenly detached itself, then snaked out and clasped around her left wrist. "Agrippa's book is yours, as am I."

Both tailor and goat faded from view, leaving only Solomon's Seal on the cover, and the book floated to her free arm, padlocks unclasping one by one until the cover flew open, and she found herself looking at an even more elaborate Solomon's Seal, etched with the head of Baphomet, demonic patron of the Knights Templar.

What do you wish of us?

The words appeared below the seal and the demon within.

Clothilde considered. The candle of the Yule lantern was growing low. "Show me whatever magic Saint Nicholas used to go up chimneys."

The pages of the Agrippa turned by themselves until Clothilde found herself looking at a spell for a mortal to no longer be composed of the Four Elements of Aristotle, but only two—fire and air—taking the form of smoke. No words required, simply an arcane gesture, precisely performed, and Clothilde could play piano. One moment she was making the magic gesture, and the next she was at once Salamander and Sylph, fire and air.

She passed as smoke up the spiral stair, under the crack of the secret door, then up the chimney like the witch in Keller's story, flying off with the wind to heaven knew where, though Clothilde had a suspicion, it being *Walpurgisnacht.*

The wind blew her almost directly west. She drifted along, but not alone, for chained to her wrist by smoke was the Agrippa, smoky as well, and in the center of the smoke ring that was the Seal of Solomon perched the goat-horned imp Rumpelstiltskin.

"We're headed to the Brocken, aren't we?" Clothilde asked, not so much surprised as glad she could still speak.

"Of course, mistress," giggled the imp. "It's *Walpurgisnacht.*"

Clothilde had dreamed of attending the witches' sabbath ever since reading *Faust* as a schoolgirl, and even more when she'd seen Murnau's silent film seventeen years ago, with Faust flying along atop Mephistopheles's cape like it was a magic carpet, but the truth was much stranger, with witches and conjurers riding in on steeds and conveyances of all kinds, horses and goats, broomsticks and pitchforks, all alighting on the *Hexentanzplatz*, the witches' dance floor, high atop the Brocken.

Clothilde attempted Saint Nicholas's gesture in reverse, and it worked, smoke becoming flesh once again, and she fell, but not totally, held aloft by a book flapping like a giant bat chained to her wrist.

It was a stylish entrance to the witches' ball, and Clothilde had attended enough dances over the years to understand such things, witches and wizards giggling and gossiping as much as folk anywhere, with obvious cliques and coteries.

Clothilde decided her best course of action would be to play the mysterious newcomer, talking little and listening more. Soon, exactly as in *Faust*, she came upon an enchanting young witch ladling youth potion from her cauldron, much like a barmaid serving up *Maibowle*—May punch—at a May Day fair, her cauldron bobbing with strawberries and green sprigs of *Waldmeister*, sweet woodruff, the herb of spring. The witch maid accepted all forms of payment, but with a good deal of haggling. Wizened wizards and haggard hags traded poppets pierced with pins and other grisly curios in exchange for her wondrous brew, sipping it down as years fell away from their forms.

Clothilde had only pennies in her pocket, but having the demon Rumpelstiltskin bound as her familiar, Clothilde commanded him to bring her three bags of gold.

It was done quick as a wink, the demon disappearing from the seal, then reappearing again as three sacks appeared beside her. Clothilde opened one and found it was stuffed with golden apples from Midas's banquet table.

The bewitching witch maid inspected the loot. "These will do nicely." She offered Clothilde a cup of brew.

Clothilde considered. She should probably haggle, but then again, a show of wealth was good for gossip. "*Prost*!" Clothilde downed it in one gulp. It tasted like May wine, too, but sweeter, Riesling fortified with more than *Waldmeister* and wild strawberries. It tasted, in fact, like spring, and as its sweetness stole through her, so did youth, the myriad aches and pains of age fading, as did the spots on her hands. Clothilde did not have a mirror handy but unpinned her hair and saw her gray locks returned to their youthful golden brown.

"Youth becomes you, Fräulein von Penzlin." A man's voice. "Herr Himmler would hardly recognize you."

Clothilde whirled, seeing a man in a German army cap. More handsome as well, and younger, without glasses, his left eye rakishly covered by a patch. "Wotan?" Clothilde hazarded.

"No." He laughed wryly, then gestured to his eyepatch with his left hand, which had only three fingers remaining. "But good guess, and I am in need of Valkyries to lend me a hand." He gestured with his right arm where his hand was missing altogether, like Týr after sticking his hand in the mouth of Fenris-wolf. "My name is Claus von Stauffenberg, and since it seems you've found the Agrippa that Himmler's been looking for, I have a proposal for you, as one member of the old nobility to another . . ."

Claus von Stauffenberg, as it turned out, was a Wehrmacht colonel, a count, and a cupbearer, which was an old office from the Holy Roman Empire dating back to Charlemagne, which also made him a hereditary warlock. That explained his presence at *Walpurgisnacht* and his flying horse that took them back to his castle in Bavaria before the devil showed up at midnight, fashionably late for his own party. But more than that, Claus was a patriot, who had the same concerns Clothilde did for Germany under the Nazis, and moreover, had a plan to do something about that—namely, kill Hitler and Himmler at the same time, and Göring, if they could get him. It was named Operation Valkyrie.

The trouble was, Himmler was something of a magician

himself. "Petty little necromancer," von Stauffenberg cursed him, "but a slippery one. He has the skull of Agrippa on his desk and the tooth of Albertus Magnus set into the cap of his fountain pen, and they whisper warnings to him, so he's evaded our trap yet again. Him and Göring. Canceled this morning. There's no help for it—we'll have to deal with Hitler now and take care of Himmler and Göring later."

Clothilde might not have had Agrippa's skull, but she had his book, and with it the services of Rumpelstiltskin. But the trouble was that demons, much like men, had their specialties, and Rumpelstiltskin was not good at general divination. The secrets he offered were where things were buried—mostly treasures, but also bodies. But, as a demon of earth, he could make gold, or porcelain, or poison.

Or bombs . . .

RASTENBURG, GERMANY, JULY 1944

It was also a swelteringly hot July day, so Hitler had decided to move his general meeting from the underground *Führerbunker* to the *Wolfsschanze*, the Wolf's Lair, an airy wooden hut designed for him by Albert Speer. Clothilde was not part of the inner circle, so she was not allowed into the meeting room with the Führer, but Claus von Stauffenberg was, and being one-handed and one-eyed, no one questioned him bringing a pretty young secretary with him, even one handcuffed to a large book, which Clothilde had disguised with a false cover.

But the cover had to be off for Rumpelstiltskin to spin straw into gold—or in this case, booze into bombs, specifically turning a bottle of French Cointreau from the Führer's private stash into an explosive suitable to blow his head off.

A series of knocks sounded, startling all but the imp. "Colonel von Stauffenberg? The meeting is just about to begin!"

"Just a moment!" von Stauffenberg called back, gesturing with his remaining hand for Clothilde to hurry.

"Just one will be fine!" Clothilde hissed to the imp. "Keep the other and drink to the Führer's demise!"

Rumpelstiltskin leered and disappeared, taking a second bottle of Cointreau with him, leaving Clothilde to toss the one bomb into von Stauffenberg's briefcase and fumble the cover back on the Agrippa as Heinz Brandt, aide to General Heusinger, chief of staff, barged into von Stauffenberg's office.

Colonel von Stauffenberg stood there holding the booby-trapped briefcase. Clothilde knelt before him. Heinz Brandt blushed.

But Colonel von Stauffenberg outranked him. "I told you 'just a moment'!" He stormed out of the room, leaving the hapless aide to catch up.

Clothilde checked her watch. She had set a relatively short timer. As von Stauffenberg had informed her, Hitler liked meetings to start promptly, but reserved the first fifteen minutes for idle chitchat and minor business, making it such that von Stauffenberg, as a high-ranking officer and decorated hero, could excuse himself for a brief phone call, then fifteen minutes after, the bomb would go off, with himself and Clothilde away from the scene.

That was the plan, anyway. Clothilde waited for him to collect her. Fifteen minutes passed, then twenty. Then just after twenty-four minutes, when she'd gone beyond anxious, the door opened, but it was not von Stauffenberg, but Heinz Brandt, and worse, he held the briefcase. "Where is Colonel von Stauffenberg?" Brandt demanded. "He said he was going to make a phone call, but he forgot his briefcase." It was still locked tight, but Brandt shook it till it rattled.

"He made his phone call," Clothilde lied, "but he had to use the bathroom. He has war injuries!" Clothilde took the briefcase from Brandt, scolding him. "You should be ashamed of yourself! Now let me get this back to the colonel so the poor man doesn't have to carry it again. He is not as strong as he looks!"

Clothilde shoved past, walking at her briskest clip to the office where the Führer was, Brandt running to catch up.

"There is no need, fräulein! You are not authorized here! I can take the briefcase!" Brandt caught up just as she was opening the door, wresting the briefcase from her and shoving past to sit down, slamming the briefcase onto the floor, but on the other side of the legs of the heavy oaken conference table from where the Führer sat.

She heard a brief *clink*, then a *click*, then an earth-shattering *kaboom!*

Clothilde instinctively made Saint Nicholas's gesture, trying to transmute herself to smoke and fire, but she was smoke and fire already, fried to a crisp.

But not completely free, for shackled to her by chains of smoke was the imp Rumpelstiltskin. "Now you are mine, naughty girl," the goaty little devil laughed, "and off to hell we go!"

"Hold!" a voice cried out, and while not a chorus of angels, it was a soloist from the choir eternal—a cherub exactly like the one depicted by Wilhelm Busch's pen in *Hypocritical Helena*. "Unhand her, evil one! She's a holy martyr!"

"She's a witch!" cried Rumpelstiltskin. "And she's mine!"

The cherub grabbed Clothilde's free right hand while the imp pulled on her chained left, then proceeded a tug-of-war, equal parts the battle from *Hypocritical Helena* and the finale from Murnau's *Faust*.

Clothilde didn't know how it would end but considered it a fitting fate for a librarian, if the matter were left for readers to debate and decide.

THE SCENIC ROUTE

JEREMY ROBINSON

RAMREE ISLAND, BURMA, FEBRUARY 1945

I dream of death's smell. The nightmare resumes when I wake.

"Captain," whispers the man whose hand is over my mouth. "Captain Moss, wake up."

I open my eyes to Sergeant Jeremy Brewer. He's got that look in his eyes. Real wide, like he's seen Death himself just over the hill, sickle perched against one of the endless palm trees, taking a shit in preparation for the coming day. It's the same look frozen onto the faces of every man left in my company.

We were two hundred strong two days ago. Today we're twelve men, spread across a mile-long proverbial line in the sand. We were sent to this godforsaken island with a simple mission—push the Japs back. No one told us why. The orders were given with a smirk, like there'd be a prize at the bottom of this particular Cracker Jack box of bullshit. I have yet to find it, and I fully expect to meet my maker by the day's end.

Because something is out there, lurking in the swamp, and it ain't one of the Japanese, though it seems to be fighting for them.

I give Brewer a nod to let him know I'm awake. He lets go

of my mouth, points to his eyes, and then out at the jungle surrounding the barren hill upon which we've dug in.

"Company?" I ask.

"Something," he says. "Ripples in the water."

Only been here three days, and we all know that the best way to spot a hidden enemy is to watch the water. The ripples tell a story, sliding through the knee-deep water left behind by a monsoon storm that rolled through a week ago.

I sit up in the two-foot-deep, mud-filled foxhole. Only thing it protects me from is being easily seen. The mud is impossible to escape. We're soaked through all the time—if not from rain, then from sweat. Fingertips are permanently raisined. If we survive this nightmare, which is doubtful, I'm going to move to Arizona.

Looking down the thirty-foot slope, the hot chocolate water below is shaded from the early morning sun by a thick canopy of palm leaves. The whole island is like this—random hills held together by thick grass, surrounded by low-lying jungle and swampland. During the recent storm, water submerged most everything below the hilltops. Below, a pattern of ripples flows past. I take in the space between them, how fast they're moving, and how many offshoots there are—created every time the water flows past a tree.

"It's distant," I say. "Moving east."

"It?" Brewer asks. "You're sure?"

"It's not a man," I tell him.

"Maybe a pig? They have those here, right? I mean, there are crocs on this island. They gotta eat something, right?"

"You see any pigs yet?" I ask him.

He thinks on it. Shakes his head.

"Whatever is out there, it's eating everything it comes across. Including the pigs."

"Including . . . our men?"

"I've heard the screams," I say. "We all have. The calls over the radio. The reports. We know they're dying. Their blood swirls through the water. You can smell it. But . . . I haven't seen a body. Have you?"

He sits in the mud, the gumption gut-kicked right out of him. "Well, shit."

"Look at it this way. Today will be your last day in hell, one way or another."

He frowns. "Death . . . or victory?"

I give him a nod.

"But, sir."

"You can call me Tyler out here, Brewer. Or Moss. Just leave out the formality. So long as everyone does as I say, we can do away with pretense when we're risking our lives." I pat his scrawny shoulder. "Tell the others to eat everything they've got left. We're pushing until we drop today."

He sighs, nods, and then stands. "I hate crocs. They're like sharks that can chase you onto dry land."

Leaves me to my thoughts.

I've sent hundreds of men to their deaths at the hands of an unknown foe. Today . . . it's my turn.

Splitting up doesn't feel like a great idea, but this is one situation where safety in numbers doesn't apply. If we're all bunched up, one submerged land mine could do us in.

I've broken the men up into three squads of four. My crew—Alpha Squad, as of an hour ago—is pushing down the territory's center. Bravo and Charlie are on our left and right. Upon contact with the enemy, the unengaged squads will flank and unleash hell—whether it's the Japanese, who currently outnumber us a hundred to one, or whatever man-eaters lurk in these murky waters. We'll overcome the obstacle with strategy and discipline. And balls. If we make it through and find the enemy camp believed to be two miles deep, we'll use the explosives we have left to cause maximum damage, before hightailing it back to our meager foxholes, where we'll continue praying that our promised reinforcements will show up soon.

We move with tortoise-like slowness, down into the water, keeping our ripples to a minimum by stepping as close to tree trunks as possible. Makes the journey a lot longer, but we've got a full day to travel from point A to point B without dying, and we'll be sprinting the whole way back.

"Hey," Corporal Phil Ward whispers from behind me. "Is it weird to drink your own sweat? Because I've been doing it all day, and I'm starting to think it tastes good."

"That's because you've been lyin' in mud and shit," Corporal Tom Moore says. "Probably tastes better than that swill coming out of your mama's well."

Moore and Ward were friends before the war. Somehow ended up knee-deep in the shit together. As a result, their southern-tinged banter often takes on a personal tone that might cause a ruckus between strangers. Generally serves to entertain the rest of us, but I don't feel much like having a laugh.

"Keep it down," I tell them.

Brewer brings up the rear, looking squirrelly, like he might shoot at the first thing he sees. Would normally be a cause for concern, but I'd feel better if the other two looked the same. If something moves out here and it's not walking on two feet, dressed in olive drab, and speaking English, well, better put a bullet in it, just to be sure. Call me old-fashioned.

"Okay, being serious this time," Ward says. "There's Burmese villages all over, right? If I—being the liberating hero—were able to woo a local girl and marry her, do you think that would be legally binding back home?"

"If you manage to marry a filly out here in the jungle," Moore says, "I suspect anything is possible."

"You'd need paperwork," Brewer says. "As proof."

"I suppose we could scrawl something on a big leaf," Ward says. "Captain, you can officiate a wedding, right?"

The southern duo have managed to worm their way past my defenses. The knots in my back loosen. A grin slips onto my face.

And it's eradicated a moment later by a scream.

"Who's that?" Brewer asks.

"Don't matter who," Moore says. "That's Bravo."

"Stay close, boys," I say, shifting direction and double-timing it through the swampy water, heading toward the scream, toward danger and heartbreak, and toward my death. My heart pounds. Vision narrows. After just a few steps, all my concerns, and the reality of my situation, are lost in a mental bloodlust that lets men do the unimaginable. Some men get lost in that place. I don't like to stay in it for very long. Leaves a stain that can build up over time, impossible to wash out.

Picking a direction is a trick at first. No one's made a sound since, and I'm not about to call out. Then I see approaching ripples mixing with our own. Gives me a direction and conceals our approach. I motion for the others to follow, adjust course, and move as quickly as I can without splashing.

Until the shooting starts.

Then I lift my knees high and charge through the knee-deep water. "If it ain't our men," I shout, "shoot it dead!"

Approaching a stand of large ferns, I draw my machete and put all my childhood tennis lessons to good use. One solid backhand is enough to lop through the bunch and provide a clear view of what can best be described as a scene straight out of Dante's ninth circle of hell.

Three Bravo team men leap around, rifles aimed down at the water. A fourth man, bloodied, leans against a tree, rifle lost, knife drawn. A swirl of water reveals the predator's position. The men with rifles dance about, firing into the water, afraid to let their legs stay submerged for more than a second. It looks ridiculous, but the state of the wounded man justifies the behavior. We've all seen how quickly a croc can dismember a human being.

Their target thrashes in the water—hit perhaps—but far from dead.

I raise my M1, hoping to add my ammunition to the effort, but it's impossible to get a shot while everyone is hopping around.

Then the wounded man—Private Mike Hall, I think—catches us all off guard when he shouts a battle cry and shoves up and away from the tree before diving onto the croc's back, plunging the knife into the water. A white froth explodes into the air as the pair fight and thrash. White turns pink from blood, and then the water goes still.

The ten-foot-long croc surfaces . . .

Belly up.

A moment later, the man rises from the water, coughing, still holding his knife. He staggers a step and then lifts his fists in victory. His squad mates join in, filling the jungle with hoots and hollers that are bound to attract attention. They know as much.

Just aren't expecting it to arrive when it does.

A wake cuts through the swamp's surface, spraying water as something races toward the men.

I track it with my M1, but I can't find a target above the surface.

"Incoming!" I shout, but they don't hear me over their victory celebration.

I fire the rifle, target be damned. The round punches through the water, but there's no way to know if it struck home. But it gets the men's attention. Doesn't take long for them to notice the oncoming bus-sized wake.

Two men stand their ground and fire.

The other two run.

Can't blame the man who killed the first croc. He's wounded and unarmed now, except for a knife. But the other man? If he survives, we'll have to have a talk about bravery, brotherhood, and—

The creature surfaces.

A crocodile the likes of which I have never seen, with jaws large enough for a man to bed down in. The armor plating covering its body is thick and dark, covered in spiky protrusions partially concealed by moss and ferns growing from the flesh. If this thing laid still, you'd never know it was nearby.

Pocks of red burst from the creature's face. Bullets burrow into flesh, but they don't get past the skull.

All that makes some kind of sense. I know crocs can get big—thirty feet plus—but this thing is more than just big.

It's also . . . different. Alien almost.

The massive jaws snap open, but the beast's aim is off. The croc is barreling toward the gap between the men. It's going to miss. I feel a momentary hope, until I see a bulge of pink flesh roiling up out of the creature's throat. Then all at once, eight twisting limbs burst out like streamers at a parade.

Each tentacle is covered with suckers and tipped with a single spike, larger and sharper than a lion's tooth.

The two fleeing men are caught first, snagged by the ankles and yanked back into the water.

The two brave men are attacked second, but they meet their ends first. One is struck in the head. The spike burrows deep, ending his life in a moment. He's the lucky one. The other man is yanked forward, into the crocodile's mouth, and dragged down whole, into the beast's massive gullet. The ensnared men are quickly yanked back, drowned, and torn apart. It happens with such unnatural speed—seconds from start to finish—and the scene is so mind-numbingly horrific that I forget to fire.

Though I suppose it wouldn't have made a difference.

"It's a croctopus . . ." Moore whispers.

I turn to the men and croak, "Run . . ." They stand paralyzed by fear. I shove them along with a growled whisper. "Run!"

I've never been much of a long-distance runner. Mom always told me I had muscles like my grandfather, built for power and speed, not endurance. That was just fine with me. Girls are more impressed when you can pick them up than they are when you can outpace them.

Now? I could use a little endurance. Disoriented by panic, we've been charging toward the enemy encampment for ten minutes. Probably not more than a few hundred feet from their defensive line.

Those of us in Alpha Squad, who saw what happened to Bravo, are in the lead. Charlie has nearly caught up to us, fifty feet back, but they're raising a racket. Shouting at us to stop. Asking what happened. I can hear them. Can make sense of the words. But they're filtered out by some primal urge to survive—or at least to be killed by a bullet rather than eaten by a nightmare.

"Hey," Brewer says, glancing back at me. "Eleven o'clock."

I shift my eyes a little to the left and spot it. A sandbag foxhole, partially submerged, likely built before the monsoon. I raise my rifle, knowing I won't be able to hit the dang thing while running.

But there's no one to shoot at.

The position has been abandoned . . . and its mounted machine gun left behind. I adjust course, running up to the foxhole. Feeling pretty good about our find, until we get close. Until we see the blood. And what's left of the Japanese men who'd been stationed here. All that remains of them is a string of intestines bobbing in the water. The machine gun is spent.

"It got them too," Moore says, bent over, catching his breath. He looks up, hopeful. "Maybe it got all of them?"

I shake my head.

We're not that lucky.

"Hey! Hey!" It's Lieutenant Rob Foster, Charlie leader. "What the hell, Captain? What happened? Where's Bravo? What—" He spots the gore behind me. "What the fuck?"

"Bravo's KIA."

"Only heard our rifles," Foster says. "Didn't hear any Japs firing back."

"It was a crocodile," I say.

Foster shakes his head. "No way one croc took out four of our guys. Not that fast."

"Wasn't a croc," Ward says.

"Croctopus," Moore says. "Thing was all kinds of ugly. Big as one of them fancy long cars."

"Limousine," Ward says. "Armored too. And out of its mouth . . ."

Moore uses his fingers to mimic the creature's tentacles coming out and retracting. "It just grabbed hold of 'em. Pulled 'em in. Didn't stand a chance."

"Fellas," Foster says, losing his patience. "I'm not in the mood to be—"

"It's all true," I say. "They're not even exaggerating."

"Not even a little," Brewer says. "We all saw it."

"Captain," Foster says. "There's no such thing as a—"

A tentacle slaps over Foster's mouth from behind, cutting him short and lifting him off the ground. When he's yanked back, I see the rest of Charlie in the creature's grasp, pulled in and torn apart with its spare tendrils.

My stomach twists in revulsion. "No!" I scream. Out of pure instinct and desperation, the four of us who are still alive lift our rifles and fire. The croctopus bucks and flinches, feeling pain from each strike, but we're unable to deliver a killing blow. Not even close.

"Aim for the eyes!" Brewer shouts. I line up one of the large eyes, hoping to put a bullet through and into the brain beyond, or at least to partially blind the creature. Before I get to pull the trigger, the monster slips beneath the water, taking the Charlie men with it.

"It was hunting us that whole time," I realize aloud. "Just waiting for us to stop."

"Then I suggest we keep moving," Brewer says.

"Seconded," Moore says. "A POW camp would be preferable."

I give a nod. "Go."

"Land!" Ward shouts, like we've been lost at sea for days.

The hill rising ahead of us *is* a welcome sight. We hit it at full throttle, wet feet slipping over slick grass that peels away, revealing a trap of viscous mud below.

"We ain't climbing this shit," Moore says.

"Here," Brewer says, clinging to a tangle of roots jutting out from the hillside halfway up. He makes it to a tree growing out at an angle. Hauls himself atop it and then searches for the next handhold. No way to know if he'll find his way to the top, but being halfway up the hill is better than being at the bottom.

One by one, we pull ourselves up to the tree and then gingerly follow Brewer's path of roots, vegetation, and rocks, each of us driven by raw, fear-fueled determination. I flinch when a hand takes hold of my wrist from above.

"Got you," Moore says, leaning down from the hill's top. "C'mon."

With a final heave, I slide up into a field of tall grass and lie on my back, staring up at the sky, watching as more storm clouds roll in from the east.

Just one day without rain . . . one day.

We're not exactly safe here, in Japanese territory, pursued by a monster. But we'll be able to see, and hear, it coming now. So I take a moment to catch my breath.

"Captain," Brewer says, standing over me. "Moss. Sir."

"Brewer, I told you—"

"I know," he says. "I just . . . you need to see this."

"See what?" I ask.

He turns away from me, motioning with his head. Whatever it is, it's close. With a sigh, I roll onto my stomach, push myself up, and come face-to-face with an aberration. In a jungle of muck and filth, filled with crocodiles and death, perched atop the hill . . . is a concrete structure that resembles an oversized pillbox, stretched out in the middle, like some kind of oblong fortress.

"Why would the Japs build something like this, in a place like this, so far from any part of the world that people care about?" Moore asks.

"We're here," I say. "Someone cares about it."

"Not me," Ward says.

"File up," I tell them. "Pistols only. Worst-case scenario, it's full of the enemy. Best-case scenario, it gives us a place to hide until that storm blows over or reinforcements arrive."

Moore draws his pistol and holds it out as mud and water drip from the muzzle. "Gonna be lucky if this thing still fires."

"Luck is all that's keeping us alive so far," I tell him, and then I head for the concrete structure's metal door, which is slightly ajar.

The door shudders and squeaks as I push it open with my foot. I brace for some kind of defense, but the only thing that assaults me is the smell. The four of us wince as one, reeling back.

"Good God," Ward says, smacking Moore's shoulder. "Smells like your mama's cooch."

Moore just nods, trying not to gag.

After placing a wet handkerchief over my mouth and nose, I push into the cool, dark interior, illuminated only by several long slits in the far wall. The air is damp, thick with humidity, but it's different from what's outside. It's . . . sticky. Tacky.

I motion to Ward and Moore as Brewer closes the creaky door behind us. "You two head left. We'll go right. Quick sweep, then meet back here in the middle. If we can hide out here, great. If not, we should keep moving."

The pair nod and head off into the shadows.

Brewer joins me. "Lock is busted. Something broke it from the inside, headed out."

Without another word, we head deeper into the building, sweeping back and forth with our handguns. Repulsive as the aromas are, it's a relief to not have to struggle through waist-high water. The breather is short-lived. I slow a step when my feet stick to layers of coagulating blood covering the floor. Slow again when I come across a side room full of crocodile parts. Heads, limbs, and tails, all removed from bodies with surgical skill. Some lie on shelves, still fresh. Others are contained in jars of clear liquid. The smell of blood, crocodile intestines, and formaldehyde nearly doubles me over.

"Hey," Brewer says, motioning to a desk. It's covered in paperwork and folders, jostled from some previous scuffle. I rifle through the pages, but as expected, everything is in Japanese. I pick up a folder, pausing to look at several anatomical sketches. Of humans. Of animals, including several octopuses. Of . . . hybrids between the two, including a man with a crocodile's head. The last sketch depicts a crocodile's head, carved open, a human brain sitting inside. "What the hell?"

"Seven thirty-one," Brewer says, pointing to a folder's cover.

"You can read Japanese?"

"Just numbers," he says. "One through ten. And this . . . is seven-three-one."

The number's importance isn't lost on me. We've all heard of Unit 731, of the horrific experiments they've been performing on civilian populations throughout Asia—and on prisoners of war.

"What do you think they were doing out here?" he asks.

I put the folder down. "I think we've already seen it." I move down the long space, a cage at the far end coming into view. It's forty feet wide, ten feet tall, and its door is bent down from the top. Surrounding the destruction are the remains of a dozen Japanese scientists, all in various stages of mutilation and decomposition.

"They *made* it," I say, turning around with widening eyes. "This is that creature's birthplace."

A gunshot draws my eyes to the slit in the concrete wall. I move closer. The view reveals a cleared swath of gently sloping hillside, free of the water, crisscrossed by wire-mesh cages, each of them containing a crocodile. And they're not alone. The Japanese camp lies just beyond. A thousand soldiers. Most of them focused on the crocs. On this . . . laboratory. They're ignoring their emaciated prisoners held in a series of handmade cages, waiting for an attack, but not from us.

They're afraid of it too.

The croctopus.

One of their experiments got loose and is now making both sides of this war pay the price.

"Let's get the hell out of here," I say, hurrying back toward the door.

Ward and Moore meet us there, equally hurried, both of them pale.

"What did you find?" I ask.

"Couple of operating tables," Moore says, and he nearly vomits.

"Lots of bodies. People. Women. Children . . . God . . . children with crocodile parts sewn on. We need to—"

The door creaks open. For a moment, the illuminated rectangle of daylight remains empty. Then . . . a reptilian head the length of my body slides inside.

Fuck me.

The four of us leap back, weapons aimed.

"Should we shoot it?" Brewer asks, his hands shaking. "How come we're not shooting it?"

"Because," I say, looking in the creature's eyes and seeing a soul reflected back. Between the eyes is a poorly stitched incision. "It didn't want this." I lower my gun. "Did you?"

"The hell are you doing, Cap?" Moore asks.

"You see any human heads missing brains?" I ask.

"One," Ward says. "One . . . of ours. Holy shit." He lowers his weapon. "You don't think?"

"Lower your weapons," I tell Brewer and Moore. "Both of you. Now."

They obey, but they take a few steps back. If I'm wrong, the first person to be eaten will be me.

Eaten first. Eaten last. What's it matter? Dead is dead.

I take a step forward, palms extended. "We aren't the people who did this to you. They're our enemies too."

A low, guttural growl vibrates from the croc's throat. Close enough.

"The people who did this . . . your enemy. They're on the other side of this building. Just over there." I point to the slit in the wall behind me. The croctopus's head shifts to the side for just a moment. "And they're planning to do it again. They have crocodiles. Hundreds of them. Penned up. Being tortured. People too. Innocent people. The people you—and us—were sent here to protect. To liberate. And our mission, it's not done yet."

I take a breath. Stand a little straighter. "Do you understand?"

The croc's mouth opens slowly. I can see the pink arms just inside, coiled up, ready to spring out. It takes everything I have not to flee.

Then the jaws snap shut.

The creature backs out of the door, and out of sight. I can hear its footsteps, the sound of its body sliding through tall grass. Then it's gone.

"Ho-lee-sheit," Ward says, letting out a sigh. "I can't believe that worked."

I lean forward, hands on shaking knees. The room spins around me until a hand rests on my back.

"You did good, sir," Brewer says. "Saved our bacon."

"Can't say the same for the Japs," Moore says, looking through the slot. The pop of gunfire fills the air. Slowly at first, coupled with shouts of warning and then the steady staccato sound of battle.

"Here," Ward says, plucking a ladder from beside the door. He hurries outside with it. Leans it against the building and starts climbing. We follow him, one after the other, scrambling up onto the roof—safe from things with teeth—and getting an eyeful of the action in the distance.

"What's it doing?" Ward asks.

"Freeing them," Moore says. "The other crocs. It's letting them go."

I shake my head. "It's recruiting them."

The croctopus moves through the grid of fencing like a rocket, flattening everything in its path. The moment a croc is freed, it sets upon the men around it. In minutes, the enemy ranks are decimated by the powerful jaws of hungry, tortured, vengeful crocodiles. All led by a creature built by mad scientists who gave it the mind, and perhaps the soul, of a man.

As the swamp on the hill's far side turns red with blood, we sit and watch the carnage play out. Just twenty minutes later, the last bullet is fired. Soon after that, the final scream.

I lie on my back, looking at the sky, the bluest I've ever seen.

The storm had moved off.

Before I can relax, I hear the distinct sound of a round being chambered. It's followed by indistinct whispers.

I get back to my feet along with the men. Rifles in hand, we creep to the roof's edge, look down, and see—

—reinforcements.

Hundreds of American soldiers in green, fresh-faced, with clean rifles and a complete lack of horror in their eyes. Some of them look downright eager.

I clear my throat, and a dozen Garand rifles snap up toward me.

"Hey, boys. You can lower your weapons. Fight's over."

"We're here to reinforce Captain Tyler Moss," a young officer says, stepping forward.

"And you found him."

"Did . . . did you say the fight was over?" he asks.

"In this small part of the world," I say. "They won't be coming back."

"In that case," the man says, "our orders—your orders, I suppose—are to push through to the mainland."

Beside me, Ward huffs, and Moore throws up his hands. I calm them with an outstretched hand and say, "No one's going through the swamp on the other side of this hill."

"But—"

"The locals don't take too kindly to strangers. I'd have you ask the Japs, if they weren't all eaten." That sobers up the fresh faces. "Find a way around. On dry land. Away from the crocodiles. Take the scenic route off Ramree Island, and you might just make it home."

The man looks like he's smelled something foul, but he's trained well enough not to argue with an order.

"Eh, eh, eh," I say as he turns away. "While you're at it, call in a duck boat. My men have spent enough time in the water."

With that, I step back and take a seat, waiting to watch the sunset from my high perch, or an approaching DUKW, whichever comes first. Down the hill, the water roils from the sweeping tails of unseen crocs, dispersing into the swamp, reclaiming lost territory, guided by a man-made monster turned protector.

APELDOORN

TANYA HUFF

APELDOORN, THE NETHERLANDS, APRIL 1945

Henry watched the staff car slow and come to a stop just past where he stood in the shadows at the side of the road. Over the pings of the engine cooling, he heard the constant background noises of an encamped infantry division, the deep distant thrum of bombers, and the higher-pitched hum of fighter planes, more distant still.

The staff car had three visible bullet holes down the driver's-side door, possibly more under the thick coating of dried mud, and had seen some hard use. So had they all at this point in the war. Leaving the shadows just to the left of the front bumper, Henry paused, empty hands well out from his side to let the occupants get a good look at him.

Muttering under his breath, the corporal behind the wheel got out, favoring his right leg. He gave Henry's clothing a suspicious once-over and limped around to lean against the hood of the car like a sullen hood ornament.

Henry waited until he lit a cigarette, then slid into the back seat.

Major General Harry Foster, unlike General Crerar, who

seldom moved TacOps more than five kilometers from his headquarters, was no stranger to the front lines. He'd led the First Canadian Infantry through Italy, then was deployed with his division to northwest Europe as part of Operation Goldflake. He wore that ridiculous, narrow mustache most of the Canadian commanders had adopted in order, Henry assumed, to look British. His sidearm braced on his thigh, muzzle pointed at Henry, he said, in a flat, unfriendly tone, "Hockey."

Henry almost smiled. "Puck."

Foster's shoulders relaxed. Slightly. "Are you Fitzroy, the *special forces* man General Crerar insisted I speak to?"

"Yes." Crerar, in command of the First Canadian Army, didn't know exactly who Henry was, but he was one of the Allied commanders who knew *what.* His Grace, the Duke of Suffolk, who'd been in charge of Henry's military training, had taught him that pressure applied in the right place would end a war faster than wholesale slaughter, and Henry had been applying that pressure since 1939. Granted, he'd originally been trained in blades and bows, but death had been a constant over the centuries, and he was very good at death.

"All right," Foster growled. "What is it that Crerar thinks you can do for me?"

Henry met the general's well-known bluntness with bluntness of his own, subtlety buried under six years of war. "I'm a weapon. Aim me."

"A weapon?" Foster spat the words at him. "Don't waste my time, boy. If you can't give me the Netherlands, I've no use for you."

"It's not mine to give," Henry agreed. This was the first time he'd done anything other than pass through the Netherlands since 1530, when, as Duke of Richmond and Somerset, he'd represented his father at the court of the new Prince of Orange. The prince had been unable to decide whether the presence of

England's bastard prince had been intended as an insult. Henry had been eleven.

"You're damned right it isn't yours." Foster gestured with the gun, the motion too minimal to shift his aim. "Now stop wasting my time. I have work to do."

"So do I." Henry let the Hunger rise.

Foster's pupils dilated and knuckles whitened on the hand holding his weapon. Nostrils flared, and, breathing heavily, stinking of fear, he whispered, "Enough. There was a woman in Italy, at Valguarnera . . . you're . . . what she was?"

"Possibly."

"And Crerar thinks you can *help*?" The general swallowed audibly and shook his head.

Well aware of what the other man was denying, likely more aware than the man himself, Henry pushed the Hunger back. "I fight for the Allies, General. What can I do?"

"What can you *do*?" His laugh had edges.

Henry rephrased the question. "What do you need?"

After a long moment, Foster shook his head, shaking the memory of a woman in Valguarnera away. He didn't so much sag as his rigid posture collapsed in on itself, letting Henry see he was as exhausted as the men he led. "What do I need? I need the war to be over. I need my men to stop dying. Apeldoorn's filled with refugees, so if I use artillery, call in the bombers Montgomery's promised, I kill hundreds of civilians. I'd rather surround the old city, isolate it—not a guarantee given the canal and the flooded ground—and force a surrender." He laid his pistol flat on his thigh and flexed his hand. "Unfortunately, we intercepted an order, signed by Himmler, threatening battle commanders with death if they neglect to take adequate measures to defend towns and communication centers. War's almost over. Everyone knows it. Us. The Germans. But people are still dying. You ask me what I need; I need the Germans out of Apeldoorn."

A few days ago, a werewolf in the Dutch Resistance had told Henry that one, *maybe* two bridges were left over the canal. Not that it mattered; one or two, the Germans would blow them before the Canadians arrived. And depending on the Germans to surrender was a shit plan. If Foster wouldn't call in bombers, it'd be a house-to-house fight, and no one wanted that . . . ghouls were still feeding in Aachen. He opened the car door.

Foster straightened. "Where are you going, then, *special forces*?"

Henry paused and stilled the driver's move toward him with a glance. "To get the Germans out of Apeldoorn."

Needing a refuel, Henry had left his motorcycle with the First Canadians, *encouraging* those he couldn't avoid contact with to believe him a courier carrying top secret documents. Walking through the camp to retrieve it, he passed a group of men curled over cigarettes, refighting the clearing of the Scheldt. Henry hadn't been there—even the night battles had been amphibious—but a couple of selkies from the Fifty-First Highlanders had helped out.

"Fucking Monty," muttered a skinny private.

Henry agreed. He'd taken himself out of Montgomery's memory after the field marshal had said, one too many times, "If you're so dangerous, why don't you just kill Hitler?"

There was no *just* about it. The Nazis—or Hitler and his inner circle, at least—believed in his kind and guarded accordingly, negating most of Henry's advantages. He would have never got close enough to Hitler to kill him.

With April shortening the nights to barely ten hours, he

gunned the bike past a sentry and once on the road opened the throttle, the sentry's profane observation about crazy couriers turning the air blue behind him.

Henry reached Apeldoorn just before dawn on April 12, having left the Norton in a barn a half mile out. There were, indeed, two bridges still standing; he could see the second from his perch on a roof overlooking the first. He could also see concrete bunkers and earthen ramparts. The Germans had been in the Netherlands long enough to dig in like ticks, and like ticks, they were bleeding the country dry.

With dawn snapping at his heels, he had no time to cross the canal into the old city and took shelter for the day in a forgotten crypt under the ruin of a church. "Life imitating art," he muttered, shoving ancient bones aside. He'd seen Dracula at the Little Theatre in London in 1927, and the hints of truth made him wonder just who Stoker had known.

The next night, hidden by the dark of the moon, he slid under the closer bridge and crossed the canal on its substructure. Unfortunately, the explosives set to take it down were up on the road. No reason to hide them when both friend and foe knew they were there.

Getting into the town, past the multiple concrete barriers the Germans had built to obstruct approaching tanks and shield their defenders, made Henry feel like a mouse in a maze. Had the men on guard not been more interested in outdoing each other's complaints about the war, he wouldn't have made it. From the town side, the Dutch Resistance—the purely human Dutch Resistance, for the werewolves stayed out of towns and cities—could have taken it out with a few well-aimed bricks had they not known how the Germans would react. One dead soldier meant ten Dutch civilians shot.

Fortunately, Henry had no intention of killing the guards. He didn't want the Germans to believe he'd slipped past their defenses, leaving them an opening to dismiss him as nothing more than an Allied trick. He wanted them to believe he'd been there all along.

Like most medieval city centers, the old town hadn't been planned so much as it had grown to fit the needs of the inhabitants. Had the oddly angled streets, the alleys, and unexpected dead ends nagged at the orderly souls of the Dutch back before the war had added the destruction of the Germans to it? He'd have to return after to see what they'd made of it.

After the war was over.

After the Germans were gone.

It wasn't late, although it was after curfew, and any Dutch civilians visibly on the streets were no doubt part of the traitorous NSB or collaborators. More than once he skirted shadows already occupied. It could have been the Resistance, out because they knew, like everyone knew, the war was nearly over. Or it could have been civilians desperate to find food because the war wasn't over yet.

The roadblock on Reigersweg denied access to nothing Henry could see unless it was the left turn just past it, heading north toward the train station. There were four men by the barricade, talking with a pair of privates in an ancient truck probably confiscated from a Dutch farmer, and another four off to one side, smoking. While he watched, a grizzled sergeant pinched out his cigarette and muttered something to the man beside him before shuffling off into the shadows to relieve himself.

He was tucking himself away as he turned. His eyes widened, his mouth opened . . .

Before he could give the alarm, Henry let the Hunger rise. He caught the sergeant's red-rimmed gaze and held it, ripping open his uniform to expose his throat, fabric tearing before buttons gave way. The sergeant moaned and trembled as Henry leaned forward and breathed in the rich aroma of the blood that flowed beneath the thin skin.

Terror was a temptation. He'd fed on it more during this war than was safe, could feel the addiction lapping at the edges of the Hunger, a darkness he could fall into as so many of his kind did until fear became as great a need as the blood.

The sergeant whimpered, his breathing fast and shallow.

Fighting his own nature, Henry drove his teeth into flesh, missing the major blood vessels. One swallow, two, then he lifted his head, giving the sergeant a good look at the blood running off his teeth and down his chin. Then he sent him staggering back toward the roadblock, carrying his terror with him, blood running from a double puncture in his throat.

He was on the roof by the time the shouting started.

Officers were a distant authority. A sergeant, marked in so obvious a way, gasping out that he'd seen a monster in the night, would be believed.

The Hunger, aroused but unsatisfied, stirred.

He soothed it like he might a leashed beast and reminded it, reminded himself, there'd be blood enough before he was done.

At a second roadblock, he caught the gaze of a young corporal and drew him into shadow.

At the third, word had arrived before him. He could have used fear to cut his prey from the herd, but he took the time to lure a burly-chested nonbeliever, a stalwart Son of the Fatherland with little imagination.

He could see no pattern in the positioning of the roadblocks and very little point, as only the Germans used the roads. The Dutch, with no vehicles and no fuel for any they might have had hidden, traveled as he did—only with more knowledge of their surroundings and the courage to face an occupying army with at most a bowl of watery potato skin soup in their bellies.

At the fourth roadblock, reinforcements had arrived. Over the last year, many of the operational commands in the Netherlands had been given to the *Waffen-SS*, although Henry hadn't thought Apeldoorn had been one of them.

"Might have been nice had Foster mentioned it," he murmured, watching an *SS-Untersturmführer*, roughly equivalent to an Allied second lieutenant, berate the men. He was young, his uniform didn't quite fit, and he was obviously annoyed at being called out to deal with . . .

". . . superstitious nonsense! The Dutch play on your fears, and you fall for it like idiot peasants!"

In Henry's experience, much of the Wehrmacht, while complicit in SS atrocities either out of fear of reprisal or true belief, considered them to be arrogant, elitist bastards. This particular *Untersturmführer* was certainly fulfilling expectations, and Henry gave thanks this roadblock hadn't drawn an officer less likely to be shot by his own weary troops. Perhaps Fate wanted the war to be over as much as those fighting it.

The lack of moonlight allowed him to position himself dangerously close, and he snarled from the shadows, pitching the sound to vibrate in blood and bone.

The Germans shuffled in place—half with their weapons up, half poised to run.

The *Untersturmführer*'s nostrils flared. "Don't just stand there! You and you, investigate!"

One of the men was honestly terrified; Henry could feel it lapping at his self-control. They shuffled forward at a speed guaranteed to annoy any officer, let alone one so desperate to prove himself in charge.

"It's probably nothing more than some mangy dog!" he

snapped, drew his sidearm, whirled dramatically, and fired. "There! Taken care of!"

Henry could see three of the older men roll their eyes. The *Untersturmführer* couldn't.

"But, sir, what if it's not dead, sir?" asked one.

"Still afraid? Go and check it, then!"

"Y-yes, sir."

Henry thought the quaver was a bit over the top, but the young officer, clearly believing in the superiority of the SS, did not.

"Cowards! Never mind. I'll do it myself."

More time passed than anyone would have needed to find a dead dog.

No one stepped away from the barricade to find out why.

When life barely lingered, the *Untersturmführer*, locked in his own darkness, crawled back toward his men. He'd live if they got him medical attention.

Henry wondered if they would.

There were soldiers billeted in the Onze Lieve Vrouwekerk, the nearest Catholic church, and with sunrise dangerously close, they'd begun to stir. Sometimes a shadow, sometimes just another soldier in the half dark, Henry moved past and among them. Rumor spread quickly when fanned by fear, so rather than risk a daylight search of the crypts for the monster in the night, he went up to wait out the day in one of the lightless recesses builders used so that the artistic demands of the Catholic Church could coexist with gravity.

He remained in the church for the first part of the night, propping thralled and bleeding men in the nooks and crannies every church seemed to accumulate, the overindulgence of the night before keeping the Hunger in abeyance. Just after midnight, when the first of those men were found and the terrified shouting began, he stripped a young corporal of his tunic and slipped out a side door.

Planes passed in the distance, bombers heading for Germany, and he heard machine guns significantly closer.

"Reconnaissance first," he murmured, stripping out of his bloody shirt and shrugging into the tunic.

The First had reached Apeldoorn. The Hastings and Prince Edward Regiment had dug in by the canal, taking cover to the east of the bridge Henry had crossed the night before. At some point during the day, the Germans had blown the bridge. The Canadians would have to move north to the last remaining bridge, but that wouldn't happen tonight, so Henry went back to work.

Three men snatched from the rear of patrols and left wandering, dripping blood. He split the fourth patrol in half, and it opened fire on itself.

Just as sunrise began to make itself felt as a nagging itch, he found where the Germans kept their Dutch prisoners. It had been a warehouse, and he assumed that, with resistance so active, there were usually more than four guards. Action at the canal had probably pulled the others away.

The first guard moved within a rank miasma of cheap alcohol. Henry used his fangs but didn't feed, Hunger recoiling from the taint. The second guard came around a corner, saw the lines of dark blood running down pale skin, and froze. His mind had darkness enough to hold him. The third guard was sneaking a cigarette tucked away where he couldn't be seen.

The fourth guard took Henry by surprise. A bullet ripped through his left shoulder, a second through his left thigh. He spun around, dropped down, and the bullet that would have gone into his skull missed.

"Just a man, then." The guard snickered. "Men can be ki—"

He didn't have time to scream, but he fought, first with fists and feet and then against the thrall. In the end, the Hunger won. The Hunger always won. Driven by pain and blood loss, Henry drank deeply and finally surfaced, almost amused by the lack of terror and the guard's fury at being so used.

Leaving the smaller man draped across the rifle half driven into the warehouse wall, Henry unbarred the one door not nailed shut and eased it silently open. A defiant question spat toward him in no way muffled the sound of a child weeping.

Well . . . fuck.

He didn't speak Dutch, and he was running out of time.

German would send the wrong message.

Hopefully, someone in there spoke English.

"Get out quickly so I can bar the door. Run and hide; it's almost over."

"Is the English army here?" This voice was young. Not a child, but not much past it.

"On the other side of the canal." The Canadians spoke English. Close enough. "Now go!"

And still, they hesitated.

His sudden vision of charging forward, scattering them like geese, was shattered by a quiet Dutch command from behind him.

The speaker was tall and thin—by this point all the Dutch were thin—her hair almost the same red gold as Henry's. A scar lifted the corner of her mouth, and her accent suggested she'd learned her English in Liverpool. "The innocent will pay for those you killed."

"No one's dead."

"Too many are dead. Go. Take care of your wounds. I have it from here."

But he watched from shadow as the prisoners surged free,

waiting so long he had to race the sunrise to a shattered sewer entrance, barely managing to scramble over the rubble almost blocking a smaller side branch before daylight claimed him.

He had a rat bite on his wrist when sunset roused him. Vermin no longer considered him food, but it wasn't his first bite and was unlikely to be his last. Rats were opportunists at heart. Both bullet wounds had healed to patches of shiny pink skin, no surprise given the amount of feeding he'd done. In another hour or two, there'd be no sign, although he suspected his shoulder would still ache where the bullet had gone through bone. Pain or the memory of pain? And did it matter?

He had to find another way out of the sewers, his entrance blocked by new rubble, and when he finally made his way up into the city, it was obvious that the two sides had been exchanging artillery fire for much of the day. Every now and then, searchlights shone north over the canal, turning the smoke rising over burning buildings a lurid yellow. If the First wasn't at the last bridge yet, they would be soon. Not that it would matter as long as there were German troops behind the concrete barriers with *Panzerfausts*. It hardly mattered that the antitank guns were single-shot when there were so many of them.

The streets were busy with running soldiers. Heading toward the canal, being carried away from the canal. Henry snagged a straggler.

"Who's in charge of the troops in the city?" he asked in German.

The boy, and it was a boy, despite the gun, in spite of the uniform, stared at him, whites showing all around his eyes. Did he even know? The Twenty-Fifth Army under General Kleffel had been broken up a mere seven days ago, and with the end of the war in sight, no one was paying much attention to reorganization. The boy swallowed, prominent Adam's apple bobbing up and down inside the sagging curve of his filthy collar, his pupils dilating as the Darkness took him. "*Oberst* Haas," he stammered at last.

"And where is the colonel billeted?"

The boy pointed north, to the other side of the railway lines.

Henry pulled the rifle from a trembling grip, throwing it and its magazine separately toward the fires. "Stay out of sight for a couple of days," he said. "The Canadians . . ."

Pale eyes widened. "Canadians?"

". . . will be across soon. Surrender. Make it through the war alive."

He ran when Henry released him. To report the enemy was inside the city? To add fangs and terror to the interrogation? It didn't much matter. Either option would get the Germans moving.

Henry headed north, toward the railway, keeping close to the canal in order to check out the railway bridge. If the abutments were still in place, the engineers might be able to . . .

The abutments were not still in place. Even the steel was gone, the tracks ending well back from the water. He stood there for a moment, looking south, watching howitzer rounds from the First destroy German antiaircraft guns and most of the buildings around them, the Canadians no doubt frustrated by their inability to get across to the rest of the city.

Artillery on both sides were engaged in an unsuccessful battle of mutual annihilation and likely had been for much of the day. Fortunately, that meant buildings along the canal, most of them long taken over by the occupying army, were taking the brunt of the damage. Foster might have ordered artillery, if it had been Foster's orders, but the gunners were doing what they could to limit civilian casualties.

Limit, not prevent; artillery didn't have that kind of precision.

He was running out of time.

He'd have to assume rumor had spread sufficiently through the ranks; time to pay a visit to Colonel Haas.

He turned, shadow moving within shadow, in time to see three men exit the old station, black uniforms making them walking shards of darkness in their own right. It looked like the SS had repurposed the building as their headquarters, not the first time they'd kept themselves separate from the Wehrmacht. He heard them laughing, saw them turn as the searchlight swept across the rail yard, assumed he'd been seen as one raised his weapon, and he realized an instant later they hadn't seen him; they'd seen a skinny, barefoot child sieving coal from the cinder heap.

He couldn't reach the boy before the bullet, but he tried.

Most of the child's head was gone.

They were still laughing.

Until they saw him.

They'd destroyed so much of the present. They didn't get to destroy the future as well.

This time, when the Hunger rose, it slipped from his control.

Or maybe, he let it go.

Flesh ripped and torn. Terror used as a weapon. As a feast. Bodies thrown into burning buildings to be further destroyed.

By the time the approaching sun forced him to find shelter, most of the SS in Apeldoorn were dead, their broken bodies burned beyond recognition. Henry had been shot four times, but he'd fed and fed and fed again, healing almost instantly. Had the Blackshirts worked together, or had one of them grabbed a larger weapon, he wouldn't have survived. But Hitler believed in Henry's kind, and the SS were Hitler's. They'd been taught he had to be beheaded or have a stake driven through his heart. Both of which *would* kill him, but swords and axes were in short supply, and terror left little time for carving stakes. The one group large enough to have been a danger to him had broken when he'd thrown the heads of their friends down from a rooftop, then leaped into their midst before they could run. Those shot by their own people in panic he left where they lay.

He woke at sunset to small-arms fire, turned over, and vomited, scrambling backward on hands and knees to avoid the steaming puddle of blood.

He'd gone to war because once he'd been a prince of England.

He'd become a weapon because that was what they needed from him.

That wasn't all he was.

That *couldn't be* all he was.

He forced the Hunger back. Fought to forget the sweet taste of blood and terror together. Fought to remember who he was. For four hundred years, he'd hung on to his humanity, surrendering to the darkness only once when the Inquisition had tortured and killed a woman he'd loved. This time he had no holy man to remind him of who he was. No Franciscan to remind him of the light.

This time . . .

. . . he had to . . .

. . . find himself . . .

. . . by himself.

And he had no time for this.

Princes of men had slaughtered as many.

Hell certainly knew his sisters had slaughtered more while on the throne.

So he'd hold on to that, to *humanity's* darkness, until he had time to deal with the rest.

He stripped the first civilian body he found of trousers and a hand-knit sweater, the evidence of death by Allied artillery an improvement on clothing dragged through an abattoir.

Then he went looking for Colonel Haas.

Fighting continued by the canal, although the artillery on both sides had dropped to intermittent firing—a few rounds from one, a few from the other, about fifteen minutes apart. The city was mostly intact, so either General Foster had refused to call bombers or Montgomery had deployed them elsewhere, as he had in the past, his own plans more important than anyone else's.

Haas had taken over what had once been a wealthy merchant's home, the presence of his headquarters easy to identify by haphazardly strung telephone lines, three antennas on the roof, and the sound of shouting through a large bay window, unshuttered and still miraculously unbroken. Cars drove up, men ran in, men ran out, and cars drove away. More arrived. The shouting changed tone and timbre, but never entirely stopped. The First had tried to take the bridge and lost two tanks. Hold the bridge. The Fourth Armoured Division was having a hard time moving around the north side of the city. No reason to send more *Panzerfausts*; let the flooded land do its job, then finish them off.

Two soldiers stood ready, one to either side of the front door. Two by the rear gate leaned against a shed, sharing a cigarette. All four were clearly walking wounded, one of the two in the rear beginning to bleed through the bandaging around his head.

Henry stared at the dark stain for a long moment, then slipped past to the back of the house, ignoring the Hunger that burned just under his skin. A single-story kitchen extension gave him easy access to the second floor, and he was up and in too fast to be seen should anyone have turned to look. The colonel's sleeping quarters were easy to find. Another time, he might have given the man credit for the lack of ostentation.

Haas had been in Apeldoorn long enough to surround himself with confiscated luxury, but he'd settled for utilitarian comfort.

There was a line of salt on the window ledge, and Henry nearly laughed. He didn't. He wasn't sure he could stop if he started. Footsteps passed in the upper hall, and he froze. He could slaughter Haas and his staff. He could slaughter everyone in the house.

Instead, he left the way he'd come and headed for Het Loo Palace. The Germans were using the Dutch royal residence as a hospital—although local patients were vastly outnumbered by refugees from Arnhem—and no one, not even the Germans, guarded a hospital in the middle of an occupied city. They should have guarded the last of their chloroform.

Returning to the colonel, crossing the park with its few remaining trees—cutting wood in the city was a crime punishable by death—Henry picked up the first of the bodies. Deserters were shot and left in the park as a warning. The body on the top of the pile had been added recently, traces of rigor still holding muscles stiff.

With the new moon not due until the nineteenth, the lane behind the colonel's headquarters held a series of impenetrable shadows. Darkness hiding him from the guards, Henry tucked the first body into the closest shadow and went back for another.

Back and forth, carrying the dead. Nineteen . . .

Eighteen and three-quarters.

Even in the cool of April, bodies in the bottom of the pile had begun to rot.

Henry was Catholic, had always been Catholic regardless of how his father had split the church. He recognized penance when maggots squirmed under his collar to be crushed between sweater and skin.

At 3:00 a.m., with the bodies hidden in the lane and Henry waiting predator-patient in a heavy oak armoire, Colonel Haas stumbled up to his room, announcing that Satan himself could be stalking the city, for all he cared—they would hold!

"Wake me in three hours," he shouted from the doorway. "Three! And not a minute more! Or a minute less!" His shoulders slumped as he closed the door, and his hands shook as he pulled a full bottle of brandy out from under his mattress. "Seems as good a time as any," he muttered, breaking the seal.

Henry let Haas drink half of it before he used the chloroform.

On his way to retrieve the bodies, he chloroformed the guards on the gate, using the physical strength granted him but nothing more, nothing that might tempt him with blood and terror.

Haas's room was spacious, but the eighteen-and-three-quarters corpses, moved one at a time to the kitchen roof and through the window, filled it.

Sitting.

Standing.

Decaying.

He stripped the colonel to his underwear and tucked him into the bed, three-quarters of a body, of a young man who'd been frightened and tried to run, tucked in beside him, facing what was left of the boy's face. Then he'd used the colonel's blood—no more than he could spare, the wound obvious on his wrist—to paint GET OUT on all four walls.

His three hours were almost up when Henry slid back out the window and through the back gate. Exhausted, he wanted to be clean more than he'd had at any time in the last four hundred years, but the shadows in the lane weren't quite so impenetrable, and he could feel the approaching dawn. He took shelter three houses away in a root cellar under a stable-turned-garage, long emptied, and almost thought he heard screaming as the day took him.

He could hear nothing at all when he woke. No guns. No people.

The colonel's house was deserted of everything but the dead, and hastily stripped of anything that might be useful. A stained map was still spread on the what had once been a dining-room table. Two broken radios had been abandoned on the sideboard.

The streets were empty of Germans.

The Dutch, trained by years of deadly force, remained inside.

Henry headed toward the last bridge over the canal.

He was still two streets away when he began to hear angry Dutch voices—a woman and two men. They stood in shadows near the bridge, a pair of bound German soldiers, probably part of a small rear guard left behind to delay pursuit, slumped against the base of the nearest pillbox.

It was the woman he'd last seen leading the prisoners to freedom. He had to admit—he wasn't surprised. Hands held up, clearly visible, he approached until he was close enough they could see him, even in the limited light, and, because he was tired or lonely or damned or all three, said, in English, in as neutral a tone as he could manage, "What's the problem?"

Unfortunately, they *hadn't* actually seen him.

He ducked under a swinging piece of steel pipe, managed to keep himself from killing the man attacking him, and stopped, just out of reach, hands up again. The woman spoke quickly. One man listened, scowling. The other, still holding his length of pipe, backed away.

The scowling man protested. She cut him off, looked between Henry and the man with the pipe and said, more wary than afraid, "They don't believe me."

"They?"

A jerk of her head toward the other side of the canal. "The Canadians. I told them the Germans are gone, and they don't believe me."

"No one's shooting at them."

She rolled her eyes. "I know that! They said the Germans have been ordered to hold, and those bastards don't run. The ones I talked to . . ." Another head jerk toward the canal. "They're like . . . like an explosive with the fuse nearly burned down, and they're ready to explode! They won't listen!"

"Do they know you're Resistance?"

"They do."

Stubborn sons of bitches. "If they won't listen to you, they won't listen to me."

The scowling man, still scowling, asked a terse question.

She shrugged, answered, and turned her attention back to Henry. "I told him we can't stop you; we might as well talk to you. We know what you are. I saw you take out those guards, and I heard what the Germans said. You made them believe they'd roused a monster in the night, and unwilling to face their fear, they ran." Another shrug, she'd been facing monsters in the daylight for the last five years. "If you aren't with the Allies, why are you helping us?"

He was with the Allies; most of them just didn't know it. "Because it was the right thing to do."

She raised both brows.

Henry remembered blood and terror. "Because it was the necessary thing to do." Hands still raised, he pointed to their bound prisoners. "Send one of them."

"I wouldn't trust them to shit! They'll spew whatever filth they think will save their miserable lives."

"Not if I send them."

She stared at him for a long moment, cut off a protest from the scowling man, and finally said, "Do it. And put your hands down; you look like an idiot."

It only took a moment.

They stood together watching the chosen soldier cross the bridge.

"Will he tell them everything?" she asked.

"No."

When she turned to ask another question, he'd already reached the shadows.

By the time he heard shouting from the far side of the canal, he was three streets away.

He needed to feed on something other than terror.

Soon.

Not for a while; there was still a war on.

At least the Germans were out of Apeldoorn.

BOCKSCAR

DAVID MACK

THIRTY THOUSAND FEET ABOVE THE WESTERN PACIFIC OCEAN, AUGUST 1945

"Nobody move!"

There was no going back now: Bombardier Captain Beahan and five of his crewmates had crossed the line that separated protest from mutiny. He stood behind Major Sweeney in the B-29's cockpit, his Colt 1911A1 aimed at the pilot's head. "We're not doing this!" he hollered over the engine noise, his voice shaking almost as badly as the .45 semiautomatic in his gloved hand. "Take us back to Tinian!"

Sweeney and his copilot, Captain Albury, remained still. Almost in unison, they turned their heads slowly aft to assess the situation. Beahan's coconspirators, *Bockscar*'s five sergeants, stood with sidearms drawn behind the Superfortress's navigator, Captain Van Pelt, and backup copilot, Lieutenant Olivi, both seated at their stations. Albury's crooked features betrayed his anxiety, but Sweeney was surprisingly sanguine for a man looking into the muzzle of a loaded pistol.

The major pushed his headphones back, exposing one ear.

He raised his voice to be heard over the engine's roar. "Beahan? What the hell are you doing?"

"We can't let this mission proceed, Major. Turn us around."

"I can't do that." Sweeney glanced aft. "What'd you do to the weaponeers?"

"Nothing. They aren't taking sides."

"I find that hard to believe."

"Their orders are to protect the device. Whether we drop it is up to us. And since I'm the one who does the dropping—"

Albury cut in, "Think before you finish that sentence, Beahan."

"I have." Beahan took a deep breath to steady his hands, but with *Bockscar* at angels thirty, the air inside the Superfortress was thin and cold. Acid churned deep inside his gut, which strained against the canvas belt he wore cinched above his hips to hide his modest paunch. "All the training ops, all the briefings—none of them told us what these things really do. But now we know."

Sweeney shook his head in disappointment. "You don't know half of what's true, and what you think you know is bullshit."

Beahan rejected Sweeney's assertion with a shake of his head. "This mission's been jinxed from the get-go. Changing planes at the last second, taking off in a typhoon, a gremlin nearly triggering the bomb in flight, all the fuel we wasted in a holding pattern 'cause *Big Stink* missed the rendezvous—how many signs from God does it take before you realize we need to turn back?"

Grim resolve deepened the lines on Sweeney's fleshy face. "God can send all the signs he wants, Beahan, but we're not going home till that bomb hits Nagasaki."

Heavy clanks echoed through *Bockscar*'s forward bomb bay, announcing the opening of the pressure hatch to the command deck.

Watching the hatch from inside the bomb bay, Lieutenant Beser and his fellow weapon specialists tensed. The two naval officers, Commander Ashworth and Lieutenant Barnes, drew their pistols and converged like sentinels in front of the Fat Man atomic device. The huge, vaguely pumpkin-shaped munition, painted like a bumblebee—yellow with a black ring around its blunt nose and a crenelated ring of black around its midsection—dangled from a huge hook attached to the fuselage overhead. Knowing the pair of navy men had his back, Lieutenant Beser drew his own sidearm and blocked the hatchway.

The hatch swung open toward the command deck. First to stick his head through the open portal was Master Sergeant Kuharek, the mission's flight engineer. At his back was the assistant flight engineer, Staff Sergeant Gallagher. Both mutineers recoiled when they saw Beser's Colt 1911A1 aimed at their faces.

Kuharek raised his empty hands. "Whoa! Stand down, sir!"

"Not one step further, Master Sergeant."

The engineer put on a genial smile. "Captain Beahan's orders, sir. We just need to confirm the weapon's properly secured." He nodded at the assistant, who tried to slip past him toting an open box of tools.

Beser cocked the pistol's hammer and steadied it with both hands. "The weapon's plenty secure. I'm bettin' Captain Beahan really sent you to sabotage the drop gear. Or am I bein' paranoid, Sergeant?"

Kuharek wore an insincere smile. "He just wants to make sure we don't drop without his say-so." With another tilt of his head, the engineer cued his assistant again to try to step through the hatchway. Gallagher started forward but halted when Beser's pistol touched the bridge of his nose.

Beser stared into Gallagher's petrified eyes. "One more inch and you're dead."

The assistant engineer backed off.

Kuharek did his best to sound reasonable, but needing to shout over the din of the engines was enough to make anyone sound at least a little bit insane. "What gives, Beser? Beahan said you guys weren't taking sides."

"We ain't helpin' you; we ain't fightin' you. But if you try to touch this weapon, I'll blow the top o' your head clean off."

Gallagher wedged himself into the open hatchway beside Kuharek. "Beahan thinks the major might try to break protocol. Give his own order to drop."

Commander Ashworth shouted from behind Beser, "Let *us* worry about that, Sergeant. Now close that hatch and get back to your post."

Kuharek chewed on that, unhappy with being rebuffed.

He looked at Beser as if he expected some degree of sympathy. "How can you go along with this?"

"Why wouldn't I?"

"Weren't you on *Enola Gay* when it bombed Hiroshima?"

"You *know* I was, John."

Desperation infused Kuharek's voice. "So you've *seen* it."

Beser nodded. "Yeah, I saw it."

The engineer looked perplexed. "Then you know they lied to us. Told us we were just dropping a big but totally ordinary bomb."

"What's your point, John?"

"Now that you know what these things really are . . . how can you justify dropping *another* one?"

He understood the engineer's confusion and his moral outrage. But he also remembered the sight of nuns and nurses coming back from Japanese POW camps with their tongues cut out—and being told those women were the lucky ones. He refused to feel any pity for the Japanese people.

More importantly, the detonation and aftermath of the Little Boy atomic device on Hiroshima three days earlier was seared indelibly into his memory, alongside a hundred other horrors he wished he could forget but knew he never would. He had seen enough to know this mission had to happen, now, without delay—but he also had been sworn to silence. And he would not break his vow.

"I won't debate you, gents—but I *will* shoot you, if I have to."

He moved forward, his Colt steady, and forced the flight engineers to retreat from the hatchway, deeper into the command deck compartment. Holding his weapon in one hand, he used his free hand to grab a handle on the hatch and pull it toward him. "Sort your shit out and do it fast, 'cause we're *runnin' out of fuel.*"

Beser slammed the forward hatch shut.

Ashworth checked his watch. "Patience, gentlemen. One way or another, an hour from now this will all be over."

Beser frowned. "Yeah. I just hope it don't end with us down in flames."

None of the practice runs had addressed what to do if the crew mutinied in midair, leaving Major Sweeney with no idea what he was supposed to do next. Looking into the barrel of Beahan's sidearm wasn't helping his concentration either. By some rhetorical magic, he had to persuade Beahan to drop that bomb.

That meant he had to improvise, which wasn't his forte.

"Captain, would you mind lowering your Colt just a bit?"

"I *would* mind. It ain't goin' nowhere till you turn this bird around."

Staticky chatter spilled from the radio operator's station, just behind Beahan and his cohort of mutineers. The crew of *The Great Artiste*, their companion B-29 on this mission, was trying to contact *Bockscar*. Sweeney tilted his head toward the radio console. "Somebody gonna get that?"

Beahan shook his head. "No comms till we turn back."

Copilot Albury couldn't mask his disapproval or his alarm. "Are you trying to get us shot down? If we don't answer them, they have orders not to let the Japs capture the device. Even if that means blowing us out of the sky."

The bombardier shrugged. "If that's what it takes to prevent a war crime."

Sweeney wanted to shout, but he also didn't want to give Beahan a reason to shoot him in the face. "*War crime*? Are you fucking kidding? *What* war crime?"

"What else would you call droppin' a single bomb that can wipe a city clean off the map?"

"Our job."

"No, our job is to destroy *military* targets. *Strategic* targets. Munitions plants. Shipyards. Refineries. Bridges. *Not* civilian populations."

A cynical chortle slipped out before Sweeney could edit himself. "Tell that to the sixty thousand civilians killed by Hitler's *Drachenkrieg* attacks on London."

Albury rolled his eyes. "Or our boys who firebombed Tokyo."

Their examples irked Beahan. "First, the Nazis ain't our fuckin' role models. Second, Tokyo's an enemy capital. *And* it had training grounds for the *oni*. Were we supposed to let the Japs overrun the Marshall Islands with ogres?"

Sweeney wondered what argument would sway his mutinous

bombardier. "What about Dresden, Beahan? Twenty-five thousand civvies dead."

Beahan shook his head in denial and frustration. "We *had* to bomb Dresden. It was sheltering the Nazis' *Werwolf-Korps*."

"Says who?"

"FDR. And Churchill."

"Right, because our side *never* lies or uses propaganda."

Beahan's face reddened with anger. "Stop making excuses, Chuck! How can you drop that bomb when we know what a *smaller* one did to Hiroshima?"

Sweeney's temper frayed. "I said it before, I'll say it again. You *don't know* what you're talking about."

"I know we flattened Hiroshima with one shot."

Moral calculus had never been something Sweeney cared about, but he knew sophistry when he heard it. "Who cares how many bombs it takes to destroy a city? Or how long? Whether it takes three months, three days, or three seconds, the city's still gone. Say what you will about the A-bomb, at least it's *efficient*."

"That kind of efficiency might kill every living thing on earth, Chuck—including us. Unless we take a stand, right here, right now, and end it."

Sweeney stared straight ahead, into the clouds over Japan, and kept his hands steady on *Bockscar*'s yoke. "That's where you're wrong, Captain. It's true, every living thing on earth is in peril because of the A-bomb—but aborting our mission won't prevent Armageddon. The only thing that'll save humanity from extinction now is dropping this bomb. Here. Today."

The major's obstinate refusal to see reason left Beahan perplexed and enraged. Why couldn't the commander see the madness inherent in atomic weaponry? How could he possibly think that unleashing such a terror on unsuspecting Japanese civilians was in any way justified? How could he fail to see it was a moral horror?

"You're talking in circles, Chuck. Piling lies on top of lies."

"I've told you nothing but the truth, Captain."

Behind Beahan, the voice of *The Great Artiste*'s radio operator crackled from the console's speaker. It was impossible to tell what he was saying because his words were drowned in the great roar of *Bockscar*'s engines, but it was clear his tone was growing more frantic by the minute.

Beahan struggled to steady his Colt. "Forget the excuses. You know as well as I do there's *no reason* to drop this bomb. We *made* our point at Hiroshima. The Japanese have been suing for peace, and we've been ignoring them because we want to show off our new doomsday weapon to the Russians. This is all about scaring the Reds into keeping their troops out of Hokkaido."

Sweeney's voice was flat but laced with sarcasm. "Got it all figured out, don't you, Beahan?"

"Tell me I'm wrong, Chuck."

"That's what I've *been* telling you, Captain. *You're wrong.* What's it gonna take before you believe me?"

"How about the truth?"

The major sighed. "All right, Captain. But remember—you *asked* for it."

The aircraft was dangerously low on fuel; low-hanging smoke and cloud cover were growing thicker in the sky ahead; and unless the Japanese military had collapsed overnight, there would soon be a squadron of Zeros in the air on an intercept course for *Bockscar.* This was no time for a debate, but Beahan had forced the issue; for Sweeney to have any hope of completing his mission, he had to make the bombardier and his contingent of mutineers see reason.

Sweeney steeled himself. Telling Beahan and the rest of the crew the truth about their mission would likely result in his own court-martial—assuming any of them made it back alive from this glorified suicide run.

"Three days ago, the crew of *Enola Gay* dropped a fifteen-kiloton atomic device on the city of Hiroshima. The damage to the city has been widely reported. What's been kept quiet is that the attack had an unintended secondary outcome."

Beahan narrowed his eyes in suspicion. "That sounds like army doublespeak for a fuckup."

"That would be an understatement."

"What *really* happened?"

With a nod, Sweeney handed over control of the aircraft to Albury. Then he turned to look back at Beahan and the other mutineers. "The blast woke something. A monster bigger than anything anyone's ever seen. The Japanese call it a *kaiju.*"

The bombardier's face scrunched in disbelief. "What do you mean the blast woke it? How?"

"Based on film and photographs from *Necessary Evil,* just after detonation, a three-headed monstrosity rose from Hiroshima Bay and waded ashore into the smoking remains of the city. It's been wreaking havoc ever since."

Looks of confusion passed back and forth among the mutineers. Flight engineer Kuharek was the first to protest. "Bullshit. That's a fairy tale."

"I assure you, Sergeant, it is not. The creature's been on a nonstop, three-day rampage, on a southwesterly heading. We were supposed to stop it at Kokura, but we wasted too much time and fuel waiting for *Big Stink* at the rendezvous, and the creature is faster than we thought, which is why we're now en route to Nagasaki."

Beahan lowered his pistol a few degrees but remained too tightly wound for Sweeney's comfort. "Are you nuts? You really think *dropping an A-bomb* will kill less people than letting that thing stomp around for a few days?"

"What if it sticks around a few months? Or a few years? Or a few decades? Our spies say the Japs threw everything they had at the sonofabitch, but none of it made a scratch. Artillery, bombs, tank shells—this beast just shakes them all off. We hear it ate a half dozen Zeros and three Chi-Nu tanks."

"That's ridiculous. Even the biggest Nazi dragon can't eat a tank."

"You haven't seen this thing, Beahan. It makes a German *Feuerdrachen* look like one of those puny lizards on the beach in Aruba."

Beahan shook his head, sinking deeper into denial. "Impossible."

"What if I tell you there's someone on this aircraft who saw it with his own two eyes? An honest-to-God witness?"

That snared Beahan's interest. It even shut him up for a few seconds and made him think. To Sweeney's relief, the mutineers' ringleader lowered his Colt a few more degrees as he asked with cautious suspicion, "Who?"

"It's true. I was on *Enola Gay* when we bombed Hiroshima."

Beser stood in front of the open hatchway, looking through it at the clutch of mutineers. Beahan had left one of the sergeants to guard the pilot and copilot so he could hear Beser directly.

The bombardier's expression was taut and dubious, but he kept quiet and let Beser say his piece.

"We all shut our eyes when the flash came. It was like the sun rose through the deck. Rest of the guys had those black goggles, but I couldn't use 'em, 'cause I had to watch my instruments. It was quick, just a second or two, but I was seein' spots for almost a minute after. Colonel Tibbets banked away from the mushroom cloud. Then the shock waves hit. Felt like an earthquake knockin' my guts 'gainst my bones. But we made it out, and the colonel called all-clear.

"Then Bob, our tail-gunner, calls out over the headphones, 'What the fuck is that?' None of us could see shit, but Bob said we needed to see it, so the colonel swung us around for a look.

"We were facin' the mushroom cloud again when we saw it. Hiroshima Bay was like a pot at full boil. I thought it was somethin' from the bomb, but then the smoke on the water ripped apart, and I saw it: the monster.

"Three heads on long, sinewy necks. Huge body, four legs, massive wings, all risin' from the water, lightnin' dancin' over its body like Saint Elmo's fire. It was like watchin' a god get born. Or a devil . . . The moment I saw it, I knew we'd done somethin' terrible. Somethin' irreparable. Somethin' unforgivable.

"The colonel didn't want to get too close to whatever the fuck it was, so he told the observation bird to get photos and films to take back to command. Then he turned us around and hightailed us back to Tinian."

Beser lit a cigarette, took a long drag, and exhaled a gray plume of acrid smoke before he continued. "The next day, the brass had a closed-door meeting with Colonel Tibbets, Captain Marquardt from the observation bird, and all the weapon specialists. Some bigwig from Los Alamos was on the secure phone. They argued for three hours. Couldn't tell if it was just a coincidence the creature was there when we bombed the city, or if triggerin' an A-bomb had ripped open the 'fabric of reality,' or some other jibber-jabber. Then they got reports from spies in Japan. The beast was on a tear, layin' waste to cities, settin' the countryside on fire, and nothin' the Japanese could throw at it made a lick of difference."

Another long pause, another slow pull on the coffin nail.

Beser exhaled through his nose before he spoke again.

"I don't know what the eggheads think it is, and to be honest, I don't really care. But if you ask me, that thing is *not* of this earth—and it's our fault it's here."

It sounded almost credible—Beahan had to admit that much. But even in a world that secretly harbored living, breathing creatures of legend, he had never heard of anything like what Beser had described. The only things that even came close were behemoths like the kraken or the serpent Jörmungandr. But those titanic horrors were just myths . . .

Weren't they?

Colt in hand, he left the open hatchway and stalked forward, through the clutch of sergeants holding the officers hostage, to stand behind Major Sweeney and Captain Albury. "Even if I accept that Beser's telling the truth, so what?"

The question seemed to irritate Albury. "Are you serious?"

"As far as I'm concerned, nothing's changed."

Sweeney sounded baffled. "How can you say that?"

"I can't believe we're okay with killing a hundred thousand civilians just to stop one monster, no matter how big it is."

Captain Van Pelt, the navigator, was so angry he was almost laughing. "Damn it, Beahan, are you deaf? Didn't you hear what this thing can *do*?"

Keeping his pistol aimed at Sweeney, Beahan answered Van Pelt, "I heard just fine, Jim." To the major, he continued. "But none of this makes sense. The math just ain't adding up for me."

Albury regarded Beahan with an arched brow. "Have you considered what happens *after* that thing finishes eating Japan? I mean, it came out of the sea, walks on land, and has wings. It can go anywhere on earth. What if its next stop is Hawaii? Do you want to wind up dropping an A-bomb on American citizens because we didn't finish the job here when we had the chance?"

From behind Beahan, Beser cut in, "We might not have that option."

Beahan turned to see the weapons specialist had emerged from the bomb bay to stand near his instruments at the radar station. "Why not?"

"A-bomb cores don't grow on trees, Captain. Gettin' just two into shape for this operation was nothin' shy of a miracle. Truth is, if we blow this, we might not get another shot. It could be a year or even longer before we get another workin' core. And if what our spies say about the *kaiju* is true . . . I don't think it's gonna wait for us to get ready before it comes callin'. So you gotta make a choice, Captain: Do you want to fight this thing here and now—or at home later?"

The air inside *Bockscar* was still frigid, but Sweeney's palms were coated in sweat. He felt the minutes ticking away, the fuel reserves dwindling, the erratic chop of engines starting to taste fumes. But most of all, he was transfixed by the barrel of Beahan's pistol, which hovered mere inches behind his head.

"What's it gonna be, Captain?"

Beahan's gun hand trembled. "Shut up, I'm thinking."

From behind the mutineers, a steady stream of panicked hails issued from the radio board. Sergeant Spitzer, the radio operator, looked nervously at his console, and then he offered an apologetic frown to Beahan as he lowered his sidearm, abandoning the mutiny to dart back to his station. "Sorry, Cap, but we need to know what they're saying."

Beahan pivoted to split his attention between Sweeney at the controls and Spitzer on the radio. The bombardier grew more anxious by the second. "Everyone just stay calm and let me think."

Contact pings rang out from the radar console. Sergeant Buckley, the radar operator, reacted by instinct. He, too, gave up on the mutiny, holstered his pistol, and lurched back to his station. It took him only seconds to assess the blips on his screen. "Bogeys! Ten of 'em. Fast, coming in from the north. Pretty good bet they're Zeros."

Albury frowned at Sweeney. "There's our welcoming committee."

Beahan glanced at the radar screen. His voice was sharp with sarcasm. "Why don't we just tell 'em we're here to save 'em by vaporizing Nagasaki?"

The copilot turned a stink eye at Beahan. "Because, in this case, the enemy of our enemy still hates our guts."

Buckley's voice grew louder and pitched higher. "Zeros, closing fast! Two minutes to intercept—and no one's manning our tail gun."

Panic crept into Sweeney's thoughts. He had never actually flown in real combat before, just milk runs. He had been put in command of *Bockscar* as a favor from a friend in the command ranks, but now he wished he was anywhere else. Slick with perspiration, his hands slipped on the yoke. He wiped them dry one at a time on his pant legs. "Jesus Christ, Beahan! I'm *begging* you: Stand down."

Sergeant Spitzer swiveled his chair toward Beahan. "Captain?" He waited until Beahan looked at him, and then he took off his headphones and offered them up like a tribute. "You need to hear this, sir. Right now."

Reluctant but desperate, Beahan backpedaled away from Sweeney until he could take the headphones from Spitzer, who held his board's transmit switch open long enough to say, "*Artiste*, this is *Bockscar*. Please repeat your last. All after 'cloud cover.' Over."

An eerie silence freighted with dread settled over the crew as Beahan stood and listened to the message from their instrumentation support aircraft. Within seconds, the captain's eyes widened. He pressed the transmit switch. "*Artiste*, are you sure?" He listened a few seconds more, looking like a man in shock.

Beahan took off the headphones and handed them back to Spitzer. Holstered his weapon. Walked forward, past Sweeney and Albury, and lowered himself into position above his targeting scope. He adjusted it a few times, fiddled with its focus, and then peered through the eyepiece until his jaw slackened in horror.

All the color had drained from Beahan's face by the time he looked up and back at the rest of the crew. He said in a bold tenor of command, "Stations! Pappy, get on the tail gun! Watch our six! Beser, fire up your gear and tell your boys to look sharp. We need drop clearance on the double. Major, bring us around, hard bank left to two-six-eight and dive to angels two-five for speed. I'll talk you in once we're on approach and make the drop by visual targeting. Everybody, go!"

Sweeney nudged the yoke forward and started his turn. "Roger that. Banking hard left, two-six-eight, elevator angels two-five."

On the ground far below and dead ahead, the *kaiju* came into view through the cockpit's nose canopy, large enough for Sweeney to make out its shape even from several miles away through scattered cloud cover.

He didn't know what had changed Beahan's mind. It occurred to him he might never know, not unless he could find a safe place to land once the mission was over. But that was a problem for later.

Right now they had a monster to kill.

TWENTY-FIVE THOUSAND FEET ABOVE NAGASAKI, JAPAN, AUGUST 1945

As Beahan peered through his Norden bombsight and guided *Bockscar* to its target, guilt gnawed at his soul—only to be overpowered by an emotion far older and much more powerful: *fear*.

At precisely 11:01 a.m. local time, he gave the order to drop Fat Man.

The yellow-and-black atomic device plunged from the B-29's belly and fell like the fist of the Almighty toward Nagasaki's Urakami Valley. From *Bockscar*'s altitude, Beahan knew the device would fall for forty-seven seconds before reaching its programmed detonation height above the target.

Which meant he had forty-seven seconds to pray.

For forgiveness, for all the innocent lives that were about to be consumed in a burst of atomic fire; for peace, in a world that could no longer afford to wage war when it had such terrible weapons of mass destruction tempting humanity toward its collective annihilation; and for victory, over a monstrous foe that had proved unvanquishable by any other means, and whose clear and present threat to all humankind Beahan now saw with absolute, horrifying clarity.

He dreaded to think what the detonation of a second atomic weapon in just three days would mean for the world. He could only hope that trying to fix the crisis caused by the first A-bomb by deploying another didn't just multiply the problem. If it did, that would be an error in judgment whose grim weight he would need to bear for the rest of his life.

Perhaps history would call him and his *Bockscar* crewmates heroes; or perhaps it would call them monsters as terrible as the one they came to destroy. But in his heart, Beahan knew he'd had no other choice than to drop the bomb. Not after what he had seen through the bombsight.

If all he had witnessed had been the three-headed fiend lording like a dark god over Nagasaki, he might have told Major Sweeney to fly on, to abandon the mission, consequences be damned. But he realized the decision to drop the second atomic bomb was the right one when he confirmed the report from *The Great Artiste*—when he saw for himself what the *kaiju* was doing in the center of that vibrant city by the sea.

The damnable thing was *laying eggs.*

THE SELKIE'S JOB

JANE YOLEN

Underwater demolition
was the selkie's big ambition.
Fingers nimble, in the deep.
She could break bombs in her sleep.
But a merman caught her eye
as he paddled nimbly by.
Her fingers gripped and slipped,
and loaded . . .
The bomb, now armed, just self-exploded.
Those watery creatures learned to fly
and consummated in the sky.
And that's how bomb-birds came to be.
A mistake, a new take in nursery.

HISTORICAL NOTES

HENRY HERZ, EDITOR

While World War II is generally considered to have started with the German invasion of Poland in September 1939, some historians use the Italian invasion of Abyssinia in October 1935, the Second Sino-Japanese War in July 1937, or the Japanese invasion of Manchuria in September 1931.

These are all works of fiction, and characters' actions, statements, and attitudes should not be considered in any way factual depictions of historical people. That said, I asked each contributing author to anchor their story in a real-world battle. Below are summaries of those historical battles.

Eugen Bacon, "Kinje'kitile and the Jintu"

After the Germans lost German East Africa in World War I, it became a British mandate known as Tanganyika Territory in 1920. During World War II, the British rounded up a force of colonial units that joined Ethiopian guerrillas. Between June 1940 and November 1941, the King's African Rifles (KAR) consisted of soldiers from Kenya, Uganda, Nyasaland (now Malawi), Somaliland (now Somalia), and Tanganyika (now Tanzania). They fought in

Somaliland and Abyssinia (now Ethiopia) against the Italians. This is known as the East African (or Abyssinian) campaign.

The story also borrows from:

- The Maji Maji Rebellion in Tanganyika: In the early 1900s, the Ngoni people challenged German colonial rule. The soldiers are believed to have trusted the counsel of a witch doctor named Kinjekitile Ngwale, a spiritual medium and leader, who assured them that a magical potion would turn the white man's bullets into water—it didn't. Bullets mauled the men as they cried, "*Maji, maji!*" which means "water" in Swahili. Up to three hundred thousand Africans are believed to have died during the rebellion.
- The man-eating lions of Tsavo: During the construction of the East African railway in 1898, two rogue male lions terrorized the workers along the Tsavo River, killing an estimated 135 people, until Lieutenant Colonel John Henry Patterson shot the lions, sold their bodies to a museum, and wrote a book about it. Forensic testing on hair samples suggest the lions had eaten between 10 and 24 people, making Patterson's account rather amplified. But he had a book to sell, later adapted into a 1996 movie, *The Ghost and the Darkness*.

Ann Dávila Cardinal, "Best Behave"

Operation Avalanche was an Allied landing in Salerno, Italy, that began on September 9, 1943. Hot on the tail of the collapse of Mussolini's government, Allied forces realized Italy could be knocked out of the war, and they could open up the Mediterranean for Allied shipping. Salerno provided an ideal location to invade with its gentle surf and access to road and train systems. The landings were executed by the US Fifth Army, which included American and British troops, as well as the Sixty-Fifth Infantry, "The Borinqueneers," a regiment comprised entirely of Puerto Rican soldiers. The battalion encountered a beachhead that was heavily mined but still managed to hold it until reserve units landed. What followed were eight days of slow advance, aided by heavy mortar fire, naval salvos, and paratrooper attacks, until on September 17, General Heinrich von Vietinghoff, commander of the German Tenth Army, was granted permission to withdraw. The weeklong Battle of Salerno had cost the British and Americans a total of 2,349 killed, 7,366 wounded, and 4,100 missing. The Germans suffered 840 killed and 2,000 wounded.

Peter Clines, "The Night Crew"

Project Cerberus—later known as the Channel Dash—was a daring German navy operation to move three of their major warships from occupied France to the North Sea despite Britain's overwhelming naval superiority. While routes around Iceland and the UK were proposed, Hitler favored going straight through the English Channel, believing speed and the element of surprise would protect the ships. Through a combination of a number of factors—among them bad weather, low visibility, and poor Allied communication—the German warships and six escorting destroyers succeeded, making it up the Channel and through the Strait of Dover undamaged and undetected for most of their journey. Shortly after they reached the North Sea, however, the German flagship, *Scharnhorst*, struck a British minefield (*supposedly*) and came to a dead halt. Vice Admiral Ciliax abandoned ship, transferring to one of the destroyers, and the other vessels moved on. After half an hour, the *Scharnhorst* came back to life and limped after the battle fleet. Six hours later, *Scharnhorst* was immobilized by another mine and spent the next three months out of service. The Channel Dash was considered an overall success for Germany and a severe morale blow to the British.

Readers interested in learning more about Dr. Ken Kraft and Dar Carter can read Peter Clines's supernatural World War II stories, including "The Banner of the Bent Cross" and "Projekt: Maria."

The *Demeter*, of course, is a wink at Bram Stoker's *Dracula*.

Jeff Edwards, "The Fourth Man"

On May 24, 1941, after exchanging just seven minutes of gunfire with the German battleship *Bismarck* and an escort cruiser, the "invincible" HMS *Hood* was ripped in half by an explosion. The ship sank rapidly, taking all but three of her fourteen-hundred-man crew to the bottom of the Greenland Strait (a.k.a. Denmark Strait).

After an investigation, the British Admiralty Board of Enquiry concluded that the *Hood* had been sunk by a direct hit to her aft fifteen-inch ammunition magazines. This finding conflicted with reports of eyewitnesses, so another Board of Enquiry was convened. The second board concluded the explosion occurred sixty-five feet forward, in the four-inch ammunition magazines. Sir Stanley Goodall, who had supervised the design and construction of HMS *Hood*, concluded that one of its MK-IV torpedoes had been detonated inside its tube by a German shell.

In recent years, explorations of the shipwreck by remotely operated submersibles haven't confirmed any of the theories. We do know this: In an age when armored capital ships often pounded one another for hours with heavy-caliber naval artillery, the *Hood* went down in minutes. Perhaps the *Bismarck* was not responsible. Perhaps it was something much older . . .

Tori Eldridge, "Gods of the Sea"

The naval battle of Guadalcanal was a chaotic, ultra-close sea engagement—the naval warfare equivalent of a barroom brawl. The prize for both sides was Henderson Field, a highly strategic airfield in the Solomon Islands, originally built by the Japanese Empire, which was seized (and later completed) by Allied forces. Imperial Japanese forces launched a bombardment fleet of battleships, cruisers, and destroyers. When the Allied forces caught wind of the attack, an American fleet was sent into "the Slot," the waters northeast of Guadalcanal Island. During the desperate naval battle, nine American warships, six Japanese warships, seven Japanese transports, and one hundred downed aircraft from both sides sank into the "Iron Bottom Sound." Over thirty-five hundred lives were lost. Despite the heavy cost to both sides in lives, ships, and planes, the Allied forces retained Henderson Field in what would become a major turning point in World War II.

Mary Fan, "The Night the Moon Burned"

In 1931 the Japanese invaded Manchuria and established a puppet state. In 1937 they launched a full-scale invasion of China. By January 1938, the Japanese seemed unstoppable. Shanghai and Nanjing had fallen, and the Chinese military had suffered tremendous losses. The Japanese then turned their attention to Wuhan, which lay westward along the Yangtze River. But in order to reach it, they had to pass through Taierzhuang, a small but strategically important village.

In March 1938, the Japanese launched an attack on Taierzhuang and breached the village. After days of fighting and heavy casualties on both sides, Chinese forces successfully drove them back. The Battle of Taierzhuang marked the first significant Japanese defeat by the Chinese since the war broke out and shattered the myth of Japanese invincibility.

Henry Herz, "Das *Mammut*"

The Germans' Operation Citadel of July 1943 was designed to pinch off the Kursk salient and destroy or capture a large number of Soviet troops. With foreknowledge of the German plans, partly thanks to British Intelligence, and afforded additional time by the Germans' decision to delay the operation until they could build up their armored forces, the Soviets constructed an extensive defense in depth.

Nearly 800,000 German troops, 2,900 tanks, and 10,000 artillery pieces assaulted 1,426,000 Soviet troops, 5,100 tanks, and 25,000 artillery pieces. The attacks ground to a halt slogging through a deep series of defensive belts consisting of obstacles, trenches, fortifications, and minefields. The successful Soviet counterattacks gave them the strategic initiative for the rest of the war, particularly as Hitler had to divert troops to counter the Allied invasion of Sicily.

Other than the fictitious *Mammut* vehicle, all equipment and locations in this story are historically accurate. The Battle of Kursk was the largest tank battle in history and is viewed by some historians to be the turning point of World War II in Europe.

Tanya Huff, "Apeldoorn"

During the clearing of the Germans from the Netherlands in 1945, the First Canadian Division was ordered to take Apeldoorn and advance on a parallel axis toward Voorthuizen to relieve the Fifth Canadian Armoured Division.

The night of April 13, a squadron of the First Hussars and a company of Royal Canadian Regiment tried to cross the canal but were rebuffed with the loss of two tanks.

"It had never been my intention to assault Apeldoorn frontally. It was a friendly city, filled with refugees, and I was not prepared to use artillery on it. The plot was to isolate the city, by having one Canadian infantry brigade face up to it and thus keep the enemy garrison there occupied," remarked Major General Foster, commander of the First Canadian Infantry.

Enemy resistance in the city collapsed on the night of April 16–17, although small-arms fire was exchanged over the canal until 3:00 a.m., when the Dutch Resistance reported that the Germans had suddenly evacuated.

Readers interested in learning more about Henry FitzRoy, the vampire and bastard son of Henry VIII, can read Tanya Huff's five-novel Blood series.

Jonathan Maberry, "A Terrible Aspect"

Monte Cassino is a hilltop abbey founded in 529 by Benedict of Nursia. The Battle of Monte Cassino was a series of four Allied attacks against the German "Winter Line" (actually a series of German and Italian military fortifications) as they fought northward toward Rome. Mistakenly believing the abbey was being used by the Germans, on February 15, 1944, Allied aircraft devastated the Benedictine abbey with fourteen hundred tons of bombs.

Readers interested in learning more about Deacon (a.k.a. Mr. Church) can enjoy his exploits in Jonathan Maberry's Joe Ledger series. Those with a hunger for more *benandanti* can read the Sam Hunter series.

David Mack, "*Bockscar*"

This story is based on the real aircraft *Bockscar*'s mission on August 9, 1945. The names and likenesses of the crew members of the B-29 Silverplate Superfortress nicknamed *Bockscar* are faithful to those of the real crew who flew the mission to drop the second atomic bomb on Nagasaki, Japan.

Other details borrowed from history include the aircraft's

interior configuration; the early troubles the bomber experienced during its flight toward Japan, which in the story are attributed to interference by "gremlins"; *Bockscar*'s missed early morning rendezvous with its photographic observation aircraft *Big Stink*, which occurred in real history because the crew of the *Big Stink* were in a holding pattern at the wrong altitude; and the precise hour and minute at which the crew of the *Bockscar* deployed the Fat Man atomic bomb over Nagasaki.

In David Mack's Dark Arts trilogy, the Allied and Nazi war efforts are aided by sorcerers who temporarily gain power from demons.

Kevin Andrew Murphy, "Bound and Chained"

Throughout the war, there were twenty-three assassination attempts on Hitler, ranging from individuals on their own to plots by high-ranking army officers. In Operation Spark, a bomb, disguised as a box containing two bottles of Cointreau, was placed in the cargo hold of Hitler's plane, but the detonator failed due to cold.

The July 20 plot to assassinate Hitler was part of Operation Valkyrie, after which the Wehrmacht would take over Germany. The leader of the conspiracy, Claus von Stauffenberg, took a briefcase of explosives to the Wolf's Lair, but it failed to kill Hitler because Heinz Brandt moved the briefcase behind a heavy oak table leg, which resulted in his own legs being blown off but Hitler escaping with singed pants and a perforated eardrum.

The conspirators, however, did not immediately know that the assassination had failed and so continued forward with Operation Valkyrie as a coup d'état, which then failed because Hitler was still alive. Von Stauffenberg, along with almost five thousand others deemed to be affiliated with the assassination attempt, was executed.

Lee Murray, "Breakout"

The midnight dash in June 1942 across the Egyptian desert by the New Zealand "Kiwi" troops to rejoin the rest of the British Eighth Army ahead of the second battle of El Alamein, was, quite simply, the stuff of movies. Field Marshal Rommel's Afrika Korps encircled the Kiwis at Minqar Qaim. Vastly outnumbered and with limited ammunition, the Kiwis had little option but to make a run for it. It was a remarkable feat, the Kiwis creeping past the enemy under the cover of darkness, the soldiers hitching a ride on any available vehicle. Given the odds, the losses were surprisingly light. The Axis forces, confident that they had the Kiwis trapped, were taken unawares, the breakthrough coming at specific points on the line and achieved, for the most part, by the Māori forces using the shock combat tactics for which they're renowned and heralded by their famous traditional war cry.

One criticism of the Minqar Qaim breakthrough was an attack on a German medical unit, an action that might have constituted a war crime. But given the nature of the breakout and the extreme circumstances of that night, it's believed the assailants could not have known who they were attacking.

Bishop O'Connell, "Nachthexen"

The 588th Night Bomber Regiment, known later as the 46th "Taman" Guards Night Bomber Aviation Regiment, was one of the first all-woman battle regiments. Formed in 1941 after Marin Raskova, often referred to as the Russian Amelia Earhart, approached Joseph Stalin personally. Stalin agreed, generally believed for propaganda purposes, to form three all-woman regiments. The "Night Witches" earned their nickname from their tactic of attacking at night and gliding in silently with their engine idling. The only sound came from the wind through the rigging of their Po-2 biplanes, which were said to sound like brooms sweeping.

Throughout World War II, the Night Witches flew more than twenty-three thousand sorties, dropped over three thousand bombs, twenty-six thousand incendiary shells, and even supplies. Twenty-three of the personnel were awarded the Hero of the Soviet Union, the highest distinction available. All this in antiquated, wooden-framed aircraft, covered in flammable fabric, with no radios, defenses, or parachutes.

Jeremy Robinson, "The Scenic Route"

While the story goes off the deep end into monster madness, this tale is more rooted in reality than might be first apparent. Not only was there an actual battle on Ramree Island, located off the coast of Myanmar (then Burma), during World War II but it really was, and still is, covered in swamps and marshes teeming with crocodiles. Moving troops through knee-deep water was the least dangerous of the challenges faced by both the Japanese and American forces. In fact, when American troops pushed across the island, the retreating Japanese were forced into the swamps, where upward of one thousand soldiers were reputedly killed and eaten by crocodiles!

While the croctopus might not exist, the infamous Unit 731 did. They performed horrific experiments on human beings, including vivisections, rapid freezing and thawing, burning, gassing, and amputation and reattachment of limbs between people.

Readers interested in learning more about Unit 731 or reading about their other fictional creations, including the croctopus, can read Jeremy Robinson's *Island 731*.

Scott Sigler, "Svart Hund"

The German effort to develop nuclear weapons focused on production of deuterium oxide, also known as heavy water. Heavy water allows uranium 238 to undergo fission. The Germans used the Vemork hydroelectric plant outside Rjukan in Nazi-occupied Norway to produce heavy water.

In October 1942, Operation Grouse dropped an advance force of Norwegians into the area around Rjukan. The Norwegians had been trained by the British Special Operations Executive (SOE). Their drop was followed by Operation Freshman, a glider insertion of British engineers. The gliders crashed, resulting in the death or capture (and subsequent execution) of the British force.

Operation Freshman alerted the Germans to Allied interest in Vemork. The Grouse team waited for months in their location, surviving on moss, lichen, and reindeer. By staying operational, they allowed British command to mount another effort—Operation Gunnerside. While the Germans might not have developed a weapon in time for use in World War II, Operation Gunnerside significantly delayed their efforts.

Catherine Stine, "Grigoriy's Army"

The final Battle of Stalingrad, in February 1943, was one of the most pivotal battles on the Eastern Front in the Second World War. In November 1942, Soviet forces launched a counteroffensive against the Germans who had taken Stalingrad in bloody urban warfare. They quickly surrounded the German Sixth Army of over 220,000 soldiers. Their intention was to shrink the pocket of encircled Axis troops and hopefully set the stage for the army's surrender. Hitler promoted his commander, General Friedrich Paulus, to the rank of field marshal to stiffen his resolve. But the lack of supplies and the Soviet armies closing in as part of Operation Ring made the situation hopeless. In addition, the Germans were woefully unequipped for the brutal minus-thirty-degree temperatures. German counterattacks to relieve their encircled forces failed. On January

31, Paulus disobeyed Hitler and surrendered his forces, including twenty-two generals. On February 2, 1943, the last of the 90,000 freezing and starving men surrendered.

Andrea Tang, "Guardian of the Burma Road"

The Battle of Mount Song was pivotal to a broader campaign on the part of Chinese Nationalist forces during World War II to retake supply routes along Burma Road. In order to stymie their efforts, the Japanese army turned nearby Mount Song and its surroundings into a surprisingly effective defensive fortress. Between June and September of 1944, the Japanese army held off the Allied powers, taking cover underground and retaliating against Chinese military forces via ambush setups. Ultimately, however, the Chinese troops prevailed, thanks to ample American aid, which helped enable an extensive bombardment campaign.

The success of Chinese and American forces at Burma Road allowed supply routes into China to reopen. Although Allied powers proved victorious at Mount Song by the end of those three months, the battle is considered notable by modern military historians for the ability of the small Japanese forces, with its lack of air power, to hold off the Chinese for such an extensive period of time.

Gaby Triana, "*CS-13*"

On May 15, 1943, the Cuban merchant ship *Camagüey* and the Honduran *Hanks* set sail for Havana. Just two days before, the German submarine *U-176* had sunk the US merchant ship *Nickeliner* and the Cuban *Mambi*, both carrying molasses through the Florida Straits. With the possibility of more U-boats lurking in hostile waters, the merchant ships were escorted by *CS-11*, *CS-12*, and *CS-13*, three escort subchasers.

CS-13, an eighty-three-foot vessel commanded by Alférez de Fragata (ensign) Mario Ramírez Delgado, located the U-boat with the help of skilled sonarman Norberto Abreu. They attacked *U-176* using depth charges. After a few minutes, a dark, viscous substance reeking of gasoline rose to the surface. The *CS-13* had accomplished a miraculous feat—they were the only non-American naval ship to sink a German submarine during World War II without the assistance of Allied forces. *CS-13*'s sinking of *U-176* is considered a major victory in the Battle of the Caribbean, and Delgado was both promoted to lieutenant and awarded the honor of Meritorious Naval Service with Red Badge.

Harry Turtledove, "Gorgopotamos Bridge"

The bridge over the Gorgopotamos River lay on the only railroad line in Greece that connected German-held Thessalonica with German-held Athens. The Italians occupied the area around the bridge, though the garrison defending it had both Italian and German troops. In November 1942, for the first and only time in the war, British operatives in Greece got Napoleon Zervas's EDES monarchist rebels and Aris Velouchiotis's band of ELAS Communist rebels to cooperate with them and work together in attacking the bridge. On the night of November 25, the assault went in. At the cost of only four casualties, none fatal, it toppled two piers supporting the bridge, keeping it out of use for several weeks, causing fuel shortages and power cuts in Athens, and showing how vulnerable the occupying forces could be.

ABOUT THE CONTRIBUTORS

Eugen Bacon is an African Australian author. She's a British Fantasy and Foreword Indies Award winner, a twice World Fantasy Award finalist, and a finalist in other awards, including the Shirley Jackson Award, Philip K. Dick Award, as well as the Nommo Awards for speculative fiction by Africans. Eugen was announced in the honor list of the Otherwise Fellowships for "doing exciting work in gender and speculative fiction." *Danged Black Thing* made the Otherwise Award Honor List as a "sharp collection of Afro-Surrealist work."

Ann Dávila Cardinal is a fiction writer with an MFA in writing from Vermont College of Fine Arts. Her young adult horror novels include *Five Midnights* (winner of a 2020 International Latino Book Award and a finalist for a Bram Stoker), *Category Five*, and horror rom-com *Breakup from Hell*. Her upcoming young adult horror comedy, *You've Awoken Her*, is forthcoming from HarperTeen in the summer of 2025. Her 2022 magical realist novel, *The Storyteller's Death*, was her first novel for adults, and her second was *We Need No Wings*.

Ann lives in Vermont in a lovely little house with a *very* creepy basement.

Peter Clines is the toy-collecting, movie-loving, *New York Times* bestselling author of books like *The Broken Room*, *Paradox Bound*, *Terminus*, *The Fold*, *14*, the Ex-Heroes series, a pair of short-story collections, a classical mash-up novel, some unproduced screenplays, and countless articles about the film and television industry.

Jeff Edwards is a retired US Navy chief petty officer and an antisubmarine warfare specialist. His naval career spanned more than two decades and half the globe, from chasing Soviet nuclear submarines during the Cold War to launching cruise missiles in the Persian Gulf. Trained extensively in naval combat tactics, he brings an experience-based edge of authenticity to his writing. Collectively, his novels have won the Admiral Nimitz Award for Outstanding Naval Fiction, the Reader's Choice Award, the Clive Cussler Grandmaster Award, and the Military Writer's Society of America Gold Medal for Navy Fiction.

Tori Eldridge is the bestselling author of *Kuleana* (May 2025) and *The Ninja's Oath*, book four in the Lily Wong thriller series, twice nominated for the Anthony Award, Lefty and Macavity awards finalist, and winner of the 2021 Crimson Scribe for Best Book of the Year. Her Brazilian dark fantasy thriller, *Dance Among the Flames*, was inspired by her Academy Nicholl Fellowship semifinalist screenplay. Tori's shorter works appear in numerous anthologies, including *Crime Hits Home*, *Joe Ledger: Unbreakable*, and the inaugural reboot of *Weird Tales Magazine*. Before writing, Tori performed as an actress, singer, and dancer on Broadway, in television, and in film, and she earned a fifth-degree black belt in To-Shin Do ninja martial arts. She is of Hawaiian, Chinese, and Norwegian descent, born and raised in Honolulu.

Mary Fan is a Chinese American sci-fi and fantasy author based in Jersey City, New Jersey. "The Night the Moon Burned" is loosely inspired by her grandfather's experiences during World War II. Her books include *Stronger Than a Bronze Dragon*, the Starswept trilogy, the Flynn Nightsider series, and the Jane Colt trilogy. She is also the coeditor of the Brave New Girls young adult sci-fi anthology series about girls in STEM and the editor of the anthologies *Bad Ass Moms* and *Magic Under the Big Top*. Her short fiction has appeared in numerous anthologies. She has also written for the official *Star Trek* blog and *Star Wars Insider*.

Canadian author **Tanya Huff** lives in rural Ontario with her wife, Fiona Patton; five cats; and an increasing number of fish. Her thirty-two novels and eighty-three short stories include horror, heroic fantasy, urban fantasy, comedy, and space opera. Her Blood series was turned into the twenty-two-episode *Blood Ties* TV series, and writing episode nine allowed her to finally use her degree in radio and television arts. Many of her short stories are available as eCollections. Her latest book is *Into the Broken Lands*, and her next will be *Direct Descendants*. She's on Bluesky and Facebook as Tanya Huff. She has never used her Instagram account and isn't sure why she has it.

Jonathan Maberry is a *New York Times* bestselling author, five-time Bram Stoker Award winner, four-time Scribe Award winner, Inkpot Award winner, comic book writer, executive producer, and writing teacher. He is the author of 50 novels, 150 short stories, 22 graphic novels, 20 nonfiction books, and has edited 24 anthologies. His vampire apocalypse book series,

V-WARS, was a Netflix original series. He writes horror, science fiction, epic fantasy, mystery, adventure, thrillers, and more. He is the president of the International Association of Media Tie-in Writers and the editor of *Weird Tales Magazine.*

David Mack is the award-winning, *New York Times* bestselling author of more than thirty-eight novels and numerous short works of science fiction, fantasy, and adventure, including the *Star Trek Destiny* and *Cold Equations* trilogies. Mack's writing credits span television (for episodes of *Star Trek: Deep Space Nine*), film, and comic books. He also has worked as a consultant on the animated television series *Star Trek: Lower Decks* and *Star Trek: Prodigy.* The International Association of Media Tie-in Writers honored him as a Grandmaster with its Faust Award.

Kevin Andrew Murphy is an American novelist and game writer currently living in Reno, Nevada. He is a graduate of the University of California, Santa Cruz, and has a masters of professional writing from the University of Southern California. He has written game books and fiction for Steve Jackson Games and White Wolf, including the solo Mage novel *Penny Dreadful*, and fiction for numerous anthologies. He is one of the contributors to the Wild Cards series edited by George R. R. Martin, for which his story "Find the Lady" in *Mississippi Roll* won the 2019 Darrell Award for Best Midsouth Novella.

Lee Murray is a writer, editor, poet, and screenwriter from Aotearoa, New Zealand. A *USA Today* bestselling author, her titles include the Taine McKenna Adventures, the supernatural crime-noir series The Path of Ra (with Dan Rabarts), the fiction collection *Grotesque: Monster Stories*, and several children's books. Her many anthologies include *Hellhole*, *Black Cranes* (with

Geneve Flynn), and *Unquiet Spirits* (with Angela Yuriko Smith), and her short fiction appears in *Weird Tales*, *Space and Time*, and *Grimdark Magazine*. A multiple Bram Stoker, Australian Shadows, and Sir Julius Vogel award winner, Lee is New Zealand's only Shirley Jackson Award winner. Winner of New Zealand's Prime Minister's Award for Literary Achievement, she is also an NZSA Honorary Literary Fellow, a Grimshaw Sargeson Fellow, and the 2023 NZSA Laura Solomon Cuba Press Prize winner.

Bishop O'Connell is the author of the American Faerie Tale series and the award-winning novel *Two-Gun Witch*, as well as a consultant, writer, blogger, lover of kilts and beer, as well as a member of the Science Fiction & Fantasy Writers of America. Born in Naples, Italy, while his father was in the navy, Bishop grew up in San Diego, where he fell in love with the ocean and fish tacos. After wandering the country for work and school (absolutely not evading mind-controlling bunnies), he settled in Richmond, Virginia, where he writes, collects swords, revels in his immortality as a "visionary" of the urban fantasy genre, and is regularly chastised for making up things for his bio.

Jeremy Robinson is the number one Audible.com and *New York Times* bestselling author of more than sixty novels and novellas, including *Infinite*, *Alter*, *The Others*, *Space Force*, *Project Nemesis*, and the Jack Sigler thriller series. Robinson is also known as the number one Amazon.com horror writer, Jeremy Bishop, author of *The Sentinel*, *The Raven*, and the controversial novel *Torment*, and Jeremiah Knight, author of the postapocalyptic Hunger series. His novels have been translated into thirteen languages. His bestselling kaiju novels, *Project Nemesis* and *Island 731*, have been released as a comic book series from American Gothic Press and Famous Monsters of Filmland.

Number one *New York Times* bestselling author **Scott Sigler** is the creator of eighteen novels, six novellas, dozens of short stories, and thousands of podcast episodes. He is an inaugural inductee into the Podcasting Hall of Fame. His podcast fans fervently anticipate their weekly story fix, so much so that they've dubbed themselves "Sigler Junkies" and have downloaded over fifty million episodes.

Catherine Stine is a *USA Today* bestselling author of historical fantasy, paranormal romance, sci-fi thrillers, and young adult fiction. *Witch of the Wild Beasts* won a second prize spot in the 2019 RWA Sheila Contest. Other novels have earned Indie Notable awards and New York Public Library Best Books for Teens.

Andrea Tang grew up in Princeton, New Jersey, and currently lives, writes, and works in the Washington, DC, area. She loves martial arts in general and Brazilian jujitsu in particular, and in her spare time, she enjoys learning new sports and checking out live theater. Andrea is the author of *Rebelwing* and its companion novel, *Renegade Flight*, as well as *The Kingdom of Without.*

Gaby Triana is the Cuban American author of twenty-five books for adults and teens, including *Moon Child, Island of Bones, River of Ghosts, City of Spells, Wake the Hollow, Cubanita*, and *Summer of Yesterday*. Her short stories have appeared in *Classic Monsters Unleashed, A Tribute to Alvin Schwartz's Scary Stories to Tell in the Dark, A Conjuring for All Seasons, Novus Monstrum*, and *Weird Tales Magazine.* She has coauthored ghost hunters Sam and Colby's horror novel, *Paradise Island*, and edited the ghost anthology series Literally Dead (*Tales of Halloween Hauntings* and *Tales of Holiday Hauntings*). Her books have won the IRA Teen Choice Award, ALA Best Paperback, and *Hispanic* magazine's Good Reads awards.

Harry Turtledove is an escaped Byzantine historian (it's all L. Sprague de Camp's fault). He writes alternate history, other science fiction, fantasy (much of it historically based), and, when he can get away with it, historical fantasy. His latest novel is *The Wages of Sin*, which turns HIV loose on the world in the early sixteenth century. Harry won the Homer Award for Short Story for "Designated Hitter," the John Esten Cooke Award for Southern Fiction for *The Guns of the South*, and the Hugo Award for Novella for *Down in the Bottomlands. Must and Shall* was nominated for the Hugo Award and Nebula Award for Best Novelette. He received a Sidewise Award honorable mention for Alternate History for *Must and Shall*, *The Two Georges*, and the Worldwar series. His novels *How Few Remain* and *Ruled Britannia* and his stories "Zigeuner" and "Christmas Truce" all won Sidewise Awards. *Publishers Weekly* dubbed Turtledove "the Master of Alternate History."

New York Times bestseller **Jane Yolen** has written 459 books. Her most popular books are *Owl Moon* and the How Do Dinosaurs series, and she has written poetry since she was in first grade. (She's gotten better!) Her latest adult poetry book is *Kaddish*, poems about the Holocaust. Jane's chapbook of science fiction and fantasy poems, *The Last Robot*, won the Elgin Award. Her books and stories and poems have won Nebulas, Caldecotts, World Fantasy awards, Storytelling awards, Christopher Medals, and more. Six colleges and universities have given her honorary doctorates for her body of work.

ABOUT THE EDITOR

Henry Herz has edited six other anthologies:

• *Beyond the Pale* (adult dark fantasy, Birch Tree Publishing)—with Saladin Ahmed, Peter S. Beagle, Heather Brewer, Jim Butcher, Rachel Caine, Kami Garcia, Nancy Holder, Gillian Philip, and Jane Yolen.

• *Coming of Age* (contemporary middle grade, Albert Whitman & Co.)—with Sarah Aronson, Nora Raleigh Baskin, Barbara Bottner, Stacia Deutsch, Debbie Reed Fischer, Debra Garfinkle, Alan Katz, Nancy Krulik, Stacie Ramey, Jonathan Rosen, Melissa Roske, Laura Shovan, and Jane Yolen.

• *The Hitherto Secret Experiments of Marie Curie* (young adult dark fantasy, Blackstone Publishing, 2023)—with Mylo Carbia, Stacia Deutsch, Sarah Beth Durst, Alethea Kontis, Susanne Lambdin, Dee Leone, Jonathan Maberry, Emily McCosh, Seanan McGuire, Steve Pantazis, Lissa Price, Bryan Thomas Schmidt, Scott Sigler, Christine Taylor-Butler, Jo Whittemore, and Jane Yolen.

• *The Festival of Lights* (contemporary middle grade, Albert Whitman & Co.)—with Kimberly Brubaker Bradley, Nancy

Churnin, Stacia Deutsch, Bridget Hodder, Nancy Holder, Alan Katz, Gini Koch, Nancy Krulik, Joanne Levy, Terri Libenson, Leslea Newman, Erica Perl, Rachael Romero, and Alan Silberberg.

• *Wink* (young adult fantasy, Brigids Gate Press)—with James Aquilone, Kendare Blake, Leah Cypess, Stacia Deutsch, David Gerrold, Tara Gilboy, Nancy Holder, Alethea Kontis, Jonathan Maberry, Seanan McGuire, Wulf Moon, Henry Neff, Alex Shvartsman, Maggie Stiefvater, and Jane Yolen.

• *Red Stars and Shattered Shields* (adult sci-fi, Yuriko Publishing)—with David Brin, Jennifer Brody, Jennifer Brozek, Adam-Troy Castro, Keith DeCandido, David Gerrold, Elana Gomel, Jonathan Maberry, Jody Lynn Nye, Cat Rambo, Alex Shvartsman, Susan Schwartz, Robert Silberberg, Adam Stemple, and Ian Randal Strock.